In the Line of Duty

By Heather Rosser

New Generation **Publishing**

Praise for In the Line of Duty

"This is an excellent novel and I really enjoyed it."
Maureen Lee – Novelist and Winner of the Romantic Novel of the Year Award

'I really liked the story and I'm sure anyone interested in early 20th century history will enjoy In Line of Duty.'
Jean Fullerton – Novelist and Winner of the Harry Bowling Prize

"I love the story and setting. I'm sure it will be a hit."
Carol McGrath – Historical Novelist

"It is a considerable achievement to come up with a novel about the First World War that avoids clichés and explores relatively unknown territory such as the Royal Naval Air Service and the terrible fate that radiographers suffered. The light thrown on the White Feather phenomenon is also interesting and poignant."
Nicola Slade - Historical Mystery Novelist

Acknowledgements

Dedicated to my mother, Hazel, whose unfinished memoirs were my inspiration.

Not long before she died, my brother and my cousins, Richard and Chris, began to investigate our grandfather's career as a seaplane pilot in the First World War. My mother started to record memories of her father but she died leaving many questions unanswered. In her unfinished memoir my mother describes her grandmother as a wanderlust and, as her grandfather was a senior detective on the LMS railway with offices in Llandudno Junction and Euston, they had free rail travel. They built a holiday home in the mountains above Conwy which remained in the family for a turbulent sixty years.

In the interests of research I have had several fascinating visits to the Conwy Valley with my husband, Adrian, and daughters Emily, Melinda and Alyrene who have all supported me along the path to publication. I have also visited the Fleet Air Arm, Imperial War, London Transport, Hampstead and Llandudno museums where the staff have taken time to give me the information I was looking for and more besides. My brother, Nigel Williams, has been my expert on seaplanes. I would also like to thank Anne Kingston for her constructive criticisms and for putting me in touch with Adrian Thomas, Consultant Radiologist with an interest in early UK radiology. Joan Ward has also been helpful in checking the accuracy of my descriptions of birds.

Many thanks, also to Shawn and Caroline White for their support and the cover design.

I am indebted to members of various writing organisations who have given friendship and support as well as enabling me to produce a polished and authentic story. Jan Henley and Peter Gutteridge who ran a course on Popular Fiction enabled me to get started in the idyllic and appropriate surroundings of Ty Newydd, last home of Lloyd George. Stephanie Hale, tutor on Oxford University Starting a Novel course, helped me work out the framework for the novel. The Romantic Novelist's Association has been a fount of knowledge and support and my thanks go to the many friends I have there, especially the Oxford Chapter. Finally I must thank my friends at Oxford Writers Group and OxPens Publishing for their encouragement during the genesis of In the Line of Duty.

I began my research when The Times was still stored on microfiche and I would like to thank the staff at Oxford City library for threading the film onto the projector for me, a technique I failed to master myself.

The First World War is a huge topic and I have sifted through information from many sources. Some of the books I used during my research are: *Llandudno* by Jim Roberts, *Llandudno Queen of Resorts* by Ivor Wynne Jones, *Emigration of Single Women to South Africa* by Cecillie Swaisland, *Family Life in Britain 1900-1950* by Edmund Swinglehurst, *The Edwardians* by Roy Hattersley, *Edwardian Childhoods* by Thea Thompson, *Edwardian England* by Donald Read, *The Great War Diaries of Georgina Lee* ed by Gavin Royan, *Women at War* ed by Nigel Fountain, *All Quiet on the Home Front* by Richard van Emden and Steve Humphries, *The Home Front* by Peter Cooksley, *The Home Front in the Great War* by David Bilton, *The First Naval Air War* by Terry C Treadwell, *The Royal Naval Air Service* by Terry C Treadwell and Alan C Wood, *Baling Out* by Robert Jackson, *The Short 184* published by Profile Publications, *A War Imagined* by Samuel Hynds, *World War 1* by Lloyd Clark,

Testament of Youth by Vera Brittain, *The Crowded Street* by Winifred Holtby.

In the novel I have used the contemporary spelling of Conway instead of Conwy, the form that is now used.

Prologue

November 1916

Oblivious to the numbing cold of the open cockpit, William peered through his goggles at the streaks of red in the grey dawn.

'Hope we get back before the storm breaks,' he muttered through cracked lips.

But the roar of the engine and whistling of the wind through the wires holding the seaplane together swallowed his observer's answer.

Suddenly everything went dark as they hit a bank of cloud and the plane began to nose-dive. William gripped the controls and tried to ignore the griping fear as huge North Sea waves appeared to leap towards them. Jamming his feet on the rudder bar, he heaved the joystick round and guided the fragile craft upwards.

As they came out of the cloud he saw the Belgian coast straight ahead. The port of Zeebrugge was clearly visible and so was the German destroyer with its guns pointing directly in his path. Fear gave way to exhilaration as he manoeuvred the plane away from the gunfire while keeping his sights on the submarine sheds at the far side of the docks. He checked the target through his binoculars and saw soldiers and marines darting for cover.

Behind him, his observer prepared to destroy the U-boats in the sheds below. William set his course, the observer dropped the bombs and they accelerated away from the explosion.

He glanced down. Standing on the edge of the dock was a young naval officer, apparently mesmerised by the approaching plane.

'Watch out!' shouted William instinctively.

He was vaguely aware of the observer releasing the last bomb.

Feeling light-headed after hours of combating danger and fatigue, William took a deep breath. Her image danced before him and he seemed to hear her laughter echoing across the sea from distant mountains. The image faded; ancient hills gave way to city streets. For an instant the cockpit was filled with her perfume and the heady scent of temptation. He turned his head.

But there was nothing. Just the acrid stench of burning and the scream of the bomb as it fell. And smoke billowing upwards from where the naval officer had been standing.

Chapter 1: Alice

The Hague and Disarmament
Discussing the programme for the next Hague
Convention the committee has decided not to raise the
question of disarmament on the grounds that it would
be premature.

The Times: April 3ʳᵈ 1914

Sounds of clanking, shunting and occasional shouts came from the locomotive sheds as Alice paused on the steps of the Station Hotel. She looked upwards, above the ugliness of the railway sheds, towards the mountains where she could just make out Mynydd Brith, although a dark cloud hung menacingly over the mottled mountain.

Stepping carefully to avoid the puddles, Alice walked briskly towards Llandudno Junction station where Humphrey, a railway police detective, had his office.

She stopped outside Rowe's, the general dealer or 'station shop' as it was known locally and smiled at a small boy, his nose pressed against the window as he looked at the brightly coloured jars of sweets. The shop bell clanged when she opened the door.

An attractive dark-haired girl stood behind the counter.

'Good afternoon Mrs Dacre. The weather's better now the rain has stopped.'

Alice responded to her friendly smile. 'Yes, it should be nice on the mountain. We're going to look at our house. Do you know if your uncle is working there today?'

'No, he sent word saying he's ill today but he told the men to carry on with the roof because he knew you wanted to see it finished before you went back to London.'

'I hope he'll be better soon,' said Alice as she looked at the sugar buns arranged invitingly in a glass case. 'We'll take some things for a picnic to celebrate.'

She took a string bag from her pocket and filled it with her purchases then walked to the door leaving the girl to enter the amount she owed into the ledger.

The train was already in the station when she arrived, its engine hissing as the fireman fed it with coal. Alice walked along the platform to the first class compartment where Humphrey was waiting. A porter hurried past to open the door and she smiled at her husband as she climbed aboard. They had been married nearly twenty-five years but they were still a handsome couple; Humphrey's urbane good looks contrasting with Alice's fair, patrician features.

They sat opposite each other, looking out of the window as the train snaked past the locomotive sheds and along the wide riverbank. The sun came out as they crossed the bridge over the estuary and the blue water softened the darkness of the castle ramparts. Alice looked up at the arrow slits high in the walls and shivered momentarily. The train wheezed to a halt at Conway station, a porter held open the door and they stepped out into the sunshine.

'Are you feeling fit for the walk?' asked Humphrey, taking the string bag from his wife.

'I'm fine but you're still togged up for the office.' Alice glanced at the fob neatly fixed to her husband's waistcoat.

They swept out of the station and started their ascent. Once they had passed the grey stone houses on the edge of the town the track became steeper and narrower with mossy banks on either side. Every now and again they passed a roughly hewn stone dwelling and sometimes a farmhouse with milk churns by the gate.

'Have you any more thoughts of a name for our house?' asked Alice.

'It would be appropriate to give it a Welsh name.' Humphrey paused to take off his jacket. He folded it carefully and placed it in the bag then strode forward singing, his rich baritone echoing off the rocks.

'I know! Trealaw!' said Alice.

'Trealaw?'

'It means Home of Song.'

'You're very knowledgeable. I like it. Trealaw it shall be. I'll order a piano and we'll have a house-warming party in the summer.'

Alice breathed the scent of wet grass and quickened her pace as she saw the mountain slopes ahead of her. They heard a dog bark and saw a shepherd with his flock in the distance. They continued up the track, following a wooden sign for the Old Church.

Humphrey was still singing when they reached the end of the main track. Ahead of them the mountain, its summit still covered in cloud, rose steeply. To their right was a gateway rutted by carts that had carried building materials and there were wheel marks across the grassy slope leading to the house. It stood straight and square like a child's drawing with two windows upstairs, two down and a front door in the middle. The roof with its grey slates was almost complete.

As they walked towards the house Alice remembered the first time they had climbed Mynydd Brith. Humphrey had been sent from London to investigate a series of thefts from the locomotive sheds and Alice had joined him for the weekend. They had walked from Conway, following signs to the Old Church. As they looked down at the beautiful Welsh coast spread out before them Humphrey had plunged his shooting stick into the soft turf and declared that he would build them a holiday home. It would be a retreat from the bustle of their London life, a place to sit and dream far away from the rumours of German arms factories across the Channel and the Kaiser's plans for domination. A year later, that threat had worsened but here on the mountain it seemed far away.

The men were putting the finishing touches to the roof when they reached the house. One stood on the last exposed rafter and the other next to a ladder leaning against the wall.

'Afternoon sir, afternoon ma'am.' Dafyd inclined his head slightly and moved towards them. 'Boss is ill so we're on our own today. Would have finished already but the rain this morning slowed us down. But we'll be finished before nightfall; isn't that right Taffy?'

'That's right, just a few more slates to lay.' The slightly built figure looked down at them, then crouched on the rafter and carefully took a slate from the pile.

'You can join us in a glass of ginger beer when you've finished,' said Humphrey genially. He went through the opening where the front door would soon be and brought some glasses and a blanket from a wooden trunk then placed them on the grass in front of the house.

'I think this calls for a cigar,' he said, taking a silver box from his jacket.

They sat drinking in the view. Just below was a small peak with clumps of wild daffodils dancing among the boulders strewn over the grassy slope.

A buzzard circled on a thermal high above the peak.

'No wonder Man has always wanted to fly,' said Alice looking upwards. 'I can understand why William enjoys flying so much.'

'It won't be many years before aeroplanes will be able to fly from London to Wales in a few hours.' Humphrey contemplated the smoke rings that were floating up from his cigar.

'Let's take a walk round the house.' Alice stood up as she felt damp seeping through the blanket.

The land rose steeply behind the house and the view was wilder with the jagged peaks of Mynydd Brith casting shadows on the landscape. They walked to where a stream bubbled down the mountain and formed a small pool.

'We'll link a pipe to the water here and bring it to the kitchen.' Humphrey scooped a handful of clear water, washed his hands then shook them to dry.

They strolled back and stood at the front of the building, watching the men working steadily.

A loud guttural croaking made Alice look up to see a large black bird circling above the house.

'Raven's back,' muttered Dafyd as he moved back to the ladder.

The sun went behind a cloud and Alice shivered as she watched Taffy lean forward to pick up another slate. He straightened and edged along the beam then bent down to place the slate in position.

'Only one left,' called Taffy as he stood up again, his dark features silhouetted against the sky.

The raven swept over Taffy's head with a raucous cry just as a strong gust of wind blew down the mountain. Taffy turned then let out a terrified scream as he lost his footing. He grabbed wildly at the air as he slithered on the wet slates then crashed to the ground below.

For a moment everyone was frozen in horror then they ran to where he lay motionless, a patch of blood seeping from under his head.

Alice gasped and clutched her throat then looked away, the jagged mountain peaks swimming before her eyes.

'Pass my jacket,' Humphrey commanded and Dafyd, his eyes round with shock, did as he was told.

Humphrey placed the expensive jacket under the builder's head, took his watch from his waistcoat and held the man's wrist. 'Pulse is slow. Where's the nearest doctor?'

'Dr Jones is on the road into Conway. Shall I run to borrow a pony and trap from Farmer Davis at the Llangwm turn?'

'There's no time, we'll have to carry him.'

Alice looked questioningly at the ladder and her husband nodded. She picked up the blanket and wished there was a cushion but they had been planning to bring everything when the roof was on. However, there was some strong twine and Humphrey and Dafyd quickly converted the ladder into a stretcher.

With great care they laid Taffy onto the makeshift stretcher then, with Alice and Humphrey at the front and Dafyd at the rear, they started down the mountain.

***

When Alice looked back on the next few days her memories were jumbled – aching wrists from carrying the stretcher; relief at the first sight of the doctor closely followed by impotence as he looked gravely at the unconscious man; pride in Humphrey for his level headedness and his generosity in paying the doctor's fees tempered by irritation at his surprise when she refused to return to London with him.

'But we've done all we can. His wife's looking after him and they don't have doctor's fees to worry about. What good will you do if you stay?'

Humphrey was right, they were outsiders and their presence was not welcome despite their money. All the same she couldn't bring herself to leave and she remained at the Station Hotel when Humphrey returned to London the following day.

Taffy was still unconscious when Alice visited the small house in Conway. She stood on the doorstep and handed his wife a box of groceries and meat but when she tried to ask how he was she was answered accusingly in Welsh. She distributed sweets to the bewildered children peering round the door then went for a long walk along the morfa, aware only of the sounds of the crashing waves and wheeling sea gulls.

She fell into a deep sleep that night but was awakened suddenly by a tapping on her window. In the grey dawn she saw a black bird hopping on the sill outside. For a moment the bird's eye held hers then with a mocking caw it flew towards the sunrise.

Unable to sleep further Alice dressed and joined the early travellers in the dining room.

After breakfast she decided to call at the station shop to see if there was any news of Taffy. She bowed her head against the wind whipping black smuts into the air and hurried along the road. Alice went into the shop and nodded a greeting to Mr and Mrs Rowe who were serving customers, mainly passengers hurrying for their train.

'It's bad news, I'm afraid,' said Jack when the shop had emptied, 'my brother-in-law sent word to say that Taffy died in the early hours this morning.'

'Yes, I, I know,' Alice stood motionless and tried to focus on the worried face of the shop keeper but all she could see was the bird that had woken her like a harbinger of ill fortune. She stared blankly at her neatly gloved hands clutching the wooden counter.

Jack and his wife looked puzzled while Alice struggled to regain her composure.

'I must give my condolences to the family,' she announced making for the door.

Jack held up his hand as if to stop her then looked enquiringly at his wife.

'It's been very good of you to stay and to visit the family Mrs Dacre. But it's still early. Perhaps you would like a cup of tea? The kettle's on if you wouldn't mind sitting in the kitchen,' Nellie Rowe said hesitantly.

Alice suddenly felt very tired. 'Thank you, I'd like that,' she said simply and followed her through the door at the back of the shop.

A red-haired girl of about fourteen was rummaging through a satchel.

'Have you got everything Cilla? You don't want to be late for school.' Mrs Rowe spoke sharply.

The girl gave an exaggerated sigh then looked directly at Alice with a conspiratorial smile. She smiled back as the girl slung the bag over her shoulder and ran out of the back door shouting 'Goodbye' as she went.

'Cilla is our youngest.' Mrs Rowe's voice was a mixture of irritation and affection. 'Now please sit down and I'll make a fresh brew.'

'And your other daughter helps in the shop,' said Alice politely as Nellie Rowe stoked the fire under the hob where the kettle was beginning to sing.

'Yes Lottie's a great help, she's just turned eighteen.'

'That's the same age as our daughter, Daisy.' Alice felt herself beginning to relax.

'That's the beds all stripped.' A girl walked into the room, her arms laden with linen, and then stopped uncertainly as she saw Alice.

'Lottie, I think you know Mrs Dacre; your Uncle Owen's building her a house up on Mynydd Brith.'

'I'm sorry to hear what happened there.' Lottie hesitated for a moment then walked towards the door and smiled sympathetically at Alice before going out into the yard with the washing.

'What a pleasant young woman,' said Alice and Nellie nodded complacently as she handed her a strong cup of tea.

'Lottie's a bright girl. She helps her father with the books as well as me in the house. And she's good with the customers too. Is everything all right Lottie?' she asked as the girl returned.

'Yes, the sheets should dry well today.' Lottie took a bar of soap from the sink and went back outside.

Alice stood up. Thank you for the tea. I shall go to the station now and telephone my husband.' Alice proffered her gloved hand to Nellie's reddened one.

They shook hands briefly and Alice, her back erect, walked briskly out of the shop.

***

Humphrey urged her to come home when she phoned him but she said she did not feel able to travel. A sense of duty made her visit Taffy's family and she was received courteously by a male relative but was not invited inside. When she returned to her hotel room she fell asleep in a chair and woke feeling stiff and uncomfortable. Rain kept her inside and she whiled away the remainder of the day reading newspapers in the hotel lounge but the international news did little to lift her spirits.

The following morning Alice breakfasted late. Her sleep had been troubled and she had overslept. The hotel dining room was almost empty when she took her usual seat by the window.

'Just a lightly boiled egg with toast please,' she said to the waiter after he had pulled out her chair for her.

She was just pouring a second cup of tea and wondering how to occupy her day when she noticed the familiar figure of her son William striding from the station.

Her pleasure at seeing him was, as usual, tinged with anxiety in case he had got into one of his scrapes again. Despite an expensive education, William had not distinguished himself at school although his easy-going charm had always deflected any major criticism. When asked about a career William claimed that the only thing he wanted to do was to fly aeroplanes but Humphrey had already arranged for him to serve an apprenticeship as a railway engineer. William accepted with good grace but spent all his spare time at the Royal Aero Club. He was only twenty-one when he got his pilot's license but, without money, there were few opportunities for "real" flying. Now, aged twenty-three, Alice sensed that William was becoming bored. He sometimes talked of going to South Africa to work on the railway there but never seemed able to tear himself away from his latest romantic attachment. Alice was aware that her son had had dalliances with a number of young women who were less than respectable but she was genuinely shocked when news of an affair with a married woman began to circulate. Humphrey was tight lipped and Alice suspected he had paid off the woman's husband.

'Good morning Mother!' William stood in the doorway beaming, his presence lighting up the room.

'William, it's lovely to see you, but what are you doing here?' Alice rose to greet her son.

'Father sent me, thought you needed bringing home. So I got the night train. And here I am!' William held out his arms and gave his mother a light embrace.

Alice couldn't help smiling but answered a little frostily, 'Don't you think I'm capable of bringing myself home?'

'Of course Mother, you are the world's most capable woman but, well Father thought I might cheer you up so he had a word with the governor to release me for a day and here I am.'

Alice nodded. 'I suppose there's nothing more I can do here. And I do have things to attend to in London. By the way, have you breakfasted?'

'Yes, on the train. But a cup of tea would be just the ticket.' William signalled to the waiter.

'Well, you won't want to go straight back so we could get the night train.'

'Capital. And we can take a look at the house this morning. Father tells me you're going to call it Trealaw.'

Alice hesitated. 'We were but I don't know now. Perhaps Home of Song isn't appropriate anymore.'

'I think it's an excellent name. We'll install a gramophone and play all the latest dance tunes.'

William's enthusiasm was infectious and Alice found herself smiling. 'There's a train to Conway in half an hour. If I'm going to return to London I think we should go and see what damage has been done to the roof.'

***

An hour later they were walking steadily along the track leading up to Mynydd Brith.

'With grazing rights included we can buy a flock of sheep, they look after themselves most of the time, it wouldn't cost anything to transport them by train and we'd get a good price for Welsh mutton in London,' enthused William.

'Most flocks have a shepherd to look after them and I don't think our free rail passes would extend to a wagon load of sheep,' Alice responded sharply.

'Well, we could rear them for wool; that would be much easier to transport.'

'And how would you shear them?'

'It can't be difficult once you've got the knack.'

'But the reason your father wanted the house was as a summer retreat, not for you to try out your hair brained schemes.'

'I know Mother. But can't a fellow dream? William strode ahead whistling.

A mouse scurried across the track in front of her and, despite a feeling of irritation with her son and sadness for Taffy's family, Alice smiled. She turned the last corner and was on the open hillside. Ahead of her was the house looking almost the same as it had three days ago. But to her over sensitive eyes the gaping holes around the door and window frames looked ominous. There were some broken slates on the ground where Taffy had fallen but little damage had been done to the roof itself.

William was looking sombre. 'Damn bad luck. Poor chap.'

He walked round the house then joined Alice standing motionless in the doorway. The sun was shining, clumps of wild daffodils danced on the mountainside and they could see white flecks on the sea in the distance.

'You've bought a wonderful view,' William said resting his hand lightly on her shoulder.

Alice stiffened. 'You don't own a view. We've bought a few bricks and mortar.' She drew in her breath sharply and added, 'Paid for in blood.'

Chapter 2: Lottie

Last Efforts for Peace
The prospect of a general European war was seen to be
more imminent yesterday.
The Times: August 1ˢᵗ 1914

Shouts and a squeal of locomotive brakes woke Lottie. She scrambled up and drew back the curtain then frowned, puzzled by the unusual amount of activity so early on a Sunday morning. Soldiers carrying kitbags were running up the steps into the station opposite. Steam from the engine billowed into the air and cinders danced above the drab street. Lottie closed the curtain and crept back to bed, shivering in the cool dawn, as she wondered why so many soldiers were travelling on Bank Holiday Sunday rather than the following day.

She glanced at her sister asleep in the other bed. Cilla's lips twitched slightly as the sound of male voices drifted through the open window but Lottie found the shouts unsettling. She tried to get back to sleep but memories of looking after her little sister came flooding back. She had been thirteen when she had arrived home from school to find her mother lying at the bottom of the stairs, the basket of laundry she had been carrying scattered on the living room floor. She had screamed for Cilla to get help, her father had shut the shop and for the next few days her mother's life hung in the balance. Relief at her recovery was mixed with a feeling of loss for the baby her mother had miscarried and worry about the effect that her mother's back injuries would have on herself. Lottie was told there was not enough money for school fees as well as doctor's bills and she was expected to take over many of her mother's duties in the shop and running the house.

As she listened to the train shunting out of the station Lottie wished that she was going somewhere exciting instead of Sunday dinner at her mother's brother and family. She decided to take her sketch book in the hope that there would be an opportunity to draw if they went for a walk in the afternoon.

***

There was a holiday atmosphere as people in their Sunday best promenaded across Conway suspension bridge. With a clip clop of horses' hooves an omnibus rattled past Lottie and Cilla. A couple of young men at the front waved their boaters and called out to them.

'Cilla!' Lottie laughed reprovingly as her sister waved her hat in return, its emerald ribbon streaming in the wind.

'This bridge gets longer each time,' grumbled Nellie as she and Jack caught up with their daughters.

'We can rest here and enjoy the view.' Jack leant against the parapet and for a while they stood silently watching the fishing boats bobbing on the incoming tide.

'It would make a nice picture,' murmured Lottie thinking about the sketch pad and pencils she had put in her basket.

Suddenly there was a low drone, a glint of silver in the sunshine and an unfamiliar shape appeared on the horizon.

'It's an aeroplane!' shouted a couple of boys and elbowed their way past Lottie to get a better view.

The noise turned into a roar as the bi-plane sped towards them, flying low over the estuary. Cheers erupted and everyone rushed to the side of the bridge to see the contraption looking like some monstrous insect searching for its prey.

Nellie screamed when the plane appeared uncomfortably close while Cilla jumped up and down in excitement. Lottie felt her heart beat faster and fixed her eyes on the helmeted figure of the pilot in the open cockpit. Just as she thought the plane would crash into them there was a rush of wind and it rose and flew over the bridge.

'Mind the turrets!' someone shouted as it circled then arced over their heads and back the way it had come.

For a moment there was silence as the crowd watched the fragile beast gain height as it flew above the fishing boats towards the headland until it was out of sight. Then everyone began talking, marvelling at the sight they had witnessed and the skill of the pilot.

'It's an omen, that's what it is,' an elderly man declared solemnly.

'What does he mean?' Cilla, still flushed with excitement looked at her father.

Jack looked uncomfortable. 'It doesn't mean anything, just a pilot showing off. He'll have stopped to re-fuel in Llandudno and he'll be on his way back to Blackpool or wherever he's come from.'

'And they'll be waiting to take the plane when he lands,' said the man.

'Who will?' asked Lottie.

'The government.' The man nodded sagely. 'They'll use these new machines to fight the war.'

'What war?' Lottie tried to dispel the image she had seen of soldiers hurrying to the train early that morning.

Nellie snorted. 'You couldn't fight a war with one of those. It might be noisy but it was just tied together with bits of wire. Now, come on girls, we don't want to be late.' She nodded dismissively at the man and began to walk away.

The sun still shone but the holiday atmosphere had evaporated. Although some of the children were talking animatedly about the aeroplane the majority of people were subdued, no longer striding across the bridge but were hunched and talking to each other in agitated voices.

The castle which had always been a familiar land mark now seemed forbidding and they walked quickly past following the town walls till they came to a house at the end of a terrace.

'Meg's feeling poorly.' Owen looked worried as he opened the door.

'I'm all right, I put the dinner in the oven but then I came over faint.' Meg placed her hands over the flowered smock that hardly concealed her swelling belly.

'You need to look after yourself in your condition. Lottie can manage the dinner, can't you?' Nellie's resentment for her sister-in-law's pregnancy hung in the small hallway.

'Of course; come on Cilla. My, you've grown.' Lottie ruffled her cousins' hair as she tried to dismiss the feeling of being trapped.

The childish prattle of the boys kept the atmosphere relaxed but Lottie was pleased when dinner was over and the washing up done. The little house was dark and Lottie guessed she was not the only one who wanted to be outside in the sunshine.

Jack helped his brother-in-law carry chairs into the small back garden.

'Are you going to draw our portraits Lottie?' asked Nellie sinking into a chair.

'Well, I thought it would be nice to do a landscape,' Lottie said hesitantly.

'She's going to sketch the mountain,' said Cilla firmly.

Nellie frowned and looked enquiringly at Owen.

'The girls can take Efan and Little Owen to look for wild strawberries and Lottie can do her sketching while they pick them,' he said.

***

They walked quickly away from the town and up a winding track. The boys scampered ahead and were sitting on a rock when Lottie and Cilla caught up.

'I see you found some strawberries,' Lottie looked at their red-stained lips.

Efan looked sheepish. 'I'm afraid they've all gone.'

'They look like little goblins sitting on that rock. It would make a nice picture,' said Cilla.

Lottie looked at the clouds building up in the sky. 'I'll just do a quick sketch. Stay there boys.' She started to take out her sketch pad.

'But there aren't any strawberries here. Come on Owen, 'Let's look further on.' Efan leapt off the rock and along the track with Little Owen running behind.

'Rascals!' yelled Cilla and chased after them.

Lottie followed at a more leisurely pace, enjoying the unaccustomed solitude and the freshening breeze on her face. The track disappeared into a fold in the mountain and for a moment she lost sight of Cilla and her cousins. When she caught up they were kneeling by a grassy bank intently picking strawberries.

'So you've found some more!' Lottie bent down and picked a couple of the tiny red berries nestling close to the ground. 'Delicious!' she said popping them in her mouth.

They put the strawberries in the basket but they barely covered the bottom.

'Let's see if there are more further up,' said Cilla.

The track climbed steeply until they were on the open mountain. To their right was a newly built house and to their left a signpost pointed to the Old Church.

'Let's go that way,' said Efan and ran along a grassy path bounded by dry stonewalls until they came to the church.

Cilla pushed open the gate.

The church stood, squat and sturdy, in the centre of a walled enclosure. The plain glass windows were small and the low roof was spotted with lichen. The graves, scattered haphazardly among the rock outcrops, were also covered with lichen making the inscriptions difficult to read.

The boys darted about peering at the gravestones and a scarlet butterfly hovered above, a flash of colour amid the grey slate.

Lottie made her way to the far corner where the ground rose steeply. She looked at the scene with satisfaction and set down her basket.

'Don't you think this will make a lovely painting?' Lottie took out her pencil and sketchbook.

'Yes, I wish I could draw like you.'

'Would you like to be in it?'

'I could be sitting on a tombstone weeping for my lost love.'

Lottie shook her head. 'That's too tragic, why don't you stand by the porch; when I paint the picture your auburn hair will be a lovely contrast to the grey stone.'

Lulled by the buzzing of a bumblebee on a patch of clover, Lottie started to draw. Every now and again she looked intently at her sister standing with uncharacteristic poise, her untamed beauty framed by the ancient porch.

After a while she heard voices and looked up to see a woman and two fashionably dressed girls about the same age as her enter the churchyard.

'What a sweet little church!' The girl looked friendly but her blonde curls and peaches and cream complexion made Lottie feel gauche.

Cilla had no such inhibitions. 'My sister's sketching it and I'm in the picture,' she said proudly.

'How splendid! Can we see? The taller girl strode across the churchyard followed excitedly by Cilla.

Lottie brushed a speck of pollen off her brown serge skirt and continued her sketching, glad that she had a new yellow ribbon in her hat. She smiled hesitantly as the girl peered over her shoulder and looked at the sketch of the church with Cilla standing whimsically by the porch.

'That's a jolly good likeness isn't it Daisy?' said the girl turning to her friend.

Lottie caught a whiff of perfume as Daisy knelt down beside her. 'It's such a quaint church. How clever of you to sketch it! And your sister will look lovely in the foreground when you've painted it. Don't you think so Mother?'

The woman studied the drawing for a moment. 'It's very good.' She looked piercingly at Lottie. 'Haven't I seen you somewhere before?'

'My parents own the shop opposite the station at Llandudno Junction.'

'Yes, I remember now; you're Mr and Mrs Rowe's daughters.'

Lottie nodded. Feeling slightly awkward she stood up and began gathering her things together then added politely, 'I hope you're settling into your house, Mrs Dacre.'

'Yes, it's going to be a lovely holiday home. This is Daisy and Hilda's first visit to Trealaw.'

'You've called your house Trealaw?'

'Yes, we thought Home of Song was a good name.'

Lottie nodded doubtfully.

'My father and my brother have lovely singing voices,' said Daisy.

There was a blood curdling cry and Efan and Little Owen appeared, brandishing sticks.

'We're pirates!' they yelled to everyone's amusement.

'I was reading that pirates used to sail along the river and pillage the homesteads in the valley,' said Alice.

'How awful! It's good that sort of thing doesn't happen nowadays,' Lottie ushered the boys towards the gate.

The others followed and for a moment the women stood by the ancient stone wall savouring the peace of the old church hidden on the mountainside.

Still pretending to be pirates, the boys ran out of the gate.

'We must go,' said Lottie reluctantly.

'It's been nice meeting you, we'll see you again,' called Daisy and Hilda with a wave.

'I wonder if we will see them again,' said Lottie as they followed their cousins down the track.

'Why? Would you like to be friends with them?' Cilla looked inquisitively at her sister.

'Don't be silly; why would they want to be friends with me?'

'I'd like to have a friend like Daisy, she's really pretty.'

'So are you,' said Lottie fondly.

Cilla grinned and skipped ahead.

…

Lottie was in no hurry to get back. Meeting Daisy and her friend had unsettled her and she found herself wondering if it was time to do something about her future.

'Did you see anything interesting on your walk?' asked Jack when they were all settled round the table laden with cakes and sandwiches.

'We met the people from the house Uncle Owen built. They've called it Trealaw.'

'House of Song indeed, sorrow would be more appropriate,' sniffed Meg.

'Taffy's death was an unfortunate accident,' her husband said defensively.

Nellie looked at her brother. 'They say that if a death occurs during the building of a house, it puts a curse on it.'

'Now then Nellie,' cautioned Jack, 'that's just an old wives' tale. I'm sure the folk from London will enjoy their holidays there.'

'At least they've chosen a Welsh name,' said Nellie. 'Although I can't understand why they need a house on Mynydd Brith when they've already got one in London.'

'It seems to be the fashion to have a holiday home if you can afford one.'

'But why choose to live half way up a mountain? The English are mad!' Meg shook her head.

'Are you calling me mad?' Jack smiled good-humouredly at his sister-in-law.

'You may be English but you had the good sense to marry a Welsh girl. And you've made your life in Wales. You and Nellie have worked hard to build up your shop.'

'Thank you.' Jack gave a mock bow. 'But quite a few of our customers are English holiday makers. Inspector and Mrs Dacre are good customers when they're up here.'

'They're very friendly,' said Lottie. 'They liked my drawing of the old church.'

'And Daisy's ever so pretty, she was wearing a pink crepe de chine blouse,' added Cilla.

'It's Miss Daisy to you,' Nellie said sharply. 'Pink crepe de chine indeed, what will you think of next!'

Cilla glared and was about to retort back when Lottie interrupted.

'I'm sure they'll enjoy their holidays, there's so much to see and do around here.'

'Well, if things continue as they are, no one will have time for holidays,' said Jack grimly.

'Why? Has something happened?' Lottie looked anxious.

'According to the newspapers, troops are mobilising throughout Europe. Martial law has been declared in Germany and people are being told not to travel to the Continent.'

'I prefer to read the adverts,' Meg said soothingly. 'If I had a guinea to spare I'd buy a Kodak camera.'

'Oh yes, I like the adverts too, especially those advertising ships going to Africa and all those other exciting places.' Cilla looked animated.

'Well no one will be going anywhere for a while,' said Jack.

'Apart from the young men,' Uncle Owen added.

Lottie felt suddenly sick and gripped the table.

'We must thank the good Lord that our sons are too young to be involved with any of it.' Meg glanced at Efan and Little Owen trying hard to keep awake. 'More tea anyone?

'Yes please.' Lottie forced a smile and passed her cup and saucer to her aunt. She glanced at her father tucking into a large piece of fruitcake and her cousins with chocolate icing round their mouths.

Everything seemed so normal. And Germany was far away from this little corner of Wales.

Chapter 3: Alice

The British Fleet in Readiness

The Times: August 3rd 1914

'You've chosen a splendid spot for your holiday home,' said Hilda as they left the church path and wandered back towards Trealaw.

Alice looked at her goddaughter fondly and then at her husband digging near the house. 'It's a lovely change from London and Humphrey is enjoying making a garden.'

'Oh look, we've got a visitor!' Daisy pointed to a man pushing a bicycle up the track.

Alice frowned. 'It's a telegram,' she said and broke into a run.

Humphrey hurried to the gate.

'Good afternoon Sir.' The man handed Humphrey an envelope then waited respectfully at a distance to see if an answer was required.

Alice studied her husband's face anxiously as he read the message.

'It's from William. He says the country's preparing for mobilisation and the trains will be used for transporting troops so we should return as soon as possible.' His voice was controlled but Alice detected a tinge of despair as he turned to the man.

'There's no reply. But I'd like you to deliver a message to the station master when you get back to Conway. Tell him to send a cab for Inspector Dacre and family immediately.' He handed the man a coin.

'Very good, Sir. Thank you, Sir.' He pocketed the coin then pedalled back down the mountain.

'But we've only just come!' Daisy stared at her father.

'Don't you understand? The holiday's over. We might even be at war by the time we get back to London.'

'But people don't want to go to war!'

Humphrey looked grim. 'Sadly, it's governments who make the decisions.'

'But it won't affect us, will it?' asked Hilda.

Alice looked at the two girls on the threshold of their adult lives. What did the future hold for them? And for William? Would he be called upon to fight?

'Let's hope it'll all be over quickly,' she said, determined to be positive. 'But for the moment we have to go home and serve our country'.

***

Soldiers milled about the platform, kitbags hoisted over their shoulders, their expressions a mixture of excitement and determination. From the comfort of her first class compartment Alice watched as, with a screech of brakes, the express steamed into Euston station and juddered to a halt.

'Oh Hilda, just look at them all!' Daisy deftly re-applied her make-up and snapped her compact shut.

'Are you ready, ladies? I'll organise a porter to collect our cases from the guard's van.' Humphrey lifted his briefcase from the luggage rack.

As they made their way along the platform a bugle sounded and they turned to see a fashionably dressed couple being swept along by a group of young people laughing and shouting instructions to the pair.

'It's a wedding party! I wonder where they're going?'

'Not as far as they'd planned.' A young man heard Hilda's question and, looking approvingly at Daisy, slowed to a walk beside the girls. 'They were going to

France for their honeymoon but the Kaiser's put a stop to that so they'll stay in London instead.'

'That's frightfully bad luck.' Daisy looked sympathetically at the bride in her elegant purple costume and hat decorated with ostrich feathers.

The station was more crowded than Alice had ever seen it. Brightly dressed holidaymakers mingled with soldiers in khaki, and the normal British reserve seemed to have disappeared as everyone talked, desperately seeking information.

'There's your father speaking to someone,' she said seeing Humphrey already at the barrier. 'I wonder if he's got any more news about what's happening.'

Humphrey looked solemn when they caught up with him. 'Germany invaded Belgium today and has declared war on France. We've given Germany an ultimatum but it runs out soon.'

'Are we at war?' Daisy asked wide-eyed.

'Not yet. But it won't be long now.' He was waiting quietly, his shrewd eyes taking in the ebb and flow of the crowd.

Alice felt her heartbeat quicken as she stood next to Humphrey, trying to take in his words. She focused her attention on a dark-haired young naval officer bearing an uncanny resemblance to William. Alice clenched her fists, pushing away thoughts about what would happen to her son if they went to war.

'You're never off duty,' she murmured to Humphrey as a porter trundled towards them with their luggage.

'That's why I like our holidays in Wales; I can forget about being a railway detective and enjoy the simple life.'

Shouts from an angry mob followed by a piercing scream made Humphrey break off and hurry towards the platform. A man, urged on by an excitable crowd, was aiming blows with his fists and feet at a fair-skinned young man cowering on the ground.

'Stop! Immediately!' he commanded.

The crowd backed away muttering but the perpetrator, a mean-faced man, glared at Humphrey.

'Filthy Hun!' he said menacingly and spat in the face of the well-dressed young man lying crumpled at his feet.

The porter hovered uncertainly near the scene.

'Porter!' Humphrey called imperiously. 'Take him to the station master. You two,' he gestured towards two young soldiers, 'help this man up.'

The porter scowled and the soldiers hesitated.

'Tell the station master that Inspector Dacre witnessed the incident,' he said sharply.

'I'm a patriot, I am!' The man faced the crowd but they shifted uncomfortably and looked away.

'An Englishman doesn't hit a man when he's down,' came a shout from the back of the crowd.

The young man moaned and reached out as if looking for something.

'Is this what you want?' asked one of the soldiers hesitantly as he bent down and retrieved a pair of spectacles.

'Thank you,' whispered the young man in perfect English.

The soldiers looked at each other in confusion then helped him to his feet.

Humphrey turned to the porter. 'I asked you to take that man to the station master,' he said sternly.

'Yes, Sir.' He grabbed the man's arm.

'You come with me,' he said importantly and marched him through the now jeering crowd.

The fair-skinned young man nodded to Humphrey and shuffled away, his arm hanging limply by his side.

Alice looked at Daisy's and Hilda's horror stricken faces and felt an overwhelming urge to protect them from whatever lay ahead. Instead she tilted her chin and called for another porter to take their luggage.

'Do you think the man was a German?' asked Hilda as they walked out of the busy station.

Humphrey looked at her sadly. 'There's no telling. As far as I'm concerned he's an innocent civilian. And if our army is going to fight to protect our civilisation then we should make sure that it's worth fighting for.'

***

August 4th dawned with the sun making sporadic attempts to shine, but the temperature had dropped and the dining room of the elegant house in Belsize Park felt cool when Alice came downstairs for breakfast.

'Good morning, Mother!' William's face was flushed with excitement as he rose from the table to kiss her. His dark hair was immaculately smoothed into place but Alice was reminded of the tousled-haired boy he had once been.

In contrast, Humphrey was sombre when he looked up from his newspaper, and Alice noticed a few grey hairs around his temples. 'We'll have to see what the day holds,' he said and poured himself a cup of coffee.

For a moment Alice said nothing as she helped herself to bacon and egg from the silver dish on the sideboard. As well as a nagging fear of the future, she was disappointed that the visit to their mountain home had been cut short by Humphrey's insistence that they return to London.

'Did you go to the flying club yesterday?' Her voice was light, betraying none of the unease she felt.

'Pardon?'

Alice followed William's gaze to the big bay window. A fashionably dressed young woman was walking past the house. William gave an approving smile then looked enquiringly at Alice.

'Your mother asked if you went flying,' said Humphrey, his eyes still on his newspaper.

'Oh yes! I took Duggie up.'

'And did he enjoy it?' Alice knew that Hilda's brother had not always shared William's enthusiasms.

William laughed. 'He was a bit green about the gills after I'd put the machine through its paces.'

'Poor Duggie! I expect he was glad when you landed.'

'Actually, he reckoned that aeroplanes could be useful to farmers in surveying their land.'

'Well, his family have certainly got plenty.'

William stood up. 'Well, we'd better be off and see what's happening.'

'Aren't you going to see Hilda before she returns to Hertfordshire?'

'There's no time this morning, but why don't we all meet in St James's Park this evening? I'm sure her parents can spare her another day now that Duggie's gone back to the estate. And there might be some news by then!' William's eyes sparkled in anticipation.

'All right,' she said quietly then looked at Humphrey. 'Will you come?'

'If I can. It depends.' He left the words ringing in the air as he folded his newspaper and followed William out of the door.

Alice stood by the window as father and son walked purposefully along the street; for once they appeared to be in step. She sighed as she wondered how they could be so different. Lost in thought, she picked up a photograph on the window sill of William and Daisy taken on their very first trip to North Wales. Daisy's curls framed her face; she was smiling at the camera and proudly holding a bucket of shells. William was standing to attention with a spade slung over his shoulder as if it were a rifle.

Then her mood lightened as Daisy and Hilda came into the room.

'I hope you're rested after the journey. William suggested we meet this evening in St James's Park. I think it would be a good idea to go to Town and try and find out what's happening.'

'That's a capital idea and it will make up for our holiday being cut short. Oh, good morning, Ethel,' said Daisy as a plump, rosy-cheeked woman wearing a black dress and white cap came in carrying a tray.

'Good morning, Miss, are you ready for your breakfasts now?'

'Yes please. Has the post been this morning?'

'There was nothing for you, Miss Daisy.' Ethel smiled sympathetically as she left the room.

'Oh, I hoped there'd be something from the hospital.'

'You'll just have to be patient,' said Alice sharply.

'I know you and Father don't think radiography is a suitable occupation but I'm determined to give it a try if they'll have me.'

'My parents say there's enough for me to do on the estate at home,' said Hilda. She ran her fingers distractedly though her straight dark hair.

'If our men are fighting there may be lots of jobs for women.'

'William won't be joining up, will he?' Daisy looked startled.

'I doubt if he'd be allowed to; the railways are going to be essential for moving troops,' replied Alice with satisfaction.

***

'Bravo!' cheered the crowd as the band stood up and took their final bow with a flourish.

Like many Londoners, Alice enjoyed strolling through St James's Park and stopping by the ornate wrought iron bandstand to listen to concerts or the latest dance tunes. This evening, however, all the music had been military and the crowd had cheered, young men had slapped each other's backs and vowed to teach the Kaiser a lesson. No one wanted to disperse, even after the band had packed away their instruments. Strangers talked as if they were old friends, everyone speculating when the announcement committing Britain to war would be made.

Daisy was talking animatedly to three young men with Hilda chipping in occasionally and smiling broadly.

Alice was pleased to see the girls enjoying themselves, although she felt that everyone's enthusiasm was misplaced. She was just beginning to feel out of place in the middle of the young people when she saw William striding towards them, his face like thunder. At first Alice thought William was angry to see his sister and Hilda being courted by the young men, but one of them appeared to be an acquaintance and he greeted everyone with his familiar joviality. After a while the men drifted away and the dark expression returned to William's face.

Daisy looked at William and raised her eyes questioningly to Alice, who shrugged her shoulders.

'What's the matter, Wills?' Daisy looked affectionately at her brother.

'I've been posted, that's what.'

Alice felt her heart miss a beat: He couldn't be; war hadn't even been declared, they couldn't be posting men yet and surely they had to enlist first?

'What do you mean - posted?'

'I've been posted to Llandudno Junction. They want me to help run the locomotive maintenance department there.'

Alice felt her heartbeat return to normal. 'But that's wonderful, it's promotion.'

'Well I don't want to be in some godforsaken place at the end of the line while everything's happening here.'

The three women looked at each other, not knowing what to say.

'Does your father know?' asked Alice.

'Oh I expect so, there's not much he doesn't know,' said William bitterly.

Alice did her best to look sympathetic but she felt almost light-headed with relief. She could still hear snatches of talk about 'giving the Germans a good hiding' as if they were rivals in the school playground, and she knew that William would be swept along with the general enthusiasm to enlist if he had the opportunity.

'I'm sorry you're disappointed but I'm proud of you.'

'Thanks Mother,' he said dismissively, and began to walk across the park towards the Mall.

'Buy a posy for your ladies, Sir?' A cheeky faced, tousled haired boy skipped in front of them as they neared the edge of the park.

'Shouldn't he be in bed?' muttered Hilda.

'That's right Ma'am.' The boy's ears were sharp. 'If the gentleman takes these last three posies I'll go straight home to Muvver.' He looked at William and gave him a knowing wink.

William laughed and fished in his pocket for some coins. 'Take these, you young rascal.'

'Much obliged, Sir.' The boy handed over the wilting flowers, gave a little bow and disappeared.

Hilda carefully tucked her posy in her belt, but Daisy laughed at the fading petals and handed hers to Alice, who lifted both bunches to her nose and nodded approvingly as she inhaled a faint scent of countryside.

They bought some cockles then drifted with the crowd towards Buckingham Palace. A wind rippled along the Mall and the air felt chill as the dusk deepened. They strolled in silence, each lost in their thoughts, waiting and wondering what the future held.

The gaslights came on, casting welcome pools of light along the path, and then a military band struck up. They cheered with the crowds as the Guards came marching towards them from Admiralty Arch and on to Buckingham Palace.

'Let's follow them, maybe there's going to be an announcement.' William broke into a run behind the Guards.

For the second time that day Alice wished Humphrey was with them. She looked around and saw wild excitement on the faces of the young people running past her. She caught the eye of a woman of her own age and they smiled ruefully at cach other as they fell into step together.

'I've got three sons,' said the woman then hurried on.

Alice could just make out the figures of Daisy and Hilda ahead of her and she too hurried forward. As she ran she looked down at the flowers still clasped in her hand and noticed a sprig of heather. All at once the crowd seemed too close, she longed for the open space of Mynydd Brith and she slowed her pace.

The girls too had halted their manic surge forward and were waiting quietly under a gas lamp for Alice to catch up with them.

'Where's William?' asked Alice.

'Gone to War!' Daisy gave a little laugh then linked arms with her mother and Hilda and propelled them forward. The band gave a long roll of drums then was silent and all that could be heard were the excitable voices and tramping feet of the crowd.

They found William sitting at the foot of Queen Victoria's statue outside Buckingham Palace. 'They think there's going to be an announcement.' His eyes were shining.

The band struck up again, this time from behind the palace gates and, once again, they found themselves surging forward with the crowd. They came to a halt near the gates where they had a good view of people and vehicles coming and going. The music was stirring, the crowd good-humoured, and the next couple of hours passed quickly.

People fell silent as a church bell chimed eleven o'clock. Everyone knew it was midnight in Germany and therefore the British government's ultimatum had expired. The King appeared on the palace balcony dressed in full military uniform. He looked a dignified figure as he solemnly declared that Germany had refused to agree to Britain's demand that she withdraw from France and Belgium.

Britain and Germany were at war.

Chapter 4: Lottie

Wales and the New Army
The Prime Minister concluded in Cardiff his mission to
call for men and still more men for the army

The Times: October 3rd 1914

Lottie looked at herself in the mirror above the fireplace and straightened her blue velvet hat. Meeting the girls from London at the Old Church had spurred her into action and she had surprised everyone by getting herself a job in Llandudno, the smart seaside resort at the end of the railway line. Her parents were against the idea at first but Cilla had been happy enough to leave school and take Lottie's place in the shop.

The tang of bacon mixed with the smells of tea, newsprint, carbolic and other household items were so familiar that she hardly noticed them as she opened the door into the shop.

'Will you be all right Cilla? I'm a bit late this morning.'

'Of course!' Cilla grinned at her sister from behind the counter.

'It's a pity Mother's ill again but Father will be with you as soon as he's finished his breakfast.'

The doorbell rang and the tiny shop was suddenly filled with customers.

As she went back into the family accommodation, she could already hear Cilla bantering with a regular buying his newspaper.

Lottie let herself out of the back gate and hurried across the road to join the passengers queuing to buy a ticket before their train departed.

'It's busier than usual,' she said to the large-bosomed woman in front of her.

'The junior ticket clerk didn't turn up this morning. Packed his bags and went off to enlist. They say his mother's heartbroken.'

'Well, she shouldn't be; her son's only doing his duty,' the young army officer next to her said sharply.

The woman looked flustered. 'I wasn't being unpatriotic. It's just, well, how will the country keep going if there's no one left to do the jobs at home?'

'Women!' Lottie heard herself say.

'I beg your pardon?'

'What I mean is,' Lottie hesitated, unaccustomed to arguing with her elders, 'women can do all sorts of jobs. I'm on my way to work right now,' she added proudly.

'Good for you. What's the job?'

'It's in Knight's Emporium in the china department.'

'Oh they've got some lovely crockery there and some beautiful figurines. Hope you're not a butter fingers.' The woman laughed.

The passengers shuffled forward grumbling quietly. Lottie kept looking at the clock hanging above the entrance to the platforms. By the time she had paid for her ticket she could hear her train steaming into the station. She ran through the barrier and along the crowded platform.

A tightly corseted woman in black was trying to persuade her Pekinese to get on board but it tugged on its leash, barking loudly. Lottie swerved to avoid the dog then gasped in fascinated horror as it ran round and round its owner, its leash encircling her ankles. The woman screamed and staggered forward. With an anxious glance at her train, Lottie leapt to steady her and almost collided with a uniformed man who was also hurrying to help. Their eyes met as they each grabbed an arm then drew away when the woman steadied herself. With an unaccountable flutter Lottie recognised the new railway engineer from London who regularly bought cigarettes from the shop. His lips were twitching as he unravelled the yapping dog and gravely handed it to the woman who glared and heaved herself onto the train without a word of thanks.

'Shouldn't it travel in the guard's van?' Lottie knew she should board her train but was reluctant to leave.

'Or the pound.' His expression was deadpan but his eyes were laughing as he escorted Lottie to her carriage and helped her on the train.

'It's Miss Rowe, isn't it? Your quick thinking saved the woman from a nasty fall.'

Lottie blushed and paused at the open window by the door. 'Thank you, but it was a joint effort.' She paused, 'Mr ….'

'Dacre. William.' He held out his hand. 'What an excellent team!' William looked up at Lottie and laughed as he shook her hand.

The train shunted forward and William let go but kept pace with the train until it halted further down the platform.

Lottie felt it would be rude to take her seat while William was still standing there. And, in any case, she was in no hurry to.

'How are you finding Llandudno Junction?'

A frown darkened William's handsome features. 'I was posted here,' he said shortly.

A shower of soot blew along the platform and clanging from the railway sheds hammered in Lottie's ears. She turned away.

'But the mountains are beautiful, don't you agree?'

Despite herself, Lottie turned back to the window.

'Yes, I like to sketch them whenever I have the opportunity.' Lottie broke off, suddenly aware of the other passengers in the carriage listening to their conversation.

A whistle blew, the guard waved a green flag and the train began to pick up speed. Lottie nodded uncertainly at William who raised his hand. She took her seat but William remained where he was, his eyes fixed on her carriage.

***

Fifteen minutes later the train pulled into Llandudno station. Some late holidaymakers and the sound of a band playing gave the town a carnival atmosphere, but when Lottie pushed her way through the crowds she realised with a shiver that the holiday was over.

Trumpeters, trombonists and tuba players in cheap suits and cloth caps were marching slowly down the main street. Bringing up the rear was a man beating a huge drum. A couple of young women walking alongside were holding placards exhorting men to enlist in Kitchener's army.

Lottie fell into step with the band but took care to distance herself from the women who had begun chanting anti-German slogans. She glanced down a side street and smiled in recognition as a lanky, bespectacled young man from Knight's haberdashery department limped towards her.

'Good morning Dylan! The music's nice, but I hope it's not going to make us late.'

'We can't risk that; we'll have to shove a bit I'm afraid.'

Despite his limp, Dylan cut quickly through the crowd but when Lottie caught up the placard-bearing women were barring his way. They appeared to know him although their expressions were unfriendly.

'Will you excuse us please?' Dylan's voice was controlled but his knuckles were clenched. 'We're on our way to work.'

'Is that what you call it? Selling needles and thread doesn't sound like man's work to me.' The woman scrabbled in her bag and pulled out a feather. 'Shall we give him this?' she asked her friend with an unpleasant smirk.

Dylan stood rooted to the spot, his face ashen.

Lottie didn't understand what was happening. As she looked from the women's jeering faces to Dylan, she recollected a story her father had told her about white feathers being given to men who were too cowardly to go to war. But Dylan wasn't a coward and, whatever the girl said about it, he had a job.

'Leave the poor sod alone!' An elderly man looked sympathetically at Dylan as he shuffled past.

Lottie blushed at the coarse word, but it seemed to galvanise Dylan.

'Come on Lottie, let's go.'

He grabbed her arm and they hurried along the street till they came to the revolving doors of Knight's Emporium. A doorman, resplendent in blue uniform and scarlet sash, greeted them and, with a feeling of relief, they stepped inside.

***

Saturdays were always busy, and after her early start with chores at home, Lottie was beginning to feel tired by the end of the afternoon. She was engrossed in wrapping a pair of breakfast cups and saucers when she was aware of a young man looking at her from behind a shelf of figurines.

'Will that be all, Madam?' she asked as she handed the package to the elderly woman she was serving.

'Yes, thank you.' The woman cast her eye longingly at the delicate figurines then walked slowly away.

Lottie glanced towards the display, then blushed with pleasure and confusion as she recognised William Dacre sporting a blue and white striped blazer and straw boater.

'May I help you, sir?' she said formally.

Out of the corner of her eye she saw the angular form of her supervisor looking at her suspiciously.

'I'm looking for a gift for my mother and I would particularly like your advice. As you know her, I think you are in a position to suggest something appropriate.' William's well-modulated tones caused the supervisor to regard Lottie curiously before giving her attention to another customer.

'But ...' Lottie was about to say that she didn't really know his mother but she was not the sort of woman one would easily forget.

'Were you thinking of something ornamental?' she asked politely.

'Maybe.' He picked up an exquisitely crafted figurine of a girl with blonde ringlets holding a lamb.

'That's Dresden,' said Lottie evenly, 'it's the last one.' She didn't add that they were due to pack away all items of German origin until the war was over.

'Do you think she'd like it?' William contemplated the porcelain girl.

'I really don't know.' Lottie was confused.

'Neither do I!' William laughed.

Lottie wondered if it was unpatriotic to recommend Dresden china, particularly in view of her supervisor's strident anti-German views.

'Maybe she'd like a brooch?' She gestured to a glass display case with a range of cameo brooches in velvet-lined boxes. 'The blue and white Wedgwood, perhaps?'

'Do you think it would suit her?'

Lottie felt flustered, he was implying that she knew his mother well. The supervisor was now looking at her approvingly and she replied with a newly found confidence.

'I think it will suit her very well.'

'Then I'll take it.'

'Would you like it gift wrapped?' Lottie took the brooch to the counter.

'Yes, please.'

She wrapped the box and hoped he didn't notice her fingers trembling.

'Is that all, Sir?' she said formally as she handed him the gift.

William's eyes twinkled. 'Yes thank you, you've been most helpful. I shall come again when I need a present for my sister.' He touched his hat and walked jauntily across the shop.

***

Lottie caught sight of her friend just ahead of her as everyone filed out of the emporium.

'Lord, what a day it's been!' Bronwen shook her dark curls as they came into the busy street. 'I was rushed off my feet. How about you? Did you have any awkward customers?'

'Oh no!' Lottie's eyes shone as she recalled the encounter with William Dacre.

'Well, we can forget about work and enjoy ourselves this evening. I'm so glad you're staying the night. We can have fun getting ready together after tea.'

Later, Lottie was dabbing scent on her handkerchief and looking out of Bronwen's bedroom window.

'I can see Dylan.' She was about to tell Bronwen about the incident that morning but her friend interrupted.

'Dear Dylan, he always calls for me if we go out and he sees me home afterwards. We've known each other since school.'

'Has he always walked with a limp?'

'No, he used to be a champion runner, but he was injured when he was working in the slate quarry. It was awful.' Bronwen shuddered. 'He lost his job of course, but was lucky to get a position at Knight's. He's the kindest man I know.'

'Are you sweet on him?'

'Dylan? No he's my dearest friend but certainly not my sweetheart!' Bronwen laughed and looked at Lottie critically. 'You look very nice, but don't you want a touch more lipstick?'

Lottie pursed her lips and peered in the mirror. 'No, I wouldn't feel right with any more.'

'They say red lips are more kissable,' said Bronwen archly.

Lottie giggled but put the top firmly back on her lipstick.

'Then I think we're ready.' Bronwen led the way downstairs just as Dylan knocked on the door.

The tiny hallway was crowded as he came in and the girls put on their coats.

'You both look very nice; have you got clean handkerchiefs?' Bronwen's mother smiled and reached up to brush a piece of fluff off Lottie's collar. 'Have a lovely time. You'll take care of them won't you, Dylan?'

'Mother, we're quite capable of taking care of ourselves,' said Bronwen.

'Of course you are! Goodbye.'

As they made their way into the town two girls and another young man from Knight's joined them. All were in high spirits as they strolled past other Saturday revellers until they came to the picture palace.

Lottie felt a frisson of excitement when she saw the poster advertising 'Mabel's Married Life' with Charlie Chaplain.

'I've heard it's a bit saucy!' giggled one of the girls as they purchased their tickets.

The pianist was already playing as they were shown to their seats in the centre of the picture house.

'We're lucky the seats in front of us are empty,' said Bronwen looking around at the almost full auditorium.

The music stopped, the lights dimmed and the pianist began playing again, hammering the keys flamboyantly. Just as the film began, two young men settled themselves in the vacant seats in front of them.

'Oh Lord!' exclaimed Bronwen.

The young man in front of her turned his head. 'I do beg your pardon.' He lowered himself so that he was low in his seat and, without looking round, his friend did the same.

Within minutes the audience were roaring with laughter at the antics of Charlie Chaplin and the flirtatious Mabel Normand. Lottie thought she would burst with laughing and felt almost relieved when the film finished.

'If that's how they behave in America I wouldn't mind taking a trip there!' she heard the man in front of Bronwen say to his companion.

'They're certainly not buttoned up like we are,' he observed. He stretched his arms and turned then his face lit up with pleasure when he saw Lottie. 'So we meet again,' he said. 'I hope we didn't disturb you arriving late.'

'Oh, not at all,' Lottie flushed.

'Are you going to introduce us?' his friend asked curiously.

'This is …'

'Lottie and I'm Bronwen,' her friend answered for her.

'Delighted to meet you. I'm Rhys and this is William.'

'I haven't seen you before, do you live in Llandudno?'

'No, we're both staying at the Junction. I'm the assistant bursar at the Station Hotel and William is assistant manager of the locomotive maintenance department.'

'I think the main film's about to start,' said Dylan.

Rhys ignored him. 'I hope you're not easily frightened, girls,' he said looking at Bronwen.

'We'll be fine with you to protect us,' she giggled.

'I'm not really sure what it's about,' confessed Lottie.

'Cabiria is meant to be a very good film, I'm sure you'll enjoy it.' William's eyes held Lottie's for a moment and then the lights went down.

Lottie's heart was in her mouth throughout the film as she witnessed battles, volcanic eruptions, and hair-raising escapes. When the lights came on she blinked then smiled as she saw William looking at her.

'Not too frightening?' he asked.

'It was really exciting,' she said then reluctantly followed her friends outside.

The cold damp air contrasted with the warmth inside but Lottie and Bronwen lingered in the busy street hoping to catch a glimpse of the two young men.

Their friends were chatting some distance away and they were just about to join them when they saw William and Rhys walking towards them. They accepted their invitation to meet for a walk on the pier the following morning with the correct amount of hesitation then strolled sedately to join their friends. The girls laughed approvingly when they told them of the invitation but Dylan peered at them through his thick spectacles.

'You don't know what you're letting yourself in for,' he said anxiously.

'A walk on the pier on a Sunday morning. You can come too if you like,' said Bronwen airily.

'No, it's all right, you enjoy yourselves.' Dylan shrugged and, linking both their arms, escorted them through the crowds.

***

'Look, there they are!' Bronwen nudged Lottie's arm as they neared the pier. 'Pretend you haven't seen them.'

They looked surreptitiously at the young men in their blazers and boaters.

'Do I look all right?' Lottie felt suddenly anxious.

'I love your jacket, blue suits you. And your hat is very chic.'

The girls walked with their eyes demurely on the ground, conscious of William and Rhys watching them as they crossed the road.

'Hello girls!' Rhys's hearty voice reached them across the noise of the cars and a horse-drawn carriage.

'Oh hello!' Bronwen's voice feigned surprise when they reached them. 'Isn't it just the right weather for a stroll on the pier,' she said gaily.

'Capital!' said William falling into step beside Lottie. 'Did you enjoy the pictures last night?'

'Oh yes! It was lovely.' She looked at him shyly. 'I expect you go to lots of concerts in London?'

'I like to in the season. The West End's a fun place to be in the winter. You ought to come sometime.'

Lottie stared in amazement. 'But London's far away!'

He laughed. 'I suppose it is. And it's dirty and noisy. Not like this.' He stretched his arm towards the sea.

'My father says this is the most beautiful coast in the world.'

William stopped and looked at her. 'That's exactly what my father said when he decided to build Trealaw with its wonderful view of the coastline.'

'And you've given it a Welsh name. Home of Song! That's such a lovely name!'

'It's lovely place. You must come and see it!'

Lottie held his gaze then, feeling unaccountably flustered, turned to bring Bronwen into the conversation. But her friend was sitting cosily with Rhys in one of the little shelters which were a feature of the pier.

'Rhys isn't really an outdoor type,' said William wryly.

'I don't think Bronwen is either.'

'And what about you?'

'Me?' Lottie thought about how, as a child, she had always longed to run out of her parents' dark little house and play on the beach. 'I like being outdoors.' She moved to the side of the pier leant over the balustrade and looked down at the waves crashing round the pier supports.

'So do I.' Lottie could feel the heat from William's body as he stood next to but not touching her.

'Do you play rugby?' she asked, thinking that he was probably a sportsman.

'Not any more. Flying is my hobby.'

'Flying? Can you fly an aeroplane?'

'I've held my licence for over two years now.' William gazed at the sky. 'It's a wonderful feeling of freedom being in the sky and looking down on the world.'

Lottie looked at him in awe. 'Aren't you scared?'

'Never!' William's face glowed. 'Exhilarated, excited but never scared.'

'Have you got your own aeroplane?' Lottie was beginning to feel out of her depth.

'No, that's for the rich boys. I belong to a flying club. Or did; most of the planes have been requisitioned by the war office.'

Lottie lifted her face to the wind as she contemplated the man by her side; so different from the Welsh boys she had been brought up with.

'Look! There's a peregrine falcon,' she said pointing towards the headland.

There were startled cries from two pigeons as the falcon swooped, its grey tail feathers fanning out and its talons ready to attack. The pigeons darted about in a mad dance attempting to confuse their pursuer but it had the smaller bird in its sights and suddenly pounced.

'Oh no!' Lottie gasped as the falcon grasped its prey then soared up and away to the cliff. Feathers from the unfortunate pigeon caught the breeze before dropping silently into the sea.

Lottie stood erect, her gloved hand grasping the rail and was surprised to feel tears pricking her eyelids.

Gently, William put his hand over hers. 'It was only doing its shopping,' he said solemnly.

'Shopping? Oh!' Lottie laughed. 'I'm glad our customers aren't like that!'

'You'd be forever sweeping up feathers!'

Lottie started to shake with laughter but did not want to move her hand away.

'Can we share the joke?'

Lottie turned to see Bronwen giving her a knowing smile as she stood arm in arm with Rhys.

'It's private,' grinned William and put his arm through Lottie's.

Rhys winked at William. 'It's a bit nippy, shall we find somewhere on the promenade for a cup of coffee?'

'What do you think, Lottie?'

'It would be lovely but I promised my mother I'd be back in time for dinner.'

William looked at his watch. 'It's still early, we can have coffee at St George's Hotel before you get your train back to the Junction.'

They retraced their steps then left the pier and ambled along the promenade past couples like themselves enjoying the fine weather. Some of the young men were in uniform and Lottie wondered if they were about to be sent to the Front.

There were shrieks from a group of children by the water's edge darting as near to the waves as they dared. A dog ran barking into the sea then splashed the children as it shook itself dry.

'My landlady has a dog,' remarked William.

'That's nice. I've always wanted one but it wouldn't be possible with the shop.'

'Maybe they're afraid it would steal the sausages.'

'But it would only be doing its shopping!' laughed Lottie.

William looked at her appreciatively. 'I sometimes take the dog for a walk along the beach; perhaps you'd like to come too?'

'Yes, that would be nice.'

They crossed the promenade to the hotel, its white facade gleaming in the sunlight. Lottie felt apprehensive as they were ushered into the lounge but William was at ease in the elegant surroundings and he ordered coffee for the four of them. Bronwen grinned and Lottie relaxed in her comfortable chair while

William regaled them with stories of flying with the Royal Aero Club.

'You ought to be flying with the RNAS.' Rhys regarded his friend admiringly.

'I know.' William looked out of the window at the clear sky. 'But we have to do our duty and I was sent here.'

There was an uncomfortable silence and Lottie glanced at the grandfather clock set into an alcove. 'Goodness! I didn't realise the time. I have to go!' She fiddled with her handbag, not wanting to leave.

'Can't you stay a bit longer?' From the way Bronwen looked at Rhys it was obvious that she was in no hurry to go.

'I promised my mother I'd be back for dinner.'

'Then you mustn't keep her waiting.' William gestured to the waiter for the bill. 'I'll escort you to the railway station.'

'And I'll walk back to the pier with you.' Rhys offered Bronwen his arm.

William gave the waiter a generous tip. As they walked back into the thickly carpeted foyer Lottie glimpsed the dining room with its starched white cloths and silver service set out for Sunday dinner. Then they were in the street and back into the world she knew.

***

Lottie didn't know whether to be pleased or irritated when she saw Cilla running towards her, her red hair flying untidily from under her hat.

'Did you have a nice time?' she asked eagerly as Lottie walked through the barrier.

'Pretty girls like her can always have a good time,' leered a soldier leaning against the wall.

Lottie gasped and grabbed her sister's hand. But Cilla turned and stared at the man, fascinated by his unshaven face and the empty bottle lying by his filthy boots.

'Even the young ones,' he added as he looked Cilla up and down approvingly.

Sensing a compliment, she started to smile then flushed as she met his insolent gaze.

Lottie tugged her hand and they marched out of the station.

'He wasn't very nice!' Cilla was indignant.

'He was horrid! You shouldn't have looked at him.'

'But he spoke to us.' Cilla half turned her head. 'Anyway, I want to hear all about last night. Did you enjoy the picture?'

Lottie thought of William's well-mannered attentiveness and her eyes softened. 'Yes,' she said simply.

'Did you meet anyone?'

'Lots of people.'

'But did you meet anyone special?'

'Do you think I'd tell you if I had?'

'Of course.' Cilla was genuinely surprised. 'We always tell each other everything.'

'So what did you do yesterday?'

'Nothing much. I was in the shop most of the time.'

'You used to say it wasn't fair that I was allowed to serve customers and you weren't.'

'I know I did! Anyway it's all right for the moment. Until I find something better.' Her delicate features hardened and her green eyes were defiant.

'Your place is helping Father in the shop,' said Lottie sharply as she side-stepped a horse-drawn cab.

'I don't see why Mother can't do more.'

'Cilla! You know Mother's poorly!'

'She's not really, not like she used to be.'

They crossed the road in silence then paused at the narrow passage alongside the house. Lottie could hear a goods train with its cargo of slate shunting along the branch line and the express from London to Holyhead hooting as it pulled into the Junction. Talking to William had given her a glimpse of a life very different from own.

Cilla seemed to sense her thoughts. 'Do you remember playing lost girls when we were little? And we said when we were old enough we'd travel the world together.'

'We did, didn't we? And now everything's changed and we can't even dream about things like that.' Unconsciously echoing William she continued, 'We have to stay here and do our duty.'

Chapter 5: Alice

British Eau-de-Cologne for British People
Boots the Chemist have on sale at all their branches the
following two brands
of Eau-de-Cologne. They entirely supersede any
German cologne

The Times: October 16th 1914

A murmur of disappointment rippled round the committee and Alice shifted uncomfortably in the afternoon sunshine that flooded the small room. She fixed her eyes on the artificial flowers encircling the speaker's hat. The secretary, more soberly dressed in black, laid her pencil on a leather-bound notebook and looked up expectantly.

Resting her pudgy fingers on a wooden gavel, the chairman continued, 'And so Ladies, it is with much regret, I propose we wind up the work of the Women's Emigration to South Africa Society for the duration of the war.'

Alice's neighbour rustled her indignation. 'But surely, Madam Chairman, we have a duty to the gels we've already sent.'

'We have discharged our duty by arranging suitable placements for all the girls we've sent to South Africa. As I have already outlined, it is unfortunate that under the current circumstances, there is no way we can repatriate them. We shall of course continue to keep in touch with them from time to time.' Madam Chairman dabbed her forehead with a lace-edged handkerchief and stared imperiously at her committee. 'Do I have a seconder for the proposal?'

Alice looked around at the silent women, most of them older than her, and understood their unwillingness to disband the society which was their link with the wider, exotic world of the Empire.

Reluctantly she held up her hand.

'Thank you Mrs Dacre. All those in favour raise your hands.'

After some hesitation the proposal was carried unanimously.

The meeting drew to a close but no one was in a hurry to leave. Although Alice did not count any of the women as close friends, they had worked together for a number of years, helping to improve the fortunes of young Englishwomen as well as providing a valuable service for the colonists in Africa. Now they lingered, discussing the different options for war work.

A sharp-faced woman, her eyes burning with zeal, turned enthusiastically to Alice. 'We could put our skills into recruiting for the army; what do you think Mrs Dacre?'

Alice shuddered. She was tempted to ask her if she had sons but was politely non-committal as she took her leave.

***

A welcome breeze blew along Pall Mall as she left the Overseas Club and made her way towards Charing Cross.

Outside the station was a line of ambulances. People pushed forward and cheered the soldiers who were being helped aboard. Alice froze in horror as she watched men younger than William, some with blood-stained bandages around their heads, hobbling alongside stretchers which carried the crippled bodies of their comrades. One or two gave a ghost of a smile as they feebly raised their hands to acknowledge the words of encouragement and cries of "God Save the

King!" But the majority looked neither right nor left, their faces expressionless, as they were shepherded onto the ambulances.

Alice clutched her collar and watched as they were driven away. Then she turned into the station and walked slowly down the steps to the underground.

The wounded soldiers had unnerved her and Alice was still feeling subdued when she got off the train at Belsize Park. She glanced up the road towards the hospital hoping to see Daisy coming home from work in the radiography department.

The street was busy with horse drawn vehicles and motorbuses and Alice stepped aside to avoid a man running to catch a bus. She paused for a moment then turned sharply when she felt a tap on her shoulder. Her face lit up as she found herself looking into her daughter's smiling face.

'I wondered if I'd see you. Did you have a good day?'

'Not bad. I had a couple of difficult patients. How was your meeting?'

Alice was about to reply when a girl of around Daisy's age blocked her way and thrust a neatly folded piece of paper in her hand.

'Excusez-moi Madam, you know zees place, plees?'

She looked at the address and then at the girl who was wearing a well-cut grey coat that hung pathetically on her thin body.

'Are you from Belgium?' she asked kindly.

'Refugee, I have work here,' she stated tonelessly. She stared at the traffic with dull eyes then pushed a blonde curl back under her hat.

Alice felt a rush of sympathy for the girl. 'It's very near, we will show you.'

The girl nodded and followed them across the main road and down a side street. Daisy offered to help carry her bag but the girl refused.

They stopped outside an imposing detached house with a flight of steps going up to the front door. For a moment the three women stood on the pavement. Alice was uncertain what to do, normally she would ring the front door bell but servants would be expected to use the back entrance. She pointed to a door at the side of the house.

'This is the house,' she said.

'Thank you.' The girl walked past the rubbish bins then put down her bag and, with an almost arrogant tilt of the head, rang the back door bell.

'Good luck!' called Daisy but her face was troubled as they walked away.

Alice wondered if the young woman, like her own daughter, was used to being received at the front entrance. If so, she wouldn't find it easy adapting to life as a servant.

'It could be me,' whispered Daisy.

'Never!' Alice quickened her pace, trying not to think of the young Belgian and the thousands of others fleeing from the fighting across the Channel.

They hurried on in silence. When they turned the corner Alice felt calmed by the familiar splash of colour in her front garden. She and Humphrey had planted two Japanese maples when they moved into the house and she delighted in their scarlet and gold leaves.

'Oh! There's Hilda!' said Daisy as she opened the gate.

Alice looked in surprise at her goddaughter waving from the drawing room window and she hurried up the well-scrubbed steps to the porch.

Daisy had already rushed into the house to greet her friend but the sound of footsteps made Alice turn and she smiled in surprise as William strode through the gate.

He stretched out his arms. 'I've been following you! Happy birthday, Mother.'

Alice felt her mood lighten as he kissed her. 'Thank you. To tell you the truth, I'd forgotten all about it. This is a lovely surprise, but why aren't you in Wales?'

'There's a job they want me to do here but I hope to be back up at the Junction again soon.'

His expression was inscrutable but Alice was relieved there was no sign of his previous anger about the posting to Llandudno Junction.

She walked into the wide hallway and hung up her hat and jacket. 'Hilda's here too so it's quite a celebration.'

However, as soon as she saw Hilda's face Alice knew that something was wrong.

'Is everything all right at home?' she asked as she kissed her.

'Not really.' Hilda stood close to Daisy and twisted her handkerchief in her hands. 'I came to London to say goodbye to Duggie. He's enlisted.'

'But he's in a reserved occupation!' William hovered in the doorway, his handsome features clouded with indignation.

'That's what we all said. My parents are patriotic of course but since Father's illness Duggie has run the farm. And the country needs food.'

Alice felt suddenly tired as she sank into the cool leather of her chair by the fireplace. 'Whatever made him do it?'

'A girl in the village gave him a white feather.'

William looked shocked. 'But white feathers are for cowards! Duggie's not a coward!'

'Of course he isn't and neither are any of the young men who are given feathers by unthinking girls,' said Alice angrily.

'Who was this girl anyway?' William glared at Hilda.

'She was no one. Just a girl from the village.' Hilda's voice was laced with contempt. She sat down heavily on the sofa and took a ball of dark grey wool from her bag. 'I'm going to knit him some socks. The Queen has asked the women of England to provide thirty thousand pairs for our soldiers.'

'That's going to keep you all busy,' William said wryly as Hilda wound the wool tightly round her knitting needles. 'There doesn't seem much point in having reserved occupations if the men enlist anyway,' he growled.

Alice's eyes met Daisy's who was still standing, shaken, by the window. 'Don't you ...,' she said then stopped.

'No, Mother, I won't leave my important job as a railway engineer to enlist. Though I must admit I did consider joining the special corps of railwaymen who've gone to work on the French railways.'

'Well I'm glad you decided not to,' she said quietly.

Apart from the clacking of Hilda's needles the room was silent. Then the grandfather clock in the hall struck six.

'I'll go and get changed,' said William.

'I'll go too. I'll be back in a minute.' Daisy looked sympathetically at her friend and followed her brother out of the room.

Alice sighed. 'I'm sorry about Duggie; it'll be difficult for you without him. Let's hope the war will be over by Christmas and he'll be back before you know,' she said unconvincingly.

'Anyway, we've got your birthday to celebrate.' Hilda seemed determined to be cheerful. 'I called in to see Uncle Humphrey when I arrived at Euston and he said you're going to see The Chocolate Soldier tomorrow evening and that he'd get a ticket for me too.'

'That will be lovely.' Alice knew how much she used to look forward to the few opportunities she had of going to the theatre in London when she was Hilda's age and living in the same village as Hilda's family.

***

By unspoken agreement, everyone put aside their distress at the news of Duggie's decision to join up. When they gathered in the drawing room before dinner it had a festive air with a vase of gold chrysanthemums and gifts on the table by Alice's chair. She felt secure with her family around her as she picked up a package and read the label in Daisy's neat handwriting.

'I hope it's all right.' Daisy watched as Alice carefully unwrapped a bottle of eau-de-cologne.

'White Heather; this must be a new fragrance.' Alice took off the lid. 'It's lovely, it reminds me of heather on the Welsh mountains.'

'I couldn't get your normal perfume, everything's British nowadays.'

Alice dabbed some on her wrist and held out her arm. 'Do you like it, Humphrey?'

He rose from his chair and lifted her hand to his nose. 'I think I prefer it,' he said playfully then handed her a square flat box with a flourish.

'I think I can guess what this is.' Alice undid the ribbon and lifted a gramophone record from the box. 'Oh, it's Caruso singing some of his arias. That's wonderful! I shall enjoy it so much. Thank you.' Her eyes softened as they briefly met Humphrey's.

There was a small box left on the table. 'This is beautifully wrapped.' Alice picked up William's gift, carefully removed the paper and opened a leather box. Inside was a brooch engraved with a Grecian figure holding a bow and arrow. 'Diana, the goddess of hunting, it's exquisite!' She held the brooch in her palm then passed it to Humphrey.

'It's a fine piece of jewellery.' He studied the cameo and glanced at his son curiously.

'Thank you, that was very generous.' Alice looked at William's beaming face and couldn't help wondering why he had bought her such an expensive present.

'May I see?' Daisy held out her hand and studied the brooch. 'It's beautiful, where did you get it?'

'A shop in Llandudno. I asked L …,'William paused and corrected himself, 'the shop assistant for her advice; I was wondering about a figurine but she thought a brooch would be more suitable.'

'She's obviously got good taste.' Daisy looked at her brother quizzically.

Alice turned to Hilda. 'And thank you for the lovely chrysanthemums.'

'I picked them this morning, I was worried they'd get crushed on the train but they're all right aren't they?'

'They're lovely.' Alice smiled affectionately at her goddaughter.

The dinner gong sounded in the hall and they made their way into the dining room.

'How's your job?' Hilda asked Daisy as she unfolded her table napkin.

Alice began to ladle soup from a flowered porcelain tureen.

'I'm enjoying it. Apart from the uniform. Oh, thank you, Mother.' Daisy took a bowl of soup then continued, 'We have to wear protective clothing made of lead rubber when we're doing fluoroscopy.'

'What's that?'

'Examining different parts of the body using a fluoroscope. We have to work in total darkness.'

'That must be difficult.'

'Yes, it can be and some of the patients don't like it because it can take a while to get the right information from the continual flow of X rays on the screen.'

William looked at his sister in admiration. 'You've really taken to the work. How do you develop the film?'

'We use glass plates from Belgium but we can't get regular supplies. Some departments in other hospitals are using chemicals instead and I expect we'll start using that system soon.'

'You'll have to be careful, I understand that some of the chemicals they use are highly inflammable.' Humphrey regarded his daughter with a mixture of pride and concern.

'There's no need to worry about me.' Daisy turned to Hilda. 'It's a pity you can't get a job in London.'

Hilda shrugged. 'That's how it is; now that Duggie's gone I'll be needed at home more than ever. Of course, Bertie's furious that he's going back to boarding school next week as usual. He thinks he should stay at home and run the farm.'

'But he's only twelve!'

'He'll be able to help out in the holidays,' Alice said, then wished she hadn't. Her remark implied that Duggie was going to be away for some time. She rang the bell for Ethel to bring the second course and clear away the soup dishes.

'My favourite mutton dish,' said William. He turned to his mother. 'How was your day?'

'Disappointing in some ways. I was at a meeting of the Women's Emigration to South Africa society and we decided to suspend our operations until the end of the war. We can't send young women to the colonies with German warships patrolling the seas.'

Humphrey listened sympathetically. 'You'll miss your work with the society. Have you thought if you might like to do something else?'

'I don't know, there's help needed everywhere. Daisy and I met a Belgian refugee on our way home this afternoon.' Alice tried to banish the image of the wounded soldiers she had seen earlier.

'I've noticed quite a few refugees at Euston recently.'

'And troops,' added William.

Humphrey nodded. 'We're already seeing soldiers arriving back from the Front. They're usually exhausted and in need of a hot drink. Only this morning a corporal asked me for writing paper and envelopes. I was thinking we should set up some sort of free buffet where they could go while they're waiting for their trains.'

'That sounds a worthwhile thing to do.' Alice had been wondering whether she should offer her services to the Red Cross but Humphrey's suggestion was an opportunity to organise something new with herself in charge. 'We'd need volunteers to run it and donations of food and drinks.'

'You could give out socks as well,' enthused Hilda.

'Yes, they'd be useful. Maybe I'll come to Euston next week and see how it can be organised.'

'That's a good idea. I'll have a word with the station master.'

'It sounds as if you're going to be busy.' William looked at his mother fondly.

'And what about you Father? You never say much about your work.'

Humphrey looked at his daughter in surprise. 'No, I suppose I don't. However, I think there is something you should know.' He sipped his drink reflectively.

Alice looked at William and raised her eyebrows but he shrugged. There was silence as everyone waited for Humphrey to continue.

'I was approached today.' He lowered his voice. 'You understand this is strictly confidential.'

Alice felt an uneasy tingling in her spine as she wondered what he was going to say.

Humphrey picked up his spoon and put it down again. 'I've been asked to join the Central Specials.'

The women looked at each other for enlightenment.

'Congratulations Uncle Humphrey. Does that mean you'll have to leave your job?' asked Hilda.

'No, the Central Specials are the secret service section of the special constables. As you know, the special constables are voluntary, working in addition to their normal jobs.'

'Will you be catching spies?' Daisy was wide-eyed.

'I haven't said I'll join yet. But if I do, I won't be able to talk about it and,' he looked apologetically at Alice, 'I'll be out a lot and you won't know where I am. I wanted to know what you thought before I accepted.'

Alice was touched, although she could see that Humphrey was flattered to be asked and had already decided to accept.

'Of course you must do it,' she said.

'Congratulations.' William leant across the table and shook his father's hand.

'Thank you.' Humphrey looked relieved. 'And now we'll say no more about it.'

'That was delicious,' said Hilda, gallantly changing the subject.

'Yes, we're lucky Ethel's such a good cook and I don't think she'll want to leave us to do war work.' Alice was surprised to hear herself reply in a normal voice.

'What's your landlady's cooking like, Wills?' asked Daisy.

'It's good, plenty of it. And she lets me come and go as I please.'

'That's good. I've heard some landladies are absolute busybodies. I suppose there's still a lot going on in Llandudno?'

'Yes it's very busy; I was surprised because we've only been there in the summer season before.'

'We were looking forward to spending more of the summer at Trealaw; I don't know when we'll get the water pipes laid.' Alice frowned for a moment then rang for Ethel to bring the pudding.

'Do you like living by the sea?' asked Hilda after Ethel had brought in an apple tart.

'Yes I do.' William looked reflective. 'It's good to come out of the railway sheds and smell the sea in the air. Did I tell you my landlady has a dog?'

'What sort of dog?'

'A mongrel collie, he's a bit crazy, loves to retrieve sticks.' William paused and smiled.

'You sound well established there,' said Humphrey approvingly.

'It's better than I expected. Though, of course I don't know how long I'll be there. I miss my Sunday flying with the Aero Club but we've all got to make the best of it. Anyway, we took the dog out last Sunday, it was windy and we were chasing him and my hat blew into the sea.' William laughed. 'Skipper brought it back then shook himself all over us.'

'Us?' asked Daisy.

'There were quite a few people on the beach,' William replied smoothly.

'I wish I'd been with you,' said Alice, 'I miss the clean Welsh air.'

'I hadn't really noticed it before but there is something special about it. And I like seeing the mountains across the estuary.'

As William spoke Alice detected a new warmth to his voice. For a moment her eyes met Daisy's in a complicit smile and they silently appraised the subtle change that had come over him.

Chapter 6: Lottie

Railway Recruits
According to recruiting officers there are many railway employees who would gladly enlist if they could obtain permission

The Times: March 22nd 1915

Lottie had been devastated when William was sent back to London soon after they met and overjoyed when he returned. For a while their courtship consisted of snatched conversations on the station and walks on the beach chaperoned by Skipper, his landlady's dog. They sometimes went dancing or to the pictures in Llandudno when Lottie persuaded her parents to let her stay with Bronwen. However, these occasions were rare because Nellie maintained she needed both her daughters at home so she could rest on Sundays. Cilla advocated defiance but Lottie preferred gentle persuasion and, by the New Year, Nellie had been won over by William's charm and invited him for Sunday tea. Immediately afterwards William was sent to Crewe for two months and Lottie missed him dreadfully.

She slipped her fingers under the pillow and touched the bundle of letters he had sent when he was away. But now he was back and her body tingled as she thought about him. Swaddling the quilt around her, Lottie found herself blushing in the darkness. She lay quite still and listened to her sister's regular breathing while her own thoughts raced. Then she heard her father go downstairs and knew that it was time to get up and light the fire.

***

Lottie nursed her teacup in her hands to warm her fingers. The staff canteen was not as busy as it used to be. A number of male employees had enlisted and there was talk of closing some departments due to problems of importing goods. The war was the main subject on everyone's lips. Lottie had attempted to sympathise with Bronwen when Rhys enlisted but she had tossed her head and said she was proud of him for doing his duty. She tried to imagine how she would feel if William was serving at the Front. So deep was she in thought that she didn't notice Dylan till he sat down opposite her.

'Penny for them,' he said looking at her through his heavy spectacles.

'Oh, nothing really.'

'You were thinking of William weren't you?'

Lottie smiled and shrugged.

'Is he treating you right?'

'Of course!' Lottie was indignant.

'Lord, it's cold today!' Bronwen strode across the canteen and sat down in the chair next to Lottie.

'They've turned the heating down again.' Lottie looked at her purple fingers.

'I suppose we shouldn't grumble.' Bronwen fumbled in her bag. 'I had a letter from Rhys this morning.'

'Is he all right?'

'He was when he wrote this. He said he was lucky but he didn't give any details. Mentioned a place called Neuve Chapelle.'

'There was a battle there last week,' said Dylan.

'Oh yes, I thought I'd heard of it. All these foreign names are confusing.'

'That's what the English say about Welsh names.' Dylan glanced at Lottie.

'And how is your Englishman?' Bronwen's voice was icy.

Lottie stared at her friend, taken aback by her hostility. 'He's all right, I don't see a lot of him, he's working hard – as we all are.'

'So he hasn't enlisted yet?'

'You know he hasn't, he's working in a reserved occupation.'

'That doesn't stop people,' Bronwen snapped.

'Would you send us all to fight?' Dylan took off his spectacles and polished them intently with his handkerchief.

'Of course not. Anyway, you couldn't go, you can't see without your glasses and you can't run.'

'I'm not man enough you mean?' Dylan's lilting voice was edged with steel as he looked at Bronwen steadily then put on his spectacles.

'You know that's not what I mean!' Bronwen's eyes filled with tears.

'You must be so worried for Rhys.' Lottie tentatively put her hand on her friend's.

Bronwen bit her lip. 'I wish he'd write more. Some of the girls get poems but that's not his way. And I wouldn't have him any different,' she added defiantly. She looked at Dylan. 'But you're right, the country would be a strange place without any men.' She put her hand over Lottie's. 'You enjoy yours while you've got him.'

***

With Bronwen's words in her ears, Lottie looked for William when she got off the train at the end of the day but he was nowhere to be seen. Reluctantly she started to cross the road when she spied him in the distance walking slowly away from the station. Instinctively she turned round and hurried after him.

'Mind where you're going!' shouted a boy on a bicycle as he swerved to avoid her.

'Sorry!' she called without stopping.

Lottie had almost caught up with William when he stopped and lit a cigarette. The light was fading but she could just make out the grim expression on his face.

'William?' she said anxiously.

He smiled sadly and pulled her towards him.

'What's happened?' she whispered.

'I heard today that a friend of mine died at Neuve Chapelle.'

Lottie gasped. 'How dreadful! Poor Bronwen.'

'Bronwen?' William looked puzzled for a moment. 'Oh no, it's not Rhys. Well, I don't know, we're not in touch.'

'No, it couldn't be Rhys, Bronwen had a letter from him today. He said he was lucky.'

'Good chap, Rhys,' he said absently and tightened his arm around her.

Lottie rested her head on his shoulder and looked at the grey sky streaked with red and gold. She was aware of the sharp tang of the sea mingled with the pungent smell of tobacco and the rough serge of William's coat pricking her cheek as she waited patiently for him to continue.

'Do you remember me telling you about Duggie?' he asked.

'Your friend who enlisted after he was given a white feather?'

William nodded.

'He was a farmer wasn't he?' Lottie looked up at William and saw the pain in his eyes.

'Yes; it's been difficult for the family without him. And now he won't be coming back.' His voice was bitter.

'Do you know what happened?' Lottie felt her question was inadequate.

'No; I just had brief letters from my mother and from Hilda; she's his sister.'

Lottie tightened her arms around him and they stood in silence as the last streaks of red faded from the darkening sky.

A cart rattled by and the driver leaned towards them. 'Nice tart, Gov!' he called out lewdly.

Lottie gasped and drew away.

'Take no notice.' William's voice was controlled but Lottie could feel him trembling as he pulled her close and kissed her. She was taken aback by the violence of his passion and of her response as she instinctively pressed herself against him.

She could hear her heart thundering against William's greatcoat and, in the distance, the clip clop of horse's hooves as the cart drove on. The driver's comment rang in her ears and she felt hot as she slowly untangled herself.

'Would you like to have supper at our house?' Lottie asked tentatively, wondering if there would be enough to go round.

William kissed her gently. 'Thank you but I think I'll go back to my digs, I need to be on my own for a little while. I'll walk you home.'

***

'You're late!' Nellie's once pretty face was lined with pain and her eyes were anxious as she stirred the stew pot on the range.

'Sorry, Mother.' Lottie kissed her and hung her coat on a hook at the bottom of the stairs.

'Hello, Lottie, where've you been?' Cilla looked up from the sink.

'I met William.' She sat down and eased off her boots.

'And …?' Cilla grinned.

Lottie looked at her sister with a mixture of affection and irritation.

'He was telling me about a friend who was killed.'

'Who's died?' Jack's eyes darted round the room as he came in from the shop. His frown made his nose seem sharper and emphasised the thinness of his features.

'A friend of William's, at Neuve Chapelle.'

'Nobody we know then,' remarked Nellie wiping her hands on her apron.

'But William knows, knew, him!' Lottie glared at her mother.

'And our hearts go out to him and to the boy's parents,' said Jack with a warning look at his wife as he sat at the table.

'Do you think William will join up?' Cilla asked.

Lottie felt her stomach contract. 'He can't! He's in a reserved occupation,' she shrilled.

'You really care about him don't you?' Jack looked at his daughter quizzically.

Lottie nodded.

'He's got charming manners,' said Nellie.

'And I've heard he's good at his job and gets on well with the men working for him. But,' Jack paused, 'he's a different class from us.'

'He's English you mean?' Lottie thought of Bronwen and Dylan's remarks that morning.

'But I married an Englishman!' Nellie looked at her husband.

'You married a railway worker, not one of the bosses.'

'I remember the excitement in the villages when they started building the branch line along the valley.'

'When all the young labourers took lodgings you mean!' giggled Cilla.

'Don't be cheeky!' Nellie began ladling out four plates of stew.

As Lottie took her place at the table she looked at the room with its serviceable furniture as if seeing it for the first time. William had always seemed at home when he called but she wondered what he thought of her family. And what he really thought about her.

'Why have you gone red?' Cilla asked as Lottie toyed with her food.

Lottie shrugged, annoyed with her sister for intruding on her thoughts. She wished she had been able to comfort William but he had left her to mourn the loss of his friend alone.

***

It was drizzling when Lottie came out of the station the following evening but her face lit up when she saw William waiting with Skipper.

'I thought we could give the dog an airing,' he said as he took Lottie's arm.

She laughed. 'I could do with an airing too, I've been in the stock room most of today.'

They walked slowly, pausing every now and again to let Skipper snuffle by the roadside.

Lottie was just about to tell William about a notice she had seen for the latest picture showing in Llandudno when he told her he was going home for the weekend and planned to stop in Hertfordshire on the way to see Duggie's family.

'That will be hard for you.' Lottie tried not to show her disappointment.

'Yes.' He stopped and tilted her face towards him. 'I wish I didn't have to leave you,' he said.

Lottie looked up at him, scarcely daring to breathe.

Suddenly Skipper barked and leapt forward, straining at the end of his lead and pulling William with him.

Despite herself, Lottie laughed and ran after them.

'Beastly dog! It's got no sense of occasion,' said William with a wry smile.

A train hooted and rumbled past sending hot sparks into the air.

'That's the London train,' said Lottie. 'I'm going to have to go, my mother wondered where I'd got to yesterday.'

'Yes of course, I'll walk you home.'

As they walked back towards the station they saw some people clustered round a poster and paused to look at it. It showed a battlefield with soldiers in the foreground, one of whom was wounded, and army vehicles silhouetted against flames in the background. The caption read: "At Neuve Chapelle your friends need you. Be a man."

Two young women were looking intently at the poster. 'My fiancé's serving at the Front,' one announced proudly.

'It looks like they're having a picnic,' a voice muttered.

'That's not a patriotic thing to say!' The woman swung round and glared at the elderly man who had made the remark.

As they stood riveted to the poster Lottie felt that the face of the wounded soldier and his friend kneeling beside him were caricatures, a propaganda tool. If she had been the artist she would have drawn it differently.

But then she had no idea what it was like out there. And she didn't want to know.

Skipper was sitting at William's feet whining quietly and she bent down to pat his head. She looked at William and tried to read his thoughts but his expression was impenetrable.

'I prefer your paintings,' he said suddenly grabbing Lottie's hand and pulling her away from the poster.

'It's a pity I don't have time for drawing these days.'

They crossed the road and came to a halt outside the shop.

'My art teacher used to tell us it was our duty to use our talents. I don't think many of us listened to him.' William shrugged. 'But, seriously, you mustn't give up your painting, people need beautiful things to look at especially now.'

Lottie was surprised by his intensity. 'Well, maybe I'll look out my paints and do something this weekend.'

'I look forward to seeing the result when I return, and if I'm delayed I'll write to you.'

'Delayed?' Lottie asked feeling suddenly anxious.

William put his arm round her. 'Don't be worried, you know I sometimes have to work at Euston. I'll see you very soon.'

***

As William had predicted, he was delayed in London and it was Saturday evening before he called. The Rowes had just finished their supper when there was a knock on the door.

Lottie's heart beat faster as she smoothed her hair and stood up.

But Cilla was already at the door. 'It's William,' she said grinning at Lottie.

'If I'd known you were coming I'd have lit a fire in the parlour.' Nellie looked flustered.

'Don't worry, the kitchen's nice and warm.' William stood by the door holding a parcel wrapped in brown paper.

'Come and sit at the table. Cilla, clear the dishes away. Lottie, pour some more hot water in the pot. You'd like a cup of tea wouldn't you William?'

'That would be lovely thank you, Mrs Rowe.' William sat down still holding his parcel.

Lottie smiled at him surreptitiously as she filled the teapot.

'So what's the news from London?' asked Jack.

'Oh nothing, just what you read in the newspapers,' William answered distractedly.

'What's in your parcel?' asked Cilla leaning across William to pick up the cruet.

'You ask too many questions,' said Nellie. 'Now you fetch a cup and saucer from the dresser, one of those new ones Lottie bought us.'

'Thank you,' said William when his tea was poured. 'I've brought you something.' He handed the parcel to Lottie and watched her as she carefully unwrapped it, smoothing the paper so that it could be used again.

She pulled out a box and inside were water colour paints and brushes.

'Oh!' she squealed and flung her arms out to kiss him then blushed and drew back.

'It's wonderful!' she said. 'Thank you so much.' She picked up one of the sable brushes and smoothed the fine hairs between her fingertips.

'You'll be able to paint some nice pictures with those, Lottie,' her mother said.

'Yes, I'll have no excuse now.' She looked at William. 'I'm afraid I was too busy to do anything at the weekend.'

'I wondered if you'd like to paint a picture of Trealaw? Perhaps we could go tomorrow if the weather's fine?'

'I'd love to!' Lottie said then looked at her father.

He shifted in his seat and frowned.

Nellie opened her mouth to say something but remained silent.

Lottie and Cilla exchanged glances, their faces taut while they waited for their father's answer.

Only William remained unaware of the tension. He drained his tea and sat back, relaxed and confident.

The young man's larger than life presence in the small room seemed to unnerve Jack. He cleared his throat. 'That part of the mountain is popular with walkers. Some go to climb Mynydd Brith and others like to visit the old church at Llanfynydd. You won't be on your own up there.'

'They'll be safe enough as long as they don't go climbing the mountain,' said Nellie although she knew that it was his daughter's virtue rather than her safety on the mountain that had been worrying Jack.

'Will you take your new paints with you?' asked Cilla.

'No, I'll just take my sketch pad and paint the picture later. Oh I do hope the weather's fine tomorrow!' Lottie smiled at William, her eyes shining.

'I guarantee it!' His smile had a touch of sadness as he looked at her intently then fell silent.

'I expect you're pleased to be back in Wales after London, aren't you, William?' said Nellie.

'Pardon? Oh yes! My mother said she envied me when I left.'

'Well you're much safer here than in London. Now will you have another cup of tea?'

'No thank you.' William stood up. 'I must be going. I'll see you in the morning.'

***

Jack had been right. When Lottie and William reached the end of the mountain track they met a group of young people with picnic baskets.

'We're going to visit the old church, would you care to join us?' one of the men asked after they had exchanged greetings.

'That's very kind, but I live here.' William steered Lottie past clumps of wild daffodils towards a new five barred gate.

'Oh right. Nice view you've got.'

'It's wonderful. My friend's an artist, she's going to paint it.'

'I'd love to be able to paint,' said one of the girls.

'Well you must come and see my friend's paintings when she has her exhibition later in the year.'

The girl looked respectfully at Lottie who was trying to stifle her giggles.

'Come on William,' she said grinning mischievously, 'I've got work to do.'

They ran up the grassy slope and came to a halt outside the house. For a moment Lottie said nothing as she took in the view. Dry stone walls zigzagged across the mountain slopes which were dotted with sheep and the occasional cottage. She could just make out the medieval walls of the town below and Puffin Island in the distance. Slowly she turned around and looked up at the jagged peaks of Mynydd Brith rising behind the house.

'It's wonderful,'' she said, looking up at William. 'I can see why your parents wanted to build a house here.'

'It's pretty good, isn't it?' He took off his haversack. 'It's a bit breezy but I'll bring the deckchairs out and we can have our picnic.'

He unlocked the door and went to the kitchen at the back of the house leaving Lottie standing uncertainly in the doorway.

'Come and look round.'

'I feel as if I'm snooping on your parents.'

'I know how you feel. It's strange that I haven't been here with them since the house was finished. I was going to come in August but then war was declared. I came up once in September to check that everything was all right.' He sniffed the air. 'It smells a bit damp in here, we're better off outside.'

William brought out the deckchairs and positioned them so they were facing the sea.

'It's too early for a picnic,' said Lottie as they settled into their chairs, 'let's just have some lemonade then I can start sketching.'

William took two glass tumblers from his haversack.

'I didn't expect glasses on a picnic.' Lottie looked impressed as he handed her a tumbler of lemonade, the bubbles fizzing on the surface.

'My landlady prepared everything and was determined that we should have the best.'

'That was nice of her.'

Lottie lay back in her deckchair savouring the view, the cool breeze on her face and her closeness to William. She let her thoughts drift and found herself replaying the previous night's conversation with Cilla in the bedroom they shared. 'Won't you be scared alone on the mountain with William?' her sister had whispered. Lottie had asked her what there was to be scared of but, as she said it, she knew that what sometimes frightened her was the intensity of her feelings for William. She glanced at him but he too seemed lost in thought.

'That hill in front of us looks so pretty covered in daffodils. I wonder if it's got a name.' Lottie leant forward in her chair.

'I think it's called Daffodil Mountain,' said William gently rubbing her back.

Lottie stood up. 'There must be a good view of Trealaw from the top. Perhaps I could do my sketch from there.'

'Excellent idea.' William held out his hand and they ran across the springy grass to the rocky outcrop.

'I don't think there's a path,' he said as they started to scramble between the rocks.

'There are plenty of sheep tracks though. Oh, look at those sweet little lambs, they must be newborn!' Lottie paused to look at the tiny twins huddled against a rock half obscured by a clump of daffodils. There was an agitated bleat and a ewe lumbered up then stood in front of them and stamped its feet.

'All right, we're not going to hurt your babies. William, look at the little smudged face on that one, I bet he'll grow up to be a rascal!'

William laughed, 'Oh Lottie I love you so much!' he said and swept her into his arms.

When they drew apart they looked at each other with a sense of wonder. Most of their kisses previously had been snatched under the cover of darkness. But here on Daffodil Mountain their faces were lit by the sun shining through the clouds scudding across Mynydd Brith and Lottie felt overwhelmed by the tenderness and passion in his face as she looked up at William.

'Lottie,' he said, 'I love you and I never want to leave you but …'

Lottie felt a sense of foreboding, 'But?' she whispered.

'When I was in London I joined the RNAS.'

'The Royal Naval Air Service?'

William nodded and held her tightly. Lottie could feel his heart beat in tune with hers. Her emotions whirled from joy that he loved her to desolation that he was leaving.

She pulled his face to hers and kissed him. 'I'm proud of you,' she said.

William slipped his hand inside her jacket and kissed her again. Lottie responded eagerly then pushed him gently away.

'You'll be able to fly again,' she said looking up at him half apologetically.

'Yes, I'm one of the lucky ones, I'll be doing something I love in the cause of duty.' He held out his hand. 'Let's climb to the top.'

Determined to be brave, Lottie put her hand in William's and strode beside him with the words 'I love you' singing in her ears.

'Trealaw looks tiny from here,' she said as they looked down on the house.

'Perhaps you can draw it bigger? Or isn't that allowed?'

'Oh yes, it's called artistic licence.' Lottie sat on a rock and took out her sketchpad. 'It's like the houses I used to draw when I was a child.'

William sat at her feet, watching as she worked.

She pursed her lips in concentration then looked up, startled by a loud mewing sound. 'Surely that's not a cat?'

'It's a bird.' William pointed to a buzzard soaring above their heads, tumbling and looping the loop.

'It's so graceful; oh look there's another one!'

The mewing sounded again and the aerobatics became wilder. 'I think that's a male buzzard putting on a show to attract a mate; yes, look she's gliding below him now. Oh, look at that dive!' William stood up and watched the bird glide downwards then soar up again almost vertically.

Lottie looked up and sketched quickly as the bird did another dive then soared up again. They watched spellbound as the male continued its display until the two birds flew off together.

'I think he managed to impress her,' said William.

'It was amazing. I made some sketches but they were moving so quickly.'

'Can I see?' William sat down beside Lottie.

She showed him her drawings and explained how she planned to use her new watercolours. 'Maybe next time, when the weather's warmer, you could bring your paints; that way you wouldn't have to remember the colour of everything.'

'Yes that would be lovely, we could…' Lottie's eyes were shining as she looked at him then her face crumpled, 'But you might not be here!'

She suddenly realised he hadn't told her when he was leaving. 'When…' she asked then burst into tears as she realised what the answer would be.

William put his arms around her and stroked her hair, 'I'm getting the night train. I couldn't bear to tell you yesterday in front of your parents.'

He took out his handkerchief and as he wiped her eyes she saw that his own were glistening.

'Lottie," he said, 'I love you; will you marry me?'

Lottie gasped, 'Marry you?'

'You do love me don't you?' William looked suddenly anxious.

'Of course I love you! It's just, I never expected….'

As William kissed her she felt ecstasy mingle with desperation that there would be a future for them to share. 'Yes,' she said looking up at him, 'I'll marry you.'

Chapter 7: Alice

Expansion of the Air Fleet
Mr Joynson-Hicks MP said he desired to call attention
to the insufficiency of the number of aeroplanes for war
service by sea and land.

The Times: June 15th 1915

Alice and Humphrey hadn't been surprised when William announced that he'd joined the RNAS. However, his engagement to the daughter of the Junction shopkeeper caused them some consternation although they could not deny that William was obviously in love and, by all accounts, the girl was respectable.

'Maybe Mr and Mrs Rowe share our concern,' Humphrey had said sagely when they were discussing the matter after William's whirlwind visit before leaving to take up his post of probationary flight officer with the Royal Naval Air Service.

Although they were pleased that Lottie's father would not give his permission for her to marry until she came of age, they thought it would be nice to have a celebration when William completed his aviator's training. They had planned to have a holiday in Wales and so decided to hold an engagement party at Trealaw. They reflected that it would be a good opportunity to get to know Lottie's family and possibly allay their misgivings about the match.

The thought of returning to Wales had sustained Alice during the increasingly troubled spring. She had worked hard to set up the free buffet on Euston station and, once it was established, continued her voluntary work there every day. Humphrey was proud of the work she did and, although it was tiring, there was satisfaction in being able to help an increasing number of men on their way to and from the battlefields of Europe and beyond.

***

'Llandudno Junction. This train terminates here. Will all passengers alight, please.'

A porter opened the carriage door and Alice felt a sudden burst of energy as she breathed in the fresh morning air. She glanced up towards the mountains, excited at the prospect of seeing Trealaw again. The welcoming shriek of a seagull made her realise how hemmed in she had been for the last few months. Co-ordinating supplies and a constantly changing army of volunteers had invigorated her at first but the sudden change of air made her realise how exhausted she had been.

As she was travelling a day earlier than Humphrey, the Rowes had invited her for breakfast and Alice quickened her pace as she crossed the road and opened the door of the shop. It was busy and she stood unnoticed at the back of the queue quietly observing where her future daughter-in-law had grown up. The shelves were surprisingly well stocked and there were a couple of hams hanging from the ceiling. Alice watched an auburn haired girl behind the counter bantering with a couple of soldiers buying cigarettes. She was in the middle of weighing out potatoes for an elderly woman when she caught sight of Alice.

'Good morning, Mrs Dacre! Lottie and Mother are expecting you.' She lifted up part of the counter for Alice to pass through. 'Just go through that door,' she said as she started putting potatoes into the woman's bag.

Alice knocked and opened the door to the Rowes' living room. There was a starched white cloth and vase of marguerites on the dining table and another on the dresser. The tiles around the range gleamed and the blue and white checked curtains fluttered crisply at the open window.

Nellie bustled from the scullery rubbing her hand on her pinafore before proffering it to Alice. 'How do you do, Mrs Dacre,' she said formally.

'How do you do,' replied Alice then smiled at Lottie hovering in the scullery doorway. Her hair was swept up and she appeared nearly as tall as Alice. She bit her lip nervously but the gentle expression in her brown eyes and the lilt in her voice when she spoke helped Alice see why William wanted to marry her.

'It was a little tiring,' she said in reply to Lottie's question about her journey, 'but the mountain air will soon revive me and we're looking forward to celebrating your engagement tomorrow.' She looked at Lottie's left hand. 'Have you got a ring?'

Lottie flushed. 'We didn't have time to get one in Llandudno but William took my ring size so he could buy me one in London, he's bringing it tomorrow.' She smiled shyly. 'It's really kind of you to have the party at Trealaw. Mother has baked a cake and Father says we can have a ham.'

'We've been saving flour and Ethel has made gingerbread and fairy cakes; Daisy and Hilda are bringing them when they come later today. And I have ordered some provisions from Conway.'

'Won't you sit down, Mrs Dacre?' Nellie pulled out a dining chair. She stood slightly awkwardly in front of Alice. 'And my brother's wife will be bringing some welsh cakes. We must thank you for letting us invite them to the party; I know Lottie's cousins are looking forward to it.'

'My brother lives in South Africa so William has only met his cousins once when they visited England years ago. It must be nice to have your nephews and nieces living close.'

'Yes; there are the two boys and my sister-in-law had a baby girl at Christmas.' For a moment Nellie appeared lost in thought as she absentmindedly stroked her stomach but she quickly recovered. 'Cilla's looking after the shop but Jack will join us in a minute. He's gone to collect some supplies that came on this morning's train. Now Lottie, while we're waiting, why don't you show Mrs Dacre that picture you painted? Lottie's always been keen on drawing,' she said proudly.

'I did this when William took me to Trealaw in the spring.' Lottie pointed to a framed watercolour of buzzards gliding above Daffodil Mountain with Trealaw in the distance. As she studied the picture Alice felt a lump in her throat.

'It's beautiful,' she said looking at her prospective daughter-in-law with new eyes.

'I'd like to paint a series of Trealaw from different angles and in different seasons.' Lottie's expression was animated as she spoke.

The back door opened and Jack Rowe appeared. Nellie carried the teapot and plates that had been warming on the range to the table. Then she opened the oven door and brought out a large earthenware dish of bacon, eggs, kidneys and fried bread.

Jack shook Alice's hand. 'I hope you're not too tired from your journey.'

'No, I slept well thank you.' Alice looked around the room and realised that the first class travel she took for granted would not be an option for the family her son was marrying into.

'You have a fine son, Mrs Dacre.' Jack hesitated then added uncertainly, 'I'm sure they'll make a happy couple.'

Alice looked at Lottie and smiled. 'I'm sure they will.'

***

Later that morning, when Alice called at the shop in Conway to check on the order she had sent by post a few days earlier, she found the cart was packed and ready to leave and she gratefully accepted the carrier's offer of a lift. As they wound up the mountain track she wondered what her volunteers at the station buffet would think if they could see her but she didn't care. Already the freedom of being high up in the open air was doing her good and she could understand why William had been so keen to fly. They stopped to deliver goods to a farm where the road forked and Alice negotiated for supplies of milk and eggs to be sent to Trealaw the following morning. She could see harebells clinging to the banks when the horse slowed its pace as the track became steeper. Then the cart swung through the gate and came to a halt outside Trealaw.

'Will you be all right Ma'am up here on your own?' The carrier looked at Alice's expensive clothes suspiciously as he unloaded the last flagon of ale.

'Oh, yes, thank you, I need a little time to myself.'

'Then I'll be going. I hope the weather stays fine for your party.'

Alice watched as the carrier turned the cart and rumbled down the slope to the lane. Then he raised his whip, the horse picked up its hooves and trotted back down the mountain.

The midday sun was warm and Alice stood on the doorstep, not wanting to go inside yet. She watched in fascination as a hawk hovered above Daffodil Mountain then swooped down to catch its prey and she was reminded of Lottie's delicate painting. Feeling bold, she defied convention and took off her hat and jacket then walked behind the house and followed a sheep track that ran alongside a tiny stream bubbling down to the sea in the distance.

The sound of a whistle made her turn. Sitting on a rock was a boy of about ten wearing a tattered shirt and bounding towards him was a black and white dog, part collie but mainly mongrel.

The boy stared at Alice. 'Are you from the new house?'

'Yes, where are you from?'

'Over there.' The boy pointed past he old church.

'And what's your name?'

'Billy Jenkins. I'll fetch your water for a penny.'

'Thank you. Come with me and I'll give you a bucket.' In her hurry to be back in her house on the mountain, Alice realised she had neglected to make arrangements for any kind of help.

While the boy was fetching water Alice lit the kitchen stove and started putting food on the shelves. When he appeared at the kitchen door his eyes opened wide at the sight of so much food. Alice scooped some water from the bucket with a jug, poured it into the kettle and put it on the hob.

'Shall I fetch some more water, Ma'am?' the boy asked eagerly.

'Yes, please.' Alice handed him another bucket.

When he had gone she brought porcelain jugs from the bedrooms, filled them and took them back upstairs in readiness for the guests.

At first she had been disappointed when Daisy had said that, instead of travelling with Alice, she would spend the night with Hilda and they would travel up together from Hertfordshire. However, she was enjoying pottering at her own pace and was keenly aware that, at this time, Hilda needed her friend more than she needed her daughter.

Since Duggie's death Hilda had put her grief aside and run the farm as best she could. Alice clenched her fist as she thought about the pointless waste of a young life. It was rumoured that Kitchener was about to introduce conscription for thousands of men but it was a different matter for some empty headed girl with a twisted idea of romance to send a young man to war through the gift of a white feather. She wondered, cynically, if the girl was really touched by his death or was wearing her mourning like a badge of honour. Hilda's mother had taken to her bed in her anguish, her father was grimly uncommunicative and Hilda had to care for her mother as well as doing jobs previously done by their farm labourers who had enlisted.

The tea had brewed by the time Billy returned with a second bucket of water and Alice poured him a cup as well as one for herself. He looked in disbelief when she told him to help himself to sugar and shovelled three heaped spoons into his mug before she had time to change her mind. He reminded Alice of the children who hung around the station buffet. They had strict rules about children but she sometimes saw a kind-hearted soldier coming back for a refill and surreptitiously passing it to one of the urchins.

Billy wiped his mouth with his sleeve when he had finished and handed Alice the empty mug. His face lit up when she gave him two copper coins and, thanking her as politely as he knew how, he clenched them in his fist and ran out of the house and across the mountain.

Alice busied herself opening windows, airing beds and sweeping the floors, stopping every now and again to look at the view and breathe in the fresh mountain air. After a lunch of bread and cheese she settled down outside with a book. As she read she was ruefully aware that having time to read was now a luxury.

It was a long time before Alice roused herself and went inside to prepare the evening meal. She enjoyed the unaccustomed domesticity and felt pleased with herself as she prepared potatoes to go with the ham and pickles she had unpacked. She set the table then lit the lamps in readiness for Daisy and Hilda then slipped on her shawl and went outside. The evening dew was rising as she stood at the top of the lane listening anxiously for the sound of a cart. She had luxuriated in her afternoon of solitude but now she needed the cheerful company of her daughter and the knowledge that she was safe. The chatter of a blackbird told her that something was moving in the lane but she could hear nothing. She waited, straining her ears, then started running as she heard the sound of girlish voices.

Daisy and Hilda appeared round the bend carrying suitcases.

'We walked from Conway,' Daisy said breathlessly.

'We were lucky we didn't have to walk all the way from the Junction.' There were dark circles under Hilda's eyes but she smiled cheerfully.

'You must be tired. Supper's all ready.' Alice gave Hilda a sympathetic smile as she kissed her.

'Doesn't it look pretty!' exclaimed Daisy as they saw the house ahead with oil lamps shining from the windows. The sun had just sunk behind the western edge of Mynydd Brith and the red-streaked sky heralded good weather for the following day.

'How are your parents?' asked Alice later when they were sitting down to their meal.

'Father's still shut up inside himself but Mother seems to be improving.' Hilda was silent for a moment. 'They sent his things, the army did, and Mother has been calmer since but, but it was terrible, seeing his things.' Hilda stopped then said brightly, 'This casserole is delicious.'

Alice nodded. She knew that the army regularly despatched blood stained uniforms stinking of the trenches to the grieving families of those killed in action and wondered how she would cope if she was ever in that position. She caught Daisy looking warningly at her and, with an effort, banished thoughts of young soldiers.

'So, William's finally got himself engaged!' said Daisy.

'Do you like Lottie?' asked Hilda seriously.

Alice considered for a moment. 'She's a very nice girl. And it's a relief to see William settling down at last.'

There was silence for a moment as Alice's unspoken reservation hung in the air.

'I'm dying to meet her again. I'm sure she'll be good for him.' Daisy smiled at her mother.

'Do you think they'll wait until the war is over before they get married?' asked Hilda.

'I wouldn't! If I met Mr Right I wouldn't want to wait.'

Alice laughed. 'Well make sure you let me know first, I don't want you eloping.' She stood up. 'Now if we've finished we'll clear away and have an early night. It's going to be a busy day tomorrow.'

...

The following morning Alice was in the kitchen when she heard male voices and delighted squeals from the girls. She hurried outside and saw William and a tall, fair-haired young man confidently swinging a cricket bat. Both looked splendid in their naval uniforms with the distinctive Royal Naval Air Service badge.

'Hello Mother, I've brought a friend. Alec, this is my mother. Mother, this is Alec Hammond.'

Alice found herself shaking hands with an extraordinarily handsome young officer. 'You're very welcome, the more the merrier.' She gave an amused glance at the girls' admiring pink faces.

'So, when's kick off?' asked William.

'Midday. Your father's coming from Crewe. He'll come up with Lottie and her family. Her aunt and uncle and their boys are arriving separately.'

William rubbed his hands together. 'I'm famished, let's have some grub then we can start making the cricket pitch.'

Over breakfast William explained that he and Alec had shared a billet during training and he had asked him to be his best man.

'And do you have a date in mind?' asked Alice.

William's face clouded. 'According to Lottie's father it can't be till she's twenty-one. That's nearly two years to wait!'

Alice felt it would not be tactful to say she agreed with Mr Rowe so she nodded sympathetically and searched for something positive to say. 'Lottie's a good artist, I saw her painting of Trealaw yesterday.'

William looked pleased. 'She is, isn't she! She wants to do a series of mountain paintings. We might even set up a little art gallery in Llandudno.'

Alice raised an eyebrow. 'So you plan to settle in Wales?'

'Who has the luxury of plans these days?' William frowned then smiled as he noticed his sister and her friend gazing at Alec. 'Are you girls going to give us a hand when you've finished helping mother?'

By the time Humphrey and the Rowes arrived preparations were well under way. Alice hadn't been able to release Daisy and Hilda as early as they would have liked but Billy Jenkins had turned up with some of his siblings and they had scampered about helping to mark out the pitch. They helped carry out the dining table and chairs but, after seeing the dirt on their hands, Alice had declined their offers of further help and they had reluctantly run home with promises to return later for the cricket match.

As soon as they heard the sound of an automobile William and Alec strode to the top of the lane and ran alongside the vehicle until it chugged to a halt. Alice began to follow but stopped by the table to smooth the white linen cloth flapping in the breeze. She watched as everyone got out and unloaded a gramophone, records and a hamper. William took Lottie's arm and hung behind while the others walked towards her.

'It really will be a house of song when we play the gramophone.' Cilla had run ahead and Alice looked at her in surprise. The girl who had been standing behind the shop counter yesterday looked several years older today. Her low cut dress, nipped in at the waist with a huge sash, was in a colour of jade that complemented her auburn hair.

'It will indeed,' said Alice then turned to welcome Nellie and Jack.

'It's a lovely place you have here,' said Jack.

William and Lottie reached the house just as Daisy came out looking elegant in a blue silk dress with a gold chain around her neck. Hilda stood behind, her severe dark blouse softened by a white lace collar.

'What an exquisite dress,' exclaimed Daisy as she kissed her future sister-in-law. Lottie smiled shyly and glanced down at the plunging neckline of her ivory frock with black polka dots and at her bare arms under the floating transparent sleeves.

'Thank you,' she said moving closer to William and twiddling the finger of her left hand.

'Your ring! Let's see!' Daisy took Lottie's hand and looked admiringly at the large solitaire diamond. As she held up Lottie's hand for everyone to see, the jewel sparkled in the sunshine.

'Golly, Lottie, it must have cost a lot,' said Cilla in an audible whisper as she hugged her sister.

'I know we're not all here yet but I think we should have a drink in honour of Lottie and William,' said Humphrey.

Alec had already lined up the glasses and was pouring ale from a flagon. Cilla wound up the gramophone and suddenly strains of a music hall number echoing around the mountain made everyone laugh in surprise.

'To Lottie and William,' said Humphrey raising his glass.

'To us,' whispered William looking into Lottie's eyes.

Despite her misgivings about the match, Alice smiled at the couple and tried not to think about what the future might hold. She went back into the house to check that everything was ready in the kitchen.

Nellie followed her carrying a large ham. 'I cooked this yesterday; shall we slice it here or on the table?'

'Here I think will be best, I've got some salt beef as well. And we've got plenty of pickles and chutney and white bread as well as the cakes Ethel made. We'll carve the meat then start taking the things out now so we can eat as soon as your brother and family arrive.'

Hilda and Cilla came in to offer their help and the picnic was soon prepared.

Alice was just putting the finishing touches when she heard a horse whinny and saw Nellie's brother, Owen, driving a small trap with his two sons hanging over the back. As soon as the trap stopped they jumped off and ran over to Lottie and William.

'My, Efan, you're nearly as tall as me now,' said Lottie as she kissed her cousin. She bent down to kiss his little brother and affectionately ruffled his hair.

Efan grinned and gave William a smart salute.

'Where's your mother, Efan?' Nellie looked worried as she bustled up.

'The baby's poorly.'

'My wife sends her apologies, our baby daughter is recovering from a cold and we thought it would be better for her to stay at home,' said Owen as he shook hands with Alice and Humphrey.

'I'm so sorry. Have you called the doctor?' Alice looked concerned.

'We didn't feel it was necessary and thankfully she's getting better now.'

'You can never be too careful with children,' said Alice as she led the way towards the picnic table.

A few minutes later everyone was sitting down with William and Lottie at the head of the table.

Cilla eagerly helped serve the food, Alec poured the drinks and everyone was laughing and talking loudly above the sound of the gramophone.

Suddenly Nellie leaned forward and started to count. 'There's thirteen of us,' she whispered to Jack in agitation.

Her husband looked embarrassed. 'It don't mean anything,' he whispered back.

Nellie wasn't placated and glared at Owen as if it was his fault.

Humphrey looked at Nellie in amusement then rose and said diplomatically, 'If everyone's glass is full I'd like to propose a toast to Lottie and William.'

Everyone stood up and raised their glasses. 'Lottie and William!'

'Hold it there!' commanded Alec producing a camera.

Alice glanced anxiously at Nellie while Alec positioned his camera. She was sitting as straight as she was able with a smile fixed to her face.

For an instant the temperature dropped as the sun hid behind a cloud and Alice felt a tremor pass through her body. 'Maybe Nellie's right,' she thought, 'and the number thirteen is a bad omen.'

Then the sun re-appeared, the camera whirred and Alice relaxed.

'Take another picture!' called Cilla clapping her hands.

'All right, now smile everyone!' Alec pressed the shutter then re-positioned the camera. 'Now, another one from a different angle,' he said and aimed so that Daisy was in the centre of the picture. He took several more shots then sat down looking very pleased with himself.

'Shall I bring the cakes Auntie Alice?'

'Thank you, Hilda, we'll do it together.' Alice looked at the girl's drawn face in sympathy as they walked into the house.

'It's nice seeing everyone so happy.' Hilda blew her nose vigorously.

Alice touched her shoulder lightly. 'Do you have a photograph of Duggie?'

'Yes, he had his portrait taken just before he left. Photographs help you remember. I'm glad William has a friend with a camera,' she added.

Alice picked up the extravagantly iced engagement cake that Nellie had brought but Hilda took it from her and, carrying it with extreme care, she laid it with a flourish in front of William and Lottie.

'Speech!' called Alec after the couple had cut the first slice.

Holding Lottie's hand firmly in his, William addressed the company. 'Today is a very special day. As you know, I have to return the day after tomorrow and nobody knows what will happen after that. But Lottie will be with me in my heart wherever I go. And I will know that Trealaw is waiting – a haven of peace in this troubled time.'

Humphrey nodded approvingly. They had built Trealaw to be a place to escape from the rigours of life in London, little knowing that it would be a place to escape from the horrors that had been unleashed throughout the world.

'So when do you start flying?' Owen asked William.

'We've finished our training but it seems there are more pilots than aeroplanes at the moment.'

'I read in the newspaper that they're building new aircraft factories.'

'Yes, and expanding existing ones; there'll soon be enough aeroplanes,' said Alec confidently.

'It's a brave man who's prepared to leave the safety of the ground for the sky.' Jack looked at William appraisingly.

'Maybe in a war situation, but when I first learnt to fly it was an exciting new hobby.'

'We certainly never thought that aeroplanes would be used as a weapon of war,' said Owen.

Alice saw the shocked look on Lottie's face at her uncle's remark.

'But they're not really, in the RNAS we'll only be involved in reconnaissance,' William assured him.

'That's a relief then,' said Daisy looking only half convinced.

When everyone had finished, the younger people got up and started to organise the cricket teams. Daisy, Alec, Humphrey, Owen and Little Owen were in Lottie's team which left William's team one short until Billy Jenkins sprang from behind a rock and offered his services.

Alice and Nellie sat back and watched for a while. It was a colourful spectacle with the girls in their new dresses and William and Alec in naval uniforms. The men soon discarded their jackets and Alice was pleased to see that Humphrey already looked several years younger. The three boys ran about enthusiastically and Alice noticed some more of the Jenkins children edging closer to get a better view. The two women looked at each other and smiled hesitantly.

A warm breeze blew up from the estuary and the sounds of curlews, the bleating of lambs and answering calls from their mothers gave the scene a timeless quality.

'Would you care to take a stroll to the church?' asked Alice.

Nellie nodded and they walked out of the gate towards the ancient church.

'Owen and I came here when we were children,' said Nellie breathlessly. 'We used to live in the valley and sometimes came up the church path looking for wild strawberries.' She pointed to a grassy path between dry stonewalls snaking steeply down the mountainside.

'We were looking forward to exploring but the war has put a stop to all that.'

Shouts from the cricketers carried on the wind; Alice strode to the high ground on the far side of the enclosure and looked down on Trealaw. Nellie was panting by the time she joined her.

Lottie's team were batting and Alec swung the bat with practised ease. He sent the ball flying and ran across the turf towards the stumps. Lottie and Daisy clapped and cheered while Little Owen jumped up and down in excitement.

William started to run towards the ball but Cilla streaked past him, her red hair flying in the wind. She lunged forwards then fell, clutching the ball triumphantly as she lay gasping for breath, her petticoat peeking out from beneath her jade dress.

'Well caught!' William's voice rang across the mountain as he came to a halt by the girl lying on the grass.

Alice felt a surge of pride as she looked down on the good-looking figure of her son, his enthusiasm dominating the group. She wondered why Nellie shifted uneasily then saw Cilla laughing up at William and holding out her hand for him to pull her up.

'You must have found Cilla a help in the shop since Lottie got her position in the emporium,' said Alice as they watched Cilla talking animatedly to William while he escorted her back to their team.

Nellie sighed. 'She's got some notion of working in a munitions factory. Of course, her father won't hear of it.'

'Well, girls are needed in all sectors now. Anyway you'll be pleased to have your daughters at home and Lottie is such a steadying influence.'

'Yes, Lottie's a good girl. We'll miss her when she goes.'

Alice looked startled and wondered if Nellie knew something she didn't. William refused to be drawn on future plans although she knew he resented Jack's insistence that they wait until Lottie was twenty-one before they married.

A feeling of unease washed over Alice. 'Perhaps we should wander back and cheer the winning team,' she said with false gaiety.

The players were having a break when they arrived back and Alec was busy taking a photograph of William and Lottie. They were facing each other, laughing and holding hands as if they were about to dance.

Humphrey caught Alice's eye and, as they smiled at each other, Alice's uneasiness about the Rowe sisters diminished.

The game continued for another half hour then everyone drifted towards the picnic table where Alice and Nellie had laid out tea, biscuits and Ethel's cakes to the accompaniment of music from the gramophone.

Owen announced it was time for him to take the boys home. 'Thank you for inviting us.' He looked around approvingly. 'You'll go a long way to find a view like this.'

They shook hands, the boys were called to say their thank yous, then they climbed into the cart and disappeared down the mountain.

'Give us a hand with these crocks, Cilla,' said Nellie as she saw her daughter about to follow her sister and fiancé along the path behind the house.

'All right Mother,' she replied cheerfully and joined her at the table.

'That was jolly good fun.' Hilda looked invigorated as she lifted up a chair to take inside.

'I think ours was the best team, don't you?' Cilla picked up a pile of plates and followed Hilda into the house.

'Definitely, that was a good catch of yours and I made a good innings.'

It was nearly dark by the time William, Lottie, Daisy and Alec sauntered into the house. They crowded in the doorway of the sitting room, their faces glowing as they looked at the adults drinking tea.

Jack stood up. 'I'm afraid we must be taking our leave, I promised I would return the automobile by nightfall.'

'It was kind of your friend to lend it.' Alice felt sorry as she looked at the crestfallen faces of the young people.

'It's a pity to break up the party but you need to return the vehicle safely, you don't want to risk it being requisitioned.' Humphrey's comment brought everyone back to the sombre reality of the situation away from the comforting bubble they had created at Trealaw.

Alice felt a sense of impotent sadness as she watched Lottie's expression take on a stricken quality and she was reminded of the farewells she witnessed every day in the course of her work at Euston station.

'Perhaps you'd like to come and do some more paintings of Trealaw; we could leave you a key.' Alice hesitated uncertainly and looked at Humphrey.

'It would be good to have someone checking on the place,' Humphrey said. 'You can bring a picnic if you like, Lottie can sketch and her paintings will be a record of Trealaw for all of us.'

'That's your first commission.' William looked at Lottie proudly and the panic left her face as she smiled up at him.

Slowly the Rowes gathered their things and everyone walked to the automobile. Alec wound the starting handle while William helped the ladies into their seats. Then he ran alongside the vehicle holding

Lottie's hand until it reached the top of the lane and accelerated into the dusk.

Chapter 8 Lottie

Air Raid Last Night
Hostile aircraft visited the eastern counties and London
district and dropped incendiary and explosive bombs.

The Times: September 9th 1915

Lottie fingered the envelope with William's familiar writing then took out the letter and read it with mounting excitement for the second time that day.

'Sorry I'm late. Isn't it a gorgeous day!' Bronwen sank down on the bench next to Lottie and gazed at the blue sea with its crests of white surf rolling towards the shore.

'Yes, wonderful!' Lottie turned to her friend, her eyes shining. 'William's got leave and he's invited me to London!'

'That's lovely Lottie; will you go?'

'Of course I'll go! Why shouldn't I?'

'What about the zeppelins?'

'Oh! I'd forgotten about the air raids.' Lottie stared at the sea, stroking William's letter. She wondered whether the sun was also shining on the German warships in the North Sea and on the fragile seaplanes whose job it was to track them.

'If William has to face danger every day then I can certainly get on a train and travel to London to see him,' she said.

'Good for you! I'd do the same for Rhys.'

'I'm lucky I won't have anything to worry about; William says his father will send me a rail ticket and his mother will meet me at the station.' Lottie was determined to be positive but Bronwen's comment about zeppelins had unsettled her.

'It'll be a real adventure. What will you wear?'

'Oh dear, I don't know, autumn's such an in-between season.'

'Why don't we go and have a look at the new collection of autumn street coats in the store? There's still twenty minutes dinner hour left.'

'All right,' Lottie said doubtfully; she didn't want Bronwen to persuade her into buying something she couldn't afford.

'I want one of those new military curve corsets.' Bronwen stood up and held herself to her full height of five feet three inches. 'It might make me look taller.'

Lottie laughed, 'You're fine as you are. Let's go and see the new collection, there's no harm in looking.'

***

'What have you got there, Lottie?' Nellie asked when Lottie arrived home carrying a large bag from Knight's.

'A new hat!' she said putting on a cream hat with a brown band around the brim with a flourish. 'And a paper pattern and three yards of linen to make an autumn coat.' She showed her mother the picture on the cover of a Butterick pattern.

'The hat suits you and it will look good with the coat. Have you bought lining material?'

'No, I won't have time to line it.'

'And where are you going in such a hurry?'

'To London; William's due home on leave next week, I had a letter from him this morning, he wants me to go for the weekend.'

'Yes, I saw you had a letter. I don't know what your father will have to say about it.'

'About what?' asked Jack as he came from the shop.

Lottie told him about the invitation and waited silently while he sat down and slowly lit a cigarette.

'I see you've got yourself a new hat,' he observed.

'Yes, I bought it today.' Lottie paused then added boldly, 'for my trip to London.'

Jack nodded. 'I know times are changing but I don't like the idea of you travelling without a chaperone.'

'But Inspector Dacre's a railway detective, he'll look out for me.'

'He'll be too busy, especially with all the unrest there is at the moment on the railways.'

'You'd best take your hat off Lottie then you can help me dish up,' said Nellie not unsympathetically.

'Where's Cilla?' asked Jack.

'She'll be home any minute. She said they wanted her to work a bit later tonight.'

'She works hard, I'll say that for her, working in the shop here then helping out at the Station Hotel. I've heard she's the best waitress they've had for a long while.' Jack paused and smiled at Lottie. 'And I've heard good reports about you too, you know that.'

Lottie held her breath, hoping her father was going to give his permission for her to go to London. She started putting things on the table.

Suddenly the door opened and Cilla burst in. 'Hope I haven't kept you waiting,' she said then noticed the Knight's shopping bag.

'Have you bought something nice?'

Lottie hesitated and looked imploringly at her father.

'Maybe Cilla could go with her,' suggested Nellie diffidently.

'Go where?'

'Lottie's been invited to spend next weekend with Inspector and Mrs Dacre and she can't travel all that way on her own.'

'Golly! I've always wanted to go to London!' Cilla's eyes shone.

'I haven't agreed yet,' said Jack as he took his place at the head of the table.

***

Jack held out for the rest of the week but the sight of his daughter sitting uncomplaining at the sewing machine each night touched him and he gruffly gave his permission for the girls to go to London.

By the time their train pulled into Euston they were almost beside themselves with excitement and trepidation. They held tightly to their bags as they got off the train and found themselves swept along the platform and through the ticket barrier. There was an acrid smell of soot and Lottie was pleased she had taken her mother's advice and worn her serviceable black coat for the journey. For a moment they stood and watched as people of all ages, many in uniform, milled around them.

'Golly! I've never seen so many people,' said Cilla putting her arm through Lottie's.

The familiar gesture gave Lottie confidence and they walked towards a group of soldiers sitting at some trestle tables. Behind them some women were serving mugs of tea and sandwiches. They saw Alice putting a mug into the shaking hand of a soldier with a bandage around his head and stood quietly waiting for her to notice them.

Alice looked up and smiled in acknowledgement. She spoke to one of the other women then picked up her bag and walked towards them.

The girls shook hands with Alice, then, after exchanging pleasantries, followed her to the Underground where they took the tube to Belsize Park.

They came out of the station and crossed the busy street into a road lined with large houses set in attractive gardens behind low walls. A horse and cart rolled past and a couple carrying a baby turned out from a side street.

'Excuse me Ma'am.' The man politely took off his cap. 'We're looking for the hospital.'

'You're going in the wrong direction, it's that way.' Alice pointed and gave directions.

'Is that where Daisy works?' asked Lottie.

'Yes, she's a radiographer.'

'It must be a difficult job.'

Alice sighed. 'It is now that the radiologist who was training her has transferred to a military hospital. She now has to run the department herself with only an elderly porter to help.'

'Does she get much time off?'

'Not as much as she should. I try and insist that we go for a walk in the fresh air after dinner but she'd prefer to stay at home and write letters.'

'Does she write to Alec?' asked Cilla with a mischievous grin.

Alice laughed. 'Yes they write often, but she also writes to William and her friend Hilda.' She paused. 'It's not far now,' she said as they turned a corner.

'The houses are as grand as the hotels on the promenade at Llandudno.' Cilla looked in awe at the rows of three and four storey houses.

'I suppose they are but sometimes I prefer the simplicity of our house on the mountain.'

'This is different from Mynydd Brith but it's very beautiful,' said Lottie admiringly.

Alice opened a wrought iron gate and led the way along the garden path to the front door protected by an elegant porch.

Ethel was in the hallway as they entered the house. 'Here we are, Ethel, safe and sound. Please show the young ladies to their room. You can come into the sitting room for some tea when you've unpacked.' Alice smiled encouragingly at the girls as they followed Ethel up the deeply carpeted stairs.

She showed them to a room at the back of the house with two single beds covered with counterpanes in deep red brocade.

'The bathroom's along the landing but there's water in the jug if you prefer to wash here.' Ethel looked at the girls appraisingly then left.

'They've got an inside lavatory!' exclaimed Cilla.

'Of course they have!' Lottie tossed her head and started to unpack her clothes into an ornately carved chest of drawers.

They put on the frocks they had worn for the engagement party, re-applied their makeup, tidied their hair then looked at each other for approval.

'We'll do,' said Lottie imitating their mother's expression.

Cilla giggled as Lottie opened the bedroom door. Then the two sisters tiptoed downstairs and stood in the doorway of the sitting room.

Alice was sitting in a fireside chair and on the table in front of her was a tea tray. 'Come and make yourselves at home.' She nodded towards the sofa. 'Did you find everything you needed?'

'Oh yes thank you, Mrs Dacre.' Both girls answered together as they perched on the edge of the sofa looking almost prim against the brightly coloured fabric printed with exotic birds and flowers.

'Would you like to pour the tea Lottie?'

'Yes, of course.' Lottie looked in surprise at the Japanese tea set laid out on an intricately carved oriental table and she handled the gold-rimmed cups and saucers with great care.

'Is that a teapot?' asked Cilla pointing to a brass samovar on the mantelpiece opposite the sofa.

'Yes, it's Russian, but it's just an ornament.'

Lottie felt Alice watching them as their eyes darted about the room while they politely sipped their tea.

On the windowsill were a couple of ebony carvings and a small sphere exquisitely carved in ivory. The alcoves on either side of the fireplace were filled with books. Above the fireplace was a plate commemorating Queen Victoria's jubilee in 1887 emblazoned with the words Empire on Which the Sun Never Sets; a map of Africa was in the centre showing the different routes from London and around the rim were African scenes including H.M. Stanley's arrival in Cape Town.

Cilla edged forward on her seat as she tried to make out the detail on the plate.

'You can come and take a closer look if you wish,' said Alice.

Cilla stood very still as she looked intensely at the plate then remarked, 'It's a pity women can't be explorers.'

'But they can. Mary Kingsley was a fine botanist and intrepid explorer in West Africa, you'll see her book on the shelf.'

Cilla ran her hand along the books. 'Story of an African Farm, is this it?'

'No, that's Olive Schreiner's book about South Africa.'

'Wouldn't it be exciting to live on a farm in Africa, Lottie?' Cilla turned to her sister.

'I think life is exciting enough as it is.'

'Look at this one – Eight Months in an Ox-Wagon,' Cilla pulled out a volume and started turning the pages.

'My brother gave me that when he and his family visited us from South Africa a few years ago.'

'Do many women go to work in Africa?'

'Quite a few. I was on the committee of the Emigration of Single Women to South Africa Society.

We receive requests from employers in South Africa and interview girls then arrange their passage to Cape Town or Durban. We've even suggested that girls go out to start their own businesses.'

Cilla listened intently. 'It must be dangerous for them travelling these days.'

'Oh no, the Society stopped operating soon after war was declared. I miss the meetings but there are more important things to do now.'

Lottie nodded seriously then remembered the gift she had brought. She took a small package wrapped in brown paper from her bag and handed it to Alice.

'I painted this for you,' she said shyly.

Alice carefully untied the string and folded the paper neatly before turning her attention to the painting in her hands. It was similar to the water colour of Trealaw Lottie had first shown her but instead of daffodils there were clumps of heather and a small tree bowing in the face of the prevailing wind.

'You have captured the spirit of the place,' said Alice gravely.

'She put me in one of her pictures,' Cilla said proudly.

'I had decided to do a view of the front of the house but the day we went the sky was cloudy and I wanted something to soften the grey slates and stonework so I sketched Cilla with her beautiful red hair in the foreground.'

'I'm holding a basket and it looks almost as if I'm walking out of the picture. Lottie's so clever and she's given the painting to me and I'll treasure it for ever.'

'And I shall treasure this.' Alice studied the painting. 'Thank you. We built Trealaw as a place to retreat to and this will keep it fresh in our memory.'

She stood up. 'You may borrow any of the books to read. Now maybe you'd like to take a stroll in the garden while you are waiting for William to arrive.'

**

'Oh Lottie! Imagine having a garden like this!' Cilla darted about then stopped to bury her face in a deep pink rose bush.

'It's lovely!" Lottie cupped a bloom in her hand and held it to her nose.

'And look! There's a little pond!' Cilla ran to the bottom of the garden and knelt down next to a statue of a water nymph.

Lottie smiled dreamily, still holding the rose, and luxuriated in the late afternoon sun warming her arms through the transparent sleeves of her best frock. She heard a door open and turned to see William walking towards her, his arms outstretched and his face lit up with a smile so tender that Lottie thought her heart would burst. She was scarcely aware of her sister's surprised expression as William swept her in his arms and kissed her passionately.

'I love you,' he whispered.

'I love you too,' she said looking into his eyes.

Then, unaccountably, she looked upwards and blushed in embarrassment as she saw Alice watching from an upstairs window.

William locked his fingers in hers and they walked towards the pond.

Cilla stood up and looked at them uncertainly.

'Hello Sis.' He kissed her affectionately. 'How are you?'

'Very well thank you. How are you?'

'Top of the world!' William laughed as he led them to a garden seat. 'So tell me about the journey and your first impressions of the big city.'

Both girls started to talk at once.

After a while Lottie, her head resting on William's shoulder, was content to let Cilla do the talking while she absorbed the peace of the garden and her happiness at being with William.

She looked up when she heard someone coming out of the house.

'You look as if you're having fun!' Daisy said gaily as she joined them.

'Oh, the fun's only just beginning! I thought we could go to the music hall in Camden this evening. I'd wanted to take Lottie to a West End show but I think we're safer staying here at night.'

'Camden will be fine, it's so tiring travelling into town these days,' said Daisy.

'Oh what's that?' Cilla leapt off the seat clutching her head.

William laughed. 'It's an apple.' He picked it up and handed it to her. 'We're sitting under an apple tree.'

'It fell right on my head!' Cilla examined the apple then bit into it. 'Mm, it's really juicy.'

'The forbidden fruit,' teased William.

Cilla took another bite and a small sliver of juice escaped and settled on her lip. 'Says who?' she said grinning back at him.

'Careful there isn't a worm in it Cilla,' cautioned Lottie.

'Oh I nearly forgot! Mother said to tell you it's time to come in and get ready for dinner,' said Daisy.

'Your garden's so beautiful, I could sit in it for ever.' Lottie rose reluctantly from the seat.

William put his arm round her waist. 'It's never been as beautiful as it is today,' he whispered in her ear.

***

Lottie and Cilla had been anxious about dining at the Dacre's but everyone went out of their way to put them at their ease and they enjoyed the meal and joined in the conversation. William took a delight in teasing Daisy but it was obvious to Lottie that he was as fond of his sister as she was of hers. She was glad that Cilla had come with her, she would have been scared on her own and they would be able to talk about everything they had seen on the journey home.

After dinner they took a bus to Camden. Cilla and Daisy talked like old friends and Lottie thought she would burst with happiness sitting with William's arm held tightly around her. She noticed one or two girls looking at him appreciatively as they queued outside the theatre for their tickets. He was taller than many of the men and cut a dashing figure in his naval uniform.

'It looks like a good show, Vesta Tilly's on after the interval,' said Daisy.

'Who's she?' asked Cilla.

'A male impersonator, she's very funny; though I gather Queen Mary didn't think so when she saw her perform a few years ago; she didn't approve of a woman in trousers,' laughed William.

They took their seats and waited in anticipation for the curtain to rise then sat back and enjoyed the music and dancing accompanied by ribald humour from the master of ceremonies.

During the interval Lottie overheard the couple in front of her talking, it was their first wedding anniversary and they had come to the theatre to celebrate. The man wasn't in uniform and Lottie wondered where they were from, then she heard him say something about working in his father's smithy. For a moment she wished that William had a nice safe job and that they were celebrating their wedding anniversary.

As if reading her thoughts, he pulled her close. 'Are you enjoying yourself?' he asked.

'It's wonderful,' she said simply.

The band started to play and the curtain rose to a roar of applause as a dapper young man took a bow at the centre of the stage. Lottie found it hard to believe that the slender figure wearing an exquisitely tailored suit and boater and sporting a cigar was in fact a woman. Strutting confidently with her cane, Vesta Tilly started to sing in her clear soprano voice: 'I'm Burlington Bertie, I rise at ten-thirty, I'm Burlington Bertie from Bow'. By the time she reached the last verse the audience were cheering wildly. She held up her hand, the music changed and the mood in the theatre quietened as she gave a soulful rendition of "Sweet Adeline". After a couple more numbers she left the stage.

'It's not finished yet?' asked Cilla.

Lottie followed William's eye as he stiffened and glanced around at the men who had suddenly appeared by the theatre exits.

'I think I know what's coming next,' he murmured.

The band struck up again and Vesta Tilly re-appeared dressed as an army sergeant. Looking directly at Cilla and Daisy she started to sing: "Girls if you want to love a soldier you can all love me." Then she focused her attention on a girl sitting next to a soldier and sang: "Jolly good luck to the girl who loves a soldier". There was a pause while Vesta Tilly waited, motionless in the centre of the stage, until the auditorium was completely quiet then she sang with a forcefulness underlying her sweet voice: "The army of today's all right".

When the cheering had finished, the singer gestured to the men standing by the doors. With compelling authority she told the audience that they had the opportunity to sign up for the army at this very moment, they only had to give their names to the recruiting officers here in the theatre. There was a murmur of voices and men began to get up and move towards the back of the theatre, some hurrying, others shuffling reluctantly. The couple in front of Lottie were whispering urgently with their heads together and Lottie found herself willing the young blacksmith to remain in his seat. She was pleased when the enlisting was over and the men returned to their seats amid patriotic cheers.

The band struck up again and Vesta Tilly began to sing: "We don't want to lose you but we think you ought to go". Looking much younger than her fifty years, the singer leapt gracefully off the stage and addressed individual members of the audience directly. Soon another batch of young men were getting out of their seats and making their way towards the recruiting officers. The couple in front of Lottie sat bolt upright looking directly ahead but the sergeant had them in her sights and she stood at the end of their row looking towards them until the song was finished. It seemed as if the whole audience turned to watch as the young man got out of his seat to the sound of hysterical sobs from his wife.

Lottie exchanged horrified glances with Cilla and Daisy while William shifted uncomfortably in his seat and squeezed Lottie's hand.

Vesta Tilly walked nonchalantly back to the stage and started to sing "And the band on the pier starts playing." As she sat holding William's hand Lottie thought back to the first time they had strolled along the pier together and she told herself fiercely she wasn't going to let anything spoil her weekend with William.

Chapter 9: Alice

Yesterday at Westminster was remarkable chiefly for a statement by Mr Asquith on the finance of the war and the position of recruiting, which was followed by a debate on the question of National Service.

The Times: September 16th 1915

'Daisy won't be coming down for breakfast,' said Ethel when Alice entered the dining room the following morning.

'Oh dear, isn't she well?'

'She said she's tired after her night out. I'll take her a tray up later.'

'Thank you. I'll go and see her straight away.' Alice hurried upstairs and knocked on her daughter's door.

Daisy had brushed her hair and was sitting up in bed reading a magazine but Alice was worried to see dark circles under her eyes and her peaches and cream complexion had a translucent quality. She smiled at her mother and assured her that she was fine but was a bit tired and she hoped that William and the girls wouldn't be upset if she didn't join them on their sightseeing expedition.

'I think her job is too much for her,' said Alice when she returned to the dining room.

Humphrey sighed. 'The job on its own might be all right, although I worry about her being exposed to so many chemicals, but in my opinion being frightened is bad for the health of a young woman.'

'Frightened?'

'She told me she can't sleep for worrying about the zeppelin raids.'

'She told me she can't sleep for worrying about Alec.'

'That's a lot of worrying!' Humphrey made a half-hearted attempt to laugh.

'Do you know where William planned to take the girls?' asked Alice.

'The usual sights I suppose.'

'Why don't we go too? It's a lovely day and it would do us both good to be out in the sunshine.'

There was a shriek of laughter from upstairs, which came unmistakably from Cilla.

'You think we should go to keep the little sister in order?' Humphrey asked.

Alice laughed. 'Maybe. What do you think of her?'

'I haven't made up my mind.'

'And Lottie?'

'I absolutely approve of William's choice and I hope he makes her happy.'

Alice looked surprised. 'I'm sure he will, they're besotted with each other!' She didn't add that she had been watching from the window when William went into the garden the day before.

They did not have the opportunity to say any more because Lottie and Cilla arrived for breakfast, followed closely by William.

William was surprised when Humphrey suggested they join them in town but acquiesced cheerfully enough and they set off soon after breakfast.

***

They took the tube to Euston and then a cab to Marble Arch.

'This way,' said Humphrey steering them towards Hyde Park but the girls were staring open mouthed at the majestic white arch towering in front of them.

'It's beautiful.' Lottie looked in awe at the ornate carvings on the archway.

William took her arm. 'It's impressive isn't it? What do you think Sis?' He turned to Cilla but she was already running into the park.

Lottie laughed. 'She's incorrigible,' she said affectionately.

Alice joined Cilla and Humphrey at Speaker's Corner where people were heckling a conscientious objector. They were jostled as the crowd surged forward and she was touched to feel Cilla's hand grip hers.

'Freedom of speech, one of the cornerstones of democracy,' murmured Humphrey and led them away from the mob.

Cilla looked confused as she pulled her hand away from Alice's.

'There's Lottie and William!' she said and hurried after them.

Alice and Humphrey followed at a leisurely pace until they reached the Serpentine. There was almost a carnival atmosphere with people promenading around the lake and children throwing scraps to the ducks. The women and children were decked in their Sunday best but most of the men, like William, were in uniform.

'Isn't it wonderful!' exclaimed Cilla, her fear at Speaker's Corner suddenly forgotten.

'There's so much to see. And so many different people!' Lottie's face was radiant as she hung onto William's arm.

'Oh listen! There's a band!' Cilla ran away from the lake towards a contingent of Scots Guards.

When Alice and Humphrey caught up with her she was watching in undisguised admiration as the guards marched past accompanied by the haunting wail of bagpipes. There were a couple of soldiers who looked no older than Cilla and, taking her cue from the other spectators, she waved and shouted encouragement. An unkempt woman ran forward, her grey hair escaping from her bun, and pressed a sprig of white heather into the hand of the youngest looking soldier.

'That was kind,' said Cilla.

But Alice noticed a wild look in the woman's eyes and wondered what tragedy she had suffered to give her the appearance of madness. She glanced at Humphrey as they walked on, but he was uncommunicative. She tried to draw comfort from Cilla's enthusiasm but the woman had unnerved her and she found herself worrying about the war. Like most people, Humphrey was working too hard as more and more young men were leaving their jobs to sign up. There were also times when she didn't know where he was but assumed he was on business with the Central Specials. Sometimes the only time they would see each other was when Humphrey called at the station buffet at the beginning or end of one of his trips away. Giving herself a mental shake Alice told herself that the fatigue lines etched on Humphrey's face were no different from the majority of the population these days and he was fortunate that, despite approaching his fifty second birthday, he showed few signs of losing his thick dark hair.

Cilla paused in front of a stall selling trinkets. She picked up a little mirror with a cheap gold plated handle and looked at herself then self-consciously brushed a stray red hair back under her hat. Alice leant over to look at a collection of framed prints of London and was just about to remark that Lottie's pictures were superior when she noticed a young, heavily made up woman lurching towards Humphrey who was standing on his own.

Alice spun round in disbelief when she heard the woman taunting, 'Who's a big toff that's afraid to go to war?'

The woman grabbed Humphrey's hand and waved a bunch of white feathers in his face.

Alice leapt forward just as the woman was about to put a feather in his hand. She pushed her aside then, boiling with rage, grabbed the feathers and struck her hard across the face with them.

'Bitch!' yelled the woman, staggering backwards.

Without a word Alice hit the woman again then slowly began to rip the feathers into little pieces.

A small crowd started to gather as the woman yelled obscenities at Alice and a policeman came hurrying towards them. He looked uncertainly at the well-dressed middle-aged couple, the beautiful girl he assumed was their daughter and the screaming woman with bright red welts on her cheeks.

Humphrey regained his composure and stepped forward. 'Inspector Dacre,' he said, taking a card from his pocket and handing it to the policeman. 'This woman was being a nuisance but she's leaving now.' He glared authoritatively at the woman who stood her ground and glared back.

'You saw what she done!' The woman turned to the muttering crowd.

As the policeman studied Humphrey's card a gust of wind sent the feathers skittering along the ground. Some were blown into the air and he absent-mindedly brushed his jacket when one of them landed on his epaulette.

The crowd waited expectantly, their sympathies appearing to shift from the brazen young woman to Alice and Cilla standing like alabaster statues. Then the mood lightened as the good-looking figure of William arrived with a smiling Lottie on his arm.

'Everything all right?' William looked curiously at his parents.

The policeman looked at William's naval uniform, taking in the sub-lieutenant's stripe and the badge of the Royal Navy Air Service. 'My nephew's in the RNAS, he's training to fly sea-planes,' he said.

The crowd murmured its approval as William replied; 'I got my naval aviator's licence a few months ago.' Then, suddenly taking in the situation, he steered Lottie towards Alice, put his arm through his mother's and said, 'I'm just home for a few days leave then it's back to fight for King and Country.'

'That's right Sir, we're all doing our bit.' The policeman handed Humphrey back his card with a gruff, 'That'll be all Sir, thank you.'

Cilla looked nervously at the crowd and moved close to Humphrey.

The young woman shook her fist at the family then turned and walked quickly away to shouts of 'Shame on you!' from some of the crowd.

'Thank you.' Humphrey gave the policeman a curt nod and started to walk away.

Lottie hung behind with Cilla and they followed Alice who walked, chin tilted, with her son and husband on either side.

'Perhaps I should enlist. What do you think William?' The quietly spoken question hung in the autumnal air.

Alice felt William stiffen. Humphrey rarely asked anyone's opinion and he had certainly not confided in his son before.

'You shouldn't take any notice of these stupid women and their feathers; they've no idea what it's like out there. It's our duty to try and stay alive as well as serve our country. And you're certainly serving your country in both the jobs you're doing. And so are you Mother. And so is Daisy with her work at the hospital. And Lottie's parents are trying to keep enough food in their shop to feed their customers and trying not to put the prices up. We're all doing our bit!' William shouted, causing passers-by to look at them curiously.

They walked in silence towards Hyde Park Corner then paused to watch a photographer taking pictures of a young soldier with his wife and baby. The couple were sitting close together on a bench with the father holding the baby who chuckled at the camera. Then the mother held the baby and the father gazed at them both with an intensity that made Alice feel like an intruder.

'That's an excellent idea! Let's have our portraits taken Lottie,' said William, regaining his equanimity.

Alice smiled as Lottie straightened her hat and smoothed her coat. 'It's a lovely coat,' she said.

Lottie blushed with pleasure. 'Thank you, I made it myself.'

'There wasn't time to make one for me as well so we stitched a new collar on mine,' said Cilla guilelessly.

They waited while the couple paid the photographer and gave him their address. Then Lottie and William took their place on the bench.

'Don't be so serious Lottie,' said Cilla after the first portrait was taken.

Lottie laughed and the camera whirred again.

'Very nice,' said the photographer. 'And now would you like a family group?'

William looked questioningly at his parents.

'Yes please,' said Humphrey.

'Could the young ladies sit on either side of the gentleman and I'd be much obliged if Sir and Madam would stand behind.' The photographer eyed them critically as they shifted into their positions. Then he put his head under the black cloth covering the camera and took the photograph.

'Thank you,' said Humphrey as he and Alice moved away.

The photographer held up his hand. 'Just one more, if I may be so bold,' he said and took a final shot of William sitting between the two sisters.

They stood up and William took out his wallet to pay.

'Put it away, I'll pay for these,' said Humphrey gruffly. He ordered two sets, one to be sent to their address and the other to Lottie. 'We'll post yours on as soon as we know where you're stationed,' he said to William.

'Thank you very much,' said Lottie. 'I'll keep them for ever.'

William put his arm round her and for a moment no one said anything as they walked through the gate at Hyde Park Corner.

Alice was pleased to be out of the park. She was feeling uncomfortable about the way she had behaved earlier. But she couldn't help feeling a tingle of satisfaction with the slap she had given even if it was not the behaviour associated with a woman of her standing.

'Where would you like to go now?' she asked.

'Are we near Buckingham Palace?' said Lottie.

'And can we see Big Ben?' Cilla added.

'We can if we take the bus and sit upstairs,' William said ushering them towards a queue of people. 'And then we can walk to Buckingham Palace.'

'I hope we're right next to Big Ben when it chimes,' said Cilla excitedly.

'That won't be possible,' said Humphrey. 'It was stopped at the beginning of the war.'

'There's a bus coming now.' Alice pointed to a crowded horse-drawn vehicle.

They got the last seats on the open upper deck. Lottie and Cilla craned their heads excitedly trying to take in everything at once.

As the bus made its way along Piccadilly they looked down on footmen standing on the steps of luxurious hotels and glimpsed people sitting under crystal chandeliers inside. Further on they saw errand boys from Fortnum and Mason on bicycles, their baskets filled with hampers and packages.

'That's the statue of Eros,' said William pointing to the magnificent bronze angel of charity in the centre of Piccadilly Circus.

Humphrey frowned as they passed the newly opened Regent Palace Hotel sporting a large board saying: "To Arms for King and Empire Join Today".

Alice felt anger welling again as she saw the hurt expression on Humphrey's face; how dare the woman with the feathers imply her husband was a coward. 'I hear it's the largest hotel in Europe,' she said conversationally. 'And it's not expensive, you can get a single room for six shillings and sixpence a night.'

Humphrey said nothing but clasped Alice's hand in his.

By the time they reached Trafalgar Square Cilla was wriggling about in excitement. The bus rounded the square and proceeded down Whitehall to the Houses of Parliament.

'There's Big Ben!' both the girls shouted at once.

They clambered off the bus and gazed at the imposing buildings in front of them. Apart from a larger presence of police and special constables, the Houses of Parliament did not give the appearance of expecting imminent invasion. The sun was shining and people seemed determined to enjoy themselves.

The girls marvelled at Big Ben and bought some post cards. Then they walked past Westminster Abbey and on to St James's Park.

'It's a pity the lake's drained,' remarked Humphrey. 'They did it so the German planes won't recognise it and know where they are.'

'But won't they recognise the other landmarks?' asked Lottie.

'You'd have thought so,' he replied wryly.

They were just about to enter the park when Cilla stopped in front of a billboard. 'Look at that!' she said pointing to an advertisement for female bus conductors. 'Wouldn't that be an exciting job!'

'You'd look just the ticket in a clippie's uniform.' William laughed, pleased with his pun.

'But Cilla you're not twenty-one.' Lottie pointed to the bottom of the notice.

'Oh!' Cilla looked crestfallen. 'But I really would like to be a bus conductor.'

'Your mother would have fifty fits,' said Alice briskly.

'You'll be twenty-one in eighteen months' time.' William put his arm around Lottie possessively. 'What will you do with the key of the door?'

'Well I don't think I'll become a bus conductor,' she giggled.

Alice wondered if that was the answer William was expecting.

'You'll be an artist and people will come from far and wide to buy your pictures,' he said proudly. Then he turned to Cilla. 'And what do you really want to be, Sis?" he asked.

'I'm going to be an explorer.' Cilla looked at them steadily then, with a defiant toss of her head, she walked into the park.

...

132

The rest of the day passed all too quickly. Daisy was looking better when they got home and her eager interest in hearing about their excursion helped to dispel the gloom that was beginning to descend on Lottie and William. The incident with the white feathers was not mentioned and Cilla gave a lively description of Buckingham Palace and her conviction that she had seen Prince Edward waving at her from a window.

Thinking that William might appreciate company after putting the girls on the night train to Llandudno Junction, Alice accompanied them to Euston. Cilla chatted happily on the journey but Lottie and William said little. When they arrived at the station Alice suggested that she and Cilla checked out the sleeping compartment. This enabled Lottie and William to say their goodbyes on the platform.

Cilla was enchanted with the bunk beds and immediately bagged the top one. Alice spoke to the sleeping car attendant to ensure that the girls received special treatment.

As she stepped back on to the platform she sensed the despair of couples clutched in desperate embraces and of the more restrained emotions of fathers and mothers bidding farewell to their sons. It was a sight she saw every day but now her own son was involved she was no longer a dispassionate observer.

Cilla leant out of a window but Lottie remained on the platform, clasped in William's embrace, until the guard blew his whistle. Doors slammed and Lottie reluctantly jumped onto the train and joined her sister at the open window. William held her hand and ran alongside the train until it pulled out of the station.

He stood with his back to Alice, watching the carriages snake between soot-stained houses as they carried Lottie away from him. When he turned, Alice could hardly bear to witness the misery on her son's face.

'She's gone,' he said brokenly, 'and I don't know when I'll see her again.'

Chapter 10: Lottie

Christmas plans at the Front
No doubt the Bosches will have plenty of Christmas
trees but they will fare very much more frugally than
our own men

The Times: December 23rd 1915

'That's another pair of socks nearly finished!' Bronwen put down her knitting and took a gulp of tea.

'I've decided to stick to mufflers, they're more satisfying because they don't take long.' Lottie's needles worked quickly and the woollen scarf slithered towards the floor.

'Is that for me? I could do with a warm muffler when I'm patrolling the streets.' Dylan put down his tray and sat next to Lottie.

'It's for the troops, as you well know!' laughed Lottie.

'Do you like being a special constable?' asked Bronwen.

Dylan shrugged. 'It's all right; bit tiring on the gammy leg after working here all day.'

Lottie looked at him sympathetically. 'Will you be able to come to the dance on Christmas Eve?'

Dylan sprinkled salt over his dinner and picked up his knife and fork.

'Dylan! Lottie asked you a question. Are you coming to the dance?'

He looked uncomfortable. 'Now that Irene's left me to become a nurse in France I haven't a partner.'

'How's she getting on?'

'I'm sure she's having a good time looking after the troops.'

'That's rather unfair.' Bronwen picked up her knitting. 'Anyway I didn't think you and she were really suited.'

'What makes you say that?' Dylan scowled.

'Because I know you so well. And, if you're not on duty, I think you should come to the dance. We're lucky that Rhys and William have both got leave and we want you to enjoy yourself too. We'll find you a partner won't we Lottie?'

'Yes, of course you must come.' Lottie thought for a moment. 'I'm sure that my sister would like to come to the dance.'

'Your little sister?'

'She's not so little these days.' Lottie didn't add that Cilla was becoming quite a flirt and she wondered how they would get on.

'I'll think about it.'

'Just say yes, Dylan. You've got to grab a bit of fun while you can these days.' Bronwen clacked her knitting needles in exasperation.

'All right. I said I'd do a duty on Christmas Day so I'm sure I'll be able to get Christmas Eve off.'

'That's settled then,' said Bronwen looking pleased.

***

Lottie was in a state of excitement all the following day knowing that William planned to arrive in the evening. She and Cilla had strung homemade paper chains across the living room and parlour ceilings and draped sprigs of ivy over the pictures.

When she got home from work she checked that everything was spotless and tried not to mind that the furniture was shabby and that their privy was in the back yard. Nellie had wanted to invite William for a meal but, since her trip to London, Lottie was diffident about her mother's hospitality. She said that William would be fed well at the Station Hotel where he was staying.

She forced herself to eat the meal Nellie had prepared because she did not want an argument with her father who was being difficult about Cilla accompanying her and William to the dance. She had warned Cilla not to mention the matter again until William arrived.

After supper Cilla volunteered to do the dishes so that Lottie could get ready. The bedroom was freezing but Lottie felt her face glowing as she put the finishing touches to her makeup. She tightened her corset then put on her new blouse with its deep V-neckline. She had bought it because it was the same colour as the rose bush in William's garden. She had just added a touch of lipstick when she heard William at the door.

As she came downstairs she was relieved to hear her father greeting her fiancé cordially.

'You and William can sit in the parlour, I've lit the fire,' said Nellie.

Lottie led William into the tiny parlour and they stood in the middle of the room looking at each other awkwardly.

'You look beautiful Lottie,' said William as he kissed her.

'This blouse is new, do you like the colour? It reminds me of your garden; that was such a lovely week-end,' Lottie gabbled then stopped and shivered for, despite the fire, the room felt chilly and slightly damp.

'Lottie, you're cold.' William pulled her onto the sofa and, taking her hands in his, rubbed them till she felt her whole body glowing.

'I'm sorry I've got to go to work tomorrow,' she said.

'Don't worry. I'll go into the locomotive sheds, I'm sure they can do with a hand. It'll be interesting to see how they've got on in my absence.'

'It will probably seem boring after all the excitement of flying.'

William frowned. 'Excitement! Oh yes, it's exciting all right.' He gripped her hand harder.

Lottie felt confused. She knew how passionate he had been about flying. But that was before he got his RNAS aviator's license, he had rarely mentioned flying since. In fact he hardly mentioned his work in his letters, concentrating instead on the camaraderie and the practical jokes they sometimes played. She wondered whether to ask him what he meant but thought better of it.

'Are you looking forward to the dance tomorrow?' she asked instead.

'Very much.' He put his arm round her. 'It will be an excuse to hold you in my arms all evening."

For a while neither of them said anything. Lottie began to feel uncomfortable in the little parlour and suspected that William did too.

He put his hand in his pocket. 'I'd like to give you your Christmas present now, there's no point in having it after the dance.' William handed Lottie a small leather box, finely gift-wrapped.

'Oh thank you!' Lottie examined the box carefully before unwrapping it. She lifted the lid and took out a necklace of three moonstones on a gold chain. As she looked at it there was a sudden draft and the fire burst into life, lighting up the room and reflecting the subtle colours of the stones. She held the necklace in the palm of her hand. 'It's beautiful,' she said.

William took it from her and, with great care, fastened it around her neck. She looked down at the jewels then lifted her face to William's. He kissed her urgently and her response was immediate and passionate. She closed her eyes and the small dark room vanished in an explosion of stars.

They were jerked back to reality by a loud clatter from the kitchen and Lottie blushed fearfully as she thought of her parents on the other side of the door.

She unwound herself from William's embrace. 'I've got a present for you too, I'll go and get it.'

'I've made a pot of tea for you and William,' said Nellie as Lottie hurried through the living room.

'Thanks,' she called and ran upstairs. She took a neatly wrapped package from the chest of drawers and paused to look at herself in the mirror.

Cilla's inquisitive eyes peered round the door. 'Has he given you your Christmas present?' she asked.

Lottie nodded and showed off the necklace.

'It's so beautiful.' Cilla held the central stone to get a better look. 'You deserve it Lottie.'

'I hope he likes his present', she said anxiously.

'Of course he will.'

Nellie had taken the tea tray into the parlour and was busy pouring William a cup when Lottie went back into the room.

Lottie was so delighted with William's gift that she didn't feel irritated by her mother's presence and showed her the necklace.

Nellie looked at William approvingly. 'It's a lovely necklace and it will go with anything.' She put a small shovel of coal on the fire then reluctantly left the room.

Lottie handed William the gift and sat close to him watching his face as he unwrapped it.

'Oh! It's a Benson's wristwatch! It's just what I wanted.' He cupped his hand around the face. 'Look, the numbers and the hands are luminous. It's just what I need when I'm flying in the dark.' He put on the watch and studied it in delight.

Lottie held his wrist, thrilled that William was so pleased. She had had the watch put by for the last two months and had paid a regular amount towards it each week.

William kissed her, but then suddenly Lottie pulled away. 'What did you say about flying in the dark?' she asked anxiously.

'It's winter, it gets dark early. On a dull day it can be dark in the cockpit; you sometimes get disorientated and forget what time of day it is.'

William's face clouded and he stared down at his polished shoes. Then he pulled Lottie towards him and kissed her again. 'But the watch will keep me on track and will be a constant reminder of you.'

They sat looking at the fire, neither quite knowing what to say.

'I'm sorry we haven't a gramophone.' Lottie wondered if she should offer to play something on the piano but she wasn't very good. We always have a sing song on Christmas Day,' she said. 'Uncle Owen and Auntie Meg and my cousins are coming. They'll stay over till Boxing Day. It'll be quite a squash.' She looked at him anxiously. 'I hope it'll be all right?'

'It will be wonderful to sit by a warm fire.' For a moment his eyes darkened and Lottie wondered what images he was seeing. His foot tapped the floor and Lottie sat in silence watching his knee moving rhythmically up and down.

A burst of laughter from Cilla in the living room made them smile.

'I love a sing song, especially at Christmas.' William rose and went towards the piano. 'What music have you got?'

Lottie showed him and he sat down and began to play. Lottie stood by the piano turning the pages until he went into a ragtime, which he played by ear.

'Bravo!' Lottie turned to see her parents and Cilla standing in the door.

'You certainly know how to get a tune out of our old piano,' Jack said.

Lottie smiled happily at her family as they sat down to enjoy the music.

***

The train to Llandudno was late and the dance was in full swing when Lottie, William and Cilla arrived. They hesitated in the doorway, scanning the room for their friends.

'Come and join the fun!' A soldier called to Cilla who was standing slightly apart from Lottie and William, her feet tapping and her eyes darting excitedly round the hall, which was teeming with young men in uniform.

'No Cilla!' Lottie caught her sister's hand as she began to move towards the soldier.

Cilla grinned as William led them through the throng to join their friends on the far side of the dance floor.

Lottie noticed that Rhys had lost weight but he still dwarfed Bronwen whose radiant face was looking up at him. He greeted them enthusiastically although she saw him look slightly wary as he took in the sub-lieutenant's stripe on William's sleeve.

'Good to see you, it's been a long time.' William seemed genuinely pleased to see him.

'It's good to be back.' Rhys turned to Cilla. 'And I see the Station Hotel has got a new waitress.'

'Yes, I can keep an eye on William while he's staying there!' Cilla laughed and swayed with the music.

'You and Cilla have met before haven't you Dylan?' said Bronwen.

'Yes, at a beach picnic last summer. Would you care to dance?' Dylan smiled shyly at Cilla.

'I'd love to.'

The three couples joined the rest of the dancers. Lottie soon lost sight of the others as William held her effortlessly and they glided in tune with the music and each other. They danced through four consecutive numbers and when they left the floor they found the others having a drink.

Cilla's glass was already empty and she was chattering animatedly. There was a cheer from the crowd as it was announced that the next number would be a tango.

'Oh, that'll be fun won't it Dylan?' said Cilla.

'I don't think my leg's up to doing the tango,' he muttered.

Cilla tossed her head towards a couple of unattached soldiers standing nearby. 'I'd love to dance the tango,' she said loudly.

The band struck up and one of the soldiers came over to Dylan.

'Would you mind if I asked your partner for the honour of this dance?'

'You'd like to, wouldn't you Cilla?' Dylan looked relieved when Cilla accepted with alacrity.

'I think we'll sit this one out,' said Bronwen as she nestled next to Rhys.

'Would you like to tango, or shall I get us drinks?' asked William.

'I'd like a drink please,' Lottie murmured, her eyes fixed on Cilla.

Her partner certainly knew how to tango and Cilla confidently followed his lead, her jade dress a brilliant contrast to his khaki uniform. When William returned with the drinks there were only a few couples remaining on the floor. Cilla and her partner were attracting particular attention with their exuberant dancing.

'I don't know where she learnt to do it so well,' said Lottie.

'The thing about the tango is that it allows the dancers to make it up as they go along,' William replied then glanced at Dylan who was staring myopically at the dance floor. 'How's your leg?' he asked.

'I don't complain.'

'No, of course you don't. But I don't suppose that patrolling the streets after a day's work does it any good.'

Dylan didn't answer but shifted uncomfortably then stood up and started to move away.

Lottie frowned, wondering why Dylan was being so taciturn when William was making an effort to be friendly. The reason became clear when two soldiers lurched drunkenly towards him.

'How's Constable Four-eyes?' The tallest soldier leered down at Dylan. He said nothing and took a step back.

Lottie saw Bronwen look frightened and whisper something to Rhys.

Rhys and William exchanged glances, stood up and took their places silently behind Dylan.

'Still tied to your mother's apron strings like you were at school?' The soldier swayed then closed in and lifted his hand towards Dylan's glasses.

'Stop it!' squealed Bronwen.

'Oh, your little tart still stands up for you even though she's got herself a soldier now. At least she's got enough sense not to be seen with a conchi.' He turned his head towards the dance floor where Cilla was tangoing with abandon. 'And your new little tart's just left you for someone who's proud to fight for his country. What are you going to do about that? Will you fight him?'

The soldier spat in Dylan's face.

Dylan clenched his fists in the air but it was William who leapt forward and punched the man's jaw. He staggered and William aimed another blow. The soldier fell to the ground as William's fist hit his chin.

A flicker of satisfaction crossed William's face. He turned and silently fixed his eyes on the other soldier, daring him to retaliate. With a show of bravado the soldier took a step forward then hesitated uncertainly as Rhys and Dylan closed ranks behind William. He was considerably shorter than both William and Rhys and he swallowed nervously as he looked down at his companion cowering on the floor and muttering obscenities.

'You all right, cock?' he asked inadequately.

The obscenities increased, loud and venomous.

The soldier looked uncomfortable. 'There are ladies present,' he mumbled, glancing at Lottie and Bronwen's stricken faces as they clung to each other for support. He gave William a sickly smile and began to back away. 'He likes to have a joke; no harm done eh?'

He sidled towards the dance floor as the band started playing another number and people began to take their partners for the next dance. William watched him go with contempt then glared at the soldier at his feet.

He scowled back through bloodshot eyes and hauled himself up, breathing heavily into William's face and cursing furiously.

Lottie bit her lip, terrified that William was going to get hurt. Aware only of the two angry men and her own

144

beating heart, she was startled when Cilla pushed through the dancers.

'Did you see me tango?' Her face was flushed with excitement and exertion. She looked at the soldier who was standing with beads of sweat on his forehead and an ugly welt already developing on his chin. 'You've had a nasty fall,' she said then stared curiously at Lottie when she let out a hysterical giggle.

'I think it's time for us to go, or it'll be my turn to cause trouble for somebody.' Rhys fixed his eyes on the parrying fists of the angry soldier.

William was standing very still, his hands clenched firmly by his side. 'You're right. This room isn't big enough for us and cowardly bullies.'

He put his arm through Lottie's and began to lead the way back across the dance floor.

'Why?' began Cilla then stopped as she saw the thunderous expression on Dylan's face. Walking stiffly he steered her towards the door.

'But why did we have to leave so early?' she persisted as they stood shivering in the cold night air.

'It's best forgotten.' Rhys spoke gruffly.

'Would you all like to come back to my house for some cocoa?' asked Bronwen, her voice agitated.

'That sounds tempting but we'd better get back to the Junction,' said William with resignation.

Lottie wanted to burst into tears.

'Enjoy your Christmas dinner,' she said in a determined to be cheerful as she kissed Bronwen goodbye. 'And keep away from criminals,' she added giving Dylan a hug.

Dylan shook William's hand. 'Thanks. And good luck with your next mission,' he said quietly.

'It seems as if I missed something,' said Cilla as they hurried toward the station.

'Nothing anyone's proud of.' William sounded grim.

...

The sisters undressed quickly in their cold bedroom. As Lottie slid between the warm sheets she blessed her mother for putting hot water jars in their beds.

'Good night,' she whispered and pulled the blankets tightly around her.

'But you haven't told me what happened.' Cilla's voice cut urgently through the darkness.

Lottie could sense her sister's excitement as she recounted how the soldiers had taunted Dylan and how William had stood up to them.

'You must be really proud of him!'

Lottie considered. 'I'm proud of him for standing up for my friend but I don't like fighting and I don't think he does either.'

'It's lucky he doesn't have to do any fighting in the RNAS.'

'Actually, I don't know what he does, he won't talk about it. He says he sometimes has to fly in the dark.'

'How does he know where he's going?'

Lottie felt her heart palpitate. She took a deep breath and said, 'He's got an observer who flies with him.'

'Yes, but how does he know?'

'Shut up Cilla!' Lottie kept her voice low but she felt like screaming. She swallowed hard. 'If you hadn't danced with that soldier this wouldn't have happened.'

'But Dylan's leg was hurting, he said I could dance with him. It wasn't my fault that soldier went on at him.'

'No. I'm sorry.' Lottie knew that it hadn't been Cilla's fault but she instinctively felt that Cilla attracted attention and the soldier couldn't bear to see someone like Dylan with a pretty girl.

'Do you think Bronwen and Rhys will get married?'

Lottie thought for a moment of William flying over the sea in the dark before answering bleakly. 'What's the point of getting married if your husband is risking his life somewhere you've never heard of and you're left at home waiting for his next letter?'

March 1916

My Darling Lottie
 Thank you for your last letter which I treasure with all the others.
 I'm sorry we couldn't be together to celebrate the anniversary of the day you agreed to marry me. The sketch you sent of Daffodil Mountain brought back wonderful memories. You are so clever. I'm not an artist like you but I have written a poem. With apologies to Mr Wordsworth!

I flew my plane above the cloud
That hovers o'er those lovely hills,
When all at once I saw a crowd,
A host of golden daffodils;
An artist sits beneath the trees
Painting a picture in the breeze.

Continuous as the stars above
That twinkle on the Milky Way,
You are my one and only love,
A love that shines both night and day.

 As you know, I wear the watch you gave me all the time. Its light shining in the cockpit during the dark winter days kept me on an even keel and I felt stronger knowing that part of you was with me.
 Things are a bit easier with the spring weather. I'm still flying reconnaissance missions but I can't tell you any more than that. When I hear about what's happening to our boys on the front line I know I'm one of the lucky ones. Knowing you are waiting for me gives me courage even when I see enemy ships looming below me. Don't worry about me. I'm getting very

sharp noting the enemy's position then heading back to Blighty.

Christmas seems such a long time ago. I hope to get leave at Whitsun. Maybe you can persuade your father to change his mind about waiting till your 21st before getting married. We could have a May wedding; it would be perfect with all the blossom and the baby birds learning to fly. Darling Lottie, please tell your father I am honourable and I will take care of you. I know your parents need you but they have Cilla to help. If you wanted, you could even carry on living at home until the war's finished.

I wait for your next letter.

All my love,

Your ever loving fiancé, William

Chapter 11: Alice

LLANDUDNO St George's Hotel
*1ˢᵗ class. Premier position. Covered balcony. Facing
sea.*

The Times: May 19ᵗʰ 1916

Alice was startled to hear the sound of weeping as she
unlocked the front door. She was exhausted after doing
an early shift at the station buffet. A young naval
officer had collapsed in her arms, she had been jostled
in the tube on the journey home and her nerves felt
ready to snap.

Forcing herself to appear calm, she paused at the
door of the sitting room. Daisy was curled on the sofa
holding a letter in one hand and a sodden handkerchief
in the other.

'Please God, don't let anything have happened to
William.' Alice prayed silently as she hurried across
the room and sat down next to her daughter.

'Alec's leave's been cancelled!' Daisy turned to her
mother and sobbed, her chest heaving as she gulped for
air.

'What's happened? Is, is he all right?'

'Oh yes. But he was meant to be coming home!'

'And - William?'

'William? His leave's been cancelled too.' Daisy
screwed the tear soaked hanky into a ball. 'I miss Alec
so much and I get so worried about him. He must be so
lonely up there!'

A feeling of relief washed over Alice as she handed
Daisy a clean handkerchief. Her son and the man who
obviously meant so much to her daughter were all right
– for the moment. She wondered why their leave had

been cancelled, were they engaged in some secret mission?

Alice put her arm round Daisy and held her like she used to when she was a little girl. She remembered William's excitement the day he got his pilot's licence. Flying had seemed such an innocent activity in those days. It was the freedom of being in the sky that had attracted William and young men like him but now the skies were neither free nor safe. Mothers and sweethearts remained at home living for news and praying for their loved ones' safe return.

She waited till Daisy's sobs had subsided then got up. 'I'll ask Ethel to make some tea,' she said and left the room.

Realising that it was Ethel's afternoon off, Alice went abstractedly into the kitchen and started to prepare the tea. She had a sick feeling in the pit of her stomach but could not work out why. For the moment her loved ones were safe – alive anyway. She did not have financial worries; they had enough to eat and even had help in the house. Alice wondered if she was still upset about the naval officer at the station but this feeling was deep, it gnawed at the core of her. As she thought about Daisy's trembling shoulders as she held her Alice realised that her beautiful daughter was turning into skin and bone. In her agitation the cups rattled on the tray she carried into the sitting room. She passed Daisy a cup of tea and noticed that her once manicured hands were chapped and raw like a servant girl's. The long hours at the hospital were taking their toll.

Alice came to a decision. 'You had asked for some time off work for Alec's leave hadn't you?'

'Yes, but ….'

'Well, I think a change of air would do us both good. Why don't we go to Trealaw for a few days?'

Daisy looked uncertain. 'It's a long journey.'

'It will be worth it. If you like, we can stay in a hotel in Llandudno for a couple of days before going to Trealaw – pamper ourselves for a bit.'

Daisy gave a wan smile. 'I think you're right, perhaps the sea air will do me good, I've been feeling so tired lately.'

***

Humphrey had insisted that they spend a week in Llandudno for Daisy to recover her strength before going on to the more primitive pleasures of Trealaw.

'I feel better already,' she said as they walked up the elegant steps of St George's hotel.

Alice felt a frisson of nostalgia as she inhaled the scent from a floral display in the foyer and her feet sank into the thick carpet. She had wondered how she would feel returning to her honeymoon hotel with her daughter but now she was pleased that Humphrey had booked somewhere that held such happy memories. A porter in immaculate uniform showed them to their rooms and Daisy gave a cry of delight on discovering they had views across the bay.

The weather was warm and on their first morning Daisy joined a group of bathers, insisting that the seawater invigorated her. Alice relaxed in a deck chair watching the women splashing about in the water. Daisy seemed perfectly at home with her new friends. At the end of the morning an elderly attendant dragged a bathing machine into the shallow water for the women to change into their clothes in privacy.

'That was lovely,' said Daisy as they made their way back to the hotel for luncheon.

'You looked as if you were enjoying yourself. I was almost tempted to have a swim myself.'

'You wouldn't!' Daisy looked shocked.

Alice laughed. 'No, I don't suppose I would. I tried it once but the bathing machine was unpleasant especially as the door jammed and it was some time before the attendant managed to open it.'

She shivered as she remembered waiting in the dark with waves crashing against the flimsy sides. 'I much prefer walking in the fresh air.' She glanced towards the mountains. 'But I'm sure the seawater will do you good.'

'It's all doing me good,' smiled Daisy as they reached the hotel.

Alice had invited the Rowes to take tea with them that afternoon in the hotel sun lounge.

Lottie arrived first, straight from work, and greeted them with a confidence that had been lacking on her visit to London the previous autumn.

Daisy looked at her admiringly and patted the chair next to her. 'You've had your hair cut, it suits you! Does William like it?'

'He hasn't seen it yet but he said he liked the photo I sent.' Lottie sighed as she sat down. 'I was so disappointed when his leave was cancelled but it's lovely that you're here.'

'It's horrid being apart all the time and everything so uncertain but I'm so pleased Mother suggested we came and it's lovely to see you again.'

'And how is your mother?' asked Alice.

'She'll probably tell you she's all right but her legs are troubling her quite a lot. She's looking forward to seeing you.' Lottie looked out of the window. 'Oh look they're coming along the promenade just now!'

Alice stood up when Nellie and her younger daughter came through the door. As she shook Nellie's hand she was shocked to see how much she had aged since their last meeting.

'Cilla, I hardly recognised you!' Alice turned to the carefully made up girl and caught a whiff of perfume.

Cilla smiled as she drew off her gloves, revealing scarlet nails and a garnet ring on her right hand.

'I love your perfume,' said Daisy as she kissed her. 'Ashes of roses isn't it?'

'She's too young for scent. She's growing up too quickly.' Nellie pursed her lips.

'They do,' said Alice. 'I can't believe Daisy will be twenty-one soon. And how old are you now?' she asked Cilla curiously.

'I'll be seventeen next birthday. Old enough to work in a munitions factory.' Cilla looked defiantly at her mother.

'Now then, Cilla,' said Nellie warningly.

'Oh Cilla, you're too pretty to be a canary. Anyway, I thought you had a job at the Station Hotel. Aren't you enjoying it?' Daisy asked.

'Yes, it's all right but I'd like to be doing war work.'

The waitress arrived with a trolley laden with sandwiches and cake.

'And how's your job?' Alice looked at her future daughter-in-law.

'It's fine; for the moment anyway.'

'She's working too hard,' said Nellie.

Lottie flushed. 'I don't suppose I've been working nearly as hard as Daisy. It must be exhausting working in a London hospital. I know one or two of the nurses in the hospital here and they're run off their feet.'

'Anyway, it's wonderful to be away from it all. And I'm enjoying bathing in the sea. I've joined a group and we go out in the bathing machines.'

'Oh, we never used to bother with those!' said Cilla.

Lottie laughed at the surprised expression on Daisy's face. 'It's true! I used to hold the towel round

Cilla while she wriggled out of her bathing costume then she'd do the same for me!'

'Maybe I should try,' said Daisy doubtfully.

'You'd have all the men queuing up to watch!'

'Cilla!' Nellie looked distressed at her daughter's risqué remark.

Alice wiped her mouth with a serviette to hide a smile. 'Would anyone like more cake?' She gestured to the silver cake stand.

'This sea air has given me an appetite. The walnut cake's delicious; go on, have another piece,' said Daisy as she saw Lottie wavering.

Alice was pleased to see everyone tucking in and relaxing as they passed comments about the people outside.

After tea they strolled along the promenade. The sun was still shining and people of all ages appeared to be enjoying the sea air. Alice was about to remark that you could almost forget the war when she noticed several young men on crutches and others propelling themselves along in wheelchairs.

However, she was delighted to see the colour return to Daisy's cheeks and hear her laugh as she linked arms with Lottie and Cilla.

'It's good to see the girls getting on so well,' she said as she watched the blonde, brunette and auburn heads bent together and giggling.

Nellie sighed. 'Sometimes I don't know where Cilla gets her ideas from. She's as different from her sister as chalk is from cheese but they get on well enough.'

'It's not always easy to understand our children,' agreed Alice as they sat on a bench and watched the sea. 'And how is business?' she asked.

'We've been having trouble getting stock and people don't seem to understand why the price of everything is going up.'

'Do you have a problem with people stock-piling?'

Nellie looked uncomfortable. 'Not from our shop, people don't have the money. But Jack says the government may have to bring in some sort of rationing if things continue as they are.'

'It must be very difficult for you.'

'It is. Not that you'd understand.' She clapped her hand over her mouth and Alice realised that Nellie had spoken without thinking.

'My father was a grain merchant,' she said. 'It's not the same of course but I do remember one year when there was a very bad harvest and my parents didn't know how they were going to pay the bills.'

'But they came through?' Nellie looked at her with a grudging respect.

'Yes, they came through. Just as we'll come through this war.'

Nellie nodded and they sat in uneasy silence until the girls joined them.

***

Daisy and Lottie seemed to have struck up a genuine friendship and they arranged to meet again after Lottie had finished work on the day before they left Llandudno.

'I've invited Lottie to visit us at Trealaw,' said Daisy when she and Alice were strolling along the promenade after Lottie had got her train back to the Junction.

'That's nice. I'm glad you get on.'

'You do like her don't you?'

Alice didn't want to spoil their last evening by saying that she had hoped William would make a more suitable match. Theoretically she and Humphrey applauded the breaking down of the rigid class barriers that had existed before the war but she found she had little in common with Nellie Rowe.

'Lottie's a lovely girl and Mr and Mrs Rowe are decent hardworking people,' she said truthfully.

'And she and really William love each other!'

Alice's face softened. 'They do and that's all that matters.'

They stopped and leant on the railing and looked out to sea. An oystercatcher hopped at the water's edge, its orange bill probing the shallows. Further out, herring gulls screeched as they dived for fish then flew off towards the headland.

'North Wales is a lovely place to live,' said Alice.

'It's beautiful here," replied Daisy thoughtfully, 'but the Junction's quite ugly. And most of the houses there only have back yards. I wouldn't like to live in a house without a garden.'

'Do you think Lottie minds?'

'I don't think she thought about it before she came to visit us.'

'No, I suppose she didn't.' Alice said nothing for a moment then added, 'And Cilla?'

Daisy frowned. 'Cilla's different. In fact, Lottie's a bit worried about her but I promised I wouldn't say anything.'

'Did she say when they plan to get married? Or is that a secret too?'

'It can't be before next March, she's not twenty-one till then.'

'No, I gather her father is adamant about that.' Alice wondered whether he had hoped his daughter would change her mind if he forced her to wait. Or whether William would call it off. 'I must admit your father and I had reservations at first but I'm beginning to think Lottie is worth waiting for, even …'

'And do you think Alec is worth waiting for?' Daisy interrupted.

'It's what you think that matters. Has he declared himself?'

'He says he loves me. And I know I love him. And his family seemed to approve of me when I met them at Christmas. If it wasn't for the war...' Daisy's voice trailed off.

'I know,' said Alice. She glanced down at the beach. A young man was dodging the waves in a show of bravado for the laughing girl with him. She felt suddenly angry on Daisy's behalf that Alec wasn't with her to share such innocent fun. But at the same time she was glad that she had her daughter to herself for these few days. She realised she had more in common with Nellie than she thought – neither of them wanted their daughters to leave home.

A low drone out to sea made her look up. Silhouetted against the evening sky was a dark shape like a huge bird swooping into the bay.

'It's a seaplane!' Daisy shouted.

Footsteps sounded along the promenade as people ran to the railings to get a better view.

'It's not the Germans, is it?' a woman's voice shrilled behind Alice.

'Of course not, their planes can't fly this far.' The young man elbowed his way next to Alice to get a better view.

Alice glared at him, but his eyes were on the plane.

'Look, you can see the RNAS emblem!' He pointed to the concentric circles of red, blue and white on the fuselage.

Daisy grabbed her mother's arm. 'Perhaps it's Alec!'

Alice shook her head but nevertheless she too strained to see the figures in the open cockpit. The plane dived then skimmed just above the waves towards the shore. Suddenly the floats on either side of the plane hit the water with a resounding splash. There was a gasp from the onlookers as it almost disappeared in the spray.

'They must be drenched.' Alice shivered.

Daisy paled as they watched the plane being buffeted forward. 'I wonder why it's come,' she said shakily.

A loud hooting blasted from the promenade and half a dozen soldiers ran down the steps and onto the beach.

'It's the Canadians!' Alice turned and saw the Canadian red ensign pennant on a vehicle that had stopped just behind them.

'They're from the camp over there.' The young man pointed towards the headland on the far side of the bay.

The soldiers, led by their captain, waded into the water as the seaplane taxied towards the shallows. The noise from the propeller blades was deafening but gradually the whirring subsided and the plane came to a tentative halt although it continued to bob alarmingly in the swell. It rested on its floats, its fragile wings giving the appearance of a mast that had slipped to a horizontal position.

There was only just enough room in the cockpit for the pilot and his observer and Alice wondered if they felt cramped. But there was no way of telling how they felt as their faces were half hidden by scarves and goggles.

The Canadian captain reached the plane and held out his hand.

Daisy leant forward to get a closer look as the pilot pushed his goggles onto his helmet and shook the captain's hand.

'It's not Alec!' she sighed.

'You didn't really think it would be?'

Daisy shook her head.

They watched the observer remove his goggles and take a package from beneath his seat.

Alice strained to hear what was said as the package was handed to the captain but the noise of the sea and excited chatter of the people around her made it impossible. The men spoke for a few minutes then the captain gave instructions to his men before wading back to the beach and up the steps to the waiting vehicle.

The pilot checked the controls, stretched his arms, then settled into his seat and readjusted his goggles. The soldiers manoeuvred the seaplane around and pushed it out of the shallows. When the water reached their knees the pilot gave the thumbs up sign and they backed away. There was a roar from the engine and the plane began to move forward on its floats. Alice heard Daisy's intake of breath as the plane gained speed leaving a spume of water in its wake. Then suddenly it was airborne and flying across the bay.

'So now we know what they do,' said Daisy shakily.

'I think they do more than deliver packages,' replied Alice quietly. Although it had presumably been a straightforward flight she was shocked by what they had witnessed. Taking off and landing on the sea was entirely different from the little trips William had made when she and Humphrey had watched him at the flying club.

People started to move away but they remained leaning over the railings following the path of the plane as it flew east into the darkening sky.

'I wonder where it's heading,' said Daisy when it finally disappeared from view.

'Liverpool maybe?' Alice shrugged. They would never know. Just as they would never know what mission William and Alec were engaged in that caused their leave to be cancelled. And just as she rarely knew where Humphrey was whcn he was on his duties with the Central Specials.

'It's not easy being left behind, is it?' Daisy seemed to sense what she was thinking.

'But you wouldn't want to go, would you?' For a sickening moment Alice wondered if Daisy was thinking of joining up.

'No, I'd hate it. I just wish things were the same as they were before.'

'I don't think you'd like everything to be exactly the same.' Alice smiled as she turned away from the sea.

'Good heavens no! If it hadn't been for the war I'd never have met Alec.' Daisy's eyes opened wide at the thought. 'It's wonderful how good things can come from bad!'

Alice was pleased to see Daisy looking happy. She only hoped her optimism was not misplaced.

Chapter 12: Lottie

Work or Play at Whitsun
The announcement that the government contemplate
making a general appeal to the nation to give up the
Whitsun holiday in order to strengthen Mr Lloyd
George's special appeal to munition workers was
received with loyalty but without enthusiasm.

The Times: May 31st 1916

As her train rumbled beside the golf course Lottie reflected on the pleasant evening she had spent with Daisy and how fortunate she was at the prospect of having her as a sister-in-law, especially as she was still slightly in awe of William's mother. She could just make out some rabbits scampering over the turf in the dusk and, sighing contentedly, she started to compose in her head the letter that she would write to William when she got home.

Lottie was still thinking of William when she got off the train and stopped in surprise when she saw his landlady's dog snuffling the ground at the entrance to the station.

'What are you doing here Skipper?' she asked and patted his head.

He wagged his tail and barked in recognition.

Lottie looked around but he didn't appear to be with anyone.

'I'd better take you home.'

Skipper barked again and ran in front of her, stopping to check she was following. They walked past several rows of terraced houses until she saw Mrs Jones standing outside her house, one hand on her hip, as she talked to a neighbour.

'Why it's Lottie! Did Skipper come looking for you? He misses his walks.' She turned to her neighbour. 'You know Lottie don't you?'

The woman smiled. 'Yes, I've shopped at the Rowes for many years. And how's that handsome fiancé of yours?'

'He was fine when I last heard. His leave was cancelled.'

'Everything is being cancelled - trains, food supplies; and now they're talking about cancelling the bank holiday.' The woman sniffed. 'Where is it all going to end? That's what I want to know.'

'Well, they're not about to tell us, that's for sure,' said Mrs Jones.

'How's your leg, Mrs Jones?' asked Lottie.

'Could be better. It's not good enough to go running after dogs who stray.'

'Perhaps I could come sometimes and take him out like I used to when William was staying with you.'

'That would be lovely, my dear. You come whenever you like.'

'I will. I'd better go now before it gets completely dark.'

'Go carefully, there's some funny goings on these days.' Mrs Jones's neighbour seemed determined to be pessimistic.

'I'll be fine. Goodbye.' Lottie turned and made her way back towards the station.

There was a patch of wasteland between Mrs Jones's terrace and the next. As Lottie started to walk past she heard a man's voice and then a giggle. She quickened her pace then stopped and listened. The girl giggled again and Lottie felt her heart beat faster. The voice was unmistakeable. She turned and could just make out a couple leaning against a tree. The man had his back to her but the girl was facing her, her arms entwined around the man and her breath coming in sharp rasps as he thrust himself against her in a frantic rhythm.

Lottie clapped her hand to her mouth to prevent her from shouting her sister's name.

She felt sweat break out under her armpits as she stood rooted to the spot. She knew she should carry on walking but her legs felt numb. A train hooted behind her and she jumped in fright. There was a hiss of steam as the goods train rumbled past and Lottie was dismayed to find herself showered in black smuts.

Gritting her teeth, she walked on quickly past the Station Hotel and down the passage leading to the back yard of the shop. She opened the gate and inhaled the heady scent of lilies growing in a pot by the back door.

Her father was sitting at the table, his head bent over his ledgers. He smiled as she came in but she noticed that his face had become careworn.

'Did you have a nice evening?' he asked absently.

Lottie felt her head swim and she leant against a chair. She managed to banish the image of Cilla, compromised on a patch of waste ground, and answered truthfully, 'Daisy and I had a lovely time, she's such a nice person.'

She looked around the room. 'Where's Mother?'

'She said her leg was playing her up and she wanted an early night.'

'Mrs Jones is having trouble with her leg too.'

'Mrs Jones?'

'William's landlady.' Lottie told him about finding Skipper at the station.

'I don't know why Cilla isn't home. The hotel doesn't usually stay open late in the week.'

Lottie swallowed. 'Actually I did notice some people inside as I walked past. People are staying up later at this time of the year, it's such a relief after the blackout all winter.'

Jack yawned. 'Well, they can't have to get up early in the morning. My brain's getting fuddled with these accounts. I think I'll turn in.'

'Let me do them for you. I always used to help you.'

'That was before you got your smart job. But it would be nice if you could give me a hand. I don't have so much time since your mother stopped working in the afternoons.'

'Poor Mother; I didn't realise she was that bad.'

'Well it can't be helped.' Jack went to the foot of the stairs. 'Goodnight. You're a good girl Lottie.'

Lottie took off her hat and jacket and shook them outside. She was pleased to find that there was only a small black mark on her collar which she would try and remove the next day. She grimaced as she looked at herself in the mirror and wondered if her father had noticed the smut on her cheek. She washed her hands and face, poured herself some water and sat down to wait for Cilla.

It wasn't long before she heard the gate click and footsteps tiptoeing across the yard.

'Hello. Did you have a nice evening?' Cilla asked brightly.

'Yes thank you. Did you?'

'It was all right. I was working.'

'And what time did you finish?' Lottie looked steadily at her sister.

'I can't remember. I chatted for a while afterwards. When did you get back?'

'I would have been home an hour ago. But Mrs Jones's dog was at the station and I took him back to her,' said Lottie quietly, her eyes still fixed on her sister.

Cilla flushed and looked at the floor.

'You were with Len weren't you?'

She tossed her head. 'I might have been.'

'Cilla, I saw you.'

'You couldn't have!' Cilla looked aghast. 'It was dark.'

'I'm your sister; I knew it was you. Cilla, how could you?'

Cilla twisted the ring on her finger. 'Lottie, I wasn't born good like you. And anyway he might be dead next month.'

'That's a terrible thing to say!'

'But it's true,' she said passionately. 'William might be …'

Lottie put her hands over her ears. 'You must never even think such a thing.'

'I'm sorry, I didn't mean to upset you. Lottie...' Cilla suddenly looked very young, 'You won't say anything will you?'

'Of course I won't say anything. I don't know what Father would do if he found out.' Lottie glared at her sister. 'When's Len leaving?'

'Soon, I don't know exactly.'

'You must write and tell him you can't see him again.'

'But I have to see him again!'

'Why?'

'Because he loves me.'

'If he loved you he would treat you with respect,' flashed Lottie. For a moment neither sister said anything then Lottie said quietly, 'Do you love him?'

'I don't know.' Cilla looked down at the cheap jewel on her right hand. 'He gave me this ring.'

'But he didn't propose.' Lottie felt secure as she touched her diamond engagement ring. 'When you do meet the right person, you'll know,' she said and smiled for the first time since she had said goodbye to Mrs Jones.

'But what if there aren't any of the right ones left?'

Lottie shuddered. 'Don't be stupid, Cilla, of course there will be. Now it's time for bed.'

***

The weather was set fair for the next few days but Lottie scarcely noticed. Occasionally she looked up at the sun shining on Mynydd Brith and was pleased that Daisy and her mother were having good weather but most of the time she worried about her family.

She wondered if her parents noticed the tension between her and Cilla and was surprised when Jack commented that Cilla seemed to be settling down. Lottie was finding the house rather dull but she supposed her parents were pleased that their younger daughter was quietly doing chores without being asked.

She missed the cosy chats they had in their bedroom at night but she was so tired that she fell asleep quickly and slept soundly all night.

On the fourth morning since confronting Cilla, Lottie awoke to the sound of the mail train pulling out of the station. The shunting of the train was accompanied by trills and whistles from the dawn chorus. Lottie drifted back to sleep as the birds welcomed the new day.

She awoke much later to the sound of her mother calling and looked at the clock then sprang out of bed. She dressed quickly and ran downstairs.

'I see Cilla was up before me this morning,' Lottie said cheerfully to Nellie who was dishing up the breakfast.

Her mother stared at her. 'Cilla's still in bed.'

'No, her bed's empty. She must be in the privy.'

Jack came in from the yard. 'Good morning Lottie. Where's your sister?'

Lottie felt suddenly sick. 'I'll go and see,' she said and ran upstairs.

The room was empty but on Cilla's pillow was a folded piece of paper. As Lottie picked it up she wondered how she had missed it earlier. It had her name but she did not dare look at it. Instead she opened the wardrobe then sat down heavily on Cilla's bed and stared at the empty rail where her sister's clothes were usually hanging.

She unfolded the paper and scanned the contents.

'Lottie!'

'Coming, Mother.' Lottie felt the weariness in her voice as she went down to break the shocking news to her parents.

***

The next couple of days passed in a blur. Lottie did not know which was worse, her mother's hysteria or her father's simmering anger at learning that their youngest daughter had run away to London with a soldier. Cilla's letter was brief, she said she would stay in Len's sister's boarding house and would write again when she had found work. Lottie begged her parents to get in touch with Len's battalion in the hopes of finding an address but they were determined to keep their daughter's immoral behaviour a secret.

When Nellie had calmed down Jack despatched Lottie to the Station Hotel to tell the bursar that Cilla had been called to Crewe to look after her widowed aunt who had been taken ill after the death of her only son on the western front. She felt the lie stick in her throat but he didn't appear to notice and she hurried away, already very late for work.

It took a great deal of willpower to keep the secret from Bronwen and Dylan but, shaken as she was, it wasn't difficult to feign feeling unwell.

Lottie had been looking forward to visiting Daisy at Trealaw on Sunday and was surprised when her father raised no objection as she began to get ready. She bit back an angry retort when he said they should carry on as normal and concentrated on lacing her boots. He disappeared into the shop and came back with a packet of biscuits.

'Mrs Dacre and Miss Daisy may be running out of supplies by now.' Jack's face took on a servile expression as he handed Lottie the biscuits and for an instant she glimpsed why her sister had run away to find a better life.

'It doesn't matter because they're leaving tomorrow.' She snatched the packet and crammed it in her bag. Then, seeing the bewildered look on her father's face, she gave him a peck on the cheek.

'I won't be too long,' she said and hurried out of the house.

***

As Lottie crossed the bridge she bent her head against the wind that was sweeping up the estuary and pummelling the grey swirling water. She glanced up at the mountains but Mynydd Brith was lost in cloud. A roll of thunder reverberated round the castle walls and she ran along the cobbled streets in a desperate effort to reach Trealaw before the storm broke. She was heading up the mountain track by the time the second clap of thunder sounded followed by a jagged streak of lightening. Spats of rain bounced off the dry stonewall but the sunken lane was relatively sheltered and Lottie slowed her pace as she climbed higher. The bleating of lambs and answering calls from their mothers became suddenly urgent and were almost obliterated by a crash of thunder overhead. The heavens opened and soon rivulets of rain were pouring down the track. Ignoring the water dripping off the brim of her hat Lottie stepped determinedly on. Her hands felt clammy through her wet gloves and her boots began to squelch. As she reached the end of the lane a gust of wind shook the branches of a mountain ash and deposited its unwanted rainwater down Lottie's neck. Salt tears stung her eyes as she plodded across the slope towards the house. She had wanted to look her best for William's mother and his beautiful sister but she wondered if they would even recognise her with hair plastered to her face and her clothes clinging to her body like wash rags.

'Lottie!' Daisy's shocked voice called from the open door.

Lottie stumbled inside and burst into tears.

**

A quarter of an hour later she was sitting on the sofa wearing Daisy's clothes and savouring a hot cup of tea. Daisy sat beside her and brushed her hair with a silver hairbrush. For a moment Lottie forgot about the shame Cilla had brought to the family and her sense of bereavement that her sister had gone.

'How are you feeling now?' William's mother looked at her kindly and Lottie felt less in awe of her.

'Much better thank you.' But her hand trembled as she her held cup.

'How are your parents?'

'They're very angry,' Lottie replied without thinking.

Daisy put down the brush. 'Why? What's happened?'

Lottie bit her lip. 'They said we shouldn't tell anyone.'

There was a distant roll of thunder as the storm moved away. Lottie glanced at the window; the rain was no longer lashing against the panes. She would be able to go soon. But she didn't want to leave; she was desperate to unburden herself.

'Cilla's run away to London,' she whispered.

'Good heavens!' Alice was shocked. 'Do you know where she is?'

'No, the note didn't say. She, she's run off with her soldier!'

'Oh my! The one who gave her the ring?' Daisy appeared to be relishing the drama of the situation.

'Yes, they weren't engaged or anything. I didn't take it seriously at first, not until…' Lottie paused as she re-lived the scene she had witnessed just a few nights ago. 'Cilla changed after a few months at the hotel. She's so pretty and men started to ask her out but she usually had to say no because my father is very strict.'

'But that didn't bother her did it?' Daisy said knowingly.

'She used to sneak out of the house sometimes.' Lottie's voice was scarcely audible.

Alice frowned. 'And what did her note say?'

'She says Len's sister runs a boarding house and she'll be helping her out till she finds a proper job.'

'I can't see Cilla enjoying being a chamber maid!' laughed Daisy.

'My sister's not afraid of hard work,' flashed Lottie.

'I'm sorry, I didn't mean it like that. Don't worry Lottie, Cilla will be all right.'

'And what of the soldier – Len did you say his name is?' Alice asked.

'I don't know much about him except that he expects to be sent to France soon.'

'Do you think Cilla intends to remain with the sister?'

'I doubt it; she said in her letter that she'll let me have her address when she's got a job and accommodation in a hostel.'

'She won't really work in a munitions factory will she?' Daisy looked horrified.

'I think she wants something more responsible than that.'

'She's so young to leave home.'

'It's happening all the time,' said Alice. 'Some of the soldiers I see at the station can't be older than fifteen.' She looked at Lottie quizzically. 'How is your mother coping with this?'

'She's worried what the customers will think.' Lottie didn't say that the customers thought Cilla was doing her family duty in Crewe.

'That's understandable. And she'll feel better once she knows where her daughter's living. If there's anything we can do to help we will. Cilla knows where to find us if she needs us.'

'Thank you. Yes, I'm sure it will all work out,' said Lottie doubtfully.

'Oh, this horrible war!' exclaimed Daisy.

'I wish it was all over!' Lottie ran her fingers distractedly through her hair. 'It's almost dry. And the rain has stopped. But what about my clothes? They won't be dry for a long time.'

'Don't worry, you can keep mine.'

'I couldn't do that!'

'Of course you can. The skirt's a bit short on you but the blouse fits well.'

Lottie fiddled with the cuffs of the cream coloured blouse and luxuriated in the feel of silk on her arms.

She glanced at Alice, wondering what she thought of her daughter's casual generosity.

'It suits you. And you can always let down the hem of the skirt,' she said practically.

'That's really kind of you, Daisy. Cilla was always wanting to borrow my clothes but I'm taller than her and they didn't fit.' Mentioning her sister made her feel like crying again and she continued hurriedly, 'Are you looking forward to going back to London?'

'In a way, even though it isn't as safe as here but it's time to go home. And there might be some letters from Alec!'

'I haven't heard anything from William since the letter saying his leave was cancelled.'

'We'll all hear soon enough,' said Alice.

Lottie stood up. 'I promised my parents I wouldn't be long. I help my father with the accounts,' she said to Alice in explanation.

'You're welcome to stay longer but it might be better to leave while it's dry.' Alice glanced out of the window at the dark clouds still hanging over the estuary.

'I'll put your wet clothes in a bag.' Daisy hurried into the kitchen.

Lottie rubbed her hands uncertainly. She could think of nothing to say to Daisy's mother who, with her commanding presence and elegant good looks, was so different from her own. She was already regretting blurting out her family's shameful secret and she felt herself flushing as she wondered if Mrs Dacre feared that she too was capable of such immoral behaviour. She looked at the floor, desperately wishing William's leave hadn't been cancelled. But more than anything, she wished that her father had given permission for her to marry before she was twenty-one. She remembered Cilla's defiant despair as she said, 'But what if there aren't any of the right ones left?' And she wondered if she would ever forgive her father if William was taken from her before she became his wife.

Chapter 13: Lottie

Losses in the Ranks
Lists of over 5,880 names

The Times: September 4th 1916

Lottie came out of the imposing doors of the emporium and lingered by the window, not wanting to go home. Since their daughter's dramatic departure, her parents had rarely mentioned Cilla's name. It felt as if she had taken all the laughter with her and Lottie had increasingly relied on her friends at work for companionship, particularly Bronwen. She watched the doors anxiously, waiting for her friend to appear.

'Hello, Lottie. Have you seen Bronwen?' Dylan peered short-sightedly at the revolving doors he had just come through.

'No, I haven't seen her all day.'

'Neither have I.' Dylan frowned and kicked a cigarette carton that was skittering along the street.

A couple of gulls fought noisily over a morsel in the gutter.

'Beastly things,' said Dylan then added, 'I don't suppose I'll miss them but it'll be strange not hearing them every day.'

'Why? Where are you going?' Lottie felt an irrational panic welling.

Dylan took off his spectacles and chewed on one end. 'My call-up papers have arrived.'

Lottie stared him, thinking how different he looked without his glasses. 'But you can't.'

'Can't fight?' He put his glasses back and glared at Lottie.

'That's not what I was going to say.' Lottie sighed. 'When do you leave?'

'The day after tomorrow. I've got to report to Aldershot.' He looked agitated. 'I must see Bronwen before I go.'

'It's unusual for her not to be at work, especially on a Saturday. 'Perhaps she's ill.'

'I was wondering that; shall we call and see?' Dylan started to limp away from the emporium.

Lottie was torn by a desire to see her friend and her duty to her parents who relied on her help with the household chores and the shop accounts. 'Yes,' she said, making up her mind quickly and hurrying after Dylan past the pier and up the lane of terraced cottages to Bronwen's house.

Her mother must have seen them coming because she was standing at the door. She looked unusually frail and there was no trace of her welcoming smile.

'I'm so pleased you've come.' Her voice cracked as she ushered them into the tiny parlour.

Lottie and Dylan exchanged worried glances and sat bolt upright on the edge of a small sofa.

'Is Bronwen all right?' Lottie immediately felt the inadequacy of the question.

'She's not ill.' Bronwen's mother paused then said quietly, 'There was a letter waiting when she got back from work yesterday. It was from a soldier who was a friend of Rhys. He said they went over the top together but Rhys didn't come back.' She looked despairingly at the ceiling. 'Bronwen went straight to bed and hasn't been up since. She was in such a bad way I nearly sent for the doctor.'

Suddenly the war that was being fought on the Continent seemed to invade the parlour, making everything in the neatly arranged room appear insignificant. The delicately carved love spoon by the wedding photograph of Bronwen's parents seemed irrelevant now that their daughter's chances of happiness had been dashed

Lottie's eyes filled with tears. 'I'm so very sorry. Can I go and see her?' She was surprised to feel her legs shaking as she stood up.

Dylan started to get up then sat down again, realising it would be inappropriate for him to visit Bronwen in her bedroom. 'Tell her, her friends are thinking of her.' He leant forward with his elbows on his knees and an impenetrable expression on his face.

'I'll make a brew. I hope you can persuade Bronwen to have a cup,' said her mother as Lottie left the room.

'I'll try.' Lottie walked purposefully up the stairs and knocked on Bronwen's door.

She could hear muffled crying but there was no reply so she went in.

Bronwen lay with her face to the wall, a patchwork quilt drawn tightly around her hunched body.

Lottie knelt down beside the bed. 'Bronwen,' she said softly, 'It's Lottie.'

Her friend gave a shuddering sob then turned and stared at her blankly. Lottie was shocked to see her hair hanging limply around her pallid face and purple bags, like bruises, under her eyes. She took a deep breath and inhaled the odour of stale scent and despair.

'Your mother told us what happened, I'm so terribly sorry.' Lottie knelt by the bed and took Bronwen's clammy hand in hers.

Bronwen sniffed but Lottie felt her give her hand a gentle squeeze. With her other hand she smoothed the hair away from Bronwen's face. Her mother's anxious chatter accompanied by the deeper tones of Dylan's voice drifted upwards.

Bronwen looked puzzled. 'Did you say 'us'?' she whispered.

'Yes, Dylan and I came together. We wanted to see if you were all right.' Lottie's voice broke. 'Your mother's so worried about you. She's making a brew. Will you come down and have a cup with us?'

'I'm too tired.'

Lottie got up. 'You need fresh air.' When she pulled back the curtains the evening sunshine filtered into the room and the sound of seagulls could be heard through the window.

'Dylan says…' Lottie stopped, realising this was not the time to tell Bronwen that her childhood friend was leaving imminently.

'What?' Bronwen croaked.

'He says he's thinking about you. And that you should drink the tea your mother's making for you.'

A ghost of a smile crossed Bronwen's face then the blank expression returned.

'You'll feel better if you wash your face.' Lottie poured some water from a jug into the washing bowl by the side of Bronwen's bed. 'Let me help you sit up,' she coaxed. When her friend was propped against the pillows, Lottie wet the face cloth and smiled encouragingly as she handed it to her.

Bronwen washed her face then, with childlike obedience, waited for Lottie to tell her what to do next. For an instant Lottie was reminded of Cilla when she was little.

'Would you like me to brush your hair?'

Bronwen nodded and shifted forward in the bed while Lottie tenderly brushed and combed her dark curls taking care to tease away the tangles.

'That's better,' she said approvingly and held out a blue woollen dressing gown that had been hanging on the back of the door.

'I can't go downstairs!'

'Of course you can. We'll go slowly and there'll be a nice cup of tea waiting for you.' Lottie determinedly pulled back the covers.

With a look of resignation, Bronwen swung her feet out of the bed and into her slippers then Lottie put the gown round her shoulders and helped her up. Bronwen's fingers fumbled as she fastened the gown then she gripped Lottie's hand and shuffled to the door.

'Bronwen!' Her mother hugged her daughter when she appeared, shaking, in the parlour doorway.

Dylan stood awkwardly by the fireplace as Bronwen's mother led her to the settee. 'You sit next to her,' she said to Lottie, 'I'll pour the tea.' The older woman fluttered about the girls making sure they were comfortable.

Dylan passed round the cups of tea then sat down in a straight- backed chair opposite the settee. Everyone was silent as they concentrated on their drinks.

Lottie looked up and cleared her throat to say something about Rhys but the expression on Dylan's face made her stop. Behind his glasses, his eyes were shining with love as he gazed at Bronwen. Lottie drew in her breath and felt a sharp pang when she remembered that he would be leaving Wales the day after tomorrow. She wondered if Bronwen had noticed, but her eyes were cast down.

They left soon afterwards with Dylan promising to call again the next day and Lottie saying she would see her on Monday.

'I'll walk you to the station,' said Dylan.

'Thanks, but I'd rather not say goodbye to you there.' Lottie shivered as she recalled her goodbyes to William on Llandudno Junction station.

They stopped at the end of the lane. 'Well, I suppose I'd better go home and pack.' Dylan sighed. 'Will you write?' he asked diffidently.

'Of course. And I know Bronwen will too.'

'Yes. Anyway there's no need to worry about me.' He gave a bitter laugh. 'I'm only going to push a pen around at Aldershot.'

***

'You're late today.' Nellie sounded anxious rather than annoyed.

'Yes. I'll tell you about it later.' Lottie hung up her coat then slumped into a chair.

'There's a letter for you.' Nellie handed her an envelope with William's familiar script. Normally she preferred to read his letters away from her mother's prying eyes but she was too tired to move. She tore open the envelope and read the single page.

'William's got leave! He's getting the night train! He'll be here in the morning!' Lottie's face was radiant.

'So everything's all right then.' Nellie looked relieved at her daughter's happiness.

'Well, not everything.' Lottie told her about Rhys' death and Bronwen's distress.

'It's too much,' said Nellie wearily as she filled the kettle. And Lottie knew she was referring to the deaths of thousands of others as well as Rhys.

'And Dylan's been called up,' added Lottie.

'Everyone's leaving,' said Nellie bitterly and glanced at the chair that used to be Cilla's. 'Anyway,' she attempted a smile, 'William's coming tomorrow and that's all you need to think about for the moment.'

***

Lottie was up early the next morning. She washed from head to toe and agonised over what to wear, finally deciding on a heather-coloured skirt and cream blouse. Her fashionable bob was beginning to grow out but she had washed her hair the previous evening and brushed it till it shone.

As Lottie applied her make-up she wondered how Bronwen was and hoped that she would take some comfort from Dylan's visit and not be too upset that he had been called up. When she looked at herself in the mirror she couldn't help contrasting her shining eyes with Bronwen's despair but she was only too aware that her own circumstances could suddenly change.

Pulling back the net curtain, Lottie stood by her bedroom window her eyes riveted on the passengers leaving the station. Suddenly her heart fluttered as she saw William in his naval uniform hurrying down the steps. He paused and looked up then his face broke into a smile as he waved and ran across the road, narrowly missing a cart.

She rushed downstairs, through the house and opened the back gate just as William reached the end of the passage. She tumbled into his arms hardly able to believe that they were together again.

'You smell so fresh,' William murmured when they finally drew apart.

Lottie smiled and stroked his cheek.

'I need a shave,' he said ruefully. 'And a wash. And a chance to get out of this uniform for a while.'

'You can change here,' Lottie said.

'I've booked a room at the Station Hotel. I'd better go and check in but I'll be back as soon as I've changed.' He kissed her fiercely and was gone.

***

A few hours later they were sitting on the grass outside Trealaw, eating the picnic that Lottie had prepared.

181

'I can't tell you what a treat it is to have home-made food.' William looked relaxed in his striped blazer as he half lay on the rug looking up at Lottie.

'But it's only sandwiches!'

'Made with care, just for us. You don't know how often I've dreamt of this.'

'I've dreamt of it too.' But as Lottie spoke she knew that many of his dreams would have been of horrors that she would never even wish to share.

When he had finished the last sandwich William took an apple and a penknife from his pocket. 'I picked this yesterday from our garden at home.' He rubbed the fruit for a moment then peeled it in one piece. He arranged the peel into the shape of an L and presented it to Lottie on his outstretched hand.

'Is that all I get?' She laughed then blushed when William grinned at her unintended double-entendre.

'Not at all, I picked the apple for you.' He cut a small piece then tilted her face towards him.

She opened her mouth and he popped the fruit inside.

'Mm, delicious,' she said as she bit into it and felt the sweet tang of the juice on her tongue.

He fed her another piece then she held out her hand for the penknife.

'We must share,' she said softly and cut a wedge of fruit.

'We must,' he said then took it from her and brought it tantalisingly near her mouth before taking it away.

Lottie laughed and bent her face towards the apple dangling from his fingers. He put the tip in his mouth and turned his face to hers so that the fruit brushed her lips. She held it with her teeth then nibbled until the apple was finished and their tongues were entwined. As they kissed she luxuriated in William's touch and the scent of his skin against hers, and the lingering scent of apple holding a memory that danced out of reach.

As Lottie thought she was about to explode with joy she had a fleeting memory of her happiness the previous September when they had sat under the apple tree in William's garden, and of his mother watching from an upstairs window.

'I love you,' she said fiercely then shifted away, suddenly afraid of the passion burning inside her. 'Let's go for a walk.'

'A walk?' William looked hurt. 'Is that what you want?'

Lottie shook her head. 'What I want,' she whispered, 'is you.'

'And I want you too, I love you so much.' He looked at her with eyes filled with tenderness and hope.

Lottie tore herself away. 'It wouldn't be right.'

William sat motionless for a while then took Lottie's hand. 'I'm at your command, where shall we go?'

For a moment Lottie wished she hadn't said anything but she knew she couldn't have answered for the consequences if she hadn't.

'Let's go that way.' She pointed to a sheep track leading west towards the sea.

'That's a good idea,' said William with determined cheerfulness.

Lottie felt a mixture of relief and regret as they packed away the picnic things.

They talked easily as they walked and Lottie pointed out landmarks across the estuary that held memories for her. The track led downhill to a gate in a dry stone wall. As they leant against the gate there was a whinny and a black horse trotted towards them. William held out his hand and stroked the horse's nose.

'Did I tell you about the times I went riding?'

'No, where did you go?'

'Duggie and Hilda's farm, it was great fun. We used to follow the local hunt.'

Lottie listened, spellbound, as he recounted hair-raising experiences of leaping across ditches and fences.

'Did you ever fall off?'

'Only once.' He grinned.

'Were you hurt?'

'No, I was fine, I rolled away from the hooves.'

Lottie blanched as the horse pawed the ground, snorted, then trotted away. 'You do like to live dangerously,' she said more lightly than she felt.

They carried on their walk and William continued his reminisces of escapades with his childhood friends.

Lottie laughed as he described how he had almost fallen out of a tree rescuing Hilda's kitten. His enthusiasm was one of the many things she loved about him and she didn't know how she was going to bear to say goodbye. She fell silent, lost in thought.

'I don't think you've been listening!' William laughed accusingly. 'What were you thinking about?'

'I've been thinking,' she said slowly, 'that in six months I'll be twenty-one.'

'And we can get married!' William shouted joyfully then added, 'But why don't we get married now? We can get a special licence!'

Lottie shook her head. 'We'd need my father's permission. And where would we live?'

'We could take lodgings on the south coast so I'd be near enough to come home when I was off duty. Or,' he continued when she looked doubtful, 'You could stay with my parents; I sometimes go up to London on a twenty-four hour pass but I need leave to come as far as Wales.'

'Live with your parents?'

'Daisy's at home. It might be better than staying in lodgings where you don't know anyone.'

'But I want to live with you. In our own little house.'

'And we will do. When the war's over,' William said desperately.

'But the war will be over by next spring won't it?' Lottie felt panic welling up inside her.

'For God's sake, Lottie, you read the newspapers; you know what's happening in France as well as I do!'

Lottie hung her head to hide her tears; it was the first time William had raised his voice to her. 'Of course I know,' she whispered, 'after all, I spent yesterday afternoon comforting Bronwen.'

William hugged her. 'I'm sorry I shouted. Let's continue our walk. And we can make plans for our wedding in the spring.'

***

William was waiting when Lottie left work the following day.

'I thought we could have tea at St Georges's Hotel,' he said as they strolled along the promenade.

'I wonder if they still have those lovely cakes.' Lottie's mouth watered as she remembered the last time she had been there.

'I'm sure they will. We'd better hurry, it looks as if it's going to pour in a minute.'

Lottie felt exhilarated as they ran along the promenade with the wind blowing in their faces. They reached the hotel steps just as the rain started and were ushered to a table overlooking the sea. The waiter took their order and they amused themselves watching people scurrying from the rain.

'I'm glad we're not still outside.' Lottie pointed to people hurrying with their heads down and a man battling to put up his umbrella.

'Bad luck old chap,' grinned William as the umbrella folded itself inside out.

'These sandwiches are delicious,' said Lottie.

'Not as good as yours.'

Lottie was embarrassed by the intensity of William's gaze especially when she noticed the waiter hovering by her chair.

'More tea, Madam?'

'Yes, please.' She waited till he had filled their cups. 'What did you do today?'' Lottie asked as she stirred sugar into her tea.

'Not a lot; it was good not having to obey orders. I talked to a couple of chaps in the bar and looked forward to being with you. And I called in at the shop.' William took a letter from his pocket. 'I almost forgot; your mother asked me to give you this.'

'It's from Cilla!' Lottie tore the letter open and her face crumpled. 'Oh no! Poor Cilla!'

'What's happened?'

Her voice was expressionless. 'Len's dead. Killed in action on the Somme.'

William's face darkened. 'Running off with your sister was unforgivable but it's still a damn shame. How do you think she's taking it?'

'She doesn't say much.' Lottie's hand trembled as she passed him the letter. 'I can't bear to think of her all alone, who will comfort her?' she asked as she thought of Bronwen too grief-stricken to get out of bed.

'I'm sure the girls in the hostel will rally round. And maybe she'll come home.'

'Do you think she will?' Lottie looked hopeful.

William turned over the page and shook his head. 'I don't think so,' he said gently. 'She says her colleagues on the buses have been good to her.'

'But that's not the same!'

'When you're away from home the people you work with can seem like family.'

'Nobody can take the place of family!'

'That's not what I said,' William said patiently.

'I just wish I was there to look after her.' Lottie thought for a moment. 'Perhaps you could visit her, just to see she's all right.'

'But I'm due back in Dover the day after tomorrow.'

'I know,' said Lottie miserably. 'There wouldn't really have been time to get married would there?'

William held her hand across the table. 'There might have been. But we wouldn't have had much of a honeymoon.' He chuckled. 'And that would have been a shame!'

Lottie blushed. 'Do you think you might have time to see Cilla?' she persisted.

'I don't want to leave you any earlier than I have to.'

Lottie felt a sinking in the pit of her stomach. 'I don't want you to leave either. But it would be a great relief if you could see Cilla, she's so young and I worry about her.'

'She may be young but she's managed to convince people she's old enough to work on the buses.'

'But will you try and see her?'

'Lottie, it's you I want to see. But if that's what you really want, I'll do what I can.' William took a fountain pen from his jacket and copied Cilla's address on to a cigarette packet.

Chapter 14: Alice

Bombs on Zeebrugge and Ostend
British Naval Air Raid
An attack was carried out in the early hours of this
morning on the harbour and submarine shelters at
Ostend and Zeebrugge by a squadron of naval
aeroplanes.

The Times: November 11th 1916

It is a moonless night. Enveloped by silence Alice sits alone at the top of Daffodil Mountain. Her feet are bare and she is clad only in her nightgown but she feels neither cold nor discomfort from the rock-strewn terrain. She gazes out to sea, her eyes fixed on a dark shape in the sky above the bay. It is huge, cylindrical and glides towards her with a low mesmerising whoosh. Alice stands and faces the apparition. It hovers above the ancient turrets of Conway then travels inexorably on to Mynydd Brith. She feels its menace as it floats past and turns, watching in horror when it stops above Trealaw, its malevolent presence appearing to fill the whole sky. High above she sees a tiny red sphere and from it a beam of light streaks down with a ferocious velocity. There is an unearthly howl as the zeppelin explodes and the Home of Song becomes engulfed in a fireball.

In the distance Alice heard a woman screaming. She sat up in bed, drenched in sweat, and realised the woman was her.

'What's the matter? Is it a raid?' Humphrey struggled to wake up beside her.

Alice crept to the window and opened the blackout curtain a fraction. She was unnerved to see a shaft of moonlight shining onto the pillared porch of the house opposite and illuminating a cat, its body taut, ready to pounce. She watched, transfixed, as the cat leapt into the air and sprinted after its prey before disappearing into the shadows. Then she dropped the curtain, shutting out the deserted street.

'No, it was nothing. Just a nightmare.' Her body was clammy now in the cold air and she shivered.

'Well come back to bed and get some sleep, we've got enough real problems to deal with in the morning,' Humphrey said irritably. But he pulled Alice close to him as she slid back between the sheets.

She felt comforted by the warmth from Humphrey's body but lay awake for a long time as images of zeppelins showering their bombs on crowded streets flashed through her overactive mind. She longed for the solitude of Mynydd Brith but the picture of Trealaw in flames remained and she knew nowhere would be safe till the war was over.

It was dawn before Alice drifted back to sleep and when she awoke, Humphrey had gone. She got up, opened the curtains and returned to bed contemplating the dreary November sky.

***

It was later than she'd planned when Alice left the house and hurried to Belsize Park station, her head bowed against the drizzling rain.

She joined the passengers in the lift, the attendant clunked the doors shut and, with a loud hum, it began descend.

'Are you all right Madam?' The attendant looked worried as he saw Alice clutching her throat.

She put her hand on the rail, aware that she was descending to the deepest station in London. 'I'm fine thank you, I …' She was going to say that the humming of the lift reminded her of the zeppelin she had seen in the night but finished, 'I'll be all right in a minute.'

'Would you like me to take you back to the surface Madam?' the attendant asked as he opened the doors by the platform.

'No, thank you, I'm perfectly all right.'

The platform was unusually crowded and she gathered from snatches of conversation that people had been waiting some time. However, it was only a couple of minutes before she felt the rush of air through the tunnel heralding an approaching train.

She sat down thankfully, the doors clanged closed and the train left the comforting light of the station and plunged into its tunnel. Standing passengers were forced to hang on tightly as the train swayed when it picked up speed. The man opposite Alice was reading a newspaper and she caught some of the headlines then looked away, sickened by the unremitting awfulness of it all.

A few passengers got off at Camden Town but more got on. A couple of young corporals stood in front of Alice and she shifted as she felt a kit bag against her leg. The soldiers had obviously been in the rain because their khaki greatcoats smelt damp and slightly fetid. However, Alice was unperturbed because the next stop was Euston and she would be in the high-ceilinged main station in a couple of minutes.

Suddenly the train jolted forward and shuddered to a halt. A few people muttered to each other in exasperation but most, like Alice, waited stoically in silence.

Then the lights went out.

Panic began to ripple through the train, slowly at first but then it gathered its own momentum. There was little movement but Alice was aware of feet tapping, knuckles cracking and breath rasping all around her. A low moan could be heard from one end of the carriage answered by a keening wail from the other.

'Must be a raid,' someone said authoritatively.

'Thought we'd sent Jerry packing last month,' a comfortable West Country voice responded.

A child's clear voice rang through the carriage, 'Are the Germans coming to get us?'

'Of course not, darling, Papa's ship won't let any Germans hurt you.' The confident, well-modulated tones staunched the flow of panic; the moaning subsided and the keening became a whimper.

Alice waited, her muscles taut, her mind blank. Minutes passed. Then a glimmer of light showed in the adjoining carriage and the guard appeared holding a torch and issuing instructions to stay calm and not strike matches or cigarette lighters. He briefly shone the torch into the faces of the passengers and made his way over pieces of luggage and into the next carriage. Alice was aware of her heart pounding as she craned her neck to watch the light bobbing as the guard moved slowly down the train.

The light had only just disappeared from view when there was a cranking sound and the train moved forward in the darkness. Then without warning the lights blazed and people blinked at each other.

A few minutes later the train halted at Euston station. Alice rose stiffly from her seat and was swept along by the throng hurrying to the exit. When she asked a ticket collector what had caused the delay she was relieved to find that the problem had been mechanical and that there had not been an air raid.

**

The afternoon passed quickly and it was dusk by the time Alice left the station buffet. She paused at the platform where the express was leaving for Llandudno Junction and looked longingly at it for several minutes. Then she made her way past exhausted soldiers sprawled on the ground to the stairs leading to the underground. She hesitated when she reached the top of the steps and held onto the rail feeling breathless. A soldier carrying a large kit bag ran towards the stairs and leapt down the first three, narrowly missing Alice. She looked at the mass of people coming up, their pale faces appearing ghost-like as they emerged from the dimness of the underground station.

'Beg pardon Ma'am,' shouted a second soldier unconvincingly as his kit bag touched Alice's shoulder.

'That's quite all right,' she murmured automatically as more people pushed past her into the semi-darkness below.

She noticed her knuckles straining through her black leather gloves clasped tightly to the rail and felt herself swaying as she stood looking down, mesmerised by the mass of humanity surging beneath her. She could move neither forward nor back.

'How do they do it?' she thought. 'How do soldiers force themselves to live in trenches under the ground?'

Still grasping the rail Alice turned and looked out into the station. She felt relieved as her breathing began to return to normal and she smiled in recognition as one of Humphrey's colleagues approached the stairs.

'Good afternoon, Mrs Dacre, are you returning home?' he asked politely.

'No,' she replied haughtily, 'I'm on my way to catch a bus.' She swept away leaving the man staring in surprise.

Outside, Alice gulped in the damp air like a drowning man rising to the surface. She quickly crossed the road then slowed her pace as she saw the queue snaking along the pavement ahead of her. She hoped she wouldn't have to wait too long.

A horse-drawn vehicle stopped and passengers at the front climbed aboard. Alice shuffled forwards, her feet like lead weights. The woman behind tried to engage her in conversation but she answered in monosyllables and the woman gave up.

Suddenly the queue went quiet as a distant rumble was heard and then a rhythmic pounding. Alice caught the eye of a young serviceman leaning on a stick then looked away. For an instant she inhaled the scent of cordite but, even in her nervous state, she knew it was her imagination. The sound of gun batteries on the Somme could travel across water but, God forbid, not the stench as well.

'They're working late tonight,' said an elderly man in an attempt at humour but people just shifted uneasily and looked ahead.

Undaunted the man tried again. 'There goes Old Bill.' He pointed to a bus passing on the other side of the road.

'I was driving one of them at the Front,' the soldier with the stick said proudly. 'It were like home from home for the new recruits, we'd take them down to the line in style, some of them thought they was on holiday.'

'Some holiday,' thought Alice looking at the man's leg.

'A Jerry bullet got me, but I'll be back in a couple of months to give it back,' the soldier continued in response to Alice's glance.

'That's the spirit,' said the woman behind Alice.

Alice wondered if William would be so anxious to return to flying if he was wounded. She knew he was fortunate to be doing something he had previously loved and he had spoken enthusiastically about the exhilaration of flying in a clear sky. She glanced at the leaden sky, trying to imagine what it would be like guiding a fragile plane as darkness fell, and didn't notice the queue was moving until the woman behind tried to elbow her way past.

Alice gave her a look of disapproval and hurried forward. She was relieved to see that the bus was motorised and not a horse-drawn boneshaker. As she lifted her foot to get on she saw an advertisement on the step proclaiming the reliability of Iron Jelloids and made a mental note to buy some for Daisy. She was about to climb the outside staircase to the upper deck when the conductress motioned her inside.

'The fog's coming down, you'll be more comfortable with a roof over your head,' she said chirpily and pointed to a vacant seat at the front.

Alice didn't like to say that she liked the feel of the wind on her face and she sat down between a pallid young woman in black and a man in a shabby suit. From where she sat she was able to observe the conductress in her navy blue serge skirt and smart jacket with white piping on either side of the brass buttons. Her paddy hat, strapped loosely beneath her chin, also had piping around the brim.

The conductress brushed a strand of red hair under her hat as she asked Alice her destination.

'Belsize Park,' Alice said automatically and ferreted in her bag for some coins.

'I'm sorry, Mrs Dacre, we don't go to Belsize Park. You'll need to change at Marylebone.'

'Oh yes, of course. How much is that?'

'One penny please.' She took a ticket from the machine on her belt, clipped it and handed it to Alice. It wasn't until Alice handed her the copper coin that she looked into the conductress's face.

'Oh, goodness me, it's Cilla!' she exclaimed.

'I thought you didn't recognise me.' Cilla smiled.

The naïve young girl who had accompanied her sister on their first visit to London the year before had blossomed into a striking young woman and the bloom on her cheeks was in stark contrast to the washed out faces of most of the passengers.

'I heard you were working on the buses. Do you enjoy it?'

'Oh yes, everyone's very friendly. Excuse me a moment.' Cilla walked along the bus. 'Any more fares please?' Her lilting Welsh accent lightened the drab atmosphere and Alice noticed that people smiled with pleasure when she handed out the tickets.

Cilla returned to Alice's seat. 'We're just arriving at your stop, Mrs Dacre. You'll need to cross the road and hail a motorbus for Hampstead. I hope you don't have to wait long for your next bus.'

'Thank you.' Alice hesitated. 'Please come and see us sometime, you are always welcome.' There were lots of questions she wanted to ask but instead she found herself walking down the bus and automatically getting off when it stopped.

She felt disorientated as she stood on the pavement remembering Cilla's visit to London when she saw the advertisement for lady bus conductors and William jesting that she would look 'just the ticket' in the uniform. He had been right about that, she looked almost voluptuous in her navy serge. Alice glanced back at the bus and saw Cilla standing at the top of the stairs directing the passengers.

Suddenly a young naval officer leapt onto the bus as it was moving. He was laughing as he ran up the stairs then he stopped and said something to Cilla. At that moment the bus turned sharply and for an instant they were thrown against each other. The couple started to laugh uncontrollably as the bus gained speed but not before Alice realised the naval officer was William.

She stared, uncomprehending, until the figures of William and Cilla were no longer distinguishable. Feeling confused, she crossed the road and joined the queue for the Hampstead bus.

A whiff of cheap scent reached her as a couple of brightly painted girls sauntered past, arm in arm, joking about the Tommies they had been with the night before. Alice frowned and tried to put the image of William and Cilla out of her mind. She wrinkled her nose as the stale scent of Devon violets became mingled with the sharp tang of meths. Huddled in a doorway was a woman swaddled in a blanket; her tangled grey hair framed her ravaged face and her hand shook as she raised a bottle to her parched lips.

'She's been there every night this past week,' a large bosomed woman confided to Alice with a mixture of pity and contempt.

'Oh really?' Alice couldn't think of anything to say. She felt unnerved by the raw humanity of the street. She had thought that the station buffet had made her immune to the sufferings of her fellow human beings but she now realised that she had been insulated behind her table and by her position as Lady Bountiful. The station was orderly with porters in uniform, timetables, announcements and the trains ran on lines. But the street was exposed, anarchic and unfamiliar.

There was a clattering of hooves, shouts and a deafening noise as half a dozen horns hooted. A horse and cart had veered out of control and bicycles, horse buses, motorbuses and pedestrians were scattering in its path.

'What am I doing here?' thought Alice. 'I'd be home by now if I'd taken the underground.' Then she remembered the pitch black as the train stopped in the tunnel and the zeppelin hovering in the darkness of her nightmare.

Suddenly a cheer rang out followed by angry shouts as the driver of the horse and cart brought it under control. A trio of young men in khaki staggered across the road singing, 'There's a girl for every soldier' and in the distance she could see a bus for Hampstead approaching.

***

Both Daisy and Humphrey were home when Alice arrived, anxious to know why she was late. They were concerned about the incident on the tube although Humphrey implied that it had been unnecessary for her to come home by bus. She was about to tell them about her encounter with Cilla and the scene she had witnessed between her and William when Ethel announced that dinner was ready.

After the meal they retired to the sitting room and sat reading by the fireside until a loud knocking at the front door interrupted them. Humphrey got up to open it and William burst in, bringing with him a blast of cold air and a distant whiff of the sea and of danger.

'William!' Daisy's smile lit her face as she leapt up and kissed him affectionately.

'I thought I'd surprise you.' William bent over and kissed Alice then shook hands with his father.

'It's lovely to see you, are you all right?' Alice half rose in her chair, wondering if she should mention seeing him earlier but said nothing, subconsciously hoping she had been mistaken.

'Yes, I'm fine.' William rubbed his hands together in front of the fire.

Humphrey regarded him appraisingly. 'Do I see two stripes on your cuff?'

'What?' William looked at his sleeve in surprise. 'Oh yes! I've just been promoted to flight lieutenant.'

'Well done, son. I'm proud of you.'

'That's wonderful news!' said Alice. 'What did you have to do to be promoted?'

William shrugged. 'Fly my sea-plane across the Channel.'

'I gather the RNAS is to be congratulated on its recent successes in Belgium.' Humphrey looked quizzically at his son.

'Was it your squadron that bombed the submarine sheds at Zeebrugge?' asked Daisy in awe.

William's face darkened and he drummed his fingers on the arm of his chair.

'Of course not, Daisy, William's role is reconnaissance,' said Alice sharply.

There was a heavy silence and Alice added, 'I believe you use pigeons to relay messages.'

'Oh yes! Me and my pigeons have seen a thing or two!' William said jovially but his eyes were unfathomable.

Daisy took up the bantering tone. 'Who can fly fastest – the pigeon or you?'

'Oh, the pigeon every time!'

'So, do you pack a picnic basket for the pigeon?' Alice spoke with a lightness she did not feel.

'Sadly that's not allowed; we've had special orders not to overfeed the pigeons or to make pets of them.'

'So how exactly do you send messages?' Daisy was more serious now.

'They have a small tube attached to their leg. I fly around to see what the Hun's up to, scribble the info on a thin sheet of paper, pop it in the tube, release the bird and she flies back to port!'

'They say that carrier pigeons are more reliable in the trenches than wireless but of course you can only send them one way.' Humphrey looked at his son with pride.

'How long are you home for?' asked Alice.

'Only twenty-four hours, worse luck. If I had longer I'd be on the train to Wales by now.' William slumped in his chair.

'I had a letter from Lottie this morning; she says she's missing you.' Daisy looked at her brother sympathetically.

'I just wish Wales wasn't such a bloody long way away!'

'Well son, that's how it is at the moment. Anyway, I think we should celebrate your promotion. I have a bottle of whisky hidden away, I think now would be a good time to open it.' Humphrey had a satisfied expression as he left the room.

'I'll put some music on, what would you like, Wills?' Daisy busied herself at the gramophone.

'Pardon? Oh, you choose.' William gave his sister a half-hearted smile.

The animation Alice had witnessed on the bus was gone and she again told herself she had been mistaken. It was nearly dark, her eyes had deceived her. The man she had seen couldn't have been William.

Chapter 15: Alice

Marching The New Year In
New Year's Eve! There was a subdued air of expectant
animation about the huddled sentry groups in the
sploshy trench. These men gathering together their
bedraggled belongings were going out to a new camp.

The Times: January 2nd 1917

The sun streaming into the bedroom made Alice think it was summer, then she saw the spider's web delicately etched with frost suspended on the window frame. She sat up and stretched her arms. A fire was burning in the grate but she knew she would not need it today. She cleared her throat; the rasping cough had gone and her chest no longer ached.

Humphrey had warned her that she would be ill if she continued to travel by bus but the feelings of claustrophobia had remained and she refused to use the tube. She had developed a persistent cough and the doctor advised her to stop travelling to Euston. Reluctantly she gave up her work at the station buffet but was immediately asked to serve on the committee of the local Waifs and Strays society. With characteristic enthusiasm she had set about organising Christmas boxes for the children and gone out in all weathers enlisting donations and support.

By Christmas Eve Alice was exhausted but determinedly accompanied Humphrey to church on Christmas Day. The following day the doctor was sent for and confirmed that Alice had bronchitis. Humphrey had insisted that Daisy give up her job to look after her mother. The hospital told her that she could return whenever she wanted but, as she was becoming increasingly tired, Daisy was relieved to have a reason to stay at home.

The sound of footsteps thundered up the stairs and Daisy burst into the room wearing her coat and hat.

'Daisy, whatever's the matter? Where are you going?'

'Alec's plane has been shot down. He's in a military hospital in Surrey.' Daisy's face was white but she had a calm dignity as she told her mother about the letter she had just received from Mrs Hammond telling her about Alec's injuries, which included a broken ankle, fractured wrist and several cracked ribs.

Alice got out of bed and hugged her daughter. 'He'll pull through. Have you got everything you need?'

'Yes, I shouldn't be gone long.' She kissed her and ran out of the room.

Alice spent the day attending to things she had neglected since her illness but her thoughts were with Daisy rushing to be with the man she loved. It was late evening by the time Daisy returned and both Alice and Humphrey were becoming anxious as they sat in the sitting room listening to the gramophone.

The front door opened with a bang and they hurried into the hall. Daisy's face was radiant as she pulled off her coat.

'I'm engaged!' she shouted and flung her arms around Alice.

'And don't I have any say in the matter?' asked Humphrey, though he was smiling as he kissed his daughter.

'Oh yes! Alec's going to write to you. We want to get married on my twenty-first birthday!'

'But that's in three weeks!' Alice looked at her daughter in disbelief.

'I know but he'll be almost recovered by then and we must have time together before they send him back.' For a moment a look of fear crossed Daisy's face.

'Do they think he'll be fit enough to fly?' asked Humphrey.

'Probably not.' Daisy smiled. 'He thinks he'll be involved in planning operations.'

***

The next three weeks flew past. Dressmakers were becoming adept at making bridal gowns at short notice and Daisy chose a simple high-necked style with long sleeves. She had asked Hilda to be her bridesmaid and William was to be best man provided he could get leave.

The guest list was short, no more than a dozen on each side. Daisy was delighted that all the invitations had been accepted, despite the problems of wartime travel, particularly for Lottie who had furthest to come.

Alec was discharged from hospital a week before the wedding and Daisy visited him at his parent's home in Gloucestershire. On her return she was full of praise for Alec's family and for the cottage they were giving them as a wedding present.

'It's like Trealaw,' Daisy told Alice breathlessly, 'only more convenient, it's got running water and a lovely view even though it's in the village.'

'It doesn't sound like Trealaw at all,' said Alice dryly.

'It's been in the family for some time; they used to rent it out but Alec's father wants us to have it and we can sell it when we need to buy a bigger house. It will be lovely to have a home of our own from the very beginning.'

'It will.' Alice looked at her gravely, 'and what will you do when Alec's away?'

'His mother says there's lots to get involved in and I'm sure the country air will do me good, and of course I'll come and visit you whenever I can.'

'Of course you will.' Alice's voice was calm but she felt her heart judder.

***

'They're here!' Daisy shouted.

Alice entered the hall and looked up at Daisy elegantly poised at the top of the stairs. She was about to ask her daughter if she felt nervous but her radiant face told otherwise. She gave an inward sigh and realised that it was she who was feeling anxious. In less than twenty-four hours Daisy would have a different name and a new family to consider. The house would feel very empty without her.

The doorbell rang and Ethel rustled past, her uniform starched to perfection. Alice and Daisy took their places in the sitting room and waited for Ethel to announce the arrival of Alec and his parents.

'Mr and Mrs Hammond and Alec Hammond.' Ethel's voice rang out clearly as she ushered in the guests.

Alice found herself shaking hands with an older version of Alec and a pretty, elegantly dressed woman with a fox fur round her neck.

'I hope your hotel is comfortable,' she asked solicitously.

'Yes, thank you for recommending it. I don't think I'd feel safe in the centre of London but it's quieter here. The service is good; you wouldn't think there was a war, would you?' Mrs Hammond looked to her husband for confirmation.

Daisy drew Alec to the window then let out a little squeal and waved as she saw William coming through the gate.

'Ah! The best man!' said Alec's father jovially as William entered the room. 'Alec was worried whether you'd get leave.'

'I've only got a two day pass,' he said as he shook hands then looked around the room distractedly. 'Where's Lottie?'

'She's not here yet but Father said he'd bring her from the station, they'll be here soon.' Daisy kissed her brother.

'Perhaps you'd like to serve some drinks, or do you want to get changed first?' Alice noticed the dark rings under William's eyes and the tenseness of his mouth.

'We must fill our glasses!' William picked up the decanter and relaxed as he passed everyone a drink. He joined Daisy and Alec near the window.

'Humphrey said he'd try and get home early today.' Alice said apologetically to Alec's parents.

'It's impossible to make plans these days,' said Mrs Hammond drinking her sherry a little too quickly.

'I think the young people have the right idea,' her husband remarked as a gale of laughter came from the other side of the room. 'They grasp their happiness while they can. And good luck to them I say.' He drained his glass and poured himself another from the decanter.

Mrs Hammond's eyes darted about the room. 'Is that painting of your cottage in Wales?' she asked looking at Lottie's watercolour of Trealaw.

'Yes, do you like it?'

'It looks beautiful. Alec has told us about it, he said he found the wildness appealing.'

'It is. Ours is the highest house on the mountain. We built it as a place to escape to. And we love the freshness of the mountain air.'

'Yes, I find London very dirty compared with Gloucestershire.'

Alice was at a loss how to answer and was relieved when she heard the front door open and Humphrey and Hilda walked in.

'Hilda! How was the journey?' Daisy ran across the room to greet her friend. 'But what's happened to Lottie?'

'There was a derailment at Crewe just before the Llandudno train arrived. I've asked the stationmaster to find Lottie a room in the Station Hotel there and she can get the first train out in the morning. That's why I'm late,' said Humphrey as he shook hands with Mr and Mrs Hammond.

'Has anyone been hurt?' asked Alec's father.

'Not seriously, but it will take a while to lift the wagons off the track. Anyway, the Hertford train wasn't affected and I had the pleasure of travelling home with Daisy's bridesmaid,' Humphrey said gallantly.

'Poor Lottie.' Daisy looked at William sympathetically. She linked her arm through Hilda's. 'Let's take your bag upstairs, I expect you'd like to wash before dinner and I'm dying to see your dress.'

'If you'll excuse me, I'll go and have a wash and brush up too.' William strode across the room, his fists clenched and his face etched with disappointment.

***

Alice had planned dinner with care and had even managed to engage a young girl to help Ethel serve. Although Lottie's absence made the table seating easier, Alice's heart went out as she imagined the girl whiling away the hours in a hotel in Crewe.

However, once everyone was seated for dinner, Alice forgot about Lottie as she slipped into her role of mother of the bride. Both the fish and the beef were good, they had managed to get plenty of vegetables and Humphrey had procured some excellent wine. Daisy and Alec's happiness and optimism lit up the room and the talk was of childhood memories and future plans.

Alice was pleased to hear Hilda's roar of laughter as William and Alec vied with each other in telling jokes. Egged on by Alec's father, the jokes turned to anecdotes about their flying experiences. Alice leant forward to catch what they were saying as William never mentioned flying these days. Humphrey raised a warning eyebrow but William ignored him and filled his glass then graphically explained to Mr Hammond how his plane was hit by enemy fire and nose-dived into the sea.

Hilda's laughter stopped abruptly as she stared at William in horror.

'But you extricated yourself all right didn't you?' Alec's father asked jovially as he drained his glass.

'Yes, it happened near our ship. I scrambled out then hung onto the plane, thankful the fuel tank wasn't hit and after a while someone threw me a line and I climbed aboard.'

'Good man. My son and yours are heroes aren't they, Mrs Dacre?'

There was an embarrassed silence.

'My brother was a hero,' said Hilda, her fingers gripping the ivory napkin ring by her plate. 'A girl in the village gave him a white feather and he enlisted. We never saw him again. But he died for his country.'

For a moment Humphrey looked down the table directly into Alice's eyes. 'He was a farmer, a reserved occupation,' he said quietly. Then he turned to Hilda. 'Are you managing to get enough labour?'

'Now and again, but it's hard and I find it tedious working on the farm all the time.' She paused. 'I wanted to be a radiographer like Daisy. But I've learnt to drive and that's good fun.'

'How splendid!' Mrs Hammond smiled at Hilda then turned to Alice. 'I noticed a fine piano in the sitting room, do you all play?'

'Some of us are better than others, Daisy has a lovely touch and William sings as well as plays; perhaps we can have a sing-song after dinner.' Alice was grateful to Mrs Hammond for steering the conversation away from the war.

Humphrey filled everyone's glass and the atmosphere returned to its previous conviviality.

It was late by the time dinner was finished, with much praise for Ethel's lemon meringue pie and the excellent selection of cheeses. However, no one was in a mood to leave and Alice led everyone into the drawing room.

Daisy seated herself at the piano and Alec, William and Hilda gathered round. She began to play the Last Rose of Summer and soon everyone was joining in. After several songs Mr Hammond suggested 'It's a Long Way to Tipperary' but Alec put his hand on Daisy's shoulder and started to sing 'I'll Walk Beside You'.

'That was beautiful Alec,' said his mother as she wiped away a tear with her lace handkerchief.

Daisy stood up and leant against Alec, her face flushed with happiness.

'Have we finished?' asked Hilda disappointedly.

'I think we should be going; it's been a wonderful evening.' Mrs Hammond looked at her husband.

'Just one more.' William sat at the piano and began to accompany himself to 'The Rose of Tralee'.

Alice sat back and listened to the rich baritone then smiled as he changed Tralee to Trealaw. She glanced at the young faces around the piano and noticed Hilda looking at William as he sang, her face a mixture of admiration and profound sadness.

'Bravo!' cried Mr Hammond as William closed the piano.

William gave a mock bow and everyone clapped then started to make their way into the hall.

It was cold after the warmth of the sitting room and they said goodbye quickly although Daisy dallied in the doorway and watched until they rounded the corner, their way lit by the moon shining on the frosty road.

**

Everyone rose early the following morning and, after a quick breakfast, hurried to their rooms to get ready.

Alice looked at herself in her midnight blue V-necked gown and smiled as she heard giggles from Daisy's room. She was unaware that Humphrey had come into the bedroom until their eyes met in the mirror.

'Blue suits you.' Alice felt the warmth of his hand as it rested on her shoulder. 'The sapphires bring out the colour of your eyes.' His other hand reached over her shoulder and stroked the jewels around her throat.

A flush crept up her body as she stood motionless, silently admiring her husband dressed in his morning suit.

'What a handsome couple!' Humphrey's half playful tone reminded Alice of William.

'I think we'll do Daisy proud,' she whispered.

'I'm sure we will.' Humphrey's hand imperceptibly brushed his wife's breast as he drew away.

There was a knock on the door and Alice turned as Humphrey opened it. For a moment she thought she was seeing double as father and son stood in the doorway dressed in identical suits.

'Which cuff links should I wear?' William held out a pair of solid gold and another with diamond studs then glanced at his father's gold links on his starched white cuffs and said, 'I think I'll wear the diamond.'

'That will be nice and you can wear the diamond tie pin you had for your twenty-first birthday.'

'Good idea.' William frowned and studied his pocket watch. 'I wish Lottie was here.' There was a gale of laughter from Daisy's room. 'The poor girl's missing all the fun.'

'I'm going to see if they need any help. Shouldn't you be going soon to give Alec moral support?' said Alice as she tried to ignore the lost expression on her son's face.

'I suppose I should. I'll get the diamond tie pin, then I'll go.' William banged on his sister's door. 'Don't keep the groom waiting too long.'

'We will if we like!' Hilda called.

Alice laughed. 'Now, be off with you,' she said to William as she went to join the bride and bridesmaid.

'We've just finished, Mrs Dacre.' The young hairdresser cocked her head on one side as she appraised her handiwork.

Alice had always considered her daughter beautiful and she smiled with satisfaction at Daisy's radiant face framed by her golden curls.

'You look lovely. And you too, Hilda.' Alice looked in admiration at her goddaughter whose normally straight hair curled softly round her face.

'I'll be at the church so I can see you in your wedding dress,' said the hairdresser as she gathered up her things.

'Thank you so much, I'll show you out.' Alice led the way downstairs.

There was no sign of Humphrey or William and Alice felt suddenly alone as she stood in the doorway watching the hairdresser walk down the road. She looked anxiously towards the station but there was no sign of Lottie. She could see the church spire rising above the houses in the next street and wished that the bells could ring out for Daisy and Alec as they had done for her and Humphrey in Hertfordshire twenty-six years ago. But this was 1917; the bell ringers were gone far and wide – the North Sea, Gallipoli, the Somme. She shivered and closed the door.

The activity of the last three weeks, the late night and early morning and the realisation that she was about to lose her daughter made Alice feel weary. She climbed the stairs slowly and paused for breath on the landing.

'Are you frightened?' she heard Hilda ask in a low voice.

'No, why should I be?' Daisy sounded surprised.

'Well, you know….' There was a pause and Alice found herself unable to move.

'I'd never be frightened of Alec.'

'Not even, well, the first night?'

'No, I love him and I don't want to wait any longer.' Alice could imagine Daisy's honest eyes shining.

'But, will you know what to do?'

Daisy laughed. 'Of course, after all…' she paused.

Hilda gasped. 'You haven't done it already?'

'No, of course not. Well, not really.'

'Oh! It's funny that you and Alec have only been engaged three weeks and William and Lottie have been engaged for two years.'

'But I've known Alec for two years. They've just done things the other way round. William loves Lottie very much.'

'Yes, I know he does.'

Alice coughed and stepped heavily. 'Can I come in?'

'Yes, of course. What do you think?' Daisy stood before her, looking demure in her wedding dress with her gold cross and chain around her neck.

'Perfect.' Alice smiled then turned to Hilda. 'What a beautiful colour, maroon really suits you.'

'Thank you. Auntie Alice, where did you go for your honeymoon?'

'We went to Llandudno. That was the first time I had seen mountains. It was wonderful.'

'Do you wish you were going further away?' Hilda asked her friend.

'Two nights in a hotel in the Cotswolds will be lovely. And I'm really excited about moving into our cottage.'

There was a loud knock at the front door and they heard Ethel's firm footsteps in the hall as she went to answer it.

'The flowers have arrived!' she called.

'I'll get them.' Humphrey's voice came from his study.

He brought the bouquets upstairs – pink orchids set in maidenhair fern for the bridal bouquet and a posy of white roses for Hilda.

'Considering it's January the florist has done very well,' he said approvingly. He looked at his watch. 'We'll have to be going soon. I see there's no sign of Lottie yet.'

'I hope she's all right,' said Daisy anxiously.

'Ethel will have to stay and let her in, although she had hoped to come to the church,' Alice said.

'Is Lottie used to travelling?' asked Hilda.

'No.' Alice looked worried then added, 'But she's sensible and she would have been well looked after in the hotel last night.'

'It was a shame she missed last night, it was good fun,' said Hilda.

'Yes, I know William was upset she wasn't there but he hid it very well. Anyway, Humphrey has arranged for her to be met at Euston and put into a taxi so I'm sure she'll be here any moment,' Alice said to reassure herself.

Chapter 16: Lottie

Railway Travel
A resolution was passed calling on the Board of Trade
to restore the old rates of fares and suggesting the
abolition of Pullman cars and first and second-class
bookings

The Times: January 29th 1917

Lottie plumped the single pillow and slipped between cold sheets then pulled the blankets up to her chin. She knew she should be grateful to have had a good meal and her own room in the hotel instead of being crammed in the station waiting room but, now she was on her own, she could not stop the tears. She had forced herself to be cheerful at Christmas and tried not to think about the happy occasion it had been the previous year celebrated with both Cilla and William. When Daisy's wedding invitation arrived she was overjoyed at the thought of being with William and of having the possibility, however remote, of seeing Cilla. William had told her in a letter that he had seen Cilla and she was fine. Cilla herself had written enthusiastically but sporadically about her life on the buses. Lottie also welcomed the opportunity to have a break from the confines of what her life had become. Her mother's arthritis had worsened and the pain made her increasingly bad tempered. At first she had ignored Nellie's hints that she give up work to help more than she was already doing, but by October Lottie realised that her father was finding it difficult running the shop and so she handed in her notice. Lottie resented the fact that she now rarely saw the friend she had shared so many confidences with and was not there to comfort her in the months following Rhys' death. She had been surprised how upset she had been, not just for Bronwen, but also for herself and William and the good times they had shared.

As she lay awake listening to the shunting of railway wagons Lottie began to understand her sister's unwillingness to return to their little bedroom opposite the busy station. Since Cilla's departure, Lottie had been more aware of the noises outside and she had missed the sound of her sister's regular breathing in the bed beside hers.

She heard light footsteps on the stairs, a door creaked and someone went into the room next to hers. She realised it was a woman when she heard her humming while she was getting ready for bed. It wasn't long before the woman was asleep and Lottie felt comforted as she listened to her breathing, then she too fell asleep.

***

As she had her breakfast in the Pullman car the following morning, Lottie felt privileged to be travelling in the luxury that most passengers could not afford. In order to save time later she had dressed in her wedding clothes and she felt able to hold her head up among the other first class passengers. However, despite the fact that a cab was organised for her at Euston, she was frantic that she would not get to the wedding in time.

Ethel must have been watching from the window because, as Lottie got out of the cab at the Dacre's house, the front door opened. She waved and ran up the steps, followed by the driver with her luggage. Ethel explained that Inspector Dacre had asked her to accompany Lottie to the church in the cab.

'They haven't been gone long, we won't be too late,' she said reassuringly.

Lottie barely had time to look at the grand houses before they pulled up outside the church. She looked at Ethel enquiringly when she saw the heavy wooden door was closed then watched her turn the iron handle and pull the door open. There were some women sitting in the pews near the door and Lottie went to join them.

'No, you go further down,' whispered Ethel giving her a little push.

Feeling too scared to move, Lottie watched as Daisy and Alec stood in a pool of sunlight in front of the vicar who was reading from the Book of Common Prayer: 'Forasmuch as Alec and Daisy have consented together in holy wedlock and have witnessed the same before God and his company, and thereto have given and pledged their troth either to other, and have declared the same by giving and receiving a ring and by joining of hands: I pronounce that they be Man and Wife together.'

A ripple of satisfaction went round the church and Alice turned her head. She smiled at Lottie and beckoned her forward. Glad that the rest of the congregation had their backs to her, Lottie walked towards the altar then slipped into an empty pew behind the guests. Her knees felt weak when she saw William standing erect next to his father. She glanced around and saw an extravagantly dressed woman she assumed was Mrs Hammond dabbing her eyes as Alec tenderly lifted Daisy's veil from her face. The couple bowed their heads reverently as the congregation recited 'The Lord's Prayer'. The vicar gave a brief address then the first bars of 'Praise my Soul the King of Heaven' rang out on the organ. Lottie sang lustily, happy in the knowledge that she would soon be twenty-one and then it would be her and William's turn to get married.

At the end of the hymn William turned and saw Lottie. His face lit up and he took a step towards her then stopped and followed the bride and groom to the vestry to sign the register.

Lottie waited impatiently for them to return and was relieved when the 'Wedding March' struck up and Daisy and Alec walked radiantly down the aisle. She felt a pang of jealousy at the sight of William's arm through Hilda's but when they reached her pew William paused and kissed her then, with a girl on each arm, he gallantly proceeded to the door of the church.

***

Lottie sat through the sumptuous wedding breakfast with a fixed smile on her face. She had looked forward to being with William with every fibre of her being and she wasn't even sitting next to him. He made an excellent speech as best man but Lottie's smile was forced when he proposed a toast to the bridesmaid. She told herself she had no reason to be jealous of Hilda, but the long journey was beginning to catch up with her and the rich food was making her feel bilious. As soon as the meal and speeches were over Daisy and Alec left to change for their honeymoon. Hilda accompanied Daisy, and the guests began drifting into the lounge where coffee was being served.

Lottie stood up and suddenly William was at her side.

'I think that went well, hope you didn't find it an awful bore,' he said and gently kissed the nape of her neck.

'No, of course not,' she said truthfully. 'I enjoyed looking at everyone's clothes and your speech was very good.'

'And did Uncle Charlie behave himself?' asked William referring to the elderly gentleman who had sat next to Lottie.

'Yes; he seems quite a character.'

'He's a bit of a black sheep. When I was a boy my father used to say that I mustn't end up like his brother Charlie. But he's a decent sort. Now, I'd better introduce you to a few people then we might be able to find a quiet corner.'

They made their way into the lounge and paused by a huge mirror in a gilded frame. The reflection of the room with its elegant décor and richly clad people appeared to stretch to infinity.

'What a handsome couple!' exclaimed an immaculately dressed white-haired woman. 'I'm Alec's grandmother. And you must be the future Mrs Dacre,' she said looking appraisingly at Lottie.

'She is indeed,' said William proudly.

'Ah, William!' called Uncle Charlie. 'Bring your beautiful fiancée and sit over here, I want to hear what you've been up to recently.'

They settled themselves on a deep sofa next to William's uncle and a waiter brought some coffee. It wasn't long before Lottie felt relaxed and happy for the first time that day.

After a while Daisy and Alec re-appeared. Alec was in his officer's uniform while Daisy was wearing a blue two-piece jersey costume and matching cape. The guests crowded round and followed them to the hotel entrance where their cab was waiting. They waved and shouted advice until the cab was out of sight.

Gradually people started to leave. Mr and Mrs Hammond insisted that everyone remaining should be their guests for dinner. William did not leave Lottie's side and she spent the evening in a bubble of contentment.

***

Lottie fell asleep almost as soon as her head touched the pillow.

She dreams that William is beside her, she smells his skin against hers and the scent of his hair. She entwines her arms around his neck as she turns towards him and feels his lips on hers. She moans as his hand caresses her breast.

Then she gave a startled cry and woke up.

William was lying beside her.

'What are you doing!' she exclaimed in a frightened whisper.

'Oh Lottie, I want you so much.' He wrapped his arms around her and held her in the darkness.

She lay rigid, trying to ignore the tingling in her body and the pounding in her head.

'But we can't, not yet, we're not married.'

'My darling, I know, but I don't think I can wait any longer.'

Lottie stroked his cheek. 'But we will be very soon. We can't here, your parents might hear.' She wanted to say that she had thought their love was beautiful; she didn't want it turned into something sordid like Cilla and Len.

'I'll be twenty-one in April,' she whispered. 'Then we can be married.'

'But I might not be here in April.' Lottie only just caught the words muttered into her hair.

'We planned to get married on your next leave, you'll be due for leave again in the summer,' she whispered desperately.

'We don't know that, we don't know anything.'

Lottie was shocked by the misery in his voice. 'We know we love each other,' she said fiercely.

218

William rolled on his back and lay completely still.

Lottie wondered what he was thinking; wondered what she should say; what she should do; what his parents would say if they knew their son was in her bed. Now that she was no longer enfolded by William's arms she felt cold and began to shiver. She touched him nervously, desperate for reassurance.

He flinched then sighed and gripped her hand. 'You're right,' he said. 'If it wasn't for knowing that you love me I don't know how I'd keep on going day after day; day after bloody day.' He shifted himself into a sitting position and pulled Lottie close. 'You're freezing, I think we should get some cocoa.'

'But it's the middle of the night!'

'Do you want me to leave you to lie awake in your cold bed?'

Lottie shook her head.

'Then put on your dressing gown and slippers and we'll go downstairs.' William got out of bed, picked up his dressing gown from the floor and put it on over his pyjamas.

They crept downstairs and into the kitchen. William poured some milk in a pan and put it on the gas stove to boil. He rummaged around till he found the cocoa then whisked it expertly with the milk and filled two breakfast cups with the steaming liquid.

They took their cups into the sitting room and William resurrected the fire. He pulled the sofa nearer to it and they snuggled together and sipped their cocoa.

Lottie felt the tension leave her body and she saw that William had lost the angry expression he had earlier.

'This is a lovely cosy room,' she said.

'We've had a lot of good times here. I'm so sorry you weren't here yesterday, we had a sing song round the piano.'

'I wish I'd been with you.' Lottie refused to feel sorry for herself and added, 'We used to tell stories round the fireside in the evenings.'

'Tell me a story now.'

Lottie looked at William uncertainly then saw he was serious.

'Once upon a time,' she began softly, 'there was a young girl who lived in a little house at the bottom of the mountain. She helped her parents in their shop but when she went outside she would often look up at the mountain and imagine that a handsome young man would come and take her away to exciting places. Then one day the man of her imagination came into the shop but he didn't notice the girl. She saw him again on the railway station and this time he noticed her and the girl was very happy.'

Lottie paused. 'Shall I continue?'

William studied her face intently. 'Tell me they lived happily ever after.'

'They did,' she said simply.

A flame flickered in the grate then died.

As they sat staring at the fire Lottie wondered if, like her, William was trying to make pictures from the dying embers.

'I'll put more coal on.' William gently pulled away from Lottie and shovelled a scuttle full on the fire.

'Now it's your turn to tell a story,' said Lottie, leaning her head on William's shoulder.

He looked pensive for a moment then began. 'Once upon a time there was a young man who loved flying. He was happiest when he was in an aeroplane flying over the tiny fields and houses and feeling the wind in his face and knowing he was in control of the machine. He looked forward to buying his own aeroplane one day. But then everything changed and there was a war. Lots of the young man's friends went off to fight but he was sent to work in a remote place at the foot of a mountain and he was very angry because he wanted to go to war with his friends. Then one day he met the girl of his dreams and he didn't want to leave any more. But he still loved flying and he wanted to fight for his country. So he left the girl of his dreams and flew aeroplanes for his country but they had become killing machines and that wasn't what he wanted to do any more.'

William shifted and held Lottie's face in his hands. 'He wanted to stay at home with the girl of his dreams.'

For a while neither of them said anything. As Lottie fought back the tears she could see that William's eyes were moist.

'William,' she asked hesitantly, 'you've never really told me what you do; if you did it might help me to understand.'

'We're not encouraged to talk.' He paused. 'But you're right, and anyway a man shouldn't have secrets from his wife.'

Lottie wondered what pictures William was seeing as he gazed into the fire. She nestled closer to him and took his hand.

'Have I told you about my pigeons?' he asked.

'Yes. I often think of you flying, with your pigeons cooing in their basket beside you.'

William said nothing.

Lottie reappraised her cosy image. 'But I don't suppose you can hear them over the noise of your aeroplane.'

'And the bombs,' William muttered.

Lottie shuddered and waited for him to continue. She glanced at his brooding expression and wondered if she had done the right thing by asking him to talk. She stroked his hand and listened to the clock ticking.

'Have you heard of a place called Zeebrugge?' he asked after a long silence.

'It's a port in Belgium that's used by the German navy.'

'Good girl.' William sounded surprised.

Lottie coloured, pleased by his approval but slightly irritated by his surprise.

William leant forward staring at the fire but when she looked at his face she saw his eyes were closed. She wondered if he had fallen asleep or was simply trying to blot out some bad memory.

She wished she could do something to ease his suffering then realised that she could have comforted him when he had come to her bed but she had rejected him. She felt her nipples harden and her face burned as she imagined what might have happened. But she knew she would have been unable to look his parents in the eye if she had misbehaved under their roof. Although they had shown nothing but kindness to her she instinctively felt that she would not like to incur their disapproval.

A sound made her turn and she was disconcerted to see Alice standing in the doorway wearing a floral dressing gown.

'Oh can't you sleep either?' she asked distractedly.

William sat up and looked at his mother. 'I heard Lottie coughing so I knocked on her door and asked if I could get her some cocoa,' he said smoothly.

'Poor you; I didn't hear you. How are you now?' Alice looked concerned.

'I'm a lot better now, thank you.'

'Poor Humphrey has a cough too. I hope he didn't catch it from me. He's working far too hard and I don't even know what he does. I know it's an honour but I really wish he'd never been recruited for the Specials.'

'It must be difficult not knowing where he is,' said Lottie hesitantly.

'It gets lonely. And of course it will be worse now Daisy's married.'

Lottie looked surprised, she hadn't thought of the competent Mrs Dacre being lonely. 'It was a lovely wedding,' she said.

'It was, wasn't it? And I've absolutely nothing to complain about. I must take Humphrey his medicine. I suppose there's no point in your going back to bed now?'

'No, I think we'll stay by the fire a bit longer and have an early breakfast,' said William.

'I'll see you in the morning then.'

'I thought I'd die when your mother came in the room,' said Lottie after Alice had left.

'Mother's a good sort. I hope Father will be all right. Anyway, now they know we're here, why don't we put the gramophone on quietly?'

'That would be nice.' Lottie yawned.

William made no effort to continue the conversation they had begun earlier and Lottie did not pursue it.

They curled up on the sofa and listened to love songs for a while until they both fell asleep.

***

The fire had gone out by the time they woke but, even as she went upstairs to get dressed, Lottie felt an inner warmth. She dressed with care then made her way to the dining room.

The morning was bright and crisp and after breakfast William suggested they went for a walk on the Heath. When they came back their faces were glowing.

'Did you enjoy your walk?' asked Alice.

'Oh yes! I never realised there was countryside in London,' Lottie replied.

'Daisy loves walking on the Heath,' Alice paused and for one embarrassing moment Lottie thought she was going to cry. 'But now she's got all that beautiful Gloucestershire countryside to walk in. Alec's going to get her a dog for company when he's away and the country air will be so good for her,' she continued quickly.

'And you'll be able to visit her,' said William.

'Yes, once she's had time to settle down.' Alice blew her nose. 'Oh dear, I seem to have caught Humphrey's cold.'

Lottie and William exchanged glances.

'Shall we have a game of mah-jong before lunch?' suggested William.

'That's a lovely idea, but I have a few things to attend to. You two enjoy yourselves.'

***

Lottie was taking an evening train back but she wanted to try and see Cilla so they decided to leave her luggage at Euston then walk to the hostel where she was staying.

It was beginning to get dark by the time they came out of the station and they walked for over half an hour before they came to the hostel. They rang the bell and, after what seemed an age, they heard footsteps and the door was opened by a severe looking woman.

'Is Cilla Rowe in?' asked Lottie.

'No, she left on Friday.'

Lottie's face dropped. 'Where has she gone?'

'She didn't leave a forwarding address.'

'But,' Lottie felt suddenly faint, 'she's my sister and I've brought her some presents from home.'

The woman's expression softened. 'She asked me to keep any letters for her to collect.'

'Do you know why she left?' asked William.

The woman shook her head.

'She wasn't in any trouble?' he persisted.

'Not to my knowledge. She's a nice cheerful girl, works on the buses.' She looked at Lottie sympathetically as she took the parcel she handed her. 'She made lots of friends, some of them moved on, maybe she went to stay with one of them.'

'But what shall I say to my mother? She made her a cake.' Lottie pointed to the parcel.

'She said she'd come back for her mail.' The woman began to back away from the door.

'And my father sent her favourite sweets.'

'Come along Lottie.' William took her arm. 'Thank you. If you see her, can you tell her that her sister called?'

'Yes, of course. Goodnight Sir.'

'And I knitted her a pair of gloves,' sobbed Lottie as they turned and started to walk away from the hostel.

'And she'll be wearing them very soon. Now don't worry, I expect there'll be a letter from her when you get home saying where she's gone.'

Lottie dabbed her eyes. 'I hope so. It's so lonely at home without her. But it wouldn't be so bad if I knew she was all right. I don't know what I'd do if anything happened to her.'

Chapter 17: Alice

Waifs and Strays Society
is Saving the Children
4,746 now in Homes; Total received 31,210
Will you help in the urgent national work?

The Times: March 2nd 1917

The streets were almost deserted as Alice made her way to the local Waifs and Strays society. As usual they were short staffed and she had volunteered to help with the breakfasts. A well-meaning gentlewoman had bequeathed the house to the society but it was in need of refurbishment and had a neglected air. The small front garden was overgrown and she didn't notice the pram by the privet hedge just inside the gate.

Alice was about to ring the doorbell when a cry made her turn. She frowned. She knew the girls were overworked but they surely wouldn't put the babies out so early in the morning. The cry came again, weak but insistent.

Alice strode across the wet grass and gasped in disbelief at a baby, its face screwed up and its blue eyes full of tears, looking up at her. The infant was warmly wrapped in bonnet and shawl and, attached to a thick blue blanket was a note in copperplate handwriting. Alice bent forward to read the message: 'My name is Peter. Please look after me.'

Her head swam as she looked for clues to the baby's identity. Tucked under the blanket were a change of clothes and a bottle of medicine. The baby coughed and Alice put her hand under his head and raised him slightly.

'It's all right Peter, you'll be safe now,' she said then laid him back down.

She manoeuvred the pram across the grass to the front door and rang the bell.

A red-faced, big-bosomed woman opened the door and glowered at the pram.

'We can't take any more waifs!' Her voice rasped in the frosty air.

'Of course you can! The society doesn't turn babies away. You know that as well as I do!' snapped Alice.

'Oh! Mrs Dacre!' The woman looked confused but stood her ground, her arms crossed as she barred the way.

From inside Alice could hear caterwauling as the infants had their nappies changed and bibs put on ready for breakfast. She understood the superintendent's reluctance to take in another baby; they were full to capacity and there was a shortage of volunteers but that problem could be addressed later.

Peter began to cough, causing the superintendent's expression to soften then harden again.

'Well he can't come here with his germs. Who does he belong to?'

Angrily, Alice pointed to the note. 'I've no idea but the person who brought him obviously thought he'd be cared for here.'

'You found him here?'

'Yes, under the hedge.'

Alice jiggled the pram as the superintendent chewed her lip. Both women knew that the baby had to be taken in, even if he was transferred to a larger home later.

***

For the next two days Alice assumed almost total responsibility for Peter. There was no clue to his parentage but the note, his clothes and the large carriage-built pram suggested he was not from the lower classes. She was concerned about his cough but his ready smile suggested he had been well loved.

She brought the note home to see if Humphrey could detect anything from it. As was usual these days Humphrey was late and Alice showed it to him after dinner. He put down his pipe and examined the note carefully. 'The paper is good quality,' he said, 'and I'd say it's been written with an expensive pen.'

Humphrey passed it back to Alice and began to re-fill his pipe. 'From what you've told me, the little chap seems to have come from a good home.' Humphrey sucked on the pipe and held his cigarette lighter over the bowl until the tobacco glowed red. 'Maybe he's the result of a wife's indiscretion while her husband was away.'

'And she can't face him now he's coming back. Perhaps he's injured and she's got to nurse him.' Alice's imagination raced as different scenarios flashed through her mind.

'Maybe.' Humphrey sighed. 'But, unless whoever left the baby comes to claim him, you've no way of knowing.'

'It's just so sad.' Alice focused her eyes on Lottie's painting of Trealaw, determined to keep control of her feelings. 'Peter's cough is getting worse. I told the superintendent to send for the doctor but she defied me!' Alice flashed angrily.

'Do you wish you were still running the station buffet?' Humphrey looked shrewdly at his wife.

Alice shrugged. 'I did it for two years, it was time for a change and in some ways this is more worthwhile.' She didn't add that this new work was often tedious and the overworked staff did not treat her with the respect she was used to.

'Perhaps you'd be happier concentrating on fund-raising for the society like you did before Christmas.'

Alice sometimes found Humphrey's ability to read her thoughts unnerving. 'At the moment I need to concentrate on getting Peter better.'

Humphrey nodded. 'I'll be home late tomorrow night. Will you be all right?'

'Of course.' Alice was surprised; she was used to Humphrey being late. If he was on railway business he would tell her about it but he seemed to be increasingly involved in secret service work.

***

Humphrey left early the following morning and Alice got up soon afterwards. She was surprised to see that nothing had been prepared for breakfast and went into the kitchen to look for Ethel.

Her maid, who she had first employed a quarter of a century ago, was slumped at the table, her grey hair unkempt and her normally starched white cap crumpled as she held it to her eyes.

'Ethel, whatever's the matter?'

Alice seated herself at the other side of the table, appalled, as this apparent stranger dropped the cap in her lap, clutched her arms across her chest and slowly rocked backwards and forwards staring unseeing into the distance.

Ethel seemed unaware of her presence and Alice quietly stood up and looked around the kitchen. There was a kettle of water simmering on the hob and a teapot covered by a brightly knitted tea cosy. She added a scoop of tea, poured on hot water, stirred it briskly then poured out two cups to which she added generous amounts of sugar.

'Drink this,' she said placing Ethel's hands around the cup. Alice sat down and sipped her tea, waiting for Ethel to speak.

After a while she put her hand in her pocket and took out a letter.

'This is from my sister,' she whispered.

Alice nodded. Ethel had often spoken of her nephew, a gentle boy who was reputed to have green fingers. The market gardener he worked for could ill afford to lose him but after the Conscription Act was passed he had been sent to the Front.

'Is it bad news?' she asked quietly.

'He's been shot.'

Alice was surprised at the vehemence of her voice and her choice of words. 'Killed in action. I'm so sorry,' she murmured.

'No!' Ethel sat bolt upright and glared. 'He's been shot. By a firing squad.'

'The Germans ...' Alice began.

'Not the Germans! The British! They said he was guilty of cowardice.' In her agitation, Ethel wound her crumpled cap around her fingers.

Alice frowned, not knowing what to say.

'He never was a coward!' Ethel spoke in a quiet monotone. 'There was a time when one of the ruffians in the village dived into the pond and didn't come up. There was weeds you see. My nephew jumped in and pulled him out. And animals. He was always bringing hurt animals home. He should have got a medal for the things he did. Not... '

Ethel drained her tea and looked directly at Alice. 'You won't tell anyone will you? My brother-in-law said no one's to know. I shouldn't have told you.'

'No, I won't say anything. But isn't there something we can do? Perhaps it was a mistake.'

Ethel looked incredulous. 'Of course it was a mistake. But we can't do anything, we're just ordinary people. And making a fuss won't bring him back.'

Alice sat silently as if seeing her maid for the first time. 'Would you like to go and visit your sister?'

'Do you think you can manage without me?'

'Of course, take as long as you need. And if your sister needs any help, writing letters, perhaps…'

'Thank you but we won't talk of it again.' Ethel stood up. 'Now I'll get your breakfast before you go off to look after that little baby at the home.'

***

Alice paused by her front door contemplating a hearse drawn by a single horse with a group of mourners shuffling behind. It was a sad sight, not like the splendid carriages drawn by four or even six horses before the war. She walked slowly down the path and turned away from the little procession. Her conversation with Ethel had made her late but she found herself unable to hurry, burdened as she was with the weight of what Ethel had told her combined with anxiety for baby Peter and a general feeling of war-weariness.

The feeling remained even after Alice reached the home. Breakfast was over and the bigger babies and children were in the playroom. She made her way to the room where the babies slept but all the cots were empty.

'Where's Peter?' Alice's voice was accusing as she addressed the girl busy changing sheets.

'In the isolation room.' The girl jerked her head upwards.

Alice could feel her heart thumping as she hurried upstairs. She paused before entering a small bedroom at the back of the house.

'Do you want me to stay with him?' Alice heard a girl ask.

'No, there's plenty for you to do downstairs. Anyway her ladyship will be here soon.' Alice drew in her breath at the supervisor's disparaging tone.

The girl giggled. 'You mean Madam Hoity Toity!'

'There's no need for that.' But Alice got the impression the superintendent agreed with the remark.

'Oh! Good morning, Mrs Dacre!' The girl had the grace to look flustered as she came out of room.

'Good morning,' Alice replied automatically as she watched the girl clomp down the stairs.

Summoning her strength Alice went into the room. 'How's Peter today?' she asked as she bent over his cot.

'His cough is worse so, as you can see, we've moved him away from the other children.'

'Have you called the doctor?'

'It's not the doctor's day to call.' The superintendent glared at Alice as if to say 'We've already had this conversation.'

'No, of course it isn't. And it's very good of him to come free of charge once a week anyway.' Alice felt the fight leave her as she recalled the remarks made about her behind her back. She realised that the elderly doctor's old-fashioned remedies would probably be of little use anyway to the baby lying listlessly in the little iron cot.

'I must see to the other children now.' The superintendent tweaked Peter's blanket then looked at Alice almost sympathetically. 'Perhaps you can keep an eye on him.'

As the superintendent left the room Alice nodded, not trusting herself to speak.

The baby began to cough and she swaddled him in the blanket then picked him up and lent him over her shoulder, murmuring endearments as she paced the room. When he was calm she sat him on her knee and wiped his face. He smiled at her and she had a sudden feeling of elation that he would get better and the war would end. She laid him back in his cot, pulled the chair next to it and sat down. Her eyelids felt heavy and she was overwhelmed with fatigue.

'Mrs Dacre, I've brought you a cup of tea.'

Alice started as the girl she had seen earlier came into the room. She looked at her wristwatch and realised she must have fallen asleep. 'Thank you,' she said and took the tea.

The girl gasped and Alice recoiled when she saw her panic-stricken face staring at the cot.

'No!' Alice gave a growl like a wounded animal as she followed the girl's gaze. The teacup rattled in her shaking hand and slid to the floor. Oblivious to the liquid seeping into her skirt, Alice bent over the cot, lifted up the limp body and tenderly rocked it in her arms, crooning softly as she swayed back and forth.

The girl looked at her in horror. 'I'll get the superintendent,' she said and rushed out of the room.

***

It was almost dark by the time Alice wearily stood in her porch and fumbled for the door key.

'Ethel!' she called as she dumped her bag on the hall table.

The house was cold and the familiar smells of cooking and polish were absent. Then she remembered; Ethel's nephew had been shot as a traitor and she had gone to comfort her sister.

And Peter, the little waif, was dead too.

'When will it end?' she muttered as she trudged round the house drawing the blackout curtains. She switched on a small brass table lamp in the sitting room and noticed that Ethel had thoughtfully laid the fire before she left. She struck a match and watched a flame curl round the paper and ignite the sticks and coal.

Then Alice slumped into her chair and waited for Humphrey to come home.

April 1917

Dover

My Darling Lottie

I'm glad you liked the silk scarf. I had wanted to get you something really special for your 21ˢᵗ but I rarely have time off when the shops are open. What I really wanted to give you was a wedding ring. I have no idea when my next leave will be but I promise you we will get married then. I am living for the day when we are Mr and Mrs Dacre.

I have some bad news. My friend John was killed last week. I didn't mention it in my last letter because I didn't want to spoil your birthday. As you know, John was my observer and we flew together for over a year. I really miss him, he always saw the funny side of things.

Apparently he stepped out in front of a bus; there was nothing the driver could do. To die in a freak accident in the street seems so unfair. There are rumours that too much flying leads to disorientation. But I expect that's just scaremongering. You certainly don't need to worry about me, I'm as fit as a flea.

Stan, my replacement observer, has only just got his stripe. He's from Lancashire with a wife and baby at home. His brother was killed at Arras so he's in a bit of a state, gets twitchy when we're in sight of the French coast. John and I understood each other but I can't find much common ground with Stan. Things have been tricky since the rules of engagement changed a few months ago but I can't say anything about that.

I'm glad to hear that your mother is feeling a bit better after the long damp winter. I don't know how I would have managed without all the warm socks you knitted for me. I have to wear them at night as well because the billet is always cold.

Make sure you look after yourself and try not to work too hard, you are so precious to me I couldn't bear it if you were ill.

I wait for your next letter.

All my love - now and always

William

Chapter 18: Lottie

Record of Air Service
Information as to enemy movements and battery
positions and so forth is largely got from aeroplane
observation and the value of airmen's contribution is
beyond computation

The Times: June 11th1917

'Bronwen! How lovely to see you! I'm just about to close the shop.' Lottie had seen little of her friend since giving up her job at Knight's.

'Yes, it's been too long.' Bronwen paused and looked up at the soldier who accompanied her. 'Barry, this is my friend Lottie. Lottie, meet Barry.'

'I've heard so much about you.' The soldier squeezed Lottie's hand as he shook it.

Lottie drew her hand away and looked at her friend. She had lost weight and looked almost elegant in her fashionable shorter length skirt but her bright red lips were forced into a smile that didn't reach her eyes. As Barry took out a packet of cigarettes Lottie felt he was a poor substitute for Rhys.

'So how's life been treating you?' asked Bronwen.

'Not much has happened. I haven't seen William since his sister's wedding in January.'

'You should have got yourself a local boy. Barry's at the army camp in Conway.'

'So, you're training for the Front?' Lottie felt an unaccountable need to hurt the soldier who wasn't Rhys.

'Oh no! Barry's a cook, it's his job to keep the troops in Wales fed,' said Bronwen desperately.

The doorbell rang and an elderly man shuffled into the shop. Barry leant against the door looking at the depleted shelves while Lottie served the customer.

'How's business?' asked Bronwen when the man had gone.

Lottie shrugged and gestured to the shelves.

Bronwen nodded. 'Even Knight's are having problems.'

'We've got plenty of supplies at the camp,' Barry drawled.

'I'm glad to hear it, the troops need good food,' replied Lottie.

Barry leant across the counter. 'We might be able to come to some arrangement,' he said and winked.

Lottie felt his breath on her face and looked at her friend in horror.

Bronwen had turned white. 'The arrangement he meant was, would you like to come to the pictures with us? Wasn't it Barry?'

'Of course.' He took a step away from the counter. 'We can be a foursome, I've got a friend who'd like to meet you.'

Lottie fiddled with her engagement ring. 'But I'm about to get married,' she said agitatedly.

'So, when's the happy day?' Barry's question was laced with impertinence.

'As soon as William gets leave. I'm twenty-one now!' Lottie's voice was shrill.

'He'll be home soon,' said Bronwen comfortingly. 'But in the meantime do come to the pictures, it's ages since we've been out together.'

Lottie sighed. 'It might do me good. I just seem to work, help my mother, knit for the troops and write letters. We don't even see my cousins any more since the family moved away.'

'Is there any news from your sister?'

'No, and it's a few weeks since I last had a letter from her. I asked her to be my bridesmaid but she said she didn't know if she'd even be able to come to the wedding.'

'Your sister's quite a one isn't she? I heard about her running off with a private from our barracks last year.' Barry grinned.

Bronwen ignored him. 'She'll be back.' She paused. 'I'm really happy for you. And, you'll come to the pictures on Saturday?'

'Yes, I'd love to,' Lottie replied without conviction.

***

Nellie was well enough to work in the shop the following morning and Lottie was pleased to have time to herself. Bronwen's fleeting visit had left her feeling troubled. During the long winter nights she had lain awake and wondered if she had been right to refuse William when he came to her bed after Daisy's wedding. But she had been so certain they would be married as soon as she was twenty-one. And she was terrified of being in the family way if she wasn't married. She knew that there were precautions people took but she didn't know what they were and she had no one to confide in.

She went upstairs and opened her wardrobe. Hanging at one end was her bridal gown, protected by a sheet. She had bought the fabric while she was working at Knight's and had spent the winter evenings bowed over her mother's sewing machine. Wondering just how much longer it would be before she wore the dress she took a package wrapped in tissue paper from the top shelf and carried it downstairs.

Lottie removed the tissue and laid out her delicately embroidered wedding train on the table. A needle

239

threaded with white silk rested on a flower she had embroidered the previous winter. She settled down and began to work on a pair of buzzards she had already drawn on the fabric. As she stitched, she recalled the courtship flight of the birds on the day William had proposed to her on Daffodil Mountain. Her heart beat faster as she remembered how ecstatic she had felt when William had said he loved her. Since that day she had never doubted his love and she knew that she would remain steadfast to him whatever happened.

There was a sudden draft and the back door burst open. Lottie turned and saw William standing in the doorway.

She gasped, quickly covered the train with the tissue paper, then flung her arms around his neck and kissed him.

Gently he disentangled himself and put his hands on her shoulders. Lottie stroked his cheek then drew back at the unaccustomed feel of stubble on his handsome face.

'I've missed you so much. Why didn't you let me know you were coming?' Then as William stood looking silently at her, she said fearfully, 'Are you all right?'

'Yes, I'm fine. I've come to see my parents, they're staying at Trealaw.'

'Yes, I know. Has something happened to them?'

'No, it's just that I need to see them.'

'Oh!' Lottie felt hurt. 'How was the journey?' she asked mechanically.

'Crowded. And I couldn't get a train all the way to Conway. So I'll have to walk from here.'

'But …' Lottie had been going to ask why she couldn't come too but the grim expression on his face stopped her. 'Will you have a cup of tea before you go?' she asked instead.

'Yes please.' William smiled momentarily and Lottie felt her heart lurch.

She poured two cups and added lots of sugar, despite the fact that it was strictly rationed. They sat, unspeaking, in the chairs on either side of the fireplace.

Lottie stared at the cup in her hands then looked at William but he appeared unaware of her as he sat motionless, locked in some dark place of his own imagining.

As she looked at the door into the shop, willing her mother to come and break the silence, she thought wryly that it was the first time she had wanted her mother barging in when she was with William.

Suddenly he clenched his fist and stood up.

At the same time the door opened and Nellie bustled in.

'Your father's just walked in with some supplies and …. Oh William! I didn't know you were here. Has Lottie got you something to eat?'

'I've had some tea thank you. I'm sorry I can't stop but I have to see my parents.'

'Of course you do! It's a good thing that Jack's back and I'm feeling well today so there's no need for Lottie to be in the shop. You can both go off and spend some time together while you can,' Nellie said indulgently.

Lottie looked questioningly at William.

'Yes, we'll be off then.' William grabbed her hand.

'I'm not really dressed for visiting your parents,' flustered Lottie.

'Neither am I.' William rubbed his stubbled cheek while keeping Lottie's hand firmly in his other hand.

'Give our regards to your parents and tell your father I hope he's feeling better,' said Nellie.

'I will.' William opened the door and propelled Lottie outside.

'We'll walk,' he announced and they set off at a fast pace.

Lottie was panting by the time they reached the suspension bridge across the estuary.

'I've got a stitch,' she said apologetically when they were nearing the middle of the bridge.

'I'm sorry. I wasn't thinking.' William stopped and cupped her face in his hands.

For a moment Lottie thought he was going to kiss her but he turned and fixed his gaze on some fishing boats landing their catch in the harbour. The breeze rippled the water and Lottie's stitch subsided as they leant against the rail.

She was about to comment on the tranquillity of the scene when she noticed a contingent of soldiers with rifles over their shoulders marching along the morfa accompanied by their sergeant shouting a series of incomprehensible commands.

'Did you have to drill like that when you were training?' Lottie asked.

'What?' William seemed surprised when she spoke.

'It doesn't matter.' Lottie was silent for a moment then said, 'William, I wish you'd tell me what's wrong.'

He took her hand again and started walking. 'I will. It's just I don't want to tell it twice.'

They walked quickly past the castle and through the town and up the mountain track. Lottie's heart began to pound with exertion and anxiety. She was relieved when the track ended and they were on the open mountain. Ahead of them was Trealaw, its grey walls standing straight and square with the dark slopes of Mynydd Brith rising behind.

William pulled Lottie across the slope and hammered on the front door.

***

'William! What a wonderful surprise! And Lottie too!'

As Alice kissed her, Lottie noticed lines on her face that hadn't been there in January and remembered William mentioning in a letter that his mother had been unwell after the death of a child she had looked after at the Waifs and Strays society.

Her legs were still shaking as she sank down on the sofa next to William and gratefully accepted the glass of cordial that Alice offered.

'I see you're not wearing uniform,' remarked Humphrey sternly as he sat in his chair by the fireside.

William looked down at his blazer and grey flannels. 'No, I thought I'd give these an airing for a change.'

'But you always wear uniform for travelling.'

'Yes, I usually do.' William drained his glass.

'William, are you all right?' Lottie saw her own concern mirrored in Alice's face as she questioned her son.

'I'm still a bit bruised.' He sneezed. 'And I can't shake off this cold. I suppose it's not surprising, I was in the water a good while.'

He paused then took out his cigarette case and offered it to his father.

'No thank you, son, I've got my pipe.' Humphrey concentrated on filling and lighting his favourite rosewood pipe.

Lottie's eyes met Alice's as they looked expectantly at the men, waiting for one of them to speak.

'So, what's been happening?' Some of the sternness had left Humphrey's face as he regarded William.

'Shall I start at the beginning or the end?'

'I think it will make more sense if you start at the beginning.'

'Right.' William inhaled deeply. 'Two weeks ago I took off in a Short 827 with Stan, my observer. We had the usual instructions to track enemy shipping and had our basket of pigeons ready to fly back with messages. We carried a small rack of Cooper bombs under the fuselage and Stan had a light machine gun.'

'So you could defend yourselves against the enemy?'

'No. The Admiralty doesn't care much about defence. The bombs and gun were for attacking the enemy.'

'But I thought you were only involved in reconnaissance,' said Alice sharply.

'At first, yes, but for some time now we've had instructions to attack enemy shipping.'

Humphrey frowned. 'Do you mean single-handedly? You weren't flying in a squadron?'

'Not this time. That's usually left to the boys in the Flying Corps.'

Alice went pale. 'But what chance has a tiny plane against an enemy battleship?'

'Well, I didn't think the odds were very good.' William stubbed out his cigarette. 'Stan and I seemed to understand each other. We carried on as before, flying over the Channel and using our binoculars to sight enemy ships and U boats. It was sometimes a narrow shave because we had to get near enough to identify the type of ship and direction of travel. Then we'd pull back, scribble a note stating the position, give the note to the pigeon, tip the little blighter overboard and Bob's your uncle.'

'And you continued your reconnaissance?'

'Yes, that's how it was at first. But it all changed once we started carrying the bally bombs. They were no longer scouting missions, they were suicide missions.'

William squeezed Lottie's hand and said, 'I'd got Lottie and our future to think about. And Stan had his wife and baby. He talked about the baby all the time.'

He closed his eyes for a moment and his voice was hardly more than a whisper as he continued. 'You're so, so alone up there. On a dull day everything is grey, it's sometimes hard to distinguish the sea from the sky. To keep myself going I used to imagine Lottie sitting by our fireside nursing our baby girl while I sat at the table showing our little boy how to make a model aeroplane.'

Lottie lowered her eyes, not wanting to share her tears. In the distance she could hear a skylark singing and for a moment she shared William's vision of their future together.

Then Humphrey broke the silence. 'So all this happened two weeks ago?'

'No, scouting then jettisoning the bombs has been going on for a while. Two weeks ago we crashed into the sea. And that's what changed everything.'

They sat expectantly while William lit another cigarette.

'Stan and I were on patrol a long way from shore. We hadn't seen any ships and were about to head back when the engine started to judder and then it failed completely. Fortunately the sea was calm and I managed to make a forced landing. Stan was thrown backwards against the gun and it fired. I nearly leapt out of my skin I can tell you. But Stan went berserk. He almost tipped the plane over when he leant over the side and the next thing I knew he was thrashing about in the water. I held out my hand to him but he was trying to get to the bomb rack. I asked him what the hell he thought he was doing and he screamed we'd got to get rid of the bombs.'

William's voice became louder and more urgent as he continued. 'I ordered him to get back in the plane but he became hysterical. He'd jumped in with all his kit and was beginning to sink. I took off my boots and jacket, tied a lifeline to my waist, and lowered myself into the water. I managed to get hold of Stan but he tried to push me under the water. I kneed him in the groin and when he went limp I pulled us both back onto the plane. He was thrashing about, cussing and swearing, so I tied him up firmly, scribbled a note with our position and circumstances and gave it to one of the pigeons.'

'How long did you have to wait?' asked Alice quietly.

'Several hours. I don't really remember.' William's face went blank.

'And then what happened?' prodded Humphrey.

'Stan calmed down after a while so I untied him and we both had some brandy. But he wouldn't look me in the eye and carried on muttering about the bombs. Then he cried himself to sleep. He was still asleep when the ship arrived. They thought he was concussed. I was pretty tired myself by that time. Anyway we got on board and they towed our plane back to port.'

'But that isn't the end of the story?' persisted Humphrey.

'No. I had to give a report. I just stuck to the facts. There didn't seem any point in saying that Stan had blabbed like a baby. He's avoided me ever since. But he's obviously been talking to some of the high-ups. I was called in again later. They asked me to resign my commission.'

Alice gasped. 'But it wasn't your fault the engine failed.'

'No, but Stan spilled the beans about the bombs. Of course we wouldn't have been expected to get rid of the bombs on that trip but Stan seemed to think it necessary to tell them about our little habit of ditching them into the sea on previous occasions.'

'The little rat,' said Lottie quietly.

'They might agree with you, disloyalty isn't encouraged. Anyway they were very civil. I could have been kicked out but the letter says that I'm a good pilot although I have shown little enthusiasm for engaging with the enemy.'

Humphrey busied himself with his pipe. 'You may have saved that boy's life, you certainly saved his reputation. And you're a first class pilot, we've always known that and your letter confirms it. The Navy needs to hang on to its pilots, especially men with experience like you.' He sighed as he regarded his son. 'So, what happens now?'

Abruptly William got up and went to the window. Lottie could see the tension in his shoulders as he stood with his back to them.

'I'm being posted to Calshott, assigned to technical duties."

'At least you'll be safe,' said Alice with relief.

William spun round angrily. 'Do you think that's what I want? Don't be so stupid!'

'How dare you speak to your mother like that!' Humphrey glared at his son.

Lottie fixed her eyes on William's anguished face as he attempted to control himself.

'I'm sorry Mother. But don't you understand; I failed to do my duty and as a result I'm no longer a flight lieutenant.'

He clutched his arm where his stripe had been and looked steadily at his father. 'I'm sorry for bringing shame on the family.'

'Where is Calshott?' Lottie's voice was barely audible.

'It's a naval base on Southampton Water,' said Humphrey when William did not reply.

Lottie wondered why Mrs Dacre had said William would be safe, it was common knowledge that German U boats patrolled the area and a seaplane base would be a likely target. But, at least he wouldn't be risking his life in the air.

It was some time before anyone spoke. Then Alice said, 'I've prepared some lunch. Come, Lottie, you can help me dish up.'

The food went some way to nourishing their spirits. Alice and Humphrey talked about their plans for Trealaw and Lottie said she'd like to do another painting. When they had finished Lottie stacked the plates and started to carry them into the kitchen.

'When do you plan to get married?' she heard Alice ask William quietly.

She didn't hear his reply but when she came back to the dining room she was perturbed to see the grim expression had returned to William's face and his mother had a worried frown.

***

Lottie had hoped to linger on the mountain but William was anxious to get back. His dark mood had returned and, after a couple of attempts at conversation, Lottie gave up and tried to enjoy her unaccustomed freedom.

They walked quickly down the mountain track, through the town and across the suspension bridge. When they were nearly at the station William stopped and looked at his watch.

'The London train should be arriving any minute,' he said.

'But you've only just come!'

'I've been here all day.'

'Yes, but … aren't you going to stay?'

William looked above her head. 'What for?' he asked bleakly.

Lottie looked puzzled. 'To talk about our wedding.'

William's face was a mask of pain as he looked at Lottie. 'I can't marry you now,' he said.

Lottie felt panic rising inside her. 'But I'm twenty-one now!'

'I know. But I'm no longer an officer.'

'What difference does that make?' Lottie's head was pounding.

William held both her hands in his. 'Lottie, I'm disgraced. I can't marry you. It wouldn't be honourable.'

Lottie felt a searing pain in her chest. She bowed her head and was surprised to see the diamond on her left hand was still sparkling. 'But you said you loved me,' she said desperately.

'I know. But I'm not worthy of you any more.'

Lottie pushed the ring further down her finger. 'Of course you are! What happened is nothing to do with us.'

'It's everything to do with us. I don't have a rank any more.'

'But you didn't when we met.' Lottie felt a flash of anger. 'I don't care about your rank!'

There was a hoot and they could hear the train rumbling over the bridge.

'But I do and so will your parents.'

'No they won't!'

William started walking quickly towards the station.

'Don't go!' cried Lottie and ran after him.

One or two people gave them curious looks as Lottie chased William up the steps and onto the platform.

The train wheezed into the station and a few people got off. William hurried towards a first class carriage and a porter opened the door. He looked at Lottie disdainfully as she clung onto William and begged him not to leave.

'That'll be all.' William spoke sharply to the porter.

He took Lottie in his arms, kissed her on the lips then pushed her away. Before she could follow him he jumped into the compartment and slammed the door.

With a shriek Lottie hurled herself forward and grabbed the handle. Her eyes met William's as she tried to wrench the door open. For a moment she thought her nightmare was ending when she saw his hand reach towards the door handle.

Then a whistle sounded and the train jolted forward, sending her staggering along the platform. Sobbing violently Lottie ran alongside, her eyes riveted on William's white face pressed against the window as the train snaked out of the station.

Chapter 19: Alice

Plans for 'Baby Week'
Arrangements for the celebration of National Baby Week
are being completed in London and throughout the country

The Times: June 13th 1917

'Do you think William meant it when he said he couldn't marry Lottie?' asked Alice as their train sped out of Wales towards London.

Humphrey frowned. 'I don't think the boy knew what he was saying.'

'I wish we'd called on the Rowes before we left.'

'And I think it would have been inappropriate.'

'Perhaps Daisy will talk some sense into him.'

Humphrey's features relaxed. 'Maybe. Though he's not going to find it easy telling Alec he's no longer an officer. Especially now that Alec's been awarded his medal.'

'I don't care about medals or ranks; I just want William to be happy.'

'I agree with you. Absolutely. But not everyone would.'

Alice looked at her husband. 'You're right. I wonder what Alec's parents will say?'

'If Alec's any sense he won't tell them. Anyway it's none of their business.'

The train slowed as they approached a station and they fell silent.

...

Humphrey insisted on going into his office when they arrived at Euston so Alice took a cab on her own.

She wondered if William would be home or if he was already in Calshott.

The sun was shining but even the street market they drove past looked drab. There was a long queue at a stall selling eggs with two emaciated little girls offering sprigs of lavender to people as they shuffled forward, while poorly dressed women were gathered around a second hand clothes stall fingering the fine garments that were no longer fashionable. The traffic thinned out as the cab neared Belsize Park and Alice was relieved when they turned into the familiar side street.

As the driver carried her luggage to the porch Alice noticed a young woman in the distance with a baby in her arms. Still feeling raw after the death of little Peter she paused for a moment, fighting an irrational desire to ask the woman if the baby was all right. Then she rang the bell and listened to it echo in the empty hallway.

'Ethel must be out,' she muttered as she took her key and unlocked the door. The driver lifted the bags into the hall, thanked Alice for the tip and left. She stood in the silent hall for a moment then took off her hat and jacket and put them in the carved oak cupboard. Several of William's coats and hats were hanging up but Daisy had left nothing behind when she left home to begin life as a married woman.

There were some letters on the hall table. One was for William addressed untidily in a cheap envelope. Alice picked up a letter from the Waifs and Strays society and another in Daisy's handwriting. Her eyes strayed to a sepia photograph above the table of Daisy as a baby smiling into the camera, her face framed by a halo of curls. She studied the photograph and tried to remember Daisy and William as babies but the memories were vague. She was startled to hear footsteps and jumped when Ethel emerged from the other end of the hall carrying a bunch of sweet peas.

'Oh, you're back, Ma'am. I was just in the garden picking these flowers for your return. I hope you had a good journey?'

'Yes, thank you. Is William at home?'

'He went to Gloucestershire yesterday to see Miss Daisy, I mean Mrs Hammond. He said he'd be back tomorrow and then he's off to Calshott, I think he said.'

'And there weren't any problems while we were away?'

'No, everything was fine. Shall I make some tea?'

'Yes please. I'll take my letters to the front sitting room.'

Daisy wrote regularly and not much had happened since her last letter. Alice wondered why Daisy thought she'd be interested in a description of her mother-in-law's new evening gown.

She put the letter aside and saw that the woman she had seen earlier was standing by the gate. She watched her hesitate before carefully adjusting her bundle and lift the latch. Alice looked puzzled then stood up as recognition dawned. The young woman was Cilla and she was carrying a baby. The jaunty angle of her hat and confident tilt of her head did not fool Alice who took in the tenseness of the mouth and desperation in her beautiful eyes as she walked down the garden path. Alice sat down, folded her hands and waited.

'There's a young woman to see you, Ma'am,' announced Ethel in surprise.

'Thank you. Please show her in.'

Ethel nodded and the next moment Cilla was standing defiantly in front of Alice, her arms held tightly around the baby. She attempted to smile but her teeth were chattering.

'Can you bring tea for both of us, Ethel?'

Alice smiled encouragingly at the trembling girl and stood up. She lifted the baby's shawl and gazed at the tiny face. Hardly daring to breathe she held out her arms and Cilla gave her the baby.

'He's yours. Your grandson.'

'My grandson?'

She held him silently for a moment feeling the warmth of his body against hers then looked at Cilla questioningly. 'William – and you?'

A ghost of a smile twisted across the girl's face. 'It was a mistake, I'm the wrong sister.'

The women stood silently looking at each other, then at the baby as he punched his fist in the air.

'Will that be all Ma'am?' asked Ethel as she came into the room with a tea tray and looked curiously at the baby.

Alice wondered what her maid would think if she knew the child was William's illegitimate son. 'Yes, that's all for the moment, thank you Ethel.'

She felt tears prick her eyelids. It was the first time she'd held a baby since that awful day when Peter had died. She stroked his cheek and sat down, suddenly aware that she too was trembling.

She motioned to the carved Japanese tea table. 'You can pour the tea.'

Cilla's hand shook as she poured milk into the china cups, held the tea strainer over it and poured in the tea. 'Do you take sugar?' she asked politely.

'Yes, please.' Alice inclined her head thinking that, whatever the girl had done, she hadn't lost her manners. She sipped her tea while gently rocking the infant.

Cilla sat on the edge of the settee her eyes fixed on Alice. 'So – so you like him then?'

Alice smiled proprietarily. 'Like' was hardly sufficient to describe the passion she suddenly felt for the baby in her arms, her first grandson, whatever the circumstances of his birth.

'He's perfect. What's his name?'

'Neville.'

'And how old is he?'

Cilla looked agitated. 'He's five weeks. And they don't let you stay after six weeks.'

'Who don't? Where are you staying?'

'The mother and baby home. They send the babies to the orphanage at six weeks."

Alice had an image of rows cots each with a distressed infant and involuntarily tightened her grip on the baby. 'Does William know he has a son?'

Cilla shook her head.

'And your parents? And Lottie?'

'When we were little our father said he would throw us out if we misbehaved. We are a very respectable family.'

And so are we, thought Alice grimly, but war has turned everything upside down.

'And I couldn't bear to hurt Lottie. She's so kind and good and she has a drawer full of trousseau she's been making for her wedding.' Cilla's eyes filled with tears.

'So what do you propose to do?' Alice felt her heart beat faster in anticipation.

Cilla lowered her eyes. 'I, I thought you could have him,' she whispered.

Alice remained silent, trying to check the joy bubbling inside her.

Then Cilla raised her glistening eyes and said solemnly, 'And it would be our secret.'

The baby whimpered; Alice stroked his fair hair and rocked him gently. On the table lay the letter from the Waifs and Strays society.

'You can't keep a baby a secret,' she said.

'I kept him a secret for seven months. Then I gave up my job and went to stay at the home.'

Alice had a sense of déjà vu as she said, 'Perhaps you should start at the beginning. What happened to your soldier friend?'

'He was killed at the Front three months after I arrived in London. His sister didn't really want me but she let me stay till I got the job on the buses. I moved into a hostel. They were a nice group of girls. We went out dancing most nights and drowned our sorrows.'

Alice raised an eyebrow.

'Most of us had lost someone,' Cilla said dismissively.

'And William?'

'When he heard Len had been killed he came to the hostel to see me but I was working. Then, quite by chance, he got on my bus. Was surprised to see me. Like you were. Anyway, I was finishing my shift and so he took me dancing. It was nice to be with someone who knew my family. We talked about Lottie; we were both missing her. We went out once or twice when he came to London on an overnight pass and one thing led to another. Times have changed, Mrs Dacre,' she said defiantly.

Alice crooked her finger and brushed it against the baby's cheek.

'When did you last see William?'

'The day you got on my bus. We hadn't seen each other for some time. We went out that evening but things weren't right. William was anxious about another winter flying in bad conditions. And I was feeling sick though I didn't know why. And we were both feeling bad about Lottie. So we agreed not to see each other again.'

'And what about other boyfriends?'

'Other boyfriends? I wasn't two-timing if that's what you mean.' Cilla leant forward. 'He is your grandson, I swear it.'

Alice felt the baby's heart beating close to hers as she stroked his hair and knew his mother was telling the truth. 'And how did you feel after you and William stopped seeing each other?'

'We weren't really seeing each other; he only came to London a couple of times. It was a relief to be able to write to Lottie with a clear conscience. That is, until I knew I was expecting. That's why I wouldn't see her when she came down for Daisy's wedding. I moved to another hostel where no one knew me. I carried on working as long as I could, I didn't really start to show till the last month and I was in the home then. When Neville was born I wrote to Lottie and said I was moving and I'd be in touch again as soon as I could. Do you know if she's all right?'

For a moment Alice said nothing, wishing things weren't so complicated, she liked everything cut and dried. The shame of William losing his commission was only just beginning to sink in. But an illegitimate child was far more serious. She tried to concentrate but for the moment all she could see was Baby Peter's pram abandoned under a hedge.

Alice rocked the baby in her arms. 'I don't know how Lottie is,' she said truthfully. 'I think she's worried about your mother.'

'What's the matter with her?'

'Her arthritis is getting worse. Your father needs Lottie to help in the shop and run the house. It's a …,' she began then stopped. It wasn't appropriate to say that she thought it was a pity that William and Lottie couldn't get married and live together in Southampton.

'I suppose it's time I went to see them all.' Cilla half rose then sat down with her head in her hands.

Alice held the baby closer. He coughed gently, leaving a tiny dribble at the corner of his mouth. Taking a handkerchief from her sleeve Alice tenderly wiped his lips.

'So, will you take him?' Cilla looked up at Alice, her huge brown eyes full of trust.

'And what would we tell William?'

Cilla pointed to the letter on the table. 'That you've taken in a waif and stray.'

Alice looked down at the baby, her own flesh and blood, and he gazed back at her. 'He's not a waif or a stray,' she began then stopped as she realised that's just what he was – not an orphan but an illegitimate child, a product of the war.

She stood up and handed the baby to Cilla. 'I'll talk to Humphrey. Now I expect he needs feeding and changing before you take him back.'

'Back?' whispered Cilla.

'Yes, till we've decided what to do. I'll telephone the home tomorrow.'

'But, you will take him?'

Alice was surprised Cilla couldn't hear her heart shouting 'Yes!' as she calmly replied, 'I'll let you know.'

***

As soon as Cilla and the baby had gone Alice went upstairs and ran a bath. Her eyes closed as her body relaxed in the warm, scented water but her mind was racing. Images of William in the sea struggling with his observer, of William and Lottie walking towards Trealaw, of William and Lottie joking with Cilla in London when she said she wanted to be a bus conductor, of William and Cilla ...... Alice banished her thoughts and briskly scrubbed herself.

She dressed with care and wondered, anxiously, what Humphrey's reaction would be to this second crisis of William's. And would he see that there was only one solution?

Alice peered at herself in the bedroom mirror. Her figure was still good and, despite a few grey hairs, she felt younger than her forty-eight years. The Welsh air and hard physical work at Trealaw had rejuvenated her.

She went downstairs and put some dance music on the gramophone. She hummed and swayed with the tune and didn't hear Humphrey come in a few minutes later.

'You look very gay,' he said. 'The change of air must have done you good. Is William home?'

'He's staying with Daisy, returning tomorrow.'

'It'll be good to see him before he goes to Calshott. It won't be easy for him but he'll do a good job. It's a pity he can't settle down and get married, Lottie's a good influence.'

'Yes. Shall I ask Ethel for some tea or would you like a glass of port?'

'I had tea in the office, port would be very nice. Port and lemonade for you?'

'Yes please.'

'Has Daisy any news?' asked Humphrey looking at the letter on the table.

'Not a lot. William will be able to fill us in.'

'And I see you've got a letter from the Waifs and Strays society. I admire the work you do for them. It's a sign of the times that there are so many of these poor children abandoned by their parents. A lot of the fathers probably don't even know they've got a child.'

'No, they don't. Humphrey …' Alice drew a deep breath and told him about Cilla's visit bringing news of their grandson.

He listened attentively then stood up. 'Damn the boy!' he shouted. He stood for a moment, his hands clasped behind his back. 'And Cilla? Is she a fit mother or a common little tart?'

Alice winced. 'The young woman who came this afternoon was a frightened, remorseful girl who wants the best for her son and her sister.'

'She always seemed headstrong.' Humphrey took out his pipe. 'Do you think William should marry her?'

'I don't know what to think. Cilla said she wanted to keep it a secret.'

'You can't keep a child a secret!'

'That's what I said. But I suppose, if we took him, we could keep his parentage a secret.'

'No grandson of mine is going to think he's a common bastard.'

'So, do you think we should bring him up as our son?' Alice tried to be calm but she could hear the eagerness in her voice.

'We'll let the matter rest till William comes home tomorrow.'

***

The evening sun was still warm when Humphrey came home the following day and they sat in the conservatory waiting for William to arrive. Alice had asked Ethel to prepare a cold meal and had given her the evening off.

Humphrey had just handed Alice a drink when the front door slammed and William burst in, his face glowing with excitement.

'Daisy's talked sense into me!' he shouted. 'I've been thinking about what she said all the way back and I'm going to write and tell Lottie that we'll get married and live in Southampton.' He kissed Alice and beamed

260

at his father. 'Daisy will be pleased when I tell her I've decided to take her advice; she said she'd been looking forward to having Lottie as a sister-in-law.' He laughed. 'She said she hoped Lottie would keep me in order!'

'It's a bit late for that I'm afraid.'

William laughed again but stopped abruptly when he saw his father wasn't making a joke. 'What's happened? Has something happened to Lottie?' A look of panic swept over him.

'In a way, yes.' Humphrey paused before informing him that he was the father of Cilla's illegitimate son and that he had responsibilities to the child.

The colour drained from William's face as he sank into a chair.

'Do you deny it?'

Alice winced as Humphrey addressed his son as if he were a suspect he was interrogating.

He shook his head and listened, his eyes downcast, as Humphrey proposed what they were going to do.

'There are two reasons we have to act quickly. The baby will be put in an orphanage if no arrangements are made by the end of the week and you have to report to Calshot the day after tomorrow. If you're in agreement, we will go to the mother and baby home tomorrow to sign the necessary papers and bring our grandson home.'

Alice's heart missed a beat. Humphrey hadn't spoken to her about his plans but he had obviously understood how much she wanted to care for their grandson. She made a determined effort not to show her joy.

'And Cilla?' she asked, aware that the misery on William's face mirrored that of Cilla's the previous afternoon.

'We will respect her wish that the child's identity remain a secret for the time being at least. Is that acceptable?'

William's nod was barely perceptible.

'Ethel has left us a cold meal, I think we should eat now,' said Alice and led the way to the dining room.

No one had much appetite and they did not linger over the meal. As they left the room Alice noticed the letter for William on the hall table. 'You have some post,' she said.

William frowned as he looked at the post mark. 'Dover,' he muttered and tore open the envelope. He pulled out a blank sheet of paper.

Alice gasped as a white feather fluttered to the floor.

William looked at it in horror then bent to pick it up.

'Leave it, son.' Humphrey rested his hand on William's shoulder. 'Take no notice.'

But William shook him away. He ground the feather underfoot then turned and hurried upstairs.

Chapter 20: Lottie

Baby Week
*Mr Herbert Smith MP said that it was of vital
importance to save all the infants in the country to
grow to manhood and womanhood. Some might regard
a baby merely as another mouth to feed, but if it had a
rapacious mouth it also had two active little hands
which would in time produce more than the mouths
would eat; the larger the population the wealthier the
nation*

The Times: July 6th 1917

'Now then, Lottie, it's time you pulled yourself
together,' her father said, not unkindly, when they had
finished their evening meal.

Her eyes were no longer red from weeping but her
cheeks were hollow and her clothes were beginning to
hang from her shrinking body.

'They say that flying confuses men's minds. Now
that William's no longer having to operate one of those
machines he'll see sense and come running back,'
Nellie said placidly as she massaged her knee.

Lottie frowned. 'I used to pray that something
would happen to stop him flying, something not too
serious like Alec's injury, but I never thought it would
work out like this.'

'Prayers have a strange way of being answered.'
Jack looked at his daughter thoughtfully. 'Perhaps you
should go and stay with your aunt and uncle for a few
days. It's a pity they moved to Llnrwst but Owen seems
to be doing well there. I'm sure your Auntie Meg could
do with some help, and a change of scenery will do you
good. We can manage for a day or two can't we,
Nellie?'

'Well, we'll have to manage when Lottie leaves home to get married.'

Jack looked at his wife in exasperation. 'I'll send word for them to expect you in a couple of days then?' he said to Lottie.

Lottie made a determined effort to be positive. 'Yes I'd like to see them all again. I'm sorry I've not been much help recently. Let me do the books for you before I go.'

'That's my girl.' Jack got up and brought the ledgers to the table.

***

Lottie tried hard to put on a smile for the customers the following day despite the leaden feeling in her stomach.

After supper she went into the yard to water the tomatoes she had planted in the spring. She was just about to return indoors when she heard the gate click.

'William?' she whispered and turned round, hardly daring to look.

Standing absolutely still was her sister, her auburn hair tumbling around her white face and an unfathomable expression in her green eyes.

'Cilla!" exclaimed Lottie and hugged her.

Cilla stood with her arms by her sides, her knuckles white as she clutched her bag.

'Cilla's come home!' shouted Lottie as she took her sister's bag and hurried into the house.

She regarded her parents anxiously as they looked at their younger daughter who, after a quick flicker of her eyes around the room, fixed her gaze on the floor tiles.

'It's so good you're back, we've missed you so much, haven't we?' Lottie looked desperately at her parents.

'Aye, we've missed you well enough,' said Jack.

'What you did was shameful, Cilla. I never thought a daughter of mine would behave like that. But they say blood's thicker than water and this is your home and it's right that you've come back to us.'

Cilla looked up as her mother shuffled stiffly towards her and gave her a kiss on the cheek.

'I need to use the privy,' she whispered.

'She looks all in,' said Jack grudgingly when Cilla had left the room.

'She's had a long journey and the trains are so unreliable these days. I'll make a brew.' Lottie busied herself with the teapot.

'Make it nice and sweet,' said Nellie.

'Are you all right?' asked Lottie when her sister walked slowly back into the house.

'I feel a bit funny.' Cilla sat down and looked at the teacup before her.

'Drink up,' coaxed Lottie.

'Thank you,' she said with a glimmer of a smile as she drank the tea. 'I haven't had sugar in my tea for a while.'

'It's not easy with all these shortages but we manage,' said Nellie. 'Now, how about a slice of bread and jam?'

Cilla shook her head. 'I'm not hungry.' She looked at the door to the stairs. 'Is my bed still there?'

'You didn't think we'd sold it?' Jack said gruffly.

'It's not made up, we didn't want the sheets getting damp; I'll go and do it now.' Lottie ran upstairs feeling better than she had done since William left. She wondered what Cilla would think of their bedroom after so long. If she had known she was coming she would have picked some flowers. She was dying to tell Cilla how unhappy she was but she knew she would have to wait until her sister had had a good night's sleep.

***

Cilla scowled at the elderly bus conductor as he joked with the woman sitting in the front seat.

'Do you hear that now?' He turned to the rest of the passengers and relayed the gossip, then made his way slowly down the bus, joking with everyone as he punched their tickets.

'And who will you be visiting in Llanrwst?' he asked when Lottie told him their destination.

'Our uncle and aunt. Owen the builder, I expect you know him.'

"Owen the builder, of course. How many children does he have now?'

'Three. Two boys and a little girl.'

Lottie was surprised to feel Cilla's elbow digging in her side. 'What did you say that for?' she hissed when the conductor walked on.

'I was replying to his questions.'

'But it wasn't any of his business.'

'He was only being friendly.'

'London bus conductors aren't nosey like that. We are properly trained.'

'Well, you're not in London now,' Lottie said sharply.

She was upset because Cilla had rebuffed all her attempts to confide in her. When she had told her about William breaking off their engagement Cilla had just looked blank and Lottie wondered if she had even heard.

As she twisted her engagement ring, now relegated to her right hand, Lottie wondered why Cilla had not been in contact and had then suddenly come home. She was trying to imagine Cilla's life in London when the bus backfired and she jumped with a start.

'Careful, Driver. We'll think there's bombs falling,' said the conductor jovially.

Some of the passengers laughed, but a young man in army uniform looked scared. Lottie glanced at Cilla who was sitting bolt upright, her face expressionless. She wished the conductor hadn't joked about bombs. Although they weren't directly affected by the war in this beautiful valley, most of the passengers must know people who were. She wondered what terrible sights the soldier had witnessed. Since William's last visit, she was more aware of the realities of war. She wished he had told her more about his life as a pilot before the incident that led to him losing his commission. And what about her sister who had returned home a stranger? Was it Len's death that had affected her so deeply? Or perhaps she had been caught up in one of the recent air raids over London? As Lottie looked out of the window at the heather-covered hillsides she found it hard to visualise an air raid. She shivered as she tried to imagine how it must feel to hear the sound of sirens and then the roar of enemy aircraft, not knowing where the bombs would drop.

The bus stopped to take on more passengers and when Lottie looked out of the window she glimpsed Mynydd Brith in the distance. She swallowed and closed her eyes. She had lain awake for the last two nights listening to her sister's breathing in the bed next to hers. Cilla had slept heavily until the early hours but, just as Lottie was dropping off to sleep, she had cried out. When Lottie tried to soothe her she had pushed her away then turned over and gone back to sleep.

***

The bus came to a halt in the centre of the village and the girls took their bags and walked towards a row of cottages near the river. A little girl was waving by the gate of the end cottage.

'Megan! Haven't you grown!' said Lottie as she opened the gate.

The child smiled shyly and ran into the house.

Auntie Meg came out, wiping her hands on her apron. 'It's lovely to see you both.' She kissed them then stepped back. 'My, you need feeding up, the pair of you," she said, eyeing them critically.

'My father sent some provisions.' Lottie put some packages on the table.

'They'll come in handy. Now I've made some Welsh cakes so you sit down and eat those while you tell me all your news.' She bustled about but her eyes kept darting to the drawn faces of her nieces.

'Where are the boys?' asked Lottie.

'Working with their father.'

'Little Owen as well?' Surprise made Cilla speak.

'He's nine years old now and likes to help in the holidays. And Efan has just finished school so he's apprentice to his father now.'

'He didn't want to stay on then?' asked Lottie.

'No, he's not bookish like his cousins.' Auntie Meg smiled at the girls. 'He left as soon as he could and I must say we're glad of it.'

'And, Megan's all right now?' Lottie turned to the dark-haired child munching her Welsh cake.

'Has she been poorly?' Cilla looked anxiously at the child.

'She was a poorly baby, as you know, but she wasn't so bad this winter and she's been fine since Easter.'

'You must have been so worried when she was poorly.'

'Yes, we were.' Auntie Meg looked keenly at Cilla's white face then turned to Lottie. 'I was sorry to hear about your engagement.'

Lottie nodded and fiddled with her ring.

'What about your engagement?' demanded Cilla.

'I've been trying to tell you. William and I aren't engaged anymore.'

Cilla gasped. 'But you must be! You've got to be!'

'It's not my fault!' Lottie glared at her sister. 'It wasn't me who said I wasn't good enough to marry me!'

'But of course you're good enough!'

Lottie was shaking but determined not to cry in front of Megan who was staring at her cousins with bits of Welsh cake dribbling down her chin.

'It's complicated.' She turned to her aunt, unable to bear her sister's eyes boring into hers. 'Something happened in the war.' Her voice trembled. 'I don't really understand.'

Auntie Meg looked sympathetically at each of the girls. 'Maybe you'd like to take a walk? Megan's ready for her nap and I've got a few chores to do.'

'But wouldn't you like us to help you?' asked Lottie dutifully as she fought back her tears.

'Tomorrow perhaps. I think you should catch the sunshine while you can.'

***

Silently, Lottie led the way along a path by the river.

'Let's sit down,' she said when they were out of sight of the village.

She expected her sister to throw herself on her stomach with her legs in the air as she used to when they visited the country or the beach; or even pull off her shoes and paddle in the cool water. But she seated herself carefully and plucked a blade of grass, which she proceeded to chew.

'Do you want me to tell you about me and William?' Lottie asked when she could stand the silence no longer.

Cilla pulled another blade of grass and nodded.

Lottie spoke quietly as she recounted William's last visit. She managed to keep her voice calm as she described the incident on the plane when the observer went berserk and later when he betrayed William. But her voice broke as she started to tell her sister about the scene on the station and she couldn't carry on.

'I'm so, so sorry Lottie. It's all my fault,' Cilla whispered.

Lottie stared at her sister, wondering if she had gone a bit crazy. 'What are you talking about? William says he can't marry me because he isn't an officer anymore.'

'Oh!' Cilla stared at Lottie. 'When did he say that?'

Lottie told her and couldn't make out the expression on her sister's face but was pleased to see her give a half smile.

'You must marry him. He loves you,' she said simply.

'He's got a strange way of showing it.'

'Has he written to you?'

Lottie bit her lip. 'No,' she whispered and involuntarily looked upwards at the mountain that reminded her of Mynydd Brith.

'I expect he's been busy. The shock and everything. Or maybe his letter's gone missing.'

'Maybe,' Lottie said forlornly but felt a glimmer of hope. 'And what about you?' she asked, suddenly feeling guilty that she had been too wrapped up in her own misery to find out what was troubling Cilla.

'Me? I'm all right.'

Lottie looked at her steadily. 'I was so disappointed I didn't see you when I was in London for Daisy's wedding.'

'I really appreciated the presents you brought,' she said.

'Yes, you wrote and thanked me. And then you suddenly stopped writing. I was worried about you.'

Cilla stood up. 'I know. But I'm home now. So you don't have to worry anymore.'

'But I do worry.' Lottie got up and brushed grass off her skirt. 'Was it ever dangerous working on the buses?'

'Dangerous? It depends what you mean. But, yes, I suppose it was dangerous in some ways. You never knew who was going to get on your bus.' Cilla looked thoughtfully at Lottie then began to walk back along the riverbank.

Lottie followed, upset by the way her sister had changed from a lively and affectionate child to a troubled and distant young woman. When she caught up, Cilla was leaning against a gate by a hedgerow. They stood in silence for a while, watching a young blackbird hopping in the shelter of the hedge while its mother was busily tugging up worms. When it had a beakful, it hopped over to its young and thrust them into the upturned beaks.

Lottie bent down and picked up a speckled greenish blue egg almost hidden under a leaf.

'Oh look! This one didn't hatch.' She cupped the egg in her hand and showed it to Cilla.

Cilla nodded and her shoulders began to shake. 'She lost her baby!' she wailed.

'But it wasn't a baby, it was just an egg.' Lottie looked at her sister in dismay as she began to sob uncontrollably. She fumbled in her pocket for a handkerchief. 'Let me dry your eyes.'

When she put her arm round Cilla she felt her grief like a charge of lightning and she too began to sob.

'Oh, Lottie! I've missed you so much!' Cilla clung tightly to her and Lottie felt her sister's tears mingle with her own.

She stroked Cilla's hair and, feeling comforted by the once familiar action, her sobs began to subside. 'I've missed you too. I just wish you would tell me what's troubling you.'

Cilla pulled away, her eyes fixed on a point in the distance and her shoulders heaving as she fought to control her crying. 'I'm tired,' she said after a while. 'I needed to get out of London. It's noisy and dirty and … difficult.'

'Everything's difficult these days. But things will be easier now you're home.' Lottie tenderly wiped her sister's face with the sodden handkerchief.

As they stood listening to the river babbling beside them Lottie was relieved to hear Cilla's sobs gradually subside. Her own heartbeat began to return to normal but she had an empty feeling in the pit of her stomach as they walked slowly back to the village.

Auntie Meg and Megan were walking towards the butchers.

'Shall we join them?' asked Lottie.

'All right,' Cilla said uncommunicatively.

'Hello, girls. Are you coming with us?'

'I think we'll go back to the house. Is there anything we can do for you?' asked Lottie.

Auntie Meg looked at their tear-stained faces. 'It's all right. You make yourselves comfortable. You'll be sleeping in the boys' room and they'll be downstairs.'

'I hope they won't mind giving up their beds.'

'Of course they won't. They've been looking forward to seeing you. They want to hear all about London.'

Cilla gave a wan smile. 'Then I'll have to tell them, won't I?'

***

Lottie was pleased to see glimpses of the old Cilla as they sat round the table in the evening and she told them about the fun she had with the girls she lived with in the hostel. Little Owen was intrigued that his cousin was a bus conductor and made her tell them all about her job.

'And will you be going back?' asked her uncle.

Cilla's eyes glistened as she looked down at her plate. 'No; I won't be going back.'

'Will you get a job at the Junction? I hear they're employing female booking clerks now.'

Cilla flinched. 'Actually, I've decided to work in munitions.'

'But there aren't any factories here,' Lottie said, fearful that she was going to lose her sister again.

'There's a factory in Warrington that has a hostel for the female workers.'

There was a pause as everyone stared at Cilla.

'Where's Warrington?' asked Efan.

'In the north of England.'

'It's miles away!' said Lottie.

'But it's not London!' Cilla eyed them triumphantly.

'I don't think you should be going anywhere till you're better.' Auntie Meg looked thoughtfully at Cilla's pinched face.

'Don't worry; I'm not leaving tomorrow,' she replied coolly.

As Lottie watched her sister holding everyone's attention she felt that she was losing her again. The intimacy they had shared by the river had gone and she wondered if it would ever be regained.

August 1917

Calshot
Dear Mother and Father
I hope everything is all right at home.

I keep very busy here. There's hardly any free time for the likes of me. We used to think we were hard done by but the officers have it easy compared with us – except when they're flying of course. The pilots are so young – God help them. I had much more flying experience than them when I went on my first mission. But they are brave boys and their eyesight is better than mine, though I don't know how long that will last – goggles aren't always effective against the constant glare.

The maintenance department is a bit of a shambles. I must admit, I had my suspicions when I was flying but I think it's got worse. The supply chain often breaks down and then we have to make do and mend. I just keep my head down and get on with the job as best I can.

I guess I'm here till the end of the war – whenever that is. The Yanks' arrival doesn't seem to have made any difference yet.

I had a letter from Hilda. Shame she's still stuck at home on the farm but it's essential work.

Hope you're both keeping well. Make sure you find time for a walk on the Heath, I often think of picnics there when Daisy and I were children.

Yours affectionately,
William

Chapter 21: Alice

*The Field Marshall Commander in Chief, Home
Forces, issued the following communiqué at 12.15 this
morning:
'Hostile aircraft crossed the south east coast in relays
between 10.45 and 11.50 pm on October 31st and
proceeded towards London. The raid is still in
progress.*

The Times: November 1st 1917

Alice put down her pen and rubbed her hands together
to try and warm them. She blotted the envelope and
regarded the name she had written carefully in her
copperplate hand – 'Miss Priscilla Rowe.'

Cilla's stilted letter from Warrington had remained
unanswered for some time while Alice pondered how
to reply. Finally she took refuge in formality and wrote
a short reply assuring her that Neville was progressing
well and that they were all in good health. It was only
the second letter she had received from Cilla since she
had meekly handed over her son five months earlier.

From Lottie, there had been nothing. Alice shivered,
determinedly pushing away any thoughts of the two
sisters.

It was William who concerned her. They had not
heard from him for over two months and he never
mentioned Neville. She wished he would write more
often or at least show some interest in his son.

There was a tap on the door.

'Come in Ethel.' Alice stood up.

'I'm going to give Neville his bath now, Ma'am.'

'Thank you. I'll come and give you a hand.'

Ethel was thoroughly enjoying having a baby to
look after but Alice had been unable to employ anyone

to take over the cooking and so she helped Ethel with caring for Neville and cooking. As they rarely entertained these days it was not a big issue although she didn't know how they would manage if their daily help stopped coming.

'He's come on so well, haven't you my lovely.' Ethel knelt by the bath, her hand lightly resting on Neville's back as he sat splashing and laughing.

'He's a joy,' Alice replied.

'He was such a tiny scrap when you brought him back from the home. I suppose the mother didn't have enough milk to feed him properly.' Ethel busied herself with the sponge, carefully washing between Neville's toes.

'I don't think the home had sufficient funds to give the mothers nourishing food.' Alice looked at Neville's plump little legs and wondered what would have happened to him if Cilla hadn't asked them to take him in.

'People would rather give money to our boys at the Front,' said Ethel.

I suppose they would.' Alice suddenly realised that she had had more conversations with Ethel in the last five months than in all the time they had lived under the same roof.

'He's lovely and clean now.' Ethel lifted the baby and Alice wrapped him in a large white towel, hugging him closely to her.

As she dried him she wondered, not for the first time, if Ethel had guessed his parents' identity. If she had, she played along with the fiction that Alice's voluntary work at the Waifs and Strays society had led to her and Humphrey taking in a baby. But, lurking at the back of Alice's mind was a constant fear of being forced to give up her grandson. Nothing had been officially signed because Humphrey still insisted that William should bear some responsibility for the child.

'It's time for bed,' Alice said as she carried Neville into the nursery. She dressed him in a beautifully embroidered nightgown, one of the many presents that Daisy had given. Her daughter had been full of admiration for her parents taking on an abandoned baby and Alice tried not to feel guilty about denying her the knowledge that Neville was her nephew.

'How's my little man today?' Humphrey tiptoed into the room and knelt down in front of the chair where Alice was giving Neville his milk. The baby pushed the bottle away and held out his hands when he saw his grandfather.

As Humphrey carried his grandson around the room talking to him in baby language, Alice reflected that she had no recollection of him behaving like that with his own children. She smiled as Neville's head slumped onto Humphrey's shoulder then he gently handed him back to her and left.

Alice rocked the child in her arms as he took a little more milk then she switched out the light and laid him in his crib.

Humphrey was reading the paper when she entered the sitting room.

'How was your day?' Alice asked.

Humphrey shrugged his shoulders. 'How was yours?'

When she had finished telling him, Alice realised she had given him an account of Neville's day but that amounted to almost the same as hers.

'I wrote to Cilla,' she added.

'What did you say?'

'Nothing of consequence. It was just a reply to hers of last week.' Alice paused. 'Things would be much easier if Neville was legally ours. It's what Cilla wanted.'

'Cilla is fortunate we're giving her son a good home.'

'It would be much more straightforward if Neville regarded us as his parents. What if he and Lottie do make up and get married?'

Humphrey frowned. 'That's not likely. Even though he broke off the engagement before any of us knew about Neville I think it was fortuitous.'

'But it will be a problem, whoever he marries.'

'I agree it would be a problem if he married Lottie. But that's not going to happen. He may be courting someone else for all we know. Anyway, I'm not asking William to care for the child, just accept some responsibility for him. He's our grandson after all.'

'But what will he call us? Surely he'll regard us as his parents?'

'What he calls us is irrelevant at the moment. I'm sorry Alice, I can't think about it right now.'

There was a single chime as the clock struck six thirty. Alice got up. 'I'll go and see how Ethel is getting on with the supper.'

She clenched her fists as she walked to the kitchen. She needed the security of knowing that Neville was officially their son but she knew it was a complicated legal process which few people bothered with especially at this time when the courts had more urgent matters to attend to.

However, she was unable to get rid of the nagging fear that, out of a misplaced sense of duty, William might reclaim his son, especially if he had a wife to help care for the child.

***

A walk on the Heath the following morning helped restore Alice's spirits although she still felt a sense of unease on her return.

'I've left Neville sleeping in his pram in the conservatory.' Alice warmed her hands by the kitchen range when she went to tell Ethel they were back.

Ethel looked up from her ironing. 'Did he enjoy the walk?'

'He fell asleep very soon but I'm sure the fresh air did both of us good. And meanwhile you've been busy here.'

'Pressing clothes is so much easier with an electric iron,' said Ethel with satisfaction as she expertly manoeuvred the iron round a frilled blouse of Alice's.

'I suppose it must be. We have a flat iron at Trealaw but I have never had occasion to use it.' Alice moved away from the fire, slightly embarrassed by her implication that she was too lazy to press her own clothes. She busied herself with the teapot, pleased to have something to do.

'You must take a break, Ethel, and have a cup of tea.'

'I'll finish pressing these clothes while I drink it.'

'You work too hard.'

'I'm used to it, Ma'am. And anyway, being busy stops you worrying.'

'Do you worry about the air raids?'

'No. I feel sorry for the poor people who are hit but I don't worry about it happening to us.' Ethel looked at Alice, the iron still in her hand. 'Do you worry?'

'Not really, not for myself anyway. But I worry for William and for Humphrey especially when he's late home.'

'We haven't seen Master William for a long time.'

Alice frowned. 'No. And I haven't heard from him for a while either.'

'Maybe there'll be a letter today.'

'There wasn't anything this morning.' Alice picked up a pile of neatly ironed baby clothes. 'I'll take these upstairs.'

The bell rang as she crossed the hall. She put the clothes on the table and opened the door.

'Good morning, Ma'am.' An elderly man doffed his cap.

'Oh!' Alice stood motionless, staring at the envelope in the telegraph man's outstretched hand.

The man shuffled his feet, waiting for Alice to take the envelope. 'You have a telegram, Ma'am,' he said.

Alice continued to stare at him, feeling suddenly faint.

'Is there anyone else at home?' he asked when she didn't reply.

'Ethel!' Alice turned and absently picked up a baby's bonnet from the clothes on the table.

'Is everything all right, Ma'am?' Ethel bustled along the hall.

'We have a telegram,' said Alice screwing the bonnet into a tight ball. 'Can you bring my purse?'

She took the telegram, tore open the envelope and read the contents. 'I don't understand,' she muttered then fell silent.

The man coughed discreetly. 'Is there a reply Madam?'

'A reply?' Alice looked at Ethel's worried face for inspiration.

'Should we send for Inspector Dacre, Ma'am?'

'No, this is what we'll do.' Alice regained control of the situation. 'I want the same message delivered to Inspector Dacre at Euston Station.' She watched the man copy down the message. 'Wait, there's a bit more. Add: I will meet you there.'

'Here's your purse, Ma'am.' Ethel looked anxiously at Alice.

'Thank you.' Alice counted out some coins. 'Is that sufficient?' She handed them to the man.

'Yes, thank you, Ma'am.'

Ethel closed the door then followed Alice back into the kitchen.

'I shall need some provisions, I may be there a long time.' Alice took a loaf from the bread bin and began hacking slices off it.

'Where are you going Ma'am?' Ethel's voice was agitated.

'St Thomas' Hospital. To see William.'

'Oh no!' Ethel clapped her hand over her mouth. 'What's the matter with him?'

Alice picked up the telegram and frowned. 'It says he was injured in an air raid. But that was three days ago. Why weren't we informed immediately?' Anger galvanised Alice as she wielded the carving knife and added beef to the slices of bread.

'Let me finish this for you Ma'am while you get ready.'

'Thank you, Ethel. I've asked Humphrey to meet me at the hospital. I don't know when we'll be back. Just look after Neville and hold the fort while I'm gone.'

***

The winter sun was beginning to set across the Thames by the time Alice arrived at the hospital. The reception area, with its high ceilings, was thronged with people and for a moment Alice was reminded of the station buffet. She had almost forgotten how unnerving a crowded public building could be but no one would have suspected her unease as she imperiously asked where she could find her son. She listened carefully then ran up two flights of stairs and hurried along a corridor, narrowly missing a nurse pushing a patient on a trolley. At the end of the corridor she hesitated then saw a sign pointing to William's ward. She slowed her pace and gave a sigh of relief when she saw Humphrey sitting by a bed half way down the long ward.

William attempted a smile as Alice approached. She smiled back and kissed his cheek, careful to avoid the bandage around his head and the strapping on his shoulder. He was wearing hospital pyjamas with one of the sleeves hanging empty by the injured arm.

'So what happened to you?' said Alice trying to hide her anxiety.

William smiled but said nothing and she was horrified to see that his normally bright eyes were blank.

'He has no recollection of the bombing or how he came to be caught up in it.' Humphrey stood up and motioned Alice to sit down. 'I've spoken to the sister in charge and she says he was one of the people injured in the latest air raid.'

'But why weren't we informed earlier?'

Humphrey looked at their son sitting quietly in the iron bed, a starched white sheet pulled across his chest. 'He had no identification and he couldn't remember his address till this morning.'

'But wasn't he wearing uniform?'

'Apparently not.'

Alice concentrated on a wisp of dark hair that had escaped from William's head bandage. 'Does it hurt?' she asked.

'What hurts?' William gave a bemused smile.

Alice bit her lip. 'Your head, does it hurt?'

William ran his fingers over the bandage in surprise.

'No, it doesn't hurt. Touch wood!' He tapped his finger lightly on his head and laughed.

Two nurses marched down the ward and drew the curtains round the man in the bed next to William. They spoke in low voices and Alice was distressed to hear the patient cry out.

For a moment William's eyes took on an expression of sympathy. 'Poor chap. Damn shame,' he said. Then the blankness returned.

Alice and Humphrey looked at each other helplessly.

'What did the sister say about his injuries?' asked Alice quietly.

'He's got a broken collar bone and possibly a couple of broken ribs. And he's had concussion but they don't think there's brain damage. Just memory loss.'

'Brain damage! Oh my God!'

'They don't think there is any brain damage,' Humphrey reiterated sternly.

'That's all right then.' Alice delved into her handbag. 'Do they give you enough to eat? I've brought some sandwiches if you're hungry.'

'I'm not very hungry at the moment thank you.'

The nurses pushed back the curtain and moved on to attend to another patient. William shifted his position to speak to his neighbour and winced as he turned towards him.

'Are you feeling any better?' he asked gruffly.

'A bit,' the man replied then sank back on his pillows.

'Humphrey, why don't you sit down?' Alice pointed to an empty chair by the man's bed.

'I'm all right.' He examined his pocket watch. 'Perhaps …' he began then stopped as a blonde-haired young woman accompanied by a fireman stood in the door of the ward and looked directly at William.

'That's the man!' she shouted and walked quickly towards them. Her bright make-up and fragrant scent caused a frisson of excitement among the patients. Those that were able leant forward and stared curiously at William.

Alice exchanged a horrified glance with Humphrey as she got up and stood in solidarity next to him, wondering what crisis their son was involved in this time.

'Are you sure it's him?' the fireman asked as they stopped at the foot of William's bed.

'Yes, you're William aren't you? Don't you remember me?' The woman smiled encouragingly but William looked bewildered. 'Perhaps you don't recognise me with my clothes on!' she giggled.

Alice gasped and gripped Humphrey's hand. She looked at the fireman and couldn't understand why he was smiling.

He stepped forward and shook William's hand. 'I'm Bob Brown and this is my wife, Iris. I've come to thank you for rescuing my wife and baby,' he said and beamed at Alice and Humphrey.

Alice felt weak with relief as Humphrey made the introductions and vigorously shook hands with the couple. She was aware of a hush in the ward as the patients strained to hear the drama unfold.

'William, can you remember now?' Humphrey looked at his son with puzzled pride.

William shook his head.

'He's temporarily lost his memory. Can you tell us what happened?'

'I was on night duty. I left home soon after Iris had put the baby to bed. We thought it was going to be a quiet night but then we heard that Gotha bombers were heading for London.'

'I woke up when I heard the sirens,' continued Iris. 'I was really scared. I didn't know what to do for the best. So I wrapped the baby in a blanket and came downstairs. I sat under the table in the front room shivering and holding my baby tight. I wondered whether to go back and get dressed when I heard a crash and screams and I knew the bastards had made a hit. If you'll excuse my language.' She looked half apologetically at Alice.

'And had your house been hit?' asked Humphrey.

'It didn't take a direct hit. But I couldn't open the door. I couldn't get out!' The woman's voice rose to a scream.

Her husband looked anxiously at the injured men straining to hear her story. 'Now, now. You did get out. Thanks to our friend here.'

'Have we met?' William asked, smiling politely.

Alice tightened her grip on Humphrey's hand.

'William, you helped this lady when her house was bombed,' he said quietly.

William stared at the couple, his expression suddenly lucid. 'Where's the baby?' he shouted looking wildly around the ward.

'He's with his grandmother. We're staying with Iris's parents for a while.'

'Is the baby all right?' he asked urgently.

'Yes, thanks to your bravery,' said Bob.

'That's good, the baby's all right.' William slumped back on his pillow.

'And what happened when you found you were unable to open the door?' Humphrey prompted Iris.

'I opened the window. I couldn't see much; the air was thick with smoke and dust. And it was so cold. I thought I'd catch my death. So I went to get a tablecloth to wrap round myself, there was nothing else downstairs you see. But then the baby started to cry so I picked him up and went back to the window and leant out and shouted Help! Help!' Again the woman's voice rose and her husband laid his hand on her arm.

'And this gentleman heard you and came to your rescue.'

Iris looked at William. 'You do remember, don't you?'

He shook his head sadly.

'You wanted me to hand you the baby. But I couldn't. It wasn't that I didn't trust you. I just couldn't let go. So you called for help but people were busy with the injured further along the street. You tried to persuade me to climb out with the baby but I couldn't move!' Iris looked desperately at Alice.

'And William saved you?'

'He climbed in the window and told me his name and said everything was going to be all right. I didn't feel quite so frightened but we could hear people crying in the street and then we heard a crashing and he said he thought the roof was going to fall on top of us. He persuaded me to let him hold the baby for a moment while I climbed out of the window then William leant down and passed him to me. And he was going to climb out after me but I realised I'd left my handbag on the sideboard; it had all my money in it. So he went to get it for me. I'm so sorry, William. I should never have mentioned the bleeding handbag. Excuse my language.' Iris fumbled for a handkerchief and blew her nose.

'And I assume the roof did fall down?' said Humphrey wearily.

'Unfortunately, yes.' Bob took up the story. 'Some masonry fell on him and he was trapped. Iris managed to get help and the ambulance brought him here. As you can imagine, it's been a difficult time for us and we've only just had the opportunity to track him down to say thank you.'

There was silence for a moment then a shout of 'Bravo!' from the patient in the bed opposite William.

Bob put out his hand to shake William's again. He pulled himself up and held out his hand looking bemused.

Iris handed him a box wrapped in tissue paper. 'We've brought you something to show our appreciation. I'm sure you like chocolate,' she said, suddenly shy.

'Chocolate! Thank you. That's very kind of you.' William gave the couple a dazzling smile but his eyes remained blank.

'Well, we'll be going now.' Bob shook hands with Alice and Humphrey. 'I'm proud to meet you. I'm sure your son will be out of here in no time.'

Alice followed his glance along the ward at patients in much worse condition than William. She knew it would not be long before he was physically better but she wondered, with a sinking feeling in her stomach, how long it would be before his memory returned.

***

William furrowed his brow in concentration as he glued the final matchstick on the nose of the model aeroplane he was making.

'It's coming along nicely,' said Alice, looking up from her book.

'The propellers will be a bit tricky. And I'm beginning to run out of matchsticks.'

'Daisy promised to bring all their old ones. She should be here soon.'

'Daisy…' William paused and for one horrified moment Alice thought he had forgotten who his sister was.

'I've missed her,' he continued quietly. 'She was always here when I came home. Always interested in what I'd been doing. We had such fun.' He looked at his mother questioningly. 'You must miss her too.'

'Yes I do. But it's lovely to have you home again for a little while.' Alice replied with an enthusiasm that she didn't quite feel.

Although William's shoulder and ribs were healing well and he only had a slight scar on his forehead, his personality had changed. He no longer took pride in his appearance and he refused to say what he had been doing in London on the night of the raid and had forbidden Humphrey to get in touch with the RNAS. For once, Humphrey had agreed to their son's wishes but he had asked their doctor to call. William was amenable to the doctor's examination and questioning but made no comment when he said that he was suffering from short-term amnesia probably caused by a sudden shock or trauma.

The doorbell rang and Alice stood up but William was already hurrying from the room. Alice hung back as she heard him open the front door and greet Daisy with almost childish delight. As William stood in the sitting room doorway, his hand resting on his sister's shoulder, Alice was reminded of long ago Christmases when William's face was lit up with excitement tinged with anxiety that all would be well.

Daisy looked enquiringly into her mother's eyes as she kissed her then sat on the sofa next to William.

After asking about the journey, Alice got up. 'I don't ring for Ethel anymore,' she said. 'She's often busy looking after Neville. I'll go and see about tea.'

'I'm longing to see Neville, I expect he's grown.'

'I'll see if he's awake.' Alice forced a smile but sighed as soon as she was out of the room. William still reacted badly to Neville, showing no interest in him and resenting any time Alice spent with the baby.

...

Knowing that Daisy would be there when he arrived, Humphrey came home from work early but the evening was not an unqualified success. William was taciturn when Daisy praised him for his heroic rescue of the mother and child claiming that he wasn't a hero and, as he couldn't remember it, it didn't count, even if it was true.

Alice sensed that Humphrey was losing patience with his son but Daisy's presence kept the conversation civilised even though it lacked the sparkle of family evenings in the past. William yawned throughout the evening meal and retired to bed soon afterwards.

Alec had promised to make discreet enquiries to see if he could find out what William had been doing on the night of the raid and why his superiors in the RNAS had not contacted his family to find out why he hadn't reported back for duty.

Alice smiled at Daisy's excitement the following day when a telegram arrived from Alec saying he had got compassionate leave to visit his injured brother-in-law. Daisy appeared unaware that William did not share her enthusiasm but Alice noticed a look of defeat flicker across his face. However, when Alec arrived William did his best to muster up his former charm. Alice made her excuses and left the three young people to talk. After a while she heard the gramophone playing but there was no laughter.

Daisy looked troubled when she came into the kitchen. 'William wants to wait until Father's home and then we can talk about what's happened,' she said in reply to her mother's unasked question.

'I'll ask Ethel to look after Neville this evening so we're not disturbed.'

'I'll help her put him to bed if Father hasn't arrived by then.'

Alice was about to say that it would be good practice for when Daisy had her own child but thought better of it. 'He enjoys his bath time,' she said instead.

Neville was in bed by the time Humphrey got home. He greeted his son-in-law cordially and Alice could tell he was quietly pleased by William's changed appearance. His face was still too thin and his eyes had a haunted look but his hair and nails were immaculate and his shoes shone. As they gathered in the sitting room, William courteously poured drinks.

'I owe you all an explanation,' he said as he accepted a cigarette from Alec and sat down on a straight-backed chair.

Alec nodded encouragingly at his friend and snapped the silver cigarette case closed.

'I still can't remember what happened on the night of the air raid.' William paused and drew on his cigarette. 'And I don't know how I came to be walking down that street. I was disorientated when I got off the train at Waterloo. We'd been stuck in a siding for several hours. I was trying to get home and I started walking. I should have just sat at the station till morning. But I needed to keep moving.'

'Why were you coming home?' asked Humphrey when the silence had become almost unbearable.

'I had nowhere else to go.'

Alice bit her lip and wondered why home had become a last resort. She heard Neville cry out and Ethel's footsteps hurrying upstairs and suddenly felt a wave of guilt as she realised she had given Neville William's old room. In her euphoria at having a baby to nurture she had not considered that she was displacing her son in favour of her grandson.

'The fact is,' William leant forward and stubbed his cigarette in the jade ashtray, 'I'm no longer employed by His Majesty's Government.'

Humphrey tapped the bowl of his pipe in his palm and looked steadily at his son. 'I was beginning to fear that was the case.'

'Don't be cross!' Daisy's voice broke the silence.

Humphrey's expression softened. 'Just tell us what happened.'

'As you know, I am, I was responsible for checking the planes before they take-off. Recently the turnaround has been ridiculously quick. Anyway, I mustn't make excuses. Except that I had already reported the unreliability of the Renault-Mercedes engines. In fact the new engines had been delivered and were in the sheds waiting to be installed.'

Everyone waited for him to continue but he was lost in his thoughts.

'The new Sunbeam engines are far more powerful', said Alec, breaking the silence.

'Two thousand one hundred rpm,' said William automatically. He looked at the anxious faces and continued. 'Where was I? Oh yes, we were about to go off duty when a German submarine was sighted in the Channel and there was an order to make a late in the day scramble for it. I had to check the planes in double quick time and everything seemed in order although I had my doubts about one engine in particular. Anyway, the pilot was ordered to take it.'

Alice could hardly breathe, she guessed what was coming next.

'It was getting dark, distances are difficult to judge,' continued William. 'Anyway the plane took off but had difficulty in getting airborne. It collided with a breakwater, tipped over and the pilot drowned before anyone could get to him.'

There was silence in the room.

Alec took out a cigarette and, in a graceful movement, crossed the room and put it in William's trembling fingers. He took out his silver lighter and in a touchingly intimate movement bent over and lit the cigarette. He touched his friend lightly on the shoulder and rejoined Daisy on the sofa.

Humphrey cleared his throat. 'I don't suppose you were working in easy conditions.'

William's eyes flashed. 'The conditions were abominable. It was pouring the entire time and there was very little light. But that's not the point. I failed in my duty. And as a result a man is dead. And I am disgraced.'

Despite his words, Alice was pleased to see some of the old spirit return to William's face. But then he slumped back in his chair, his eyes half closed, as the smoke from his cigarette wafted gently upwards.

Daisy got up and kissed him gently on the cheek. 'Don't be too hard on yourself, Wills,' she said. 'I'm going to check on the dinner,' she added and left the room.

Dinner was a quiet affair despite everyone's effort to be sociable. Daisy and Alec kept the conversation going with tales of life in their Gloucestershire village. From the way they told it, it seemed as if the lives of the people there were untouched by the war. But Alice knew this was not the case, they were all affected by the war. 'Though some more than others,' she thought as she looked at William.

As soon as the meal was over, William made his excuses and went to bed.

Chapter 22: Lottie

Will you help to cure War-Shock in Discharged and
Disabled soldiers?
Did you know that there are tens of thousands of such
men in our midst who are today nervous wrecks
because they have fought and suffered for you?

The Times: December 14th 1917

Watery sunlight filtered into the parlour where Lottie concentrated on her painting of Llandudno Bay. She shivered in the cold room and refused to think about William's touch when he had rubbed her hands warm before placing a moonstone necklace around her neck. The place was the same but everything else had changed.

Shocked at the way their daughter had wasted away since her broken engagement and Cilla's visit and departure, Jack and Nellie had suggested she spent some time each day on her painting. They were all delighted when she began to sell her pictures for a few shillings and even get small commissions.

Bronwen had asked Lottie to paint a picture of Llandudno as a Christmas present for her mother. She had almost finished when Nellie came into the room.

'That's a pretty scene; she'll like that,' she said approvingly as she handed Lottie a letter. Nellie rubbed the small of her back, waiting for Lottie to open it.

'Yes, I want to finish it before the light goes. I'll read the letter later.' Lottie's heart thumped as she willed her mother to leave.

'All right.' Nellie turned away disappointedly. 'I hope it's not bad news,' she said as she left the room.

Lottie looked at the delicate script flowing over the expensive envelope. She recognised Daisy's writing immediately. They had corresponded regularly after she and William became engaged but since the break-up Daisy had only written one brief but sympathetic letter.

Slowly, Lottie opened the envelope and read the single page. She knit her brows then allowed herself to smile by the time she reached the end. She was distressed that William was unwell but overjoyed that his sister was asking her to come and help him recover. Daisy explained that she had returned home to Gloucestershire but she and Alec were worried about William's lack of interest in anything since being discharged from the RNAS. There was a sentence Lottie didn't understand about William rescuing someone and suffering from amnesia. Daisy finished the letter by saying that Alec felt William needed something to hope for and suggested that Lottie arrive unexpectedly.

'You can't just turn up,' said Jack when Lottie told her parents what Daisy had said.

'Daisy says that's the best way.'

'But it's not her home to go inviting people to stay.'

'I'm not people, I'm William's…' Lottie paused, 'friend. And his sister has asked me to go and see him.'

'If Daisy thinks you should go then it's best you go, but you mustn't offend Inspector and Mrs Dacre,' said Nellie anxiously.

'Well I don't think she should go. I don't want you getting upset again. I thought you were beginning to get over it.'

'Over it? How can you think such a thing?' Lottie glared at her father.

'I'm not letting you go running off to London without a proper invitation.'

'I've had an invitation and I'm going! If you'd let me get married when we wanted to this would never have happened!'

Jack looked hurt. 'I've always done what I thought was best for you.'

'I know. And what's best now is for me to go and look after William.' Lottie felt a newfound confidence as she met her father's gaze.

***

Unlike her last visit, there was no cab waiting when Lottie arrived at Euston the following morning. She had spent an uncomfortable night in a third class compartment but standing up to her father in order to be with the man she loved had given her a sense of purpose and she walked briskly to the underground station. Half an hour later she was walking out of Belsize Park station. It took her some time to find the correct street and she wished she had paid more attention on her previous visits. When she saw the house her heart beat faster and she slowed her pace.

Lottie tiptoed up the front steps and rang the bell. She was about to ring again when she heard footsteps in the hall. She hoped that William would answer, or even Ethel, and had prepared a little speech if it was Mrs Dacre.

'Oh!' she exclaimed in confusion when Hilda opened the door.

'Ssh!' Hilda gave Lottie a friendly smile and put her finger to her lips. 'Daisy told me she'd asked you to come. Auntie Alice is out with Neville; I'll take you upstairs so you can freshen up and I'll fill you in.'

Lottie's head spun as she followed Hilda. The jealously she had felt at Daisy's wedding reared itself again but it seemed misplaced. And Hilda had mentioned a name she hadn't heard before.

'You must have come as soon as you got Daisy's letter,' said Hilda when they were in the room.

Lottie nodded.

'I hope you don't mind sharing with me. I came to see Daisy and decided to stay a few days to give Auntie Alice a hand.'

'Does William need a lot of nursing?' asked Lottie anxiously.

'No, his injuries are nearly healed.'

'That's good.' Lottie wondered why it was necessary for Hilda to help her godmother if that was the case.

'Auntie Alice has had her work cut out since she took in the baby,' explained Hilda.

'Baby?'

'Oh, of course you wouldn't know. Auntie Alice does a lot of work with the Waifs and Strays society and she brought one of them to live here.'

'Good gracious! How old is it?'

'It's a he, Neville. He's six months.'

'How long will he stay here?' Lottie stared in amazement.

'Oh he's here for good. Auntie Alice dotes on him. They both do.'

'But do they know anything about him?'

Hilda shrugged. 'I'm not sure. There was a baby left in the garden of the Waifs and Strays society, or was that anther one? I know she was very upset when one of the babies died. Maybe she thought this one would have a better life here.'

Lottie frowned as she tried to imagine Mrs Dacre being so upset when a baby died that she brought another one home to care for.

'And does William like having a baby in the house?'

Hilda regarded Lottie sadly. 'William doesn't like anything at the moment I'm afraid. You mustn't expect too much. Now, I'll leave you to freshen up. I'll be in the kitchen.'

'And William?'

'He's in the sitting room.'

'When do you expect Mrs Dacre to return?'

'She's only just left. She's taken Neville for a walk on the Heath so she won't be back for at least an hour.'

'That's good. I mean….'

'Yes, it'll give you some time with William on your own.' Hilda smiled encouragingly as she left the room.

Lottie washed and put on the rose coloured blouse that William liked. Her hair was no longer cut in a fashionable bob but she had washed it the day before and the thick waves shone as they touched her shoulders. She glanced at the diamond ring on her right hand and walked quickly downstairs.

William was sitting by the window unaware of Lottie standing in the doorway. His face was thinner but he had not lost his dark good looks. Lottie felt herself tremble as she watched him absorbed in the matchstick model he was making. She looked around the room, familiarising herself with the furnishings and pictures that were so much richer than those in her parents' home. On one wall was the watercolour of Trealaw she had given on her first visit and she felt a glimmer of hope.

'William,' she said and walked across the room.

'Lottie?' His face lit up but then his expression changed to despair.

'How are you?' she asked inadequately.

'I don't know.' He looked at her intently.

'Daisy told me you were injured in an air raid.'

'Have you seen Daisy?' William looked pleased.

'No. But she wrote to me. She said you were ill. So I've come to look after you,' Lottie said more confidently than she felt.

'You've come all this way – for me?'

'Yes.'

'But I told you before I'm not worthy of you.'

'And I told you before, I don't care about things like that.'

'But things have changed.' William turned his head to the window.

'They haven't changed for me,' said Lottie resolutely.

'Well, they've changed for me. Everything's changed.' William resumed his model making.

Lottie stood silently, willing him to look at her. She tried to speak but waves of fatigue threatened to overwhelm her.

She watched William frown in concentration as he bent over his intricate model seaplane and wondered if it was a replica of the one he had flown.

'That's really good,' she said tonelessly.

'No it isn't,' William replied without looking up.

Lottie's legs felt like cotton wool as she left the room in defeat.

***

Hilda looked up from her pastry making when Lottie staggered into the kitchen. 'The daily help left last week. Ethel's upstairs cleaning. I'll make you some breakfast.' Hilda spoke gruffly but her eyes were sympathetic as she pulled out a chair for Lottie. She put a cup of tea in front of her. 'Drink this, it's a bit stewed but it'll warm you up.'

Some tea spilt in the saucer and Lottie was surprised to see her hands were trembling. She gulped the tea then closed her eyes. She thought she could feel the motion of the train and she was vaguely aware of pans clattering and someone humming. There was a sizzling sound and a tantalising smell of cooking which made Lottie's empty stomach gurgle.

'Pardon me,' she murmured and opened her eyes.

'You're in luck,' Hilda said as she put a plate of eggs, bacon and fried bread in front of Lottie. 'Our chickens are laying well and this is bacon from our farm.'

'Thank you.' Lottie was too tired and hungry to say any more but felt her energy returning with every mouthful.

'That was such a treat,' she said when her plate was empty. 'The eggs were delicious.'

'One of the advantages of living on a farm,' said Hilda.

'Do you have enough labour?' asked Lottie politely.

'It's better now we've got a couple of land girls. And my little brother is able to do more now.'

Kind as Hilda was, Lottie wasn't interested in hearing about her life on the farm, which she suspected was rather humdrum. 'Daisy said something about William rescuing someone,' she said.

'Yes. Apparently he was very brave. That's why it's so sad he can't remember it.'

'Do you know what happened?'

Hilda had just finished telling her what she knew when Alice walked in.

Lottie quailed as William's mother stood unsmiling in the doorway.

'This is a surprise,' she said coldly.

Lottie stood up. 'Daisy sent for me.' She was surprised to hear her voice sounding clear and confident.

'Have you seen William?'

'Yes.' Lottie's eyes met Alice's clear blue ones.

'You don't expect you can help him do you?'

'That's why I came,' Lottie said with quiet dignity.

'It would have been better if you'd let us know.'

'I'm sorry. I was so worried I came as soon as I could.' Lottie was aware of Alice staring at her engagement ring on the wrong hand.

'Has Hilda made you comfortable?'

'Very. She made me a splendid breakfast and she says I can share her room.'

Alice raised her eyebrows. 'Did she tell you we have an addition to the family?'

'Yes.' Lottie couldn't think of anything appropriate to add.

'Neville's sleeping in his pram at the moment. I must go and speak to Ethel.'

Hilda looked uncomfortable as Alice swept out of the room.

'Auntie Alice isn't usually like that,' she said.

'Maybe she's harassed without the daily help,' Lottie replied tactfully. 'What can I do to help?'

Hilda found her an apron and she started on the washing up while Hilda put finishing touches to the pastry.

'Is it the concussion that has caused the change in William?' Lottie asked after a while.

'I don't think so. The doctor said the concussion is only responsible for his short-term amnesia.'

'That's so sad he can't remember rescuing the mother and child. But what was he doing there at that time of night?' For a moment Lottie wished she hadn't asked the question.

'He was coming home.' Hilda put the pastry in the oven and started to wipe the table.

'On leave?'

'I don't think it's my place to say why he was coming home.'

Lottie stared at Hilda as she dried the dishes. 'If I'm going to help him I need to know what's happened.'

'You're absolutely right. But don't tell anyone I told you.' Speaking in a low voice Hilda told Lottie about William's job checking the planes, the accident and his discharge from the RNAS as result.

Lottie looked, unseeing, at the expensive plate in her hand. She could think of nothing to say.

'We mustn't blame him. I understand he was working in awful conditions.' Hilda pulled the plug from the sink and scrubbed the sides vigorously.

'Blame! Why should we blame him? He should be flying not fiddling with the bloody engines!' Lottie looked defiantly at Hilda.

'Well said!'

Lottie bit her lip; she was glad Mrs Dacre hadn't heard her swear. She stacked the plate with the others. 'Poor William. Is he feeling really guilty?'

Hilda nodded. 'It wouldn't be so bad if he could remember his bravery on the night of the air raid. But I believe he feels worthless.'

'He felt like that when he lost his commission.'

'Daisy felt sure he acted hastily when he broke off your engagement. She was convinced you'd get back together.'

'Was she?' Lottie's face lit up then crumpled. 'But we didn't.'

'There's still time.' Hilda was about to say more when the door opened and Alice came in carrying the baby.

Lottie found it hard to believe the change in William's mother as she jiggled the child on her hip.

'Time for dinner,' she said and looked adoringly at Neville as she put him in his chair.

'Is there anything I can do to help?' asked Lottie.

'You can lay the table in the dining room for our luncheon if you wish. Hilda can help me with Neville.'

Lottie removed her apron and left the room.

***

Lottie sat miserably through lunch, hurt and bewildered by Alice's attitude. She began to wish she hadn't come until she noticed William eyeing her covertly. Hilda did her best to keep the conversation going, although afterwards Lottie was unable to remember any of it.

After lunch Alice asked them to play with Neville in the conservatory while she did the household accounts. William declined and Lottie wondered what she should do. In despair she trailed after Hilda and tried to keep awake while Neville rolled and gurgled on the floor.

'Are you used to babies?' asked Hilda.

'A bit. I have three cousins younger than me.' Lottie remembered how worried they had been for Baby Megan when she was Neville's age and felt a desperate longing for her uncle and aunt's cottage in the little village in Wales.

'How about you?' she asked politely.

'To be honest, I'm more familiar with baby animals.' Hilda wrinkled her nose. 'I think his napkin needs changing. I'll see if I can find Ethel.'

***

Lottie was in her bedroom when she heard Humphrey come home from work. She held her breath, not daring to go downstairs. She could make out Humphrey's voice then Alice's well-modulated tones suddenly rose and she felt sick with worry, wondering if they were talking about her.

After a while Lottie heard Humphrey come upstairs and she judged it was safe to go down. She was just tiptoeing along the landing when Humphrey came out of his room.

'Good evening, Inspector Dacre.' Lottie was surprised to hear her voice sounding normal.

'Good evening, Lottie. I understand my daughter asked you to come.'

'Yes, Sir.' Lottie eyed him with a coolness she did not feel.

Humphrey looked at her intently. 'You've lost weight. Have you been ill?'

'No, Sir.' Lottie was flustered by his observation.

'And your parents? Are they well?'

'My mother isn't in the best of health. And my father gets very tired. But everyone is working too hard these days.' Lottie noticed lines on his handsome face and streaks of grey hair.

'And how do you find William?' he asked abruptly.

'I don't know much about it, Sir, but he seems to be suffering from war shock.'

'I don't like the term. William had concussion and he's lost his short term memory.'

Lottie said nothing.

'So, you think you can help him?'

Lottie thought of the man who had become a stranger, huddled over his model aeroplane. 'I don't know,' she said miserably.

'Well, you'd better give it a try. For all our sakes.' Humphrey started to walk towards the bathroom then turned round. 'Thank you for coming,' he said.

***

Hilda left after lunch the following day and Lottie missed her cheerful presence. She went into the kitchen to help Ethel wash the dishes.

'I don't want to speak out of turn but it would do Master William good to get some fresh air,' said Ethel turning to look at Lottie, her arms covered in soapsuds.

'I suppose he's not really well enough,' Lottie replied defensively.

Ethel scrubbed a pan. 'He's much improved but he seems to be stuck now. Stuck inside himself somehow.'

Lottie rubbed Neville's silver cutlery. 'I'll ask him if he'd like to go out this afternoon.'

'A blow on the Heath would be good. He used to love flying his kite there when he was little.' Ethel sighed. 'How times change.'

Lottie hurried into the sitting room as soon as the dishes were finished.

William looked up as she came in. 'Look!' he said proudly. 'It's finished!'

Lottie bent over the model seaplane, marvelling at the intricacy of the detail. She wanted to tell him how clever he was but did not risk being snubbed again. 'Is it a Short 827?' she asked instead.

William stared at her. 'How did you know?'

'You told me that's what you flew.'

'And you remembered?'

'Of course.' Lottie scarcely breathed as William held her eyes, his expression unfathomable. 'I wondered,' Lottie hesitated, 'if you'd like to go for a walk?'

'A walk?'

'Yes.' Lottie had a sudden picture of her and William holding hands and running along the beach with Skipper bounding in front of them.

'There's nowhere to go round here,' he said dispiritedly.

'What about the Heath?'

'The Heath? That's much too far.'

Lottie looked at him uncertainly. She didn't think the Heath was very far; William must be really tired if he thought it was. 'Perhaps we could just go out and get some cigarettes,' she said.

'You haven't taken up smoking have you?' William looked shocked.

'No, of course not.' Lottie smiled uncertainly at his concern. 'I just thought you might need some.'

William took out his cigarette case. 'You're right. I do.' He stood up.

The room darkened and Lottie could see some children running in the street holding onto their hats. William had his back to the window and Lottie hoped he hadn't noticed that it had started to rain.

They went into the hall and began putting on their coats. The door opened and Alice came in bringing with her a gust of cold air.

'It's absolutely pouring!' she said, shaking her umbrella. She looked at William and Lottie. 'You're not going out in this are you?'

'We're just popping out for some cigarettes,' said William.

'You can't go in this weather!'

There was a crash and a dustbin rolled as the wind whistled round the house.

Lottie looked questioningly at William.

He shrugged his shoulders, slowly took off his coat and returned to the sitting room.

'I must go and see to Neville.' Alice hung up her hat and turned away.

Lottie's fingers trembled as she fumbled with the buttons on her coat. She forced herself to remain calm and asked politely, 'Is there anything I can do to help?'

Alice paused at the end of the hallway. 'You can clean the brass,' she said coolly as she opened the kitchen door.

Lottie swallowed and looked at the barometer on the wall. The brass around the face was slightly tarnished. She peered at the inscriptions and saw that the needle was pointing to 'rain' then she tapped the glass and the needle moved upwards and rested on the word 'change.'

'Is that change for the better or change for the worse?' wondered Lottie as she went to find some cleaning materials.

She carefully cleaned the barometer then moved on to the ornate brass mirror, standing on a chair to reach the top. Finally she polished the door handle and letterbox. Feeling invigorated she went into the sitting room to find some more brass to clean.

William was staring at the Japanese maples in the garden entwined in a frenzied dance by the lashing rain. The fire was unlit and Lottie quietly bent down to clean the carved brass knobs on the grate.

'Whatever are you doing?' William turned and frowned when he saw Lottie on her hands and knees.

'Your mother asked me to clean the brass.'

'She did what? How dare she treat you like a servant!' Anger energised William and his face was animated for the first time since Lottie arrived.

'It's all right,' she said vigorously rubbing her rag over the brass. 'Now that the daily help has left, the chores are mounting up. It's impossible for Ethel to do all the cleaning as well as cooking and looking after the baby.'

'But it's not your place to do it.'

'I know that. But I can't just sit around all day doing nothing.'

'Like me you mean?'

'No, that's not what I mean.' Lottie looked up at him. 'You're not well.'

'I'm not too ill to help.' William knelt by the hearth and picked up the fire tongs. 'It's getting chilly. I'll light the fire as soon as I've put a shine on these.'

Lottie tore the cleaning rag in half and, as she passed it to William, their fingers touched. She felt a sudden heat coursing through her body and when she looked at William's flushed face she dared to hope that he felt the same.

For an instant their eyes met. 'I'm glad you came,' he said then turned his attention to polishing the fire tongs.

They worked in silence but Lottie felt relaxed for the first time since she arrived.

***

When it was time for bed Lottie snuggled between sheets that had been warmed by a stone water bottle. She was tired but her sense of despair had lifted. William had made an effort at dinner, his parents had treated her cordially and Lottie had found herself telling them about selling her paintings. Everyone went to bed early and Lottie quickly fell asleep.

She was awoken in the night by a cry and thought it was the baby. Then she heard William's voice shout, 'Take cover!' and footsteps on the landing. She sat up in bed, her heart pounding as she wondered why she hadn't heard the air raid siren. She listened intently but both the street and the sky were quiet. Cautiously she put on her slippers and went to the door then paused when she heard Humphrey's voice.

'It's all right, son, you're safe at home now.'

'Is he sleepwalking again?' Lottie heard Alice ask in an agitated whisper.

'Yes, I'll take him back to bed. Don't stay; you'll be up soon enough when Neville wakes.'

As Lottie slipped back into bed she realised it would be a long time before William was better. That he would get better, with her help as well as his parents', she had no doubt.

***

The following morning Lottie felt that the atmosphere in the house had changed with the weather. A light wind was chasing the clouds away and the sun was attempting to shine. Alice was away at a meeting and had asked Lottie to help Ethel look after Neville.

When Lottie saw the dark rings under William's eyes she suggested they took the baby for a walk on the Heath but William said he would clean the windows instead. It was one of Lottie's jobs at home to clean the shop window every week but she suspected that it was a new activity for William. They started on the conservatory with Lottie cleaning inside and William out. By the time they had finished Lottie understood why people had servants, it would be impossible to keep a house of this size clean without help. They moved on to the kitchen and Lottie's arms began to ache but the smell of baking kept her going.

'What are you cooking?' she asked.

'Chelsea buns,' said Ethel. 'They used to be Master William's favourite and I thought you'd like them when you take a break.'

William came in just as Ethel was taking the buns out of the oven. 'They look delicious.' He looked at Lottie almost shyly. 'The sun's shining and it's not too cold; shall we sit outside for a while?'

'But it's the middle of winter!'

'Tea and buns will warm us and we can take a blanket.'

'You can have a picnic like you used to when you were children,' said Ethel bustling about with a tray and plates.

They put on their coats and settled themselves on the seat by the pond at the bottom of the garden. Lottie couldn't help remembering the last time she had sat there with William and Cilla when they had all been happy and full of plans for the future.

'How's your shoulder?' she asked.

'It's not too bad. I used the other hand for the windows. How are you?' William looked at her intently.

'I'm fine, just a bit tired.' Lottie felt slightly uncomfortable with their sudden intimacy.

'So am I.' William paused, 'I don't sleep very well these days.'

Lottie nodded, wondering whether to say that she had heard him in the night. A robin chirped on a branch of the apple tree and flew down when William threw some crumbs at their feet. It cocked its head at them and they watched it hopping about but when it realised there were no worms it disappeared.

They sat in silence and William closed his eyes.

'You're tired. Would you like to go inside now?' asked Lottie.

'Do you want to? Are you cold?'

'Not really.'

William moved closer to her and rearranged the blanket firmly around them. 'Tell me a story,' he murmured.

Lottie could hear his heart beating and she felt a sudden surge of anger that he had caused her so much pain.

'No William!' She turned to face him. 'I've had enough of stories! You tell me the truth. What really happened on the night of the raid? Why were you wandering round the streets that night?'

'You want the truth?' William glared at her.

'Yes. That's what I've always wanted.'

'Not at the beginning, none of us wanted the truth at the beginning.'

Lottie waited then slowly and painfully William told her about his job maintaining aircraft and how he had been discharged when a plane he checked crashed on take-off, killing the pilot.

'I didn't know what I was doing, I was so filled with shame.' William put his head in his hands. 'So I got the train to Waterloo. It was late; there weren't any buses or tubes so I decided to walk home. Then I got caught in the raid.' He looked at her beseechingly. 'And I honestly can't remember anything else of that night.'

'You lost your memory.' Lottie put out her hand then dropped it. 'But there's something else,' she said with sudden clarity. 'Something else happened didn't it?' She stared at him, watching his expression change as different emotions flickered across his face.

William shuddered. 'Things were happening all the time. Some made a bigger impression than others.' He hesitated then said, 'Have you heard of a place called Zeebrugge?'

'You asked me that last year.' Lottie remembered them sitting on the sofa the night of Daisy's wedding. He had been about to tell her something when his mother had come in.

'It was just over a year ago. I was with the squadron that flew to bomb the harbour and submarine sheds at Zeebrugge. We were flying low and could see the Jerries running for shelter. One sailor must have been too frightened to run. He just stood looking up. He wasn't fair like most of them; he had dark hair. As I looked at him it was like looking into a mirror. For a moment our eyes met. And then we dropped the bomb. I'd finished the job but he was in the way. His death was unnecessary,' finished William bitterly.

'Is that why you started jettisoning the bombs?' asked Lottie quietly.

William took her hand. 'I couldn't get his face out of my mind. I still have nightmares about it.'

'I know.' She put her other hand over his. 'But I want to help. I've never stopped loving you.'

William studied the diamond on Lottie's finger. 'I love you too.' He paused and his face hardened. 'But there's something else you should know.'

Lottie felt suddenly fearful. 'You've told me enough,' she said quickly.

'Have I?' A mixture of relief and remorse flitted across William's face as he looked half pleadingly at Lottie. 'You do still love me no matter what I've done?'

Lottie nodded, her eyes fixed on his.

He gave a ghost of a smile. 'And you think it's enough that we love each other?'

'Of course it's enough!'

'It's not just enough.' William tenderly took the ring from Lottie's finger and placed it on her left hand. 'It's everything.'

Chapter 23: Lottie

Food away from home at Easter
People who go away from home at Easter will be faced
with a restricted train service and the absence of any
guarantee that food supplies can be provided for them.

The Times: March 26th 1918

'Look! The sun's shining on Mynydd Brith!' Lottie pointed as they reached the end of the track and paused for breath at the entrance to Trealaw.

'I can't guarantee it'll be shining on our wedding day; are you sure you want to spend our honeymoon here?' William looked at her anxiously.

'Oh yes! I want to wake up to the sound of birds and look out at Daffodil Mountain.'

'We could go to a hotel if you'd rather.' As William drew Lottie close she was aware of the change in him since their first visit to Trealaw. Then he had been a confident young man, certain of his abilities as a pilot and ready to take on the enemy. Those certainties had been swept away; he was thinner and every now and again a tremor ran through his body.

'Would you rather go to a hotel?' She scanned his face to see what he was thinking.

'No, we'd have to be on our best behaviour. And I don't want to share you with anyone.' As William kissed her Lottie felt an overwhelming sense of relief and tried to ignore a nagging fear that her happiness might still be snatched away.

William's recovery had been a slow process but knowing he had a worthwhile job to go to at the Junction had helped. Mrs Jones had had several paying guests in the three years since William had left but she said he had always been her favourite and was delighted to welcome him back.

'I can't believe we'll be married in two weeks,' said Lottie as they drew apart.

'It's been a long wait.' William looked at her intently and was about to say more when they heard voices in the lane.

'It looks as if we've got company,' he said instead and put his arm through Lottie's as a group of ramblers appeared at the end of the church path. Unaware of their presence, the leader took the mountain track that led behind Trealaw. The group followed, with the exception of the last couple. The girl waved and, pulling her partner with her, came running towards them.

'It's Bronwen! What are you doing here?' Lottie laughed in delight at the unexpected arrival of her friend.

'We're with the rambling club.' Bronwen turned to her companion. 'These are my friends I told you about. They're getting married on Easter Saturday.'

The young man held out his hand. 'Captain Briggs,' he said formally.

William looked coolly into the man's eyes. 'I'm William,' he said shaking his hand, 'and this is my fiancée, Charlotte.'

'He's Robert to friends,' said Bronwen looking slightly embarrassed. 'Is this your parents' house? Lottie's told me so much about it.'

'Do your parents live here?' Robert's lip curled as he looked at William with amusement.

'Occasionally. They enjoy the change from London.'

'Oh!' He re-adjusted his expression. 'So you're a Londoner?'

'I don't really think definitions are important.'

'That's the nice thing about the rambling club; we're all the same when we're walking aren't we, Robert?' Bronwen gazed up at the handsome man beside her.

He gave her an indulgent smile. 'Why don't we ask your friends to join us?'

'That would be such fun! We've got a picnic and everything.'

Lottie felt William squeeze her arm. 'That would be lovely but we've come to get the house ready for our honeymoon.' She blushed and continued quickly, 'but we'll come a little way with you; the views will be lovely today.'

Robert led the way and Bronwen fell back to talk to Lottie.

'Where did you find him?' Lottie whispered.

'I was waiting for Barry outside the camp one evening but he didn't turn up so I started to walk away when Robert stopped and asked if I was all right.'

'And were you?'

'Well I was after I'd met him!' Bronwen giggled.

Lottie looked at the two men striding ahead. Robert was gesticulating and obviously explaining something to William who nodded politely every now and again.

'Has he seen much active service?' asked Lottie cautiously.

'He's been in Ireland and he's waiting to be sent back. But that's not like being in France is it?' Bronwen's voice was shrill with anxiety.

'No, of course not. Would you like to bring him to our wedding?'

'That would be lovely; I'm really looking forward to it.'

'So am I!' Lottie did a little skip and ran ahead to join William.

He was pointing out the boundary of Trealaw and explaining about the grazing rights that came with the land. Robert looked impressed.

'Well, we mustn't keep you from your ramble.' William took Lottie's arm.

'Are you sure you don't want to join us for the picnic?' Robert asked.

Lottie saw a flicker of irritation on William's face. 'We'll see you at our wedding,' she said. 'I do hope you can come.'

'That will be lovely, won't it Robert?' said Bronwen.

'Yes. Thank you for the invitation.' Robert held out his hand. 'We'll see you on Easter Saturday then. That is, as long as I'm not sent to Ireland before then.'

The ramblers had stopped some distance ahead and Lottie and William watched Bronwen and Robert hurry up the track to join them.

'God help the Irish with men like him in charge,' murmured William as they turned towards Trealaw.

'He's an improvement on her last boyfriend.'

'She should find herself a nice Welshman.'

Lottie looked surprised. 'I'm glad you didn't say that about me!'

'Oh there's no hope for you! Your mother set a bad example by marrying an Englishman!' Laughing, William took Lottie's hand and they ran down the slope at the back of house.

Lottie looked at William and felt the happiness she had known three years ago return. The haunted expression that had greeted her when she arrived at his parents' house in December had gone and the carefree smile she loved was back. She sometimes wondered if he would tell her more about the experiences that had led to his illness. But, since the day in his parents' garden, he had scarcely mentioned flying. Whether it was Mrs Jones' cooking, his work in the locomotive sheds, or simply being in love, William had gradually become more like the man she had fallen in love with three and half years earlier. But the war had taken its toll and everyone Lottie knew was changed in some way.

'Are you sure your mother approves of our marriage?' she asked anxiously.

'Of course!' William frowned and put his arms around her. 'Why wouldn't she?'

'I just felt, when I came to see you, she didn't want me around.'

'Well, I want you!'

Lottie smiled at him, then continued reflectively, 'I suppose it was a difficult time for her, what with worrying about you and looking after the baby with only Ethel to help.'

'Yes.'

Lottie wished she hadn't said anything when she saw the dark expression return to William's eyes.

'Anyway,' she said positively, 'I think it was marvellous of her and your father to take in an abandoned baby. They treat him as if he was their own child.'

William said nothing and Lottie could hear his heart beating as he pulled her closer. There was a cooing sound and a rock dove hopped on the edge of the pond, its beak darting towards the water. They stood quietly for a moment then watched as it flew off, its purple plumage glinting in the watery sunshine.

'It must have a nest nearby,' said William.

'Like us,' giggled Lottie.

'We'd better get on with it then.' William took Lottie's hand and they walked towards the house.

***

Nellie looked agitated when Lottie and William arrived back at the Junction just as it was getting dark.

'Is everything all right? Where's Father?' asked Lottie.

'He's gone for a walk. Now sit down, I've made your tea.' She gestured to the table and they sat down uncertainly.

'I expect you've worked hard today.' Nellie smiled fondly at William as she picked up the teapot.

'We were lucky, Billy Jenkins and his brother came to see if we had any jobs for them and they were a great help. They're going to light the range for us on the morning of our wedding day so the house will be warm.'

William exchanged a puzzled glance with Lottie as they both wondered why Jack wasn't at home. Lottie shrugged; she knew it was no use getting her mother to talk if she didn't want to.

'We met Bronwen and her new young man at Trealaw,' she said, 'they were out with a rambling club. I've asked him to the wedding. That is,' Lottie paused, 'I hope it won't be a problem having an extra guest.'

'Not at all. There'll be plenty for everyone. I've made sure of that.' Nellie tilted her head in a defiant gesture.

The fresh air had made them hungry and they ate in appreciative silence.

'I hope you were able to rest this afternoon,' said William politely when they had nearly finished.

'I made a list of all the baking I need to do for the wedding.' Nellie got up and handed Lottie a carefully written list.

She studied it. 'If I hadn't just eaten, this would make my mouth water. But you know it's impossible, some of these things haven't been available for ages.' Lottie handed the list back to her mother.

'I know. That's why I've been planning ahead. Come!' Nellie beckoned towards the cupboard under the stairs.

'I've never noticed that box before,' said Lottie as she peered into the darkness.

'It's usually hidden in the far corner but I didn't put it back after I'd shown your father. Now, William, can you carry it out for me, please?'

William did as he was told and Nellie opened the lid with a flourish. Nobody said anything as they stared at the tins of meat and fruit, packets of sugar and other carefully stored provisions.

'Well?' Nellie stood with her hands on her hips, her expression a mixture of triumph and anxiety.

For a moment Lottie was speechless as she looked at her mother then back at the treasure trove of food. 'What did Father say?' she stammered, although she was fairly certain of the answer.

'Your father doesn't understand about catering.' Nellie was dismissive. 'And I haven't done anything I shouldn't.'

William's mouth twitched. 'Mrs Rowe, you are magnificent. We'll have a banquet with all this. You must have been saving things for a long time.'

'Ever since you got engaged,' Nellie replied proudly. 'I started putting things aside out of a sense of thrift. Of course, then we had no idea of the privations we would suffer due to this dreadful war. But Jack's taken it all the wrong way and gone off in a huff.'

'But there are laws against hoarding.' Lottie looked at William.

'There weren't when we got engaged. And I suppose you just wanted to be prepared?'

'You could have come home on leave at any time and got married by special licence. And there would have been no way of getting our hands on sufficient food to give Lottie the wedding she deserves.'

Lottie looked at her mother in amazement. Whatever the rights and wrongs of the case she had shown determination. She imagined her scrimping on their rations so that she could secrete valuable foodstuff in the dark cupboard. She must have continued even after William broke off the engagement.

A tear ran down her cheek. 'Thank you,' she said simply and gave her mother a hug.

'Yes, thank you,' echoed William looking touched. He looked at his watch. 'I should be going soon. Or should I wait till Mr Rowe gets home?'

'No, I can't vouch for his mood when he returns. Perhaps you can put the box back for me.'

William returned the box to its hiding place then made for the door. Lottie followed him and they stood talking for a while by the gate.

'What do you think your father will do?' asked William.

'I expect he'll come round, he usually does. But he's a stickler for his principles.'

'You don't think your mother took the things from the shop do you?'

Lottie looked shocked. 'No, of course not. She would have just made do with less from our own allowance.'

'Then don't worry. I'm sure no one else will. The guests will just tuck in and enjoy themselves. And won't your relatives be contributing?'

'Yes, Auntie Meg has saved enough to make the wedding cake. And I think my father's relatives will be bringing some things.'

'And my parents will be and Hilda's sending some things from the farm even though she can't come. Daisy and Alec said they'd bring whatever they could when I asked Alec to be my best man. If he's that worried, your father can tell people a lot of the food has come from Gloucestershire!'

'Maybe they don't have rationing in Gloucestershire!' Lottie's eyes twinkled.

William laughed. 'Maybe they don't!' He gave her a lingering kiss then left.

***

The next two weeks passed in a flurry of preparations. Whenever there was time to spare from working in the shop, the two women devoted themselves to preparing the wedding breakfast.

Lottie tried not to be upset by Cilla's offhand attitude to her wedding though she had been hurt when her sister had refused to be her bridesmaid on the grounds that she might not be able to get leave from the munitions factory. However, when Cilla arrived on the night before the wedding all the tenderness she had felt for her little sister flooded back the minute she walked into the room.

While Nellie and Jack fussed around their younger daughter, Lottie looked forward to one last night of girlish talk when she and Cilla went to bed but Cilla fell asleep as soon as her head touched the pillow.

Lottie felt a sense of loss as she looked at the thin face of her sister but, exhausted by the preparations of the last two weeks, she too fell into a deep sleep.

A gust of wind almost snatched Lottie's exquisitely embroidered train from the tiny hands of her bridesmaid as she and William walked triumphantly out of the church.

'You look beautiful,' whispered William as they paused and waited for the two families to join them for the photographs. Lottie fingered the pearl necklace at her bare throat, William's wedding present to her.

Lottie beamed with happiness, her senses heightened as she gazed at her husband and then at the guests.

'You're a lucky man,' said Alec to his friend as he took his place next to Lottie.

'I know.' William squeezed Lottie's hand.

She watched as her mother-in-law, looking elegant in an emerald green outfit, stood between Alec and her father and flushed with pleasure when she heard Alice compliment him on his beautiful daughter.

'She's been making her wedding gown for a long time. She's a clever needlewoman,' he replied proudly.

The photographer gestured to the guests to stand together for a group photograph. There was a shuffling as the crowd of spectators, many of them customers of the Rowes, moved out of the way.

Lottie turned and smiled at Auntie Meg and Uncle Owen standing behind Megan who looked cherubic in a pink organdie bridesmaid's dress and ruffled cap.

Then she saw Cilla and Daisy standing together. Daisy's red dress and extravagant hat were a vibrant contrast to the stark lines of the church but Cilla, dressed entirely in black, seemed to mirror the bleakness of the grey slate. Her auburn hair was hidden under a black cloche hat and her skin had a translucent quality. She held herself rigid, her huge eyes fixed on the distance. Her only attempt at colour was a gash of scarlet lipstick across her face.

Two women walked past, deep in conversation about the wedding guests.

'She must have lost someone,' said one gesturing to Cilla.

'I heard that the soldier she went to London with was killed.'

'But that was nearly two years ago, there must have been another recently; you can see it in her face.'

'It's a shame she can't be happy on her sister's wedding day.'

'That's how it is these days. Anyway, Lottie seems to have made a good match even if he's not from these parts.'

The women passed out of earshot and Lottie shivered. She looked at William but he was complimenting his mother-in-law on her fashionable blue coatdress.

'Lottie made it for me,' she said proudly.

Lottie smiled faintly as she gripped William's arm.

'Darling, you're cold,' he said putting his arm around her.

'I'll be all right,' she whispered as she watched Daisy and Cilla join the group and take up their positions at either end of the front row.

The photographer asked everyone to smile then he walked back to his tripod, put his head under the black cloth draped over the camera and took the photograph. The guests waited patiently as he repeated the process several times. By the time the photographer was finished Lottie felt bathed in warmth but she could see that some of the guests were shivering. The wind had got stronger and gulls were wheeling overhead, their coarse cries bringing echoes of rough seas. She wondered if there was going to be a storm but she knew that William would care for her whatever the weather.

The guests quickly followed the bride and groom into the church room. The featureless room had been transformed by covering tables in white cloths decorated with jars of daffodils amid plates of cold meat, pickles, sandwiches, welsh cakes, fruit pies and a splendid wedding cake. If anyone was surprised by the amount of food, there was only praise as everyone tucked in enthusiastically.

Jack's speech was short and dignified. William's was also short but emotional as he thanked Lottie for helping him through the dark period after the air raid. There was a sigh among the guests as he pledged his love for his bride from now and till the end of time. The speeches finished with Alec telling a couple of light-hearted stories from their RNAS training days.

Nellie handed Lottie a knife and, accompanied by calls to make a wish, she and William cut the wedding cake.

Uncle Owen and a couple of friends had offered to play some music and they struck up on their fiddles; Efan accompanied them on his penny whistle. As William led her to the floor, Lottie felt as if she were in a ballroom rather than a church hall. Daisy and Alec joined them, followed by Bronwen and Robert then some of the relatives from Crewe. Soon the hall was alive with the sounds of music and laughter.

After a couple of numbers, Alec asked Lottie for a dance. William took Daisy's arm but she shook her head saying she was tired. As he led his sister to her seat Lottie noticed Cilla standing on her own. William hesitated for a moment and glanced towards his father. Humphrey looked at his son and then at Cilla miserably winding a tendril of auburn hair around her finger. He crossed the floor and swept Cilla up in time with the music.

'Inspector Dacre dances well,' said Alec.

'And so does Mrs Dacre,' added Lottie as her mother-in-law danced past on Jack's arm.

Alec was an accomplished dancer but Lottie wished she was still dancing with William. 'Is Daisy all right?'

she asked as she saw William hand her sister-in-law a glass of water.

'She gets tired easily,' he said sadly then nodded towards a fair-haired young man standing on his own watching the dancers. 'Who's he?' he asked.

'That's Dylan, my friend from Knight's. I'm so glad he could come. I didn't think he'd be home for the wedding.'

'Has he been in France?'

'No, he's not fit for active service. He's serving in Aldershot.'

When the music stopped Alec sat down with Daisy and William proudly took Lottie on to the floor again.

As Humphrey and Cilla were returning to their seats Dylan asked Cilla to dance. The band started to play a slow waltz and Dylan looked uncomfortable as he led his partner stiffly round the floor. They almost collided with Bronwen and Robert.

'Whoops a daisy!' giggled Bronwen.

'Careful old chap!' said Robert with forced joviality.

When the musicians took a break Robert, with Bronwen in tow, made a beeline for Alec and Daisy. The four of them exchanged light-hearted banter but Robert's over familiarity was misplaced and it did not extend to Dylan when Bronwen called him over to join them.

Cilla settled herself down with her cousins while Lottie and William circulated and thanked everyone for coming. When they had spoken to all the relatives they joined their friends. Humphrey and his brother, Charlie, attached themselves to the group and listened with interest as Alec was expounding his idea of starting a flying club in Gloucestershire when the war was over and urging William to come in with him.

'We'd need a lot of capital.' William appeared excited by the idea but Lottie was aware that, unlike Alec, he was not in receipt of a private income.

'It sounds interesting. But why not expand it? Have scheduled flights to the Continent taking passengers and freight. Air travel will take off in a big way and it would be good to be in at the beginning,' said Charlie.

Humphrey looked at his brother in amusement. 'It will never be as important as the railways.'

'Don't you believe it.' Charlie put his hand on William's shoulder. 'Let me know if you decide to go ahead and I'll see what I can do.'

'You could have your own airline.' Robert looked at his newfound friends in awe.

'Where shall we fly, Lottie?' asked William tenderly as he tightened his arm around his bride.

'Anywhere, as long as we're together.'

'You can't be together all the time if William's flying aeroplanes,' said Robert.

'Then I'll have to get my co-pilot's licence,' she replied.

'Well said!' laughed Daisy.

William looked at his watch. 'The car will be here soon to take us to Trealaw.'

'Then we'd better get ready.'

Lottie looked around for her sister. She had left her cousins and was sitting next to Dylan. Both were staring ahead, hardly aware of the other's presence. Apart from gently tapping her foot in time to the music, Cilla was sitting absolutely still. Dylan's gaze was fixed on Bronwen.

Lottie started to walk towards them but William took her arm and steered her towards the door.

Chapter 24: Alice

Recruiting Campaign for South Africa
Mr Lloyd George's appeal to the Union to reinforce its
heroic troops in the fullest possible manner and with
the smallest possible delay is meeting with prompt
response

The Times: April 2ⁿᵈ 1918

'It's good to be on our way home, I feel as if we've been away for ages.' Alice sat propped against the pillows and looked at Humphrey in the opposite bunk of their sleeping compartment.

'It's a relief to see William settled.' Humphrey carefully knocked the ash from his pipe into the highly polished brass ashtray.

'I must confess, the wedding breakfast was better than I expected. But it was strange not going to Trealaw.'

'I don't think we'd have been very welcome,' Humphrey replied dryly.

'Do you think William plans to stay in Wales when the war's over?'

'There's no reason why he shouldn't, he's got a good job.'

'Yes, and Lottie will want to stay near her family.' She tapped her fingers on the marble tabletop between the bunks. 'I wonder what Cilla will do after the war.'

Humphrey frowned. 'She'll have to make her own way. There are already opportunities for women that were unheard of three years ago.'

'Yes. Hilda's doing very well with her job at Queen Mary's. I'm so glad she's not needed on the farm now that Bertie's taken over.'

'Helping men adapt to their artificial limbs is a very worthwhile thing to do.'

'I just wish she would find a nice man to marry.'

'There aren't many of those left. But hopefully the job opportunities for young women will be some compensation for their poor marriage prospects.'

Alice tried to squash an uncharitable feeling of relief. She was sorry for her goddaughter but, as long as Cilla remained unmarried, there would be no chance of her changing her mind about Neville.

'I hope Neville's been all right while we've been away,' she said anxiously.

'He's in good hands with Ethel.' Humphrey spoke gruffly but his eyes lit up at the mention of his grandson.

'It'll be his first birthday next month. Maybe he'll be walking by then.'

'He'll be into everything.' Humphrey chuckled indulgently.

'Then he'll need watching all the time.' Alice switched off the light and was gradually lulled to sleep by the rhythm of the train.

***

Alice is standing in the middle of an empty plain, scanning the grey horizon for signs of life. She hears footsteps and rasping breath then Hilda runs past carrying an artificial leg under her arm. Her eyes are fixed on a ridge the other side of the plain and, as Alice follows her gaze, she sees it is swarming with soldiers. She chases after her goddaughter but her vision becomes clouded by billowing smoke. Noiselessly she glides across the plain and through the smoke to the top of the ridge where she looks down on to blackened sand dunes and the sea beyond. Hilda and the soldiers are nowhere to be seen but, bobbing in the shallows, Alice can see prams. A cry is blown across the wind; Alice charges down the dunes to the water and looks into the first pram. It is empty. She splashes to the next pram and, finding it empty, continues to the next and the next following the plaintive cry. Fearfully Alice looks inside the last pram then recoils as she finds herself peering at the broken body of a British airman covered in seaweed. He stares at her beseechingly then, as she stands trembling before him, the image fades and changes. Now a baby is lying in the pram, whimpering and clawing his fist in the air. Alice holds out her arms but she is pushed backwards by a wave.

'Neville!' she screamed.

There was a screech of brakes and Alice was almost catapulted from the bunk as the train came to a sudden halt.

She sat up, hugging her arms around herself and sobbing uncontrollably.

'It's all right. We've just stopped at a signal.' Humphrey put his hand on her shoulder.

'I had a dream, it was the dead pilot; his pram had crashed into the sea!' Alice gave a strangled sob.

'Don't think about it.' Humphrey said fiercely and squeezed into the bunk beside her. 'There's nothing you can do. Don't think about it,' he said again and wrapped himself around her.

***

Neville was sitting on Ethel's knee in the nursery drinking his milk when they arrived. He laughed and held out his arms when he saw them. Alice bent to kiss him and inhaled his sweet scent.

'And has the little man behaved himself?' Humphrey asked jovially.

'Oh yes, he's been as good as gold, haven't you my lamb?' Ethel beamed at her charge. 'How was the wedding?'

'It was lovely but the journey back was tiresome; we had hoped to be home earlier. We need to freshen up and Neville looks as if he's ready to go to sleep.' Alice's instinct was to scoop the baby into her arms but fastidiousness prevented her until she had washed her hands. 'We'll look in again when he's asleep.'

There was a film of dust on her dressing table and Alice realised just how much of Ethel's time was taken up with looking after Neville. However, when she had changed and gone down to the sitting room she found it spotless and there was a vase of daffodils on the windowsill.

'There's a letter for you from South Africa.' Humphrey passed Alice an envelope with brightly coloured stamps.

'I wonder how my brother's being affected by the war.' She opened the letter with an ivory paper knife and looked at the date on the letterhead. 'It was written in January, it's taken an unusually long time.'

Alice read the letter carefully. 'They're all well. He says it's difficult getting labour. Oh, that's sad; the young man he was training to take over part of the business was killed fighting the Germans in South West Africa. He says supplies from Europe are severely disrupted and that stores are going bankrupt but his investments have yielded good profits and he's bought up several shops cheaply. Well that's good news; I wonder what he invested in?'

'Arms, probably,' murmured Humphrey into his pipe.

'We don't know that.' Alice finished reading the letter. 'He's started up a wholesale business which he thinks will grow as soon as the war ends and he can get regular supplies again. But he says his biggest problem is getting educated staff. He wonders if the South African Emigration Society can help. Well, they might be able to after the war ends. I must admit, I miss my work with them.'

'I don't suppose there'll be so many women wanting to go; there'll be more opportunities here, especially when they get the vote.'

'Yes, we deserve that, even though I don't approve of some of the tactics the suffragettes have used.'

There was a tap on the door and Ethel came in. 'The little lamb's asleep. What would you like for your lunch?'

'Whatever is easiest. Don't go to too much trouble. I'll just take a peek at Neville then I'll give you a hand.'

'There's no need, you'll be tired after your journey.'

Alice nodded gratefully but she didn't feel tired as she bounded upstairs to look at her sleeping grandson.

***

The following day Alice took Neville out in the pram. Her boots needed repairing and she decided to take them to the cobbler near the station.

She parked the pram outside, told Neville to be good, and drew in her breath before going into the dark little shop with its overpowering smell of tannin. The elderly verger from her church was waiting for the cobbler to finish heeling his shoe and he politely asked after the family. Alice told him that William had just got married and he offered his congratulations. In return she enquired after his wife and expressed her sympathy on being told about an alarming number of ailments. The cobbler joined in the conversation and it was some time before the verger left and Alice handed over her boots.

They were startled to hear the raised voice of the verger outside followed by a woman shouting. Alice opened the door to see the mild mannered verger grappling with a young woman who was about to lift Neville from his pram.

The woman was hatless and her red hair tumbled down her back. She pushed the verger with her elbow then glanced triumphantly at Alice as she clasped Neville to her.

The cobbler hurried out of the shop. 'Is this woman causing trouble?'

'Cilla!' Alice mouthed and stood, shaking with fear and anger, as she watched the baby whimper in his mother's arms.

She drew in her breath then turned to the verger. 'Are you hurt?'

'No, I'll be all right.' He looked curiously at the two women.

'Shall I call a policeman?' the cobbler asked importantly as he wiped his hands on his apron.

Alice stood completely still and glared at Cilla.

'You can leave me to deal with this,' she said in answer to the cobbler's question. 'Perhaps you can give Mr Gibb a glass of water to help him with the shock.' She nodded dismissively.

He eyed the wild-looking young woman doubtfully. 'Well, if you're sure you can manage Madam.'

Fighting an overwhelming urge to grab Neville and run, Alice picked up Cilla's bag and flung it in the pram.

'We'll manage won't we?' she said coldly.

Alice turned the pram around saying, with great restraint, 'You can put him back when he gets too heavy.' Then, very slowly, she started to push the empty pram back towards home.

'I wasn't trying to steal him,' whispered Cilla as she caught up with Alice, the baby clasped tightly to her chest. 'I was coming to visit you and I saw you in the distance. When I walked past he waved to me, he must have recognised me.'

Alice felt weak with a mixture of relief, pity and fear. She was still tired after yesterday's journey and badly wanted to sit down.

Neville started to grizzle.

'Is he all right?' Cilla asked anxiously.

'Yes, he's fine; he ate well before we came out. He might be ready for a sleep now.'

'A sleep? Oh, I'll put him in his pram then.' Cilla lowered her child and tucked the expensive covers around him.

Alice held on tightly to the pram and propelled it forward. Her legs were shaking so much she was afraid she was going to collapse. She glanced along the street to check there was no one she knew.

'We'll rest for a moment,' she said and perched on a low garden wall, her hand still holding onto the pram.

Oblivious to the tension between his mother and grandmother, Neville gurgled as a shower of cherry tree petals fluttered above the pram. Alice glanced at Cilla's white face. Some of the pink petals had settled in her hair, giving her a child-like quality but Alice detected a determination beneath the vulnerability.

On the other side of the road two women wearing the uniforms of the Women's Royal Naval Service were walking towards the station.

'I was thinking about joining the WRNS,' said Cilla as she watched them.

'Really? What about your other job?'

'The money's good in munitions but I don't like living in Warrington and,' she rubbed her face, 'I don't want to turn yellow.'

'Why did you come to London?'

'I didn't mean to.' Her voice dropped to a whisper, 'I felt confused after the wedding. This morning I was at the Junction waiting for a train to Warrington then the London train pulled in so I got on it. And here I am.'

She ran her fingers through her hair and the petals floated to the ground.

'And what do you propose to do now you are here?'

'I can go and stay with my friend in Clapham. We were on the buses together and her mother said I was welcome any time.'

'Does she know you're coming?'

'No, but I'll be all right.' Cilla tossed her head defiantly.

'But Clapham is the other side of London.'

'Yes.' Cilla was silent then started scrabbling in her bag. 'I've brought Neville a present.'

'Good afternoon, Mrs Dacre.' A gentleman politely doffed his hat as he walked past then stared at Cilla who was throwing things out of her bag on to the pavement.

Embarrassed that Cilla was making a spectacle in public, Alice said sharply, 'Leave it, Cilla, you can give it to him at home.' Then added in a softer tone, 'And you can sleep in Daisy's room tonight.'

'Oh, thank you, just one night till I sort myself out,' said Cilla as if reading Alice's thoughts.

***

Humphrey was surprised to see Cilla when he got home from work but he greeted her courteously.

At dinner they discussed the different jobs that were open to her and Alice realised again that, despite its terrible toll on the male population, the war had given women opportunities unheard of only five years ago.

'Would you consider going back to Wales?' asked Humphrey.

Cilla pursed her lips. 'I think it's better if Lottie and William get on with their lives without me around. Anyway there aren't any jobs. And ever since I was a little girl I've dreamt of getting away.' She looked at Alice. 'I really enjoyed that book you lent me about Mary Kingsley's travels in Africa. And I read a book about Mary Slessor, but I don't think I'm the missionary type.'

'No, it's meant to be a vocation,' said Humphrey, then added, 'So what are you going to do about your job in the munitions factory?'

'I suppose I should go back. I've got some things in my locker at the hostel. Maybe I'll stay another week or two. But I'll write to my friend in Clapham and see if I can stay with her family and get a job in London.'

'Arding and Hobbs might be looking for staff.'

'Well, I've got experience of shop work and it would be nice to work in a posh department store.'

Through the window they could see people walking quickly in the dusk. A child cried and Cilla jumped up.

'Is that Neville?' she asked, her green eyes flashing.

'No, he's fast asleep upstairs,' Alice answered shortly.

'Shall I go and see if he's all right?'

'No, you stay and eat your dinner,' said Humphrey firmly.

After dinner they sat for a while in the sitting room but they were all tired and retired early to bed.

***

334

Alice was awakened in the night by a noise that seemed to be coming from Neville's bedroom. She hadn't heard him cry but she put on her dressing gown and slippers and, feeling her way in the dark, went to investigate.

She usually left the door ajar and was surprised to find it closed although there was a shaft of light coming from under it. She opened it fearfully and saw Cilla standing motionless by Neville's crib. The dim light from the bedside lamp cast shadows on the girl in her long white nightdress. As Alice observed her fragile features she detected a yellowish tinge to her cheeks.

'Are you all right, Cilla?' she asked quietly.

Her eyes fixed on the sleeping child she said, 'I couldn't sleep so I came to check on Neville. I thought he might be lonely.'

'He's not lonely, especially now that he has the beautiful bear you brought.' Alice looked at the honey coloured bear sitting in the corner of the crib, its boot button eyes glinting in the lamplight.

Cilla nodded, her gaze still fixed on her son. 'I thought it would be company for him.'

'Yes, it will.' Alice wondered just how much of her wages Cilla had spent on the exquisitely made bear.

In the preceding nine months she had been relieved that Cilla had made no attempt to contact them. However, William and Lottie's wedding seemed to have brought home to Cilla the enormity of her loss.

Alice shivered and wrapped her dressing gown more tightly around herself. She glanced at Cilla's bare feet. 'It's cold; you should get back to bed. Would you like another blanket?'

'I'm all right thank you.'

Alice put her hand lightly on Cilla's shoulder and steered her to the door. 'I'll get you what Daisy used to call her cuddle blanket.'

Cilla allowed Alice to help her into bed then Alice got a large knitted blanket from the wardrobe and wrapped it round Cilla's shoulders.

'You'll sleep all right now,' she said kindly but firmly.

Cilla nodded and closed her eyes.

Alice shut the door but stood outside until she could hear Cilla's regular breathing. She had a brief look at her sleeping grandson then, satisfied that all was well for the moment, she returned to bed.

She lay awake for a long time wondering what to do.

Humphrey had told Cilla he would arrange for her to collect a rail pass to Warrington when she arrived at Euston in the morning. Part of her hoped that Cilla would decide to stay in her job at the munitions factory but, for the sake of her health, Alice knew it would be unwise.

Cilla had talked of getting a job in Clapham. Although it was the other side of London it was still near enough for Cilla to visit without too much difficulty. Neville would be walking soon, then talking and understanding. Alice clenched her fists in the darkness. She had to protect Neville. And William.

She was exhausted, her head was muzzy but sleep eluded her. Fragments of the day returned to her – the bizarre scene in the street when Cilla had elbowed the bewildered Mr Gibb contrasted with the civilised conversation at dinner when Cilla said she would like to work in a posh shop because she had experience of shop work.

Alice knew that something else had been said that held a key to the future, but her mind was blank. She let her thoughts drift to the day before when they arrived back from Wales. Then she remembered the letter from her brother saying that he had bought several shops but was having problems with staff.

'I've always dreamt of getting away. I really enjoyed that book you lent me about Mary Kingsley's travels in Africa.' Cilla's words at dinner suddenly came to her and Alice felt the tension leave her body.

She would make Cilla's dreams come true. She would arrange for her to go to South Africa.

And then Neville would be safe.

Chapter 25: Lottie

Union Castle Line to South and East Africa
Royal Mail Service Frequent Sailings
Subject to Cancellation or Alteration including
Deviation without notice

The Times: November 9th 1918

Lottie leant against the promenade railings and watched the waves crashing against the pier supports. There were thin rays of sunshine in the grey sky and white crests on the waves lightened the darkness of the sea. A ship bobbed alarmingly on the horizon and Lottie felt suddenly queasy. She held her hands across her stomach and remembered the times when she and Cilla had watched the boat from Liverpool arrive with its cargo of holidaymakers. They had talked about saving their pocket money so they could go to England on a boat trip. Since then most of the boats had been requisitioned by the Navy and the trippers were mainly military people, often on convalescence.

She turned and walked towards the pier entrance then waved at the figure hurrying towards her. For a moment she hardly recognised Bronwen. She had put on weight and looked almost matronly but her eyes sparkled as she greeted her friend.

'I hope I'm not late!' she said.

'No, I was early.'

'I've got so much to tell you!' both girls said in unison then looked at each other and laughed.

They linked arms and walked along the pier to an empty shelter where they sat down facing the sea.

'You first,' said Lottie looking at her friend curiously.

Bronwen drew in her breath. 'Well, no, you first. Is it good news?'

Lottie's face shone. 'Yes,' she said.

'You're expecting!'

Lottie nodded excitedly.

'And is William pleased?'

'Of course. He says our baby will represent the future. A future with no more wars.'

'That's lovely, Lottie; I hadn't thought of it like that.'

'And what's your news?'

Bronwen slowly took off her glove and held out her left hand to show off the band of gold on her ring finger.

'You're married! Congratulations! But I thought Robert had gone away. Why didn't you tell me?' Lottie tried not to sound hurt.

'Yes, Robert's gone away,' Bronwen said grimly. 'Scarpered as soon as he knew I was in the family way.'

'You? So we're both expecting! But...?'

'You don't think too badly of me do you?' Bronwen looked anxiously at Lottie.

'Of course not. I just don't understand.' She looked at her friend's wedding ring, hoping for enlightenment.

Bronwen gazed at the sea for a moment then said quietly, 'I don't deserve to be so happy.'

'Of course you do!' Lottie waited for Bronwen to continue but she was strangely pensive. 'So who's the lucky man?' she asked when she could bear the suspense no longer.

'It's Dylan!' she said, her face suddenly radiant.

'Dylan! That's wonderful! I always thought you two were right for each other!'

'It would have saved a lot of trouble if I'd realised it earlier.' Bronwen wiped a tear from her eye.

'Dylan will make a lovely father.'

'He will. And, as long as the baby doesn't arrive early, no one will know he isn't.'

'Isn't what?'

'Isn't the father!'

'Oh!' Lottie stared at her friend as she tried to understand what she was telling her. 'I think you've had a difficult time,' she said inadequately.

'Robert was so horrible when I told him I was expecting,' Bronwen said vehemently. 'He laughed when he realised I thought he'd marry me.'

'But what did he think you'd do?'

'He wanted me to get rid of it.' Bronwen folded her hands on her lap and rocked gently on the hard bench.

'But that's not possible!'

'Oh yes it is. He tried to give me money.'

'To get rid of the baby? Bronwen, that's terrible! What did you do?'

'I spat on it!' Bronwen began to laugh. 'I suppose that proved his point that I wasn't good enough for the likes of him.'

'Well, I'll tell you now, I didn't like him and neither did William,' Lottie said indignantly. She looked at her friend hiccupping with laughter. 'Did you say you spat on his money? Good for you!' she giggled.

A couple of soldiers paused and looked curiously at Bronwen who was laughing loudly and uncontrollably. 'Can we share the joke, girls?' one of them asked.

'It's girl talk,' shouted Lottie shaking with laughter.

Bronwen blew her nose then got up. 'I'm cold. Let's go and have some tea,' she said abruptly.

As they walked along the promenade Bronwen told Lottie of the despair she had felt while trying to act as if nothing had happened. After a few days she had gone for a walk along the beach to try and pluck up the courage to tell her mother.

'That's where I met Dylan!' Bronwen pointed to a spot at the far end of the beach. 'He said he was home on leave and had called to see me, and my mother told him I'd gone for a walk. And he came to find me!'

'He must have known you were in trouble. He's always loved you.'

'That's what he said. But I didn't think I was worthy of him anymore.'

'Don't ever say that!' Lottie said passionately.

Bronwen looked at her friend with understanding.

'He was so angry when I told him how Robert had treated me. I've never seen him like that.' She smiled then said dreamily, 'And then he proposed to me.'

Lottie squeezed her friend's arm. 'And now you're married and I'm so happy for both of you.'

'Life's going to be all right isn't it? They say the war's nearly over and we've got our babies to think about.'

'And our husbands!' said Lottie with a knowing grin.

'Yes. Oh, Lottie, we're so lucky!'

***

Lottie and Bronwen scarcely noticed the lack lustre appearance of the shops as they wandered towards the station talking nineteen to the dozen. It wasn't until she was on the train that Lottie began to comprehend just how awful Bronwen's situation might have been. Even if her mother had accepted the situation she would have been an outcast, a fallen woman with an illegitimate child. Unlike her own child, Bronwen's would have grown up forever disadvantaged by being born out of wedlock. Or she would have been forced to give the baby away to a stranger and never see it again. Lottie had a sudden vision of William's mother fussing over

Neville. Fleetingly she wondered if Neville's real mother was grieving for the child she had been unable to care for. She frowned and tapped her foot on the carriage floor.

'Are you all right?' The woman sitting opposite asked curiously.

Lottie looked up startled. The train was rattling along the estuary and she could just make out the mountains in the distance. She knew the long war was almost over. Everyone bore some scars but it was time to look to the future.

'Yes,' she said and smiled. 'Everything's all right.'

The train drew into the station; Lottie crossed the road and opened the door of the shop. There were several customers waiting to be served and Jack looked agitated but, when Lottie went to join him behind the counter, he told her to go through to the living quarters.

Nellie looked up from her chair by the fire with an anxious expression on her face. 'Your sister's come home to tell us something,' she said.

Cilla stood up and looked at Lottie defiantly.

'Cilla! I've missed you!' Lottie kissed her then stepped back. 'But you're so thin. That job can't be good for you.'

'Then it's a good thing I'm leaving.'

'That's good. Are you coming home?'

Nellie gave a short laugh. 'She's going to South Africa if you please!'

'South Africa! Whatever for?'

'I've been offered a job there.'

'A job? What kind of job?' Lottie took off her hat and ran her fingers through her hair.

'I've been offered a position as an assistant manager in a wholesale store in Cape Town.' Cilla said importantly.

'But why?' Lottie looked uncertainly at her mother.

'Mrs Dacre says she'll have better prospects out there.'

'What's she got to do with it?'

'She got me the job. Her brother owns the store.'

'Oh!' Lottie slowly hung up her coat and sat down on a hard chair. 'But you'll come back?'

Cilla's voice was brittle. 'Someday, perhaps.'

'Of course she'll come back!' snapped Nellie. She heaved herself out of her chair. 'I'll make us a brew.'

'You always wanted to travel,' said Lottie slowly. 'But how did William's mother know that?'

'Don't you remember her telling us about her brother in South Africa when we visited?'

'Oh yes, and you said you'd like to live on an African farm.' Lottie twisted the rings on her finger. 'That was a lovely week-end; so much has happened since then. But, are you sure you want to go?'

Cilla blew her nose. 'Yes, I really do. I'm going to live with the family until I find my feet. They've got a big house with views of the sea. Mrs Dacre says I'll have to work hard but I'll be well looked after.'

Lottie felt her sister slipping away from her as she held her gaze. 'It does seem a wonderful opportunity,' she said quietly. 'As long as you're happy, that's all that matters.'

'None of us would be happy if I stayed,' murmured Cilla.

'Your Auntie Meg was here yesterday and she brought some welsh cakes,' interrupted Nellie.

'Oh lovely!' Lottie smiled at her mother. 'Sorry, what did you say Cilla?'

'I said I'm happy to leave the factory.'

'Oh. Yes, you must be. When are you leaving?'

'I've already left. I'm going back down to London in a couple of days to stay with my friend in Clapham

343

and then get the train to Southampton when there's a sailing. Mr Dacre is arranging it for me.'

'I wish we'd had longer to get used to the idea,' grumbled Nellie.

'I didn't want to tell you till it was definite. And Mrs Dacre said there'll be a rush for places on the boats as soon as the war's over so I'd better be at the front of the queue.'

Lottie felt a gentle movement in her stomach. 'So you won't see your little niece or nephew,' she said reproachfully.

'You must send me lots of photographs. And I'll send you photographs.' Cilla had a new poise as she looked at her sister.

'It will be an opportunity for you,' said Nellie handing Cilla a cup of tea. 'It was good of Mrs Dacre to think of you.'

Taking her cue from their mother, Lottie added 'And you'll have lots of stories to tell when you come home. Do you remember Mrs Dacre saying her brother and his family visited from South Africa?'

'Yes, she hopes they'll visit again when everything's back to normal. Maybe they'll leave me in charge!'

'As long as you don't go back to your wild ways, you should do very well for yourself,' Nellie said practically but her eyes were dark as she sank down in her chair.

***

Lottie tried not to be hurt by Cilla's reluctance to come home with her when she had finished helping her father in the shop. 'But you must see William before you leave! And you haven't even seen our house!'

'Off you go, my girl,' said Nellie, 'your father and I won't be a lot of company for you this evening. But don't be late back, high tide's at nine o'clock and you don't want to be crossing the bridge anywhere near then; there's been a lot of strong winds blowing up the estuary lately.'

'No, I won't be late,' said Cilla obediently as she put on her coat.

Darkness was beginning to fall as they walked over the suspension bridge, their heads bent low against the drizzle. They caught a glimpse of shop lights in the High Street but these gradually disappeared behind blackout curtains. Shadow-like figures trudged along the cobbles; some paused occasionally and doffed their hats with a disembodied, 'Good evening, ladies.'

Lottie turned down a side street and stopped outside a terraced house. 'Wait a moment while I draw the curtains,' she said when she had unlocked the door. As soon as the blackouts were in place Lottie switched on the lights and led her sister into the sitting room.

'It's a bit cold but it will soon warm up.' Lottie put a match to the fire. 'Do you like it?' she asked as Cilla's eyes darted round the room.

'You've made it very nice. Your paintings are lovely; this one's new,' said Cilla as she looked at a watercolour of Conway harbour. 'And there's the runner I made you when you got engaged,' she added, pointing to a cloth on the sideboard. She bent forward and looked intently at the carefully arranged photographs.

In pride of place, next to the wedding portrait, was a photograph of Lottie and Cilla standing on either side of William in his naval uniform. The photographer had captured the spontaneous gaiety of the sisters that weekend so long ago when they had visited London for the first time. William must have moved after the photographer positioned them because his head was slightly turned towards Cilla although his body leaned towards his fiancée.

'It's my favourite photograph,' said Lottie happily. 'It's a reminder of a perfect week-end.'

'Surely your wedding portrait is your favourite?'

'But that's what it is, a portrait. It shows off my dress beautifully but it's rather formal. I was trying not to shiver from the cold when it was taken.'

'Yes, it was cold wasn't it?' Cilla frowned and picked up a smaller photograph of two little girls riding a donkey. 'This is us on the beach on my eighth birthday. That was ten years ago.' She laughed for the first time since arriving.

'Hello! Have we got company?' William looked taken aback when he saw Cilla. He kissed Lottie then gave Cilla a light kiss on her cheek. 'Hello, Sis. What brings you here?'

'Cilla's going to South Africa,' said Lottie before Cilla could say anything.

William raised his eyebrows. 'South Africa? You're certainly full of surprises.'

Cilla blushed and said nothing.

'She's going to work for your mother's brother. Why don't we go into the kitchen and Cilla can tell you about it while I'm cooking the tea.'

William listened intently when Cilla told him about the job she had been offered.

'We'll miss her, won't we?' said Lottie when William was satisfied that Cilla would be treated well in her new life.

'Yes.' He hesitated, 'Of course we will.'

'How was your day?' Lottie asked when they were sitting round the table.

'Busy. And didn't it turn cold this afternoon?'

'Yes. I was lucky the rain held off while I was in Llandudno with Bronwen.'

'And how is she? Still with that captain of hers?'

'No.' Lottie's eyes widened, 'something dreadful happened.'

'Oh no!' William looked concerned. 'I must admit I didn't have a lot of time for the man but I wouldn't wish him dead. What happened?'

Lottie lowered her voice. 'He got Bronwen in the family way. And he refused to marry her.' She stopped, waiting for their righteous indignation.

William stared at his plate. 'I knew he wasn't a gentleman,' he muttered.

'He most certainly isn't!' Lottie's eyes flashed. 'He gave her money to get rid of it!'

Cilla gasped. 'Poor Bronwen. What did she do?'

'She spat on it.' The strain of the day was beginning to tell and Lottie began to cry tears of laughter while William and Cilla looked on in astonishment.

'Lottie.' William put his hand over hers. 'You're not making much sense. Is Bronwen all right?'

Lottie gave him a trusting smile. 'Yes, she's married a Welshman like you said. Dylan said he's always loved her and no one will know he isn't really the baby's father. Isn't that wonderful?'

Cilla nodded. 'So she won't have to go to a mother and baby home,' she whispered.

William blanched. 'I'm glad for both of them it's got a happy ending,' he said quietly. 'And what about Captain Briggs? There's no danger of him coming back?'

'No, he was posted to Ireland and he told Bronwen he never wanted to set foot in Wales again.' Lottie paused, 'Even though I'm happy for Bronwen and Dylan I think it's abominable that he can get away with such behaviour.'

William and Cilla glanced at each other.

'Sadly, men can't always be trusted to do the right thing,' William said.

'No, I suppose not.' Lottie looked puzzled. She was surprised by their reaction; they had appeared saddened rather than indignant.

'Dylan's only ever had eyes for Bronwen,' said Cilla. 'I wonder what happened to those soldiers who were taunting him at the Christmas party.'

'They're probably lying in unmarked graves somewhere in Flanders. It's the cripples and the cowards who've been the lucky ones in this war.'

'But they were cowards! You said so yourself!' Lottie spoke shrilly.

'Yes, they were. Then. But when their names are carved on memorials to the dead they will be heroes and the rest of us ..,' he shrugged.

Lottie drew in her breath sharply. The dark expression William had worn when she had gone to London to care for him had returned. She knew it was pointless to remind him that he had shown courage when he rescued the mother and baby after the air raid. Although his memory had almost completely returned, the events of that night were still a blank. And he refused to believe what he was unable to remember.

Cilla excused herself and went to the bathroom. Lottie began to clear the plates. When Cilla returned she had applied fresh powder and lipstick.

'You look nice,' said Lottie. 'Shall we go into the sitting room?'

'I'll give you a hand with the dishes then I'll go home.'

'There's no need, I'll do them later.'

'You need to take care of yourself in your condition, isn't that right William?

William stubbed out a cigarette. 'Yes, of course she should.' The cigarette had revived him but he seemed confused as he looked at the two sisters working harmoniously together at the kitchen sink.

'Are you sure you won't stay longer?' said Lottie when they had finished.

For a moment Cilla hesitated. 'I promised Mother I wouldn't be late.'

'All right. We'll walk you half way won't we William?'

'Yes, of course.'

The rain had stopped but the damp air folded itself around them as they hurried through the dark streets. They could hear the waves crashing against the harbour walls and the sound of a motor as a fishing vessel chugged to port ahead of the tide.

When they reached the middle of the bridge Cilla paused. 'Thank you for coming this far, I can make my own way back now.'

'We'll see you to the other end,' said William.

They continued in silence. When they reached the end of the bridge Lottie hugged her sister and felt her tremble as she rested her head on her shoulder. 'Sleep tight,' said Lottie. 'I'll see you tomorrow.'

William kissed his sister-in-law and they watched for a moment as she walked on towards the Junction.

'I hope the African sunshine will make her better,' said Lottie as they made their way back. 'She's much too thin.'

'I know you'll miss her,' William replied hesitantly, 'but I think a new life on a new continent is just what she needs.'

Chapter 26: Alice

Streets Gay with Flags
London and the country generally received with fervent
gratitude the news that the greatest war in history had
come to an end.

The Times: November 12th 1918

Sitting at her bureau, Alice felt that new beginnings were in the air. Cilla had replied with enthusiasm to her letter about the job in South Africa, arrangements had been made and she would be leaving imminently. Lottie was expecting and she and Humphrey would soon be proper grandparents.

There was a jumble of letters and pamphlets to sort out. Before Neville had arrived she had had time to keep everything in good order. 'Not that I'd have it any other way,' she thought as she put the papers into piles. At the bottom of the drawer was an envelope of photographs that William had left for safe keeping. As she looked at the snap shots of young RNAS officers she wondered how many were still alive and, not for the first time, offered a silent prayer that William had been spared.

A larger envelope bore the inscription; 'photographs handle with care.' Inside were the prints that had been taken in Hyde Park on Lottie and Cilla's first visit to London. She studied the portrait of the family group, everyone looked their best but she thought it was a pity that Daisy had not been well enough to come with them.

She examined the next photograph carefully. It was an excellent likeness of William and the two sisters and had a freshness and innocence about it that had not dimmed with the passing of time. As Alice looked at the picture she thought of Cilla, still only a child, about to leave everything she knew to start a new life half way round the world. She took an envelope, dipped her pen in the inkbottle and wrote Cilla's name. Then she placed the photograph in the envelope and sealed it. She stood up and put the envelope in a box of books she had been collecting for Cilla to take to South Africa. Feeling satisfied that she had done the right thing, Alice put the papers neatly back in the drawer and went to find Ethel.

'Neville's having his sleep,' said Ethel when Alice entered the kitchen.

'That's good, he'll be fresh when Daisy arrives.'

'He'll be pleased to see his Auntie Daisy. I hope she doesn't catch a cold travelling in this weather.'

In the event, it was nearly dark by the time Daisy arrived.

Neville greeted her enthusiastically and, as she took him in her arms, Alice hoped it would not be long before she had a child of her own. However, that was unlikely to happen until the war was over as Daisy had told her that she had hardly seen Alec since the RNAS had become part of the RAF.

'Was your train delayed?' Alice asked when they were sitting by the fire.

'No, I had to wait ages for the person I was meeting.'

'Who was that?' Alice knew it wasn't any of her business but she couldn't help asking.

'Someone I used to work with.'

'A nurse?'

'No, a doctor. Actually, he's a consultant.'

Daisy busied herself with her handbag and handed Neville a clockwork soldier. 'Let me wind it up for you,' she said and Alice realised the subject was closed.

'I had a letter from Hilda yesterday. She said she's got tomorrow off so she's going to come and see us. You don't mind do you?'

'Of course not! Hilda's always welcome.'

***

Daisy flung open the door as soon as she saw Hilda stride up the path the following morning.

'It's lovely to see you again!' she said giving her friend a hug.

'I got up really early so we could have a nice long day together.'

While the girls devoted the next couple of hours to gossiping and looking after Neville, Alice felt some of the tension that had become part of everyday life begin to recede. As she attended to household duties she could hear sounds of laughter, a musical box playing and shouts of delight from Neville.

When she went into the sitting room Neville was jumping up and down pulling funny faces while Daisy and Hilda were contorting their facial muscles into hideous expressions.

'Oh my!' exclaimed Alice, 'You've all been turned into hobgoblins!'

This made Neville laugh uncontrollably and Daisy sat him on her knee to calm him.

'He's quite hot,' she said putting her hand on his forehead.

'I expect he's over excited, he'll be all right soon won't you little one?'

Neville nodded and put his thumb in his mouth.

For a moment the room was silent then Hilda said, 'It's nice being here again, it's like old times.'

'Well, not quite,' said Daisy fondly stroking Neville's head.

Suddenly they heard shouts in the street, a horn blared and church bells began to ring.

'What's going on?' Hilda ran to the window.

Daisy joined her, still holding Neville.

More horns sounded and the unaccustomed sound of the bells made them gasp in delighted surprise.

Alice put her hand on each of the girls' shoulders, 'This can only mean one thing,' she said her voice trembling with emotion.

'The war's over!' cried Hilda.

'Alec's coming home!' shouted Daisy.

Doors were opening all along the street and people were running outside laughing and shouting, 'God save the King!'

They hurried into the hallway and found Ethel by the open front door, her careworn face lit up by a broad grin. She held out her arms and Daisy handed Neville to her, his eyes wide with excitement. The girls ran down the path and leant over the gate.

Suddenly there was a burst of fire in the sky from a maroon, which they had come to associate with air raid warnings.

'It can't be another raid!' said Daisy disbelievingly.

'What's happened?' called Hilda to two girls in nursing capes.

'The war is over! They're letting the maroons off to show everyone it's ended!' They laughed and clapped their hands.

Alice felt her eyes brim with tears as she saw the ecstatic faces of the four young women and Neville clapping and shouting, 'Over!'

'Good luck!' the girls called to each other then the nurses hurried on their way and Daisy and Hilda came back into the house.

'We must celebrate. Let's go into Town, everyone will be there,' said Daisy eagerly.

***

At first Alice had said she would stay behind and look after Neville but, by the time they had finished a quick lunch, he was sleeping soundly and the girls insisted they should celebrate the occasion together.

As they crossed the road to the station a bus crowded with passengers singing on the top deck pulled away.

'It will probably be a long wait for the next bus,' said Alice.

Daisy and Hilda looked at each other.

'The war is over,' said Daisy gently taking her mother's arm. 'You used to take the tube before.'

Hilda took her other arm. 'We'll look after you,' she said.

Alice allowed herself to be led to the lift and down to the underground platform.

A train was just pulling in and they easily found seats together. Alice had no time to feel anxious because everyone was talking and laughing. As more passengers got on they exchanged what little news they knew.

At Camden Town a gaggle of girls surged on, completely filling their compartment. They took out their lipstick and powder compacts and busily applied their make-up.

'We walked out as soon as we heard the news,' the girl nearest to Alice confided.

'Thank the Lord I'll not have to set foot in that factory again.' A blonde- haired girl peered into her compact mirror then, apparently satisfied, snapped it closed.

'We'll have to go back for our wages,' her companion said.

'Yeah, I'll take my wages but I'm not going near those machines again.'

'Wages should be doubled, the profits he's made from this war,' said another girl dosing herself liberally with cheap scent. Then, catching site of Hilda staring at her in amazement added, 'What are you looking at Miss High-and-Mighty?'

'Hold your tongue, Rose,' the girl who had spoken to Alice said sharply.

'I'll say what I like to anyone I want. The war's over and I won't go back to being pushed around and looked down on.'

'But ….,' Hilda started then stopped as Alice laid a warning hand on her arm.

'Good for you!' said Alice. 'And now women have got the vote we can make ourselves heard.'

The girl studied Alice curiously for a minute then nodded and lit a cigarette.

Alice could see Daisy looking at her anxiously when the train filled up at Euston and they were wedged in by swaying bodies hanging on to the straps as the train rattled through the dark tunnel. However, the euphoria of the crowd banished any fears that Alice might have had. Even when temporarily separated from Daisy and Hilda as they got off the train, Alice held on to the feeling of quiet elation.

They met at the entrance to the station and stood to let a patrol of boy scouts run past sounding 'All clear!' on their bugles. The cacophony of police whistles blowing, hand bells ringing, vehicles hooting and people singing was almost overwhelming. They tried to cross the Strand to Trafalgar Square but found themselves pulled towards Admiralty Arch.

Alice guessed she wasn't the only one to experience a sense of déjà vu as they were swept down the Mall towards Buckingham Palace.

'I can't believe it's four years since we were here with William,' said Daisy.

'Four long years,' added Hilda.

'And we thought it would all be over by Christmas!'

'Did you really believe that?' asked Alice.

Daisy looked confused. 'Yes, I did and so did most of my generation.'

There was a gentle toot and a young soldier in a self-propelled bath chair came alongside waving a Union Jack. On his sleeve were a crown and three stripes denoting his rank as staff sergeant. He winked at the girls as he passed and they smiled while trying not to look at the empty trouser leg pinned up under his jacket.

Drums from different regiments beat as troops from all over the Empire and from the United States headed towards Buckingham Palace.

'Look, there go the Ghurkhas!' said Hilda as a group of dark-skinned soldiers wearing shorts, knee-high boots and wide-brimmed hats marched past.

'And there's the R.A.F. I wonder if we'll see Alec!' Daisy craned her neck as they passed and received whistles and waves but there was no sign of Alec.

'And certainly no sign of William,' thought Alice feeling desolated for the first time that day.

As they approached Buckingham Palace they saw a procession of munitions girls wearing their overalls and carrying a large Union Jack. They were cheered by some Australian soldiers who had climbed onto the huge marble carving of the Victoria Memorial to get a better view. The normally severe façade of the palace was bright with crimson velvet festooning the balcony and in front people waved flags and handkerchiefs of all colours.

Cries of, 'We want King George!' caused the crowd to surge forward and once again Daisy and Hilda linked their arms through Alice's.

When the king and queen appeared on the balcony the Guards started to play the National Anthem but it could scarcely be heard for the cheers and shouts from the upturned faces below. Gradually people started to sing and Alice, Daisy and Hilda swayed with the crowd and sang at the tops of their voices. The band played 'Rule Britannia', 'Land of Hope and Glory' and other stirring tunes that had kept people going throughout the war. There were cheers when everyone sang the 'Marseillaise', then the crowd quietened to listen to the King's short message of peace.

It was dusk by the time the crowd began to disperse and there was a light drizzle. Alice, Daisy and Hilda made their way back up the Mall and, uncertain what to do next, crossed to Trafalgar Square. Someone had lit a bonfire at the foot of Nelson's Column and people of all ages danced around laughing, singing and shouting. Egged on by some munitions girls, a group of Australian soldiers started a game of leapfrog and urged the girls to join in.

'Shame on you!' shouted a woman, as one of the girls leapt over a soldier's back and was carried like a trophy by two of his comrades.

'It's just a bit of fun ma'am, we're going home soon,' one of the young soldiers said, his blue eyes shining at the thought.

But the woman was unmoved. 'You may be but thousands aren't.'

'Well, I'm sure glad to be going home,' drawled a young soldier in United States army uniform. 'My sweetheart's waiting for me in Texas. I came over here to do a job and now it's done I'm going home.'

'I don't think he understood what she meant,' whispered Hilda.

'No,' said Alice moving away. 'The newspapers are already writing about the unreturning army.'

They walked away from the bonfire and found themselves part of a sober throng heading slowly towards the church overlooking the square. As Alice looked ahead she saw that the majority of the crowd were women of all ages and social classes. She heard snatches of conversation about sons, fathers, brothers, husbands and sweethearts who would never return. Two young women walking alongside her were talking about the fiancés they had lost, friends from the same regiment.

As she looked at Daisy and Hilda, Alice was filled with gratitude that neither of them had had to endure such a loss. Daisy must have sensed her thoughts because she squeezed her arm and gave her a dazzling smile. Hilda walked steadily, lost in thought. Alice wondered if she was thinking about her brother or maybe she had had a secret sweetheart who was one of the millions who would never return. Alice hoped with all her heart that happiness would be granted to Hilda as it had been to Daisy and William.

Outside the church was a notice inviting people to attend a service for the unreturning army.

'The service is about to start, would you like to go?' asked Alice.

Daisy looked at Hilda. 'I don't mind, I will if you'd like to.'

'I don't feel like praying with all these strangers. I'd rather go to my own church. And I expect Auntie Alice would like to go home now to Neville.'

Alice nodded. 'And I'd like to be home when Humphrey arrives. I expect the station was busy today.'

They moved aside to let people pass into the church and made their way to the underground.

'Isn't it wonderful to see all the lights!' said Daisy.

'Yes, really wonderful, I didn't know how I was going to face another winter of black-outs,' Alice agreed.

'Well it's all over now and we've got the future to look forward to,' said Hilda jubilantly.

Chapter 27: Lottie

Influenza Again
From all parts of the country comes news of the disease
and the deadly pneumonia that follows it

The Times: February 18th 1919

Lottie bent her head against the wind as the train wheezed into the station. Her coat strained uncomfortably over her swelling belly and she felt self-conscious as she squeezed into a carriage packed with soldiers.

A grey-faced corporal glowered at her then turned to his companion. 'What's it all been for? That's what I want to know.'

'We were fighting to keep our country free. And now we're going home.'

The corporal snorted. 'Home! To a wife who's carrying another man's child. What sort of a homecoming is that?'

'You shouldn't put up with it,' the soldier sitting opposite Lottie said menacingly.

'You let her know who's boss.' A merchant seaman in the corner took a swig from his hip flask and handed it to the cuckolded corporal.

A wave of nausea swept over Lottie as she inhaled the odour of cheap alcohol mixed with stale sweat.

'You going far, love?' The soldier sitting next to her looked concerned.

'No, I get off at the next station.' Lottie clasped her hands in her lap as the train rattled over the estuary then ground to a halt at signals outside the Junction.

'At least we've all come back.' A sad-faced young lance corporal spoke for the first time. 'My brother was waiting for a troop ship back from the Continent and an influenza epidemic swept the camp. Half of them never made it. My mother was living for his return and all she got was his medal.'

'It's been a bad business,' said the soldier next to Lottie though whether he was referring to the epidemic or the war she couldn't tell.

Lottie glanced at the corporal whose wife had cheated on him, saw he was wearing the Military Medal and wondered what act of bravery had led to the award. She felt like saying he should be proud that his country had honoured him but then realised it was hardly adequate compensation for his wife seeking comfort elsewhere when he was away. She sometimes wondered how William felt about not having a medal then shivered as she realised they were often given posthumously or to men who had had been seriously injured as a result of their brave actions.

The train lurched forward and lumbered into the station. Lottie stood up and thanked the soldier who opened the door for her.

She hurried across the road and through the back gate into her parents' house.

'How do you like this, Lottie?' Her mother held up a length of dark blue cloth.

Lottie took off her gloves and felt the fabric. 'It's tweed, good quality. Where did you get it?'

'I did a bit of bartering. I thought you could make yourself a cape.' Nellie looked pleased with herself.

'Thank you so much, I can't wear this much longer.' Lottie hung her coat on the back of the door. 'How are your legs today?'

Nellie shrugged. 'This weather doesn't help.'

'And how's Father?'

'He's been a bit down lately. Supplies are as difficult as ever but people expect to buy everything now the war's ended. There was a to-do in the shop yesterday over the last tin of ham.'

'Poor Father, I'll go and give him a hand.' Lottie walked to the shop door.

'No, I'll take over for a bit. You can make your father a brew and read this letter from your sister.' With a flourish Nellie held up an envelope with colourful South African stamps.

'How is she?' Lottie asked eagerly.

'She says she's all right. Look, she's sent some photographs.' Nellie handed her a print of Cilla leaning over the veranda of a small bungalow and looking confidently at the camera.

'She looks well.' Lottie stared at the photograph, trying to catch hold of her sister in her new life. But it felt like an illusion. 'Is that her house?' she asked.

'She says it's the family's guest house in the garden of the big house. She's just there temporarily. Look, this is their house.' Nellie showed her a picture of four children and a dog sitting on the lawn in front of a much larger bungalow with fruit trees in the background.

'It's beautiful.' Lottie looked at her mother and wondered how she felt about Cilla leading a life they had no part in.

'And this is the last one.' Nellie fumbled with the photograph and it dropped on the floor. For a moment they looked down at Cilla's laughing face on a sandy beach with the sea in the background.

'I'll go and tell your father you're here,' Nellie said abruptly.

As Lottie bent down to retrieve the photograph she noticed her mother wipe a tear from her eye.

She studied the picture then took the letter and settled down to read in the same hungry way she used to read William's letters.

'Your sister seems to be doing all right.'

Lottie looked up startled; she hadn't heard her father come into the room. 'Yes. I can't believe she's manageress of a wholesale store and in charge of all those people.'

'Let's hope there won't be any men wanting her job when they all get back from Europe and East Africa.'

'Do you think they might?'

'Not really. I reckon most of them are pioneers, they'll be wanting to start new businesses and farms, not work for someone else.'

'I think Cilla's always been a bit of a pioneer.'

Jack sighed. 'I suppose she has. And how are you keeping? Everything all right?' His eyes softened as he thought of the grandchild his daughter was carrying.

'Yes, I'm well. William takes good care of me.'

'And so he should.'

Lottie got up and handed her father the letter. 'You'll be ready for your tea, she said.

***

There were two letters on the mat when Lottie arrived home. One, in a handwriting she vaguely recognised, was addressed to Mr and Mrs W Dacre. She laid it aside and tore open the one to herself from Cilla. It was similar to the letter she had read earlier but there were tantalising references to young men including one she had mentioned in her first letter describing the voyage to Cape Town.

Lottie put the letter in her pocket. She had been worried that her little sister would be lonely and frightened so far from home but the letters and photographs showed that Cilla's life had vastly improved since her days in the munitions factory. That didn't alter the fact that Lottie missed her, even if they hadn't seen much of each other since Cilla had run away to start her new life in London. Not for the first time, she wondered why Cilla had left her job on the buses and remained out of touch for so long afterwards.

As she started to prepare the evening meal, Lottie kept glancing at the other letter and wondering if she should open it. She was just scrutinising the postmark when she heard William unlock the door. She hurried into the hallway and lifted her face for his kiss.

'There's a letter,' she said when he followed her into the kitchen.

He looked at the envelope. 'It's from Hilda. You could have opened it.'

'I wanted us to share it.'

'Thank you,' he said absently as he read the first page.

Lottie watched as William frowned then bit his lip when he turned over the page. The colour slowly drained from his face and he slumped into a chair.

'What's happened?' she asked fearfully.

'It's Daisy,' he muttered and handed her the letter.

Alarmed, Lottie read the contents. Hilda began by saying she didn't know whether she should write but she felt they should know that Daisy had been diagnosed with cancer. Daisy had forbidden Alec and her parents to tell them because she didn't want them upset before the baby was born. Hilda said that her experience of working with relatives as well as patients at Queen Mary's led her to disagree and she had decided to take the matter into her own hands and let them know. She went on to say that Daisy was receiving the best possible treatment from a London consultant and was very well cared for at home and everyone was hopeful for her recovery.

'Poor Daisy,' whispered Lottie.

'My parents never wanted her to take that job,' said William bitterly.

'She hasn't got a job.' Lottie looked puzzled.

'Don't you remember? She was a radiographer.'

'Oh.' Lottie wasn't sure what the connection was but nodded in agreement. 'Perhaps we can go and visit?' she suggested tentatively.

'I don't want you travelling in your condition.'

'The baby isn't due for another three months. It might cheer her up.'

William hesitated. 'It probably would. But I don't think it would be wise for you to travel at the moment. Particularly with this flu epidemic.'

'It was good of Hilda to let us know.'

'Yes, Hilda's a brick.'

'I'll write to Daisy and Alec this evening. I can say we haven't heard from them for a while and we hope they are all right.'

William looked grateful. 'Yes, that's a good idea.'

***

Lottie posted the letter the following morning then walked aimlessly down a narrow street thinking about Daisy with an illness she didn't understand and her sister in a country she would never visit. The city walls towered above her and for a moment she didn't know where she was. She hurriedly retraced her steps until she was back in the main street by the draper's shop where she remembered that she needed some lining material to go with the cloth her mother had given her. As she suspected, there was none to be had but she bought some black velvet to edge the collar and a large gold button for the fastening.

Lottie only helped out in her parent's shop two afternoons a week now, so she spent the next couple of days making her new cape. As she sewed she thought about Daisy and how she had looked forward to getting to know her better now they were sisters-in-law. She knew that William had been excited by Alec's idea of running their own airline but, for the time being, everyone was concentrating on trying to get back to normality after four years of war. She smiled to herself as she remembered Daisy's laughing encouragement at her wedding when she announced she would get her pilot's licence. The baby kicked inside her and Lottie realised that she would soon have more practical things to learn. She stood up and rubbed her back, admiring the fine quality tweed as she did so.

Suddenly the door slammed and Lottie turned round feeling frightened. It was four o'clock; William wasn't expected home for another couple of hours.

'Whatever's happened?' she asked staring into his ashen face.

'My father telephoned. Daisy caught flu and she's dangerously ill.'

Lottie drew in her breath and attempted to say something comforting but the look on William's face told her there was nothing to say. She wrapped her arms around him and they rocked together as the evening shadows began to darken the room.

'I've run out of cigarettes,' William said abruptly and gently pushed Lottie away. She followed him to the door and stood in the cold air watching him stride down the street as if he was trying to outpace his troubles. Until then she had subconsciously thought that her love for Cilla was deeper than William's for his sister. She remained at the door long after William had turned the corner, remembering his stories of childhood holidays and his delight that Daisy had married a man who was worthy of her.

Lottie was stiff when she finally closed the door and the house felt cold. She lit the fire then soaked her hands in hot water and waited for William to return.

Neither of them slept well that night and by some unspoken agreement they were up before dawn.

They had just finished an early breakfast when the telegram they were dreading arrived.

'There's no reply,' said William curtly as he handed money to the telegraph boy.

Lottie looked at the stark line of typing on the telegram in William's shaking hand. There was no doubting the message. She rested her head on his shoulder but he shook her off.

'I must get to the station and telephone Father.' William pocketed the telegram, put on his hat and coat and left the house. When he reached the gate he turned and saw Lottie standing motionless by the open door. He ran back, gave her a fierce kiss and was gone.

Lottie wandered aimlessly about the house. She was missing Cilla in a way she had never done before she left for South Africa. And now her sister-in-law had been snatched from her. She jumped as she felt the baby kick and her heart began to race. Thinking that she should lie down she went upstairs but, instead of getting into the unmade bed, she opened the window and leant out despite the cold air. She turned her face towards Mynydd Brith and for an instant she thought she saw an image of Daisy, her face ringed in golden curls and her smile lighting up the mountain. Lottie held out her arms towards her but the image faded.

Slowly Lottie closed the window then rested her elbows on the sill and waited until her heartbeat returned to normal.

When her legs had stopped shaking she went downstairs, made a fresh brew and laid out the cape. The velvet-trimmed collar was ready to be attached and

Lottie saw that there was enough velvet left to smarten up her black hat. Relieved to have something to do, she busied herself putting finishing touches to the clothes that she would wear for the first time at her sister-in-law's funeral. When she had finished she put them carefully over the back of a chair then laid her head on the table and wept.

***

At first, William was against Lottie going with him to Daisy's funeral. He was terrified of her catching influenza. However, knowing how ill William had been after the shock of leaving the RNAS, Lottie was determined that her place was at his side.

By the last week of February the newspapers were reporting that the epidemic was in decline especially among the better-nourished sections of the population. Lottie and William took an express train to London and stayed at Belsize Park before travelling to Gloucestershire with Humphrey and Hilda early the following day. Alice had gone to help look after Daisy and had stayed on, too shaken to attempt the journey home.

After an early breakfast in the dining car, Lottie dozed most of the journey but was fully awake by the time they changed from the mainline to a small branch line train. The sun was shining and her spirits lifted slightly as she looked out of the window as the train chugged through picturesque sandstone villages. They saw clumps of snowdrops and a few early daffodils on the banks of a small river flowing along the valley. Sheep grazed on the slopes and Lottie took some comfort from the scene, which felt familiar but without the wildness of the Welsh countryside she was used to.

The train passed through a wooded embankment and came to a halt next to a village green. A chill breeze ruffled the catkins dancing at the station entrance and Lottie hugged her new cape around herself. Humphrey motioned to the Hammond's house with its tall chimneys and mullioned windows standing near the church. It was larger than the churches Lottie was used to but its impressive features were softened by the mellowness of the sandstone. As they made their way across the green they saw that people dressed in black were already walking towards the church.

There was only time for tearful greetings and a quick wash at Mr and Mrs Hammond's house before joining the mourners and, accompanied by the tolling of the church bells, they followed the coffin bearers the short distance to the church.

Making a conscious effort to put one foot in front of the other, Lottie walked with Hilda behind William and Humphrey who were supporting Alice. Lottie was shocked by the change in her mother-in-law; her normally upright figure stumbled as she was slowly propelled forward with her head bowed in an attempt to hide her muffled sobs. William had wanted to be one of the coffin bearers but Alec had asked friends from the village and Lottie could see that his place was at his mother's side.

The dismal notes of the organ greeted them as they followed the coffin down the aisle of the magnificent church and Lottie was aware of white faces turning to stare in a mixture of sympathy, curiosity and shared grief.

She started to take her place in the pew behind William and his parents but Humphrey motioned to her and Hilda to join them. She was relieved to be standing next to William but could take little comfort from his trembling body and grim expression.

The service was a reverent tribute to Daisy's life and, as he extolled her virtues, it was obvious the vicar had known Daisy well. William leant forward to hear the vicar telling the congregation how Daisy's cheerful kindness had encouraged even the most rowdy of the village boys to attend her Sunday school class. And in the dark times when there were no young fathers in the village Daisy had organised fishing trips and races on the village green to keep the children out of mischief.

Lottie glanced at the congregation and saw that many were weeping. She felt touched that she had been privileged to be a friend to someone who had brought so much joy and compassion to the people she knew.

The final hymn was 'Abide With Me' and Lottie thought William was going to break down as he stood silently, his head bowed, during the first verse. But he rallied and she took comfort from his strong voice as they sang the final words: 'Heaven's morning breaks and earth's vain shadows flee; In life, in death, O Lord, abide with me.'

The vicar gave the blessing then led the mourners into the churchyard past the centuries old graves to a place where the earth had been newly dug. Faintness threatened to overcome Lottie as she stood by William's side while Daisy's coffin was lowered into a grave. She stared at her boots as the vicar spoke from the Book of Common Prayer. 'Forasmuch as it hath pleased Almighty God in his great mercy to take unto himself the soul of our dear sister Daisy here departed, we therefore commit her body to the ground: earth to earth, ashes to ashes, dust to dust ..'

Lottie watched Alec, his handsome features distorted by grief, bend down to pick up a handful of soil and scatter it over the coffin. For a moment Lottie did not recognise Humphrey as he stiffly and painstakingly scooped some soil into his gloved hand

and threw it into the grave. William followed suit then Alice, clutching a clod of earth, teetered on the edge of the grave and hurled it into the hole. There was a gasp from the crowd as she threw out her arm to save herself. Humphrey caught her and with his arms tightly around her he led Alice away from the grave. Mr and Mrs Hammond, moving stiffly in their grief, scattered some earth on the coffin then stood in solidarity with Alice and Humphrey.

After the final blessing, the crowd broke up and people clustered around the family, anxious to convey their condolence and sorrow for the loss of the young woman who had been loved by so many. Lottie found herself standing alone while William embraced his friend and brother-in-law. Her head began to spin and she felt herself falling until she was caught by Hilda's capable arms and led away to a bench in the porch of the church.

'Thank you,' she whispered as Hilda, tears streaming down her face, scrabbled in her bag and handed Lottie some smelling salts.

'You've got to look after yourself,' she said brusquely.

'I'll be all right.' Lottie attempted a smile as she felt a gentle nudge from the infant in her womb.

A notice board had been attached to the ancient church wall. There was a list of services including a baptism, details of the next meeting of the Mother's Union, fixtures for the forthcoming cricket season and a notice calling upon people to discuss the construction of a memorial to commemorate the young men of the village who had died in the World War. As Lottie read the notices she realised how rich village life was and felt cheated on Daisy's behalf that she was no longer part of it. The words became blurred as she wondered how Alec would ever cope with his loss.

William found them waiting in the shelter of the porch watching the mourners make their way through the churchyard and back to their homes in the village. He held out his hands and together they followed the family and close friends to Alec's childhood home.

After the funeral breakfast, Mr and Mrs Hammond begged them to stay the night but Alice was anxious to get home and Hilda was on duty the following day. Lottie was relieved; the funeral had been an ordeal and she was pleased to be returning to the familiarity of her in-laws' home in London.

***

Ethel had prepared sandwiches for their return but Lottie said she preferred to go straight to bed with a cup of hot milk. As she took the milk from her trembling hands, Lottie resisted the urge to put her arms around the older woman whose eyes mirrored her own pain. She regretted not giving in to the impulse as soon as she reached the top of the stairs but when she turned round Ethel had gone.

Lottie slept soundly that night, although she was dimly aware of William tossing restlessly beside her.

Neville was sitting in his high chair in the dining room when Lottie and William went down for breakfast the following morning.

'I thought I'd give Ethel a break so I brought Neville in here.' Hilda helped him put porridge on his spoon and managed a slight laugh when he blew on it before putting it in his mouth.

'He's really grown up,' said Lottie. She looked admiringly at the blonde-haired little boy wearing a blue woollen jumper under a smart pair of dungarees.

'More porridge!' he cried and waved his spoon.

Alice came into the room and her strained features were momentarily transformed as she bent to kiss the child.

'Where's Uncle Humphrey? He hasn't gone to work has he?' asked Hilda.

'He'll be down in a minute. He, he didn't sleep very well last night.' Alice's hands shook as she helped herself to a small serving of porridge.

William flashed his mother a look of sympathy but said nothing.

'Have you recovered from your faintness?' Hilda asked Lottie.

'Yes, I'm fine today, thank you. When do you have to be back at the hospital?'

'I'm not on duty till this afternoon.' Hilda looked at the silent figures of William and her godmother and then at Lottie. 'Perhaps we could take Neville for a walk on the Heath after breakfast?'

'That would be nice.'

***

'That's where Daisy used to work isn't it?' asked Lottie as they walked past the hospital.

Hilda paused for a moment as an elderly woman stopped to smile at Neville in his baby chair. 'Yes,' she said then hurried on up the hill with Neville and through a gate onto the Heath.

Lottie struggled to keep up.

'I'm sorry,' said Hilda, slowing her pace. 'Seeing the hospital brings it all back. I was wrong to be envious of Daisy's job there when I was holding the fort on the farm after Duggie died. In fact, I wasn't jealous for long. I was probably the first to guess that the job was harming her.'

'I didn't realise the job was dangerous.'

'Don't you remember how tired Daisy was?'

'Oh yes, she didn't come to Hyde Park with us because she was too tired. But of course, I hardly knew her then. This must be a terrible time for you,' Lottie said suddenly realising that Hilda must be suffering almost as much as William.

'Yes it is. But,' Hilda paused as she searched for the right words, 'you know she had just begun the treatment for cancer and it was making her worse. At least she hardly suffered this way.'

'I thought Daisy was so clever having a job as a radiographer. She had to know so much about chemicals and what goes on inside us.'

'The problem is we don't know enough about the chemicals they use or the effects of the X-rays.'

Lottie's eyes widened. 'Do you think that's what caused the cancer?'

Hilda shrugged. 'It's impossible to tell. But I do know that lots of radiographers suffer from exhaustion and quite a few get very ill.'

Lottie shivered and pulled her cape more tightly around her, wishing she had been able to buy material to line it. 'And do you enjoy your job?' she asked.

'I love it!' Hilda began to explain how she helped people adapt to their artificial limbs. Lottie listened intently but Neville was bored and demanded to be unstrapped. Conversation became disjointed as they watched him run ahead of them. Every now and again Hilda sprinted after him until all three were ready to head back home.

The house was quiet when they returned and the girls took Neville to the kitchen for his mid-morning milk. They offered to help Ethel prepare the lunch and Lottie went to look for Alice to find out what time she wanted it served.

She recognised William's voice coming from the study. She couldn't catch what he was saying but he sounded dispirited. Alice said something then Humphrey appeared to be reading something aloud. Not wanting to be caught prying, she hurried upstairs to the bathroom.

She met Alice on the stairs as she came down and was surprised by the look of relief on her face. William was studying the barometer in the hall and looked startled when she tapped him on the shoulder. For a moment he looked past her then he kissed her.

'How was the walk? You didn't overdo it?' he asked anxiously.

'No, it did us good. Neville thoroughly enjoyed running on the Heath.'

'Where is he now?'

'In the kitchen.'

William hesitated then walked to the kitchen. Lottie followed and waited in the doorway. Neville was sitting in the high chair drinking his milk while Hilda and Ethel chopped vegetables. William looked at Neville for a moment then gently ruffled his hair.

'You're doing a great job,' he said to Ethel.

She looked surprised. 'I love every minute of it. This house was blessed the day your mother brought him home, poor little waif that he was then.'

'But he's well cared for now and he's got a secure home here.' William looked intently at the child for a moment then turned to Lottie. 'I'm going for some cigarettes, do you want to come?'

'If you'd like me to.'

He nodded and, with one last look at Neville, walked out of the kitchen.

For some reason she couldn't understand, Lottie felt as if a weight had been lifted. As she walked along the street beside William she realised that she had been worried that his indifference to Neville meant that he would find it hard to show affection for his own child. Watching him ruffle Neville's hair had touched her and she felt cautiously optimistic for the future.

Chapter 28: Alice

Views on the Treaty
The terms of peace and the work that must be done to
restore peace and happiness to the world in the new
conditions are inevitably the most prominent topics in
the reviews for the month of August. At present the
chief note is one of disappointment with the terms,
which appear by some writers too harsh, to others too
lenient.

The Times: August 1ˢᵗ 1919

Without Neville to lavish affection on, Alice and Humphrey would have found the months after Daisy's death almost impossible to bear.

As the days lengthened, the older couple and the little boy became a familiar sight on the Heath long after most children were tucked up in bed. On Sundays they took excursions into the countryside, sometimes visiting Hilda's family where Neville was made a fuss of by Alice's old friends. Despite labour shortages, the farm was thriving under their youngest son's management and the fields sown with barley and wheat were testimony to the emergence of new life.

Lottie wrote assiduously every week and Alice and Humphrey were touched by the regularity of her letters.

Alice had insisted they had a telephone installed although it was rarely used. At the end of April, she was startled by its loud ringing and hurried into the hall to answer it. Clamping the phone to her ear, she strained to hear William's voice above the crackling on the line.

'Pardon? I didn't quite hear you; is it a boy or a girl?'

William repeated the message excitedly; she thought she heard the words boy and girl but then the pips went and she couldn't hear the rest.

'I'm sorry, can you say that again?'

'Lottie's had twins! A boy and a girl!'

For a moment Alice panicked. 'Twins! Good gracious! Is she all right? Are the babies all right?' She slid down on the chair next to the telephone table.

'Yes, Lottie's tired but they're all fine. It was quite a surprise, I can tell you!'

'She's going to need double of everything. How …..?' Alice was going to ask her how they would manage but the jubilation in William's voice stopped her as she realised that they would manage very well. 'What are you going to call them?' she asked instead.

'Daisy and Douglas,' William said proudly.

'Oh! That's beautiful.' Alice drew in her breath in an attempt to quell the sobs of grief at hearing the familiar names mingled with joy at the birth of her grandchildren.

'Yes, we knew you'd be pleased. I must go now, I'll phone again tomorrow.'

'How much do they weigh?' asked Alice but the line went dead. Still uncertain whether to laugh or cry, she replaced the telephone receiver and hurried into the kitchen.

'Ethel! Neville's got two little cousins!'

'Cousins?' Ethel looked puzzled.

'Lottie's had twins, a boy and a girl!'

'That's wonderful!' Ethel beamed then looked uncertainly at Neville.

Alice felt herself blushing. 'They'll be like cousins, being near in age.'

'That's right. And are they all well?'

'Yes, fine. Now I must go and look out some more of Neville's baby clothes to send up.' Alice felt slightly faint as she realised that Neville was in fact the half brother to William and Lottie's children.

When she read Lottie's letters detailing every ounce the twins gained as well as visits from her parents and Bronwen with her baby, Alice couldn't help making comparisons with Cilla's experience and the bleakness of Neville's first six weeks.

Apart from a letter saying she had arrived safely, Alice hadn't heard from Cilla since she left for South Africa. Images of Cilla's haunted face kept flashing through her mind and she began to have nightmares about Neville being kidnapped. When she woke Humphrey one night to confide her dreams she was relieved that he did not dismiss them as foolish imaginings. Dealing with his son's amnesia and his daughter's death had made him more sensitive and he listened to Alice's fears.

'There's nothing to worry about,' he said soothingly. 'Cilla signed a paper at the mother and baby home when she asked us to take Neville. And William signed an agreement in February. Neville is our son now.'

Alice pulled the covers closer. 'So if Neville is our son, then Douglas and Daisy are his nephew and niece.'

'I suppose that's right. Now, will you be able to sleep or do you want me to get some cocoa?'

As Alice drifted towards sleep she wondered how William was adapting to fatherhood now that some of the euphoria had inevitably given way to exhaustion. She had been taken aback by the violence of his grief after Daisy died and hoped that having two babies to love and provide for would steady him. But part of her missed the mischievous little boy who was always getting into scrapes and the debonair young man, who before the war, had thought that the world was his oyster.

...

The twins' christening was arranged for the August bank holiday and Alice was really looking forward to seeing her grandchildren for the first time and staying at Trealaw after so long away.

They decided to take the night train and, after his initial excitement at sleeping in a bunk bed, Neville slept soundly all night. He shouted delightedly when he woke up and saw the sea for the first time. His nose pressed to the carriage window, he was hardly able to contain his excitement as he pointed to a few early risers and dogs barking as they ran along the sand or played tag with the waves.

'Are we there yet?' he asked jumping with excitement each time the train stopped, spilling out holiday makers at the resorts along the Dee estuary.

'This is where your Uncle William works,' said Humphrey as the train came to a halt at Llandudno Junction.

'Can we get off?'

'We get off at the next stop. Now look out of the window and we can see whether the tide's in or out when we go over the bridge.' Alice felt a surge of excitement as they neared their destination.

'What's the tide?' asked Neville then pointed in amazement as the train rattled across the estuary towards the castle, its dark walls lashed by crested waves.

'It's in,' Alice said ambiguously as she stared out of the window for a glimpse of Mynydd Brith.

With a squeal of brakes and a hiss of steam, the train stopped at Conway station. Alice smiled as she leant out of the window and saw William hurrying along the platform; he had always been in a hurry. He held open the door with a flourish but when he kissed her Alice was shocked to find herself looking into the face of a man much older than his twenty-eight years. She knew that it was not just tiredness for she had seen similar expressions on many of the men of his generation; aged before their time with suffering, guilt and disappointment.

Neville stared shyly at William then ran to watch their luggage being unloaded from the guard's van.

'We'll collect it later,' said Humphrey to a porter awaiting instructions as he put the luggage onto a barrow.

'We'll need to find a bigger house soon,' William said as he led the way to their terraced house in a street near the station.

Lottie greeted them enthusiastically. Her hair was shining, her figure had filled out and, although she looked tired, she had an aura of contentment about her.

'The babies are having a nap in the garden, would you like to take a peek?' Lottie took Neville's hand and led him to a gnarled apple tree in the corner of the tiny garden. She put her finger to her mouth as a warning to Neville to keep quiet then she picked him up and pointed to two little bundles at either end of the double pram.

'That's Douglas and this is Daisy,' she whispered.

Alice edged forward to gaze at two perfect little faces framed by white woolly bonnets, which were identical except for the peak on Douglas's. 'They're beautiful,' she murmured. She turned to speak to William but he was standing motionless, his expression inscrutable as he looked at Lottie by the pram with Neville in her arms. She quickly looked away; Lottie put Neville down and the moment was broken.

They returned to the house for tea and welsh cakes and talked about the arrangements for the christening the following day.

'I'm so glad you've asked Alec to be Douglas's godfather,' said Alice. 'When is he arriving?'

'He can't make it,' William said shortly. 'But Hilda will be here this afternoon so he'll have his godmother present.'

'And Daisy?'

'I've asked Bronwen to stand in for Cilla. And Efan will be godfather.' If Lottie was upset by Cilla's absence she did not show it.

'When are we going to our house?' asked Neville, beginning to fidget.

'Soon. Would you like to come with me to the station to organise a cab?' asked Humphrey.

'I'll come too,' said William. 'We can pick up the supplies I ordered for you. And I arranged for Billie Jenkins' mother to clean Trealaw and light the range yesterday so the house should be nicely aired.'

It was only when she was in the cab that Alice realised she hadn't yet held either of her new grandchildren. She smiled as she remembered how peaceful they looked as they slept and she calmly looked forward to seeing them again tomorrow and the next day. Neville wriggled on the seat beside her and her body glowed from his warmth as he leant across her and pointed at a black and white collie bounding ahead of them.

The cab ground into bottom gear as the track got steeper then swung onto the open mountain and came to a halt outside Trealaw.

***

'The weather's set for another fine day,' said Humphrey scanning the coastline from his chair next to the table they had set up outside the house.

Hilda handed him a cup of tea. 'I'm glad the sun was shining yesterday for the christening. Though it was a bit stuffy afterwards in Mr and Mrs Rowe's house.'

'It was a nice christening. Though ….,' Alice paused. She had been about to say it was a good thing Alec hadn't come, he wouldn't have fitted in with Lottie's family. But that was unfair, he might have done; Daisy certainly had no trouble in making friends with everyone. A wave of misery threatened to overwhelm her as she thought of her daughter and the life that she might have had.

'Look what I found!' Neville ran up to them holding a feather with an iridescent purple tinge.

Alice bent to examine it. 'It's very pretty. Where did you get it?'

'Over there.' He pointed to a rock near the hedge.

'I'm going to get some more!'

'Do you think Mr and Mrs Rowe will come for the picnic this afternoon?' asked Hilda.

'I don't think so. I gather Nellie's legs are quite bad again.'

'She must enjoy having her grandchildren so close.'

'Yes, she must.' Alice's features softened as she gazed at Neville running with his feather, his blonde hair blowing in the breeze.

'Especially as her other daughter's so far away,' Hilda continued.

'Yes. I think Lottie is disappointed she hasn't heard from Cilla for a while.' Alice got up. 'I'll go and make a start on the picnic. No Hilda, you relax; you work much too hard and you're only here a couple of days.'

Alice was pleased that the picnic was to be a low-key affair; a party would have had poignant memories of the engagement party four years ago. Sorrow threatened to overcome her again as she realised how much everything had changed since then. She went into the dining room and picked up a wedding photograph of William and Lottie on the sideboard. As she studied it she realised how fortunate she was to have such a steadfast daughter-in-law and that, unlike so many of his generation, William had survived the war. Determinedly quelling the thought that William's survival may have been related to his conduct as a pilot, Alice took the sandwich plates to the kitchen and began to prepare the picnic.

It wasn't long before Hilda came in to give her a hand and, despite her saying that she could manage on her own, Alice was pleased to have her help. She talked with enthusiasm about her job and Alice was genuinely pleased that her goddaughter had found a sense of fulfilment. They had almost finished when Neville ran in and announced that the twins were coming. Hilda covered the food then followed Alice who had hurried outside.

William brought the pram to a standstill by the table and put on the brake. Everyone peered at the babies lying contentedly watching the white clouds scudding across the sky.

William and Lottie sank into the deck chairs and gratefully drank the lemonade Hilda brought. For a while they talked about the christening service, the gathering afterwards and the gifts the twins had been given.

'I almost forgot!' Lottie took a package from her bag. 'This came by special delivery this morning!' She put two leather boxes on the table. 'These are from South Africa; from Cilla!'

Alice leant forward to get a closer look at the trinket Lottie was taking from one of the boxes then exclaimed in surprise as she found herself looking at a finely engraved locket in pure gold hanging from an exquisite gold chain.

'It's beautiful, it must have ….' Alice paused.

'Yes, it must have cost a lot,' said William.

'Daisy will look lovely with that round her neck when she's older,' said Lottie as she opened the other box. 'And this is Duggie's christening gift.' She held out a gold sovereign in the palm of her hand.

'Cilla must be doing well,' said Hilda peering at the coin with puzzled admiration.

'She said she had a good day at the races!' Lottie giggled uncertainly.

'Your little sister is doing all right in South Africa.' William looked amused and also relieved.

'She is, isn't she! Shall we tell them her news?' Lottie put the coin on the table. 'Cilla's engaged!'

'That's wonderful! Who's the lucky man?' asked Alice, not looking at William.

'His name's Gilbert Taylor. She met him on the boat from England; I suspected she was in love with him from her very first letter!' Lottie laughed but her eyes held a wistful expression.

'What does he do for a living?' asked Humphrey.

'His father owns a goldmine, or part of one, up country, I'm not sure where. She says they might have to move there sometime but at the moment Gilbert has some sort of export business in Cape Town.'

'It's good she's marrying someone with money, I've heard it can be a hard life over there.' Hilda picked up the coin.

'It might be worth a lot more when Douglas is twenty-one, we don't know how long these will be around,' said Humphrey.

There was a whimper from the pram and Lottie got up. 'It's impossible to imagine either of them grown up,' she said as she picked up Daisy and handed her to

Alice. 'Do you mind giving Daisy a cuddle while I feed Duggie?'

'I'd be delighted to. We can have our picnic when you've fed them both.'

***

'Have there been many walkers here this week-end?' asked William as they sat round the table having their picnic.

'There was a group going down the church path when we came back yesterday. It was such a lovely evening we took Neville for a walk as far as the spring. You liked seeing the water coming from the ground didn't you?' Alice looked fondly at the child.

He nodded vigorously, his mouth full of cake.

'Maybe you youngsters would like a walk unencumbered by the babies? We promised Neville we'd see if there were any strawberries by the church and the track's good enough to push the pram along.'

'Are you sure?' William looked at his father in surprise.

'Quite sure. We're here for the rest of the week but you've got work tomorrow and Hilda goes back to London. And I'm sure Lottie has more than enough to keep her busy. You enjoy the fresh air while you can.'

'Thanks. We'll go up the mountain for a bit then cut down and meet you at the old church. How does that sound, ladies?' William smiled at Hilda but his eyes rested on his wife.

'It sounds lovely. I often look up at Mynydd Brith and wish we had time to walk in the mountains. Not that I'm complaining,' added Lottie hastily.

'We'd better clear the dishes first.' Hilda got up and began to take the things inside while Lottie checked that the twins had everything they needed.

'Enjoy your walk,' called Alice a few minutes later as she watched the three of them set off along the sheep track at the back of the house.

'Can we go now?' Neville jumped up and down impatiently.

'Yes, come along, son.' Humphrey came out of the house swinging a basket in his hand. 'Can you manage?' he asked as Alice started to push the heavy pram across the grass.

'Yes, I'll be fine. If you want to go ahead with Neville I'll catch you up.'

Alice hummed contentedly as she watched the little boy skipping in front of Humphrey while her grandchildren chuntered peacefully as she pushed the pram towards the old church.

'No strawberries!' Neville announced when she caught up with them by the church gate.

'They look as if they've been picked quite recently.' Humphrey pointed to the plants on the bank, a couple had miniscule white petals but the others had what looked like empty cups hanging at the end of their delicate stems.

'The fairies must have been here before us,' said Alice.

Neville stared at her in amazement.

'No need to go filling his head,' murmured Humphrey.

Alice pushed open the gate. 'Let's explore the churchyard. There might be an empty nest in the wall. Neville could take it home.'

She put the pram in the shade of the wooden porch and took Neville's hand. Humphrey took out his pipe and leant against the porch while Alice and Neville made their way to a hillock in one corner of the churchyard. As Alice sat down she disturbed a grasshopper. Neville laughed and ran after it, his hands outstretched as he tried to catch it. Alice watched, savouring the tranquillity of the old church and the quiet of the churchyard, broken only by Neville's innocent laughter and snuffles from the sleeping babies.

Voices and the sound of hooves interrupted the stillness of the afternoon.

'Right ho! This is our destination!'

Alice winced at the booming tones ricocheting towards the church. She stood up and saw four horses, their flanks sweating from the climb, being brought to a halt by their riders. A fragile looking young woman on a dappled mare brought up the rear behind a young boy on a chestnut pony. In front of the boy was a woman about Alice's age on a black mare. She inclined her head in Alice's direction, leapt effortlessly off her mount and secured the reins to a post.

'It seems the infantry are ahead of us!' The gentleman leading the party joked as he pulled his black stallion to a halt and got off with surprising agility considering his portly figure. He slapped the horse's rump and tied the magnificent beast near the mare.

Humphrey left his post by the pram and walked to the gate. 'The cavalry are welcome,' he said in an attempt to meet the horseman's jocularity.

'Brigadier Phelps-Murray.'

Humphrey found his hand gripped in a firm handshake.

'Detective Inspector Dacre', he replied. 'And this is my wife,' he added as Alice joined them.

The brigadier lifted his black bowler riding hat and shook Alice's hand.

'Would you like to see inside the church?' she asked.

'Yes, we heard it's very old.' The brigadier's wife stopped at the porch and her stern features softened as she bent over the pram. 'Oh my! Twins! Are they your grandchildren?'

'Yes.' Alice felt ridiculously proud.

'We just have the one grandson,' she said sadly and looked back at the boy still sitting on his pony. He was talking animatedly to the woman on the dappled mare.

'This is for you!' Neville ran across the churchyard and thrust some harebells into Alice's hand.

'Another grandchild!' The brigadier spoke so loudly that Neville darted behind a tombstone.

'Oh no! Neville is our son,' said Humphrey firmly.

The couple appeared confused as they looked at Neville's blonde head peeking from a gravestone covered with lichen.

'We have a daughter.' Mrs Phelps-Murray glanced at the young woman who had got off her horse and was talking to her son who seemed content to remain on his pony.

Alice guessed what was coming next; stories of widows and fatherless children were all too common. 'Shall we go into the church?' she said to sidestep the issue.

Humphrey opened the door and led the way.

But the brigadier was not easily distracted. 'The fact is,' he said, his voice filling the tiny church, 'our son-in-law might be here now if it hadn't been for sheer incompetence.'

Alice opened her mouth and closed it again. It seemed unnecessary to point out that incompetence must have accounted for hundreds, even thousands, of deaths during the war years.

'Was he in the armed forces?' Humphrey asked politely.

'He was a pilot with the RNAS but his plane hadn't been maintained properly. He crashed on take-off. Didn't stand a chance.'

Alice drew in a breath and moved closer to Humphrey.

'I don't think we need bother the Inspector and Mrs Dacre with the details.' The brigadier's wife laid her hand on his arm.

Alice looked down as the brigadier took a handkerchief from the pocket of his riding jacket and mopped his brow. She focused her eyes on a beetle making its way across the stone flags.

'The man responsible would have been de-mobilised if not court marshalled. But that doesn't bring back our son-in-law,' he finished bitterly.

'No. I am sorry for your loss.' Humphrey's face was ashen. 'Did they tell you the name of the man responsible?'

'That's classified information. Good thing too. Don't know what I'd do if I got my hands on him.'

Alice shivered. 'I'm very sorry for you and your daughter and grandson.' She turned to Mrs Phelps-Murray. 'When did it happen?'

She heard Humphrey clear his throat and wished she could take back the question.

'November 1917.' The woman's voice echoed tonelessly round the church.

Alice and Humphrey said nothing as they stood, motionless, in silent misery.

'Well, we came to see the church, we'd better look around.' Their lack of response seemed to galvanise the brigadier and he strode across the church to the small wooden altar.

His wife remained near the door. 'I think the babies are waking up.' She looked enquiringly at Alice.

'It's about time, they've had a good sleep.' Alice was relieved for an excuse to leave the cold church.

Mrs Phelps-Murray followed her outside. 'I'm sorry about my husband. Everyone has suffered.' She looked enquiringly at Alice.

'Our daughter died.' She bent over the pram to hide her distress and saw Daisy screwing up her face while Douglas gurgled and punched his fist in the air.

'I'm so sorry. Are these ....?'

'Oh no, the twins belong to ...'

Suddenly a scream from Mrs Phelps-Murray's daughter rent the air.

'Oh my God!' Alice looked up to see Neville running towards the dappled mare on his stubby little legs.

'Horse!' he shouted excitedly.

The horse whinnied and reared up, its front hooves pawing the air. The young woman let go of the reins, scooped Neville up and, with a desperate look at the terrified face of her son on the chestnut pony, delivered the astonished child to the safety of Alice's outstretched arms.

Calmly inching her way forward, Mrs Phelps-Murray approached the mare and, in one quick movement, took the reins and quietened the horse.

'Mummy! I want to get off!' In his anguish the frightened boy kicked his heels against the pony's flank.

'Help me!' he screamed as the pony bolted along the path.

The twins began to wail; Humphrey and the brigadier ran out of the church, looked at the scene in horror then started to chase after the bolting pony.

'They'll never catch up,' Mrs Phelps-Murray exclaimed as she untied the black mare and swung herself into the saddle.

Her daughter stood trembling, unable to move. Then a flicker of hope crossed her face and she pointed to a figure poised on a huge rock by the side of the path.

Alice gasped as William leapt off the rock, rolled over and picked himself up just as the pony was galloping towards him. The boy had let go of the reins and was hanging onto the pony's neck sobbing violently. William managed to grab the reins and run alongside.

'Easy, easy now,' he called as he pulled on the reins.

The pony took another spurt forward and William was dragged to the ground, still holding the reins.

Alice forced herself not to scream when she lost sight of the pony as it rounded a bend. She quickly re-arranged the babies then lifted Neville into the pram and ran with it along the path behind Mrs Phelps-Murray and her daughter. For a while all she could hear was the pounding of her heart.

Then she realised the galloping hooves had stopped.

When she caught up with the others she saw Hilda holding on to the pony that was quietly chewing the fresh mountain grass. The Phelps-Murrays were comforting the little boy and Lottie and Humphrey were kneeling down looking anxiously at William.

'Is he all right?' Alice forced herself to first enquire after the child.

'He's shaken but not hurt, thanks to the gentleman,' the boy's mother said looking at William with gratitude.

'He'll be back in the saddle again in no time,' blustered the brigadier.

'Stay there, Neville,' Alice warned and put the brake on the pram.

She knelt next to William.

'Hope you liked the side show,' he said with studied nonchalance.

She smiled despite herself. 'Can you get up?'

'Oh, I expect so.' He held out his hand but winced in pain as Humphrey helped him to his feet.

Lottie started to put her arm round him then drew back.

'That doesn't look right,' she said pointing to his left arm dangling limply at his side.

'It doesn't feel too good.' William attempted to smile.

'How are your legs?' Humphrey asked.

William took a step forward. 'All right, I think.' He held on to Lottie and walked a few more paces. 'Mm, it's just the arm. I fell on it. How's the boy?'

'He'll be fine. Thanks to you.' The brigadier slapped William on the back. 'I'd like to shake your hand but I don't want to do any more damage. You deserve a medal.' He looked quizzically at William. 'But I expect you've already got one. Where did you serve?'

William was silent and a spasm of shame crossed his face as he turned his head away from the brigadier towards Mynydd Brith.

'My son and I were both in reserved occupations with the railways,' Humphrey said smoothly.

For a moment the brigadier look confounded. 'The railways eh? Where would we have been without them to keep everything moving?' He shook Humphrey's hand. 'Brave man you've got there. Pity he didn't get a chance for the army; he'd have gone far. You must be proud of him.'

'I'm very proud of him.' Humphrey's voice quivered with emotion.

Alice watched William slowly turn round and look at his father. His face was scratched and he was obviously in pain but she saw his features relax at his father's affirmation and she caught a glimpse of the young pilot who had enlisted and served his country to the best of his ability.

For a moment there was silence then Douglas started to cry. When Daisy followed suit Neville's lip quivered. Alice lifted him down and turned to Mrs Phelps-Murray. 'We have a holiday home just over there. Would you like some refreshment before you return?'

'That's very kind but we'll be all right. It will be an easy ride back down the church path to where we're staying.'

Hilda led the pony to the group. 'Butter wouldn't melt in his mouth,' she said and rubbed his nose.

The brigadier took the reins. 'Thank you.' He held out his arms to his grandson. 'Now, how about you sitting on him while I lead him at a gentle walking pace?' he said firmly.

'All right,' the child acquiesced bravely.

'Goodbye everyone. I must feed the babies,' said Lottie then took the pram and walked quickly towards Trealaw.

The family thanked William again, final good byes were said and then they parted.

***

When they got back to Trealaw Lottie was sitting on the sofa with Daisy at her breast and Douglas fidgeting beside her.

'Let me help.' William bent down to pick up Douglas then recoiled in pain.

'You're not doing anything till I've strapped you up,' said Hilda authoritatively. She and Humphrey busied themselves making a splint and triangular bandage for William's arm while Alice prepared tea and Neville showed Douglas his toy train.

'I think you'd all better stay the night.' Alice handed William a cup of sweet tea as he slumped next to Lottie on the sofa.

'I'll be all right; Hilda's given me some aspirin.'

'I think William will be better at home,' Lottie said firmly. She examined his splint. 'This looks really professional. Thank you Hilda. I hope you'll have time to call and see us before you leave tomorrow?'

'I'd love to.'

William closed his eyes and for a while no one said anything. Neville made choochoo noises as he manoeuvred his train round the furniture, the twins snuffled contentedly and the gentle cooing of rock doves drifted through the window.

Alice watched the colour return to William's face as he dozed. She caught Humphrey's eye.

'He'll be all right,' he said quietly and she knew he wasn't only referring to the injuries William had received that afternoon.

'And so will we,' she thought as Neville toddled across the room and laid his head in her lap.

William woke up, yawned and consulted the watch Lottie had given him their first Christmas.

'It still works!' He kissed her forehead and stood up.

'Are you feeling better?' Lottie asked him tenderly as she rocked Daisy in her arms.

'Yes,' William smiled. He looked at his father, 'I'm feeling much better now.'

'You must look after yourself, no more mountain rescues for a while.' Humphrey regarded his son with pride.

'I'll wait a while!' William laughed. 'And now it's time we were going.'

Lottie gathered their things and Hilda helped her put the babies in their pram. The air was cool as they stepped outside the house. Alice bent to kiss the twins tucked up in the pram then she kissed Lottie fondly.

Her daughter-in-law smiled. 'Thank you for the picnic. It's been an eventful day!'

'If only you knew!' thought Alice.

They stood for a while looking down at the castle, the estuary and the sea beyond.

William leant over the pram. 'You can see the whole world from here,' he said to his children. 'And it's all yours.'

About the Author

During her childhood Heather spent several summers at the family home above Conwy in North Wales. As a student, she returned for weekends in Snowdonia with Leicester University Mountaineering Club.

She was posted to Ghana as a VSO teacher and travelled to Timbuktu with Adrian who she married. They worked in Nigeria and Botswana where Heather was the Northern Correspondent for the Botswana Guardian newspaper. Later the family bought a smallholding in Lincolnshire where Heather set up Wold School of English for international students.

Since moving to Oxford, Heather has written Social Studies text books for Africa and the Caribbean. She is secretary of Oxford Writers Group and OxPens, the publishing arm of the group. Her stories, In Time for the Wake and Through the Mist of Time, appear in The Bodleian Murders and The Midnight Press, published by OxPens.

www.heatherrosser.com

Lightning Source UK Ltd.
Milton Keynes UK
UKOW03f2220050614

232959UK00003B/126/P